PRAISE FOR

THE TWIN DAGGERS SERIES

"Open this book and be transported into a world of magic, machines, and espionage. *Twin Daggers* is a riveting story about the length two sisters will go for each other. And be prepared—they will steal your heart."

REBECCA ROSS, author of *Sisters of Sword and Song*

"Twisting and face-paced, *Twin Daggers* is an exciting new fantasy series filled with charming magic, harrowing politics, and the bittersweet struggle of star-crossed lovers. Be careful, dear reader, for Aissa and Aro are sure to steal your heart."

MINDEE ARNETT, author of *Onyx & Ivory*

"A taut, emotionally arresting fantasy."

KIRKUS REVIEWS

"Exceptionally well crafted with a wealth of inherently fascinating plot twists and turns, *Twin Daggers* is a simply outstanding YA novel that will have a very special appeal to young readers ages 13-18."

MIDWEST BOOK REVIEW

HEARTLESS HEIRS

NEW YORK TIMES BESTSELLING AUTHOR

MARCYKATE CONNOLLY

BLINK®

Heartless Heirs
© 2021 by MarcyKate Connolly

Requests for information should be addressed to:
Blink, 3900 Sparks Dr. SE, Grand Rapids, Michigan 49546

Hardcover ISBN 978-0-310-76827-2
Audio ISBN 978-0-310-77109-8
Ebook ISBN 978-0-310-76833-3

Art direction: Cindy Davis
Interior Design: Denise Froehlich
Printed in the United States of America

21 22 23 24 25 / LSC / 10 9 8 7 6 5 4 3 2 1

WHERE TRUTH CUTS, IT LEAVES CHAOS IN
its wake. For my twin sister and me, that
becomes clearer every minute. Each shard, each
fact, chips away at the bond between us and the life
we thought we knew.

The truth about what we really are—an experiment two
hundred years in the making.

Our parents' bond, and their death because of it.

A betrayal by the man Zandria loved.

My betrayal of the entire Magi people by falling in love with a
Technocrat prince, the Heartless heir we were sent to assassinate.

The house of lies we once held dear has crumbled to pieces.

But those truths prickling around the edges of our hearts will
have to wait. First, we must get out of this cursed Technocrat city
alive. Then we can warn the rest of the Magi they're in imminent
danger.

An hour ago, we threw Palinor into chaos by destroying a
sizable section of the Palace's subterranean levels as we escaped the
dungeons with our childhood friend, Remy Gaville. Dawn hasn't
yet dared to creep over the steel roofs of the city, but the streets
and ramparts are overflowing with men. They form a net of flesh
and blood and metal, ready and waiting to catch us.

Nothing is more terrifying to the Technocrats than a Magi on
the loose. Three of us calls for every able-bodied soldier to remain
on high alert.

We managed to steal some supplies—food, a change of
clothes, and a couple water skeins—by shadowing guards while
we hid under a shield spell. Now we huddle under a window in
a shop not far from the northern gate, waiting for an opportunity

to get through. We know one way out, but the path is blocked. Guards line the alley where we once exited through a secret tunnel led by Darian Azul.

Just the thought of the traitor's name makes me quiver with rage.

My sister and I may disagree on many things at the moment, but we're united in our shared hatred of that man.

"If we get close enough, we could kill half the guards in that alley very quickly," Zandria whispers a little too eagerly for my liking.

"Right, but then the other half would be on top of us in seconds," I say. "We can't simply power through. There are too many of them, and too few of us." Zandria may be different since we rescued her from the dungeons and the Technocrats' torturous metal suits, but in one way she remains the same: she's as impulsive as ever. Now with a newer, more brutal bent.

Remy grabs my wrist. "Stop talking. Both of you."

We hold our breaths. Even before I hear it, I know what we're listening for.

The unmistakable metallic clank of the machines.

Zandria's face turns white as a sheet in the predawn light.

"We have to get out of here before they reach us," she hisses. "Let's just bring the wall down on their heads. Then we can get to the tunnel before they know what hit them." She rises, but I yank her back down.

"No. The machines will know exactly where to hunt if we do that. If we stay here until they pass, we have a shot."

"Aissa's right. We need to lay low," Remy says.

Zandria looks as if she wants to scream. Her eyes wildly glance between us as the skittering of metal legs grows louder. Remy and I each take one of her hands and squeeze tightly. She yanks her hand out of mine like she's been burned.

It feels like a slap, but I do my best to ignore it. "Breathe, Zandy," I whisper. "We'll get through this."

I peek out the window onto the street. Only guards are out there now. Any curious onlookers have been ordered back to their homes.

But they have our descriptions, and they know we're trying to escape the city.

"We need to change our appearances," I say to Zandria. She nods curtly and begins casting the spell. In moments, our red hair and green eyes are gone. In their place, I have dark hair and blue eyes, and she's taller, with brown hair and brown eyes. Remy attempts the spell too, and only manages to alter his features somewhat, likely because he hasn't had time to practice like we did.

It will have to be enough. The first mechs are the seekers, trundling like spiders over the cobblestone streets. Some turn down other streets and alleys, hunting for us. A few buildings down the road, they begin prying open shop doors. Soon they'll reach us.

"I know what to do," I say suddenly. "We can't go out on the streets, and we can't stay here much longer either. We're going to tunnel to the secret passage."

Zandria's eyes widen, but her shaking begins to subside.

We locate the latch to the cellar and drop down one by one. Remy closes it behind us and fastens the lock. Outside the front door, metallic legs prod and pry. I shudder.

My twin's hands quiver as she weaves them. The metal walls reinforcing the cellar peel away, leaving a door-sized patch of dirt behind. Remy casts his own spell to help, and soon the three of us tunnel forward, shifting the earth at full speed.

Zandria packs the dirt behind us while Remy and I continue to use our spells to dig ahead. Once we hit brick and metal again, my sister joins me in the lead. The secret tunnel is hidden in the alley just across the street from the shop where we took cover, so we've been digging in a straight line. Zandria eyes the bricks suspiciously; we don't know exactly what's beyond them. There could be guards lying in wait or no one at all.

We have no choice but to find out. We'll run out of air if we remain down here for long.

I hum softly, coaxing a brick from the wall. Beside me, Zandria casts a silencing spell so it won't make a sound as it slides free. I peek through—and relief floods my limbs. The hall is empty. The king and queen no doubt have heard how we escaped their dungeons and must've called all the guards above ground to hunt for us. If we do encounter a guard or two, we should be able to disarm or evade them.

"It's safe," I whisper. "Come on."

Zandria and I make short work of dismantling the wall with our magic, then we all step into the silent, metal-paneled hall. I take a moment to put the wall back together before we proceed; no one needs to know how we escaped.

Nerves strung tight as bow strings, we run down the hall in the direction of the gates. This tunnel goes right under the city walls. We only have a couple more turns until we're free, when I stop suddenly. Zandria and Remy pause behind me, our heaving breaths blessedly silent thanks to the spell Remy casts.

Footsteps ring out directly in front of us. There's nowhere to hide, no rooms to duck into. Zandria's expression quickly shifts from terror to rage, and her hands begin to move. I shake my head at her, then hum a shield spell that envelops us just before the guard tromps around the corner. We flatten ourselves against the wall, hearts in our throats.

The guard passes by, unaware of our presence.

When he's safely around the next corner, we wait for another minute, then finally move ahead.

"We should've just killed him," Zandria hisses. "Why are you protecting them?"

Her words surprise me. "If we leave a trail of bodies in our wake, Darian and the royals will know exactly which way we went and how we left the city. It would only expose us."

My sister grunts but doesn't respond. When we reach the end of the tunnel, we exit into the cool air of the metal forest.

We may be out of the city, but we're not safe yet.

We take off at a run, racing in the direction of the Chambers— the underground hideaway where the last remaining members of the Magi faction live. The woods are crawling with Technocrats and their fearsome machines—every one of them searching for us. The screech of metal beasts brushing against metal trees haunts the woods, setting our teeth on edge.

Finally, we enter a rocky section where real trees have begun to take root. There are still many of the lifeless metal trees the Technocrats installed after the wars to give the semblance of a forest, now brushing up against green leaves and moss-coated bark. At least they're useful for hiding when necessary.

"We have to rest," Zandria says. Her face looks paler than usual. Remy puts a hand on her shoulder.

"We can rest here," he says. "We'll make a place to hide if we have to."

Zandria straightens her spine. "Just for a few minutes. Then I can go on. We can't afford to stop for long."

"We can't afford for you to get captured again either," Remy says.

I step between them. "We'll take ten minutes to eat something and rest our legs. Then we'll get moving."

Remy starts to say something, but I hold up a hand. "Why don't you keep watch, Remy?"

"Fine," he says, and stalks off a few yards.

I sit next to my sister on a log flanked by ferns and split the few rations we were able to steal before leaving the city. We may be free now, but her expression is tight and laced with grief.

I understand why.

She's reeling from all I've told her since we rescued her from the dungeons. Our parents' deaths and Darian's betrayal most of all. She had no idea either that long ago, our parents risked the wrath of the Armory Council and used the forbidden Binding rite to irrevocably join themselves together—heart, body, and soul. Ultimately, it was their undoing. When Darian arrived that terrible night, searching for me, he only had to stab one parent to kill them both. Zandria and I both trusted Darian when we first met him. He's the Magi spymaster, after all. But his loyalty lies only with himself. And he will sacrifice anything—and anyone—in his way.

Add to all that the fact I fell for—and performed the Binding rite with—the very person I was supposed to kill: Aro. I imagine Zandria sees that as a betrayal too. My sister spent weeks in captivity, only to find the world had turned upside down in her absence.

The way she looks at me now . . . breaks my heart.

I rest my head on her shoulder. She flinches and shrugs me off.

I don't know what to say. The only comfort I have to offer her is that we've finally been reunited. After what we've been through, I'm not sure that's enough.

While we eat, my thoughts drift back to Aro. I'm worried about him. He foolishly insisted on remaining in Palinor because he believes he can make a difference.

It's futile. But I do believe his parents, the king and queen, will protect him. The wild card is Darian, their most trusted advisor and second in line to the throne—after Aro. What will Darian do now that Aro knows his plans? I've left the person I love—literally given my heart to—in a nest of knives and vipers.

I haven't told Zandy yet, but I've already made up my mind: once we get the rest of the Magi to safety, I'm going back for Aro.

Remy appears before us, scowling deeper than I've seen before. "We need to leave. Right now."

We get to our feet without a moment's hesitation. Remy's furious with us for concealing the truth about our magic, but he's been drawn into this mess by helping my sister and me escape. He won't betray us to the Technocrats.

However, his father, Isaiah—the leader of the Magi—is another matter. I don't fully trust Remy to keep our secret from him.

But that won't matter if we never reach the Chambers.

We head out again, each of us putting a protective spell in place. I cast the shield spell that conceals us, Zandria casts the silencing spell, and Remy covers our tracks.

We keep an ear out for the sounds of skittering metal, our bodies tense as we walk briskly. We won't run unless a machine or a soldier is directly upon us, or else we'll wear ourselves out quickly.

Remy is a little ways ahead of me and Zandy. When he stops short, holding up a fist, magic flares inside me, as I know it does for my companions. We're ready to defend ourselves if necessary.

After a moment of standing stock-still, listening only to the sound of our own breaths, we hear it: the click of metal. Steel parts moving in tandem, a machine with legs. I shudder. It could be any number of things, and only one or a pack.

"This way!" Remy hisses as he shoves us toward the eastern part of the forest. We need to head northeast to reach the Chambers, but the detour is worth it to evade the machines.

This time we run.

Despite our quickened pace, the machines draw closer, their noise growing louder than before. My pulse throbs in my ears.

We are absolutely not getting caught now. Not when we're so close to escape.

Soon the sound comes from all around us. It's impossible to pinpoint the exact direction. We've been careful to hide our tracks and stay under our spells. But something must've given us away.

We burst through a break in the trees into a field filled with large boulders. I scramble onto the nearest one, turning to see in all directions. Within moments, a metal beast steps onto the field at each of the four points—north, south, east, and west.

Mechwolves.

The articulated metal in their sleek bodies repeats the sound we heard. I take in the legs that allow them to run at inhuman speeds, perked ears with listening devices that can transmit back to whoever controls them, and razor-sharp teeth meant to tear apart their prey. My palms turn slick. These are not the sort of machines the Technocrats send out when they want to capture someone.

They're the kind they deploy when they want to kill.

Remy and Zandria clamber onto the boulder beside me. We're surrounded. I glance at my sister. We've never used our secret magic so brazenly before. But doing so now is the only way to defang this new threat. Remy is already muttering a spell to lift one of the nearby boulders when the mechwolves rush toward us. He knocks one aside, but another slips through. Its cold, reflective eyes bore into me as it lunges in my direction.

Anxiety and exhilaration fill me in equal parts as my magic rips its head clean off its neck. Its body clanks as it tumbles to the ground, a mess of metal legs and parts, and the head bounces once beside it.

This is what my sister and I were born—made—to do. Act on the machines and organic matter. Using my magic boldly may be risky, but it's still a thrill.

The mechwolves aren't done with us yet. Zandria makes short work of one of the two barreling down at her, and I take on the second with the same spell, dismantling it efficiently. When we turn around, we find Remy has successfully used the small boulder to crush the mechwolf he knocked off its feet earlier.

"You really can use magic on the machines," Remy says, awe creeping into his voice.

I snort. "Did you think we made up a treasonous claim just for fun?"

"No, no. But seeing it in action is something else." He puts a hand on my shoulder. "With what you can do, we could destroy the entire Technocrat army. We could—"

"We do have limits, you know," Zandria says, finally straightening up again. "We still need our hands and our breath to cast spells. And if they sneak up on us unawares or overwhelm us with sheer numbers . . ." My sister shudders. She doesn't need to finish that sentence. We both know what will happen.

An eternity captive in a metal suit within the Technocrats' dungeons. A burned-out tongue, crushed hands. No light or life ever again.

"Still, well done," Remy says. He's not happy with us, but it's evident he's beginning to realize what an asset our powers can be.

"Let's go before more of them pick up our trail," I say.

"And before they find what's left of these," Zandria says, kicking a stray piece of metal.

Finally heading in the right direction, we hike as quickly as we can with a few stops for food and rest. When darkness falls, we choose to walk all night. We're near delirious with exhaustion, but stopping for sleep will mean our deaths.

Forward is the only way if we want to live long enough to warn the others.

We trudge along on weary legs and worn-out feet until the wee morning hours. The ravine finally comes into view, slicing through the earth.

The Chambers.

RELIEF WASHES OVER ME. THE FAMILIAR

gorge yawns before us, lined on either side
with green trees and craggy rocks. The place
where we must reveal the stone steps with a spell is
nearby, welcoming as ever. Part of me was terrified we'd
arrive too late.

My eyes sting with unshed tears, but I don't let them fall. If
we want the Magi to survive, Isaiah needs to take us seriously. I
can't afford to show any sign of weakness.

Remy's expression shifts from the scowl he's been wearing
ever since we left Palinor to one that's lighter, more hopeful. "The
Techno camp . . . it's really gone."

"For now," I say, unable to release the anxious knot in my gut.

We check our surroundings one last time to ensure no
machines or guards followed us, then work the spell to open the
stairs down into the ravine and the Magi's refuge. Once we reach
the bottom, we send the stairs back into the cliff face. Then we slip
through the shadowed crack in the wall that leads into the strange
world of light and life hidden in the massive cavern system the
Magi call home.

For the first time, I don't feel safe here.

I'm surprised to see no sign of the soldiers and mechs Darian
had posted near the ravine. Not long ago, Remy and I narrowly
avoided running right into them as we left the Chambers. Darian
had plans for them to mine the vein of magic ore that runs through
this land.

Something's wrong. I can feel it in my bones.

We stumble our way to Isaiah's home. Exhausted, we fall
into the chairs around his kitchen table. The polished stone walls

dotted here and there with the green that fills this place are the same as they were a few weeks ago. Isaiah comes out of his rooms, clearly not expecting guests at this early hour, let alone three bedraggled ones.

Not much can catch Isaiah Gaville off guard, but at the sight of us, his mouth drops open. He recovers himself a moment later.

"Remy, what is the meaning of this? You and Aissa are stationed in Palinor. You already risked your post to come here recently. Why are you here again?"

Before Remy can answer, I step forward. "We must speak to the council immediately. It's an emergency."

"You will tell me and I'll decide if—"

"We will not," I say, keeping my expression as calm as possible. "We're all in grave danger, and the Armory Council must be warned."

Isaiah's deep frown informs me I've stepped way over the line. But his eyes widen when the spell that changed Zandria's features dissipates and she reverts to her normal appearance. Mine expired minutes before we went down the steps.

"Both of you?" Isaiah muses. "You went against my explicit orders and rescued your sister?"

"No, Father," Remy says with a grimace. "We were captured. But an . . . unexpected ally helped us escape with Zandria." I silently thank Remy for not mentioning exactly who that ally was. That would do us no favors with his father.

Isaiah raises an eyebrow. "And you refuse to tell me the news you bring now?"

"The council must hear it. We wouldn't do this if it weren't of the utmost importance," Remy says. "But first I have a question for you—is Darian Azul here?"

Isaiah shakes his head. "No. Why?"

"You'll understand once we relay our news," Remy insists.

His father scoffs. "Fine. I'll convene the council. But know that I'm doing it primarily to call for censuring the three of you."

He returns to his rooms and we're left staring at each other.

Zandria snorts. "Well, that went terribly."

Remy runs his hands over his face. "Yes, it did. Let's try to get some sleep before the council convenes."

Remy and I take the rooms we had before. This time Zandria joins me in mine and we sleep in the same bed. I don't want to let her out of my sight now that I've got her back. We're exhausted enough that we fall asleep quickly, our dreams filled with fears of what nightmares may come next.

We're awakened by Remy shaking our shoulders.

"The council is convening in one hour," he says. "We should eat something before we go."

Zandria and I dress quickly in the clean clothes we stole on our way out of Palinor. What we were wearing is dirtied and torn from our flight and fight.

We give each other the once-over before we leave the room. Zandria fixes my mussed-up hair, while I pull a wayward leaf off her shirt. Things almost feel as they used to between us, except that her voice and expression are cold, void of her familiar warmth. It seems like an eternity ago that Isaiah first sat in our kitchen and assigned us our mission to find the Heartless heir to the Technocrat throne. Somehow that's all led us here to deliver our dire warning.

We join Remy in a quick breakfast of toast and wild blueberry jam, then hurry to the cave where the Armory Council holds court. The lush greenery on the way is a sight for sore eyes, but the fear it could all disappear tempers any joy I might feel about being home. Our parents, for one, will never return here again.

The Magi we pass greet us curiously. They know Remy well, and me—and Zandria—they recognize from when I came here last to plead for the council to help me rescue her. My arrival, and speedy exit, were noticeable to say the least.

We don't linger, however, and when we arrive at the Armory Council room, we're ushered in immediately and greeted by unhappy, suspicious faces. I'm just grateful Darian didn't find a way to join us. The rushed meeting was necessary, even if it has angered some council members.

"Well," Isaiah says, holding his arms wide. "What is it that you three must so urgently tell us?"

Isaiah glances at his son, but Remy cedes the floor to me. I step forward, my throat coated with icicles.

"We've come directly from Palinor with dire news. We walked all night without stopping, all while the woods were crawling with Technos hunting for us."

That manages to raise some eyebrows.

"What did you do to earn such a show of force?" asks Masia Harkness, her long blue robes wrapped around her. Zandria's eyes widen at the sound of Masia's voice. We idolized her when we were children.

"We uncovered a terrible plot. One of our own, Darian Azul, spymaster, is working against the Magi. The Chambers has been compromised."

The declaration is met with silence at first, then a laugh or two. Isaiah scowls.

"This is what you came here to do? Make baseless accusations against one of the most loyal weapons in the Armory?"

"It's not baseless, Father," Remy says. "I've seen and heard the proof with my own eyes and ears."

"Darian's the reason I was captured by the Technocrats in the first place," Zandria says, her hands balled into fists at her sides.

"Yes, it is certainly . . . interesting . . . that you're free now, Zandria." Masia eyes me and Remy. "What is this proof you speak of?"

"Remy and I were searching the palace for the heir—as directed—when we happened upon some scientists heading to a demonstration of a supposed breakthrough on a new power source," I say. "We followed them and hid in the room next door. We heard Darian tell the gathered scientists and researchers the stone power source he was unveiling kept a charge after being infused with geothermal energy, but that was a lie. When he turned his machine on in the demonstration room, another lit up in ours. It contained Magi, clearly in pain." I take a deep breath, then plunge ahead. "Darian has devised a means of draining our magic."

The response is not at all what we anticipated.

"You must be joking," Isaiah says, and several council members mutter the same beside him. "This is a wild story, but it doesn't smack at all of truth."

Frustration builds inside my chest. Once again, they're going to rebuff us. But this time we all will pay the price.

Another council member speaks up. "What proof have you brought us of these grave accusations?"

"Our testimony is our proof," Remy says. "I trusted Darian as much as any of you. Even when we saw our trapped brethren in the draining machines, I argued in favor of trusting him, just as you do now. It's unthinkable he'd betray us in such a manner, but he did. When Aissa and I left the room, Darian used a spell to reveal us as Magi and oversaw our capture and subsequent interrogation."

"You expect us to take your word against that of our most trusted spy?" Isaiah says.

"Yes," I say. "He told me his whole plan in an effort to bring me—and by association, Zandria—over to his side."

Masia sits up straighter, curiosity sparking in her dark eyes. "And what is his plan?"

I pause, painfully aware of the fact I'm about to betray another Magi's secret. He may deserve it, but that doesn't make me like it any better.

"Years ago, Darian was married." That, finally, elicits some surprise among those on the council. "He married a Heartless. He became obsessed with their plight and led the charge to find a cure. When she died not long after their wedding, his work moved into dangerous territory. He didn't just want a better power source—he wanted one that would run forever and would make the Heartless loyal to him. Because while this was happening, the Armory's plan to install him on the throne was also in motion. Darian was ready to assume leadership, either through playing the role he was meant to or by building an army of supercharged Heartless who had sworn fealty to him."

"And he'd already decided to play both sides," Remy adds. "He told the Technocrat king and queen years ago that the Magi tried to recruit him, and they instructed him to play along. He's been feeding us bad intel ever since. For example, the Heartless heir was really a boy around our age, not a little girl as Darian suggested."

Isaiah's mouth is clamped closed. He knows the intel we got about the heir being female was incorrect, but he may not have informed the rest of the Armory Council.

"And why would he admit all this to you, Aissa?" Isaiah says.

I grimace, not loving the lie I'm about to tell. "Somehow he got wind of how Zandria's and my magic amplifies each other's before I even came to the council a few weeks ago. He wanted us on his side. To join his army once he stages his coup. He even set a trap for Zandria in the tunnels so he could leverage her to ensure my assistance."

"You?" Isaiah begins to laugh. More than one council member covers their mouth to hide their own laughter. "So this is your proof? An inflated sense of your own importance? Ridiculous," he says.

My anger flares, making me dizzy.

"He imprisoned me too, Father," Remy says. "He may not have tried to win me over to his cause like he did Aissa, but he was ready to condemn me to life in a metal suit without a second thought."

Isaiah blinks at this but remains unmoved. "If you were imprisoned, it was your own fault. That's the price for mistakes when it comes to the Technocrats."

Remy's mouth drops open. He's finally beginning to realize what Zandria and I long ago understood: Isaiah is a harsh taskmaster. He's as cold as the Technocrats themselves. Even his only son cannot change his mind.

"We'll all pay the price if you don't listen to us!" Zandria steps forward, visibly shaking. She can barely contain her magic. I almost put a restraining hand on her shoulder, but then think better of it. It might make things worse.

"She isn't wrong," I say. "Darian also threatened the Magi living here in the Chambers."

Masia leans forward, suddenly more interested. "What do you mean? How did he threaten us?"

"When Remy and I left the Chambers the last time we were here, a camp of Technocrat soldiers and their mechanimals were prowling along the edge of the ravine. At first, we were afraid a captured Magi had given up the location of the secret camp, but later Darian told me they were here at his orders."

"Is this army still there?" Masia asks.

"Not that we noticed. And we were very careful coming here."

Isaiah sits back in his chair, folding his arms across his chest.

"Then I suppose you have your answer. They weren't much of a threat after all, were they? If Darian meant to use them against us, wouldn't he still have them posted here?"

"I—I would've thought so," I admit. "But they may have been recalled to hunt for us."

"Ah yes, again because you're critical to Darian's nefarious plans." Isaiah's expression—mocking disbelief—is mirrored on several other faces in the room.

"It's the truth," I say between clenched teeth. Zandria simmers next to me, her face turning beet red.

"What would you have us do then? Cast Darian out?" Isaiah scoffs.

"You need to flee the Chambers," I snap. "Darian made it clear that if we didn't cooperate, he would take his disappointment out on the rest of the Magi."

Isaiah shakes his head as if he can't believe his ears. "I think we've heard more than enough."

"Wait, I have one more question," Masia says. "If you were caught in the dungeons as you claim, how did you escape?"

A muscle in my jaw begins to twitch. "We had help."

Masia frowns. "From whom? Darian and Remy were the only spies we had stationed in the Palace aside from yourself."

"A Technocrat."

She raises an eyebrow. "Why would a Technocrat help you?"

Zandria scowls. "Because he's in love with Aissa."

Heat flashes over my face.

Isaiah stands. "Hold on. Last Remy reported back, you were getting closer to an informant who you discovered was actually the Heartless heir. Is that the Technocrat who helped you escape?"

I nod. This is the last thing I wanted to tell them, but Isaiah knows too many pieces of the story, and lying will only sink our entire case.

"Your orders were to kill him. Why was he alive to help you?" Isaiah says through gritted teeth.

"He doesn't deserve to die, and I wasn't about to put Darian on the throne after discovering his treachery." Not exactly the order of events, but it's the story that will best protect Aro.

"Who are you to decide that?" he growls.

Before I can answer, Zandria reaches the boiling point. But she aims her rage at the wrong person: me.

"He was stabbed by a guard as we escaped, and she even saved his life!" she says. I gape at her, but she won't meet my eyes. She's tiptoeing around dangerous territory; she knows full well falling in love with a Technocrat is considered treason.

Isaiah's face turns purple. "You used magic to heal a Technocrat? One you were ordered to assassinate? What were you thinking?"

Something inside me snaps. "I was thinking he could be an ally, someone inside the Palace walls who is actually loyal, unlike Darian has been to the Magi."

Isaiah's hands drop to his sides and he becomes frighteningly calm and cold. "You may wait outside while we confer about what to do with this . . . information."

WE'RE USHERED INTO THE SAME LITTLE

room where we awaited the council's verdict
on whether to help Zandria only a few weeks ago.
I have the same sinking feeling in my stomach now.

"What a fool!" Zandria exclaims once the door closes
behind us. "He'd already made up his mind before we even
entered the council room. And he took issue with every single
thing we said. Ugh!"

"Isaiah is not an easy man to persuade, especially when he's
sure he's right about something." I begin to pace. "Your little outburst didn't help matters at all, thanks."

Zandria looks away again, but her cheeks are pink.

Remy sits on a bench with his head in his hands. "He's known
Darian for too long to doubt him." He lets out a small laugh. "I'm
sure the Technocrat royals would be just as difficult to convince.
Darian holds the same place here as he does with them—second
in command, essentially. Trusted advisor. The idea he could betray
the Magi is just . . . unthinkable to my father." He sits back. "I'm
not sure I can blame him. If I hadn't seen it with my own eyes, I
doubt I'd believe you either."

"Then you're a fool too," Zandria snaps.

"Zandy, that's not helping," I say.

She whirls on me but doesn't get a word in before the door
opens. Masia Harkness, Magi legend, steps out and closes the
door behind her. We all stare. Masia is rumored to have taken
down several well-positioned Technocrat men on her own. And
she's one of the best spellcasters the Magi have ever seen. She
regards us with keen eyes, then shakes her head, her short black
hair rustling.

"I'm afraid I have bad news," she says. "The Armory Council doesn't believe your story. And Isaiah is all but ready to string you up for disobeying a direct order to assassinate the heir, Aissa."

My throat closes. Did they send Masia out here to kill me?

Zandria steps closer to me, and I can't help feeling a little comforted.

"Instead, they're casting you out," Masia says.

I frown. "What do you mean, casting us out?"

"I mean you must leave the Chambers and never come back. You're no longer Magi spies, and we will not protect you or share intelligence with you. I will show you out."

In spite of her stern demeanor, there's something surprisingly sympathetic in Masia's expression and body language.

Remy doesn't seem to notice this, possibly because he's too distracted by his father disowning him. "All of us?" he says.

"I'm afraid so. Come with me, please."

Her tone makes it clear the time to argue is long past. We follow her in shocked silence. She takes us through a cavern tunnel I haven't been down before. My curiosity—and fear—grows. "Where are you taking us?"

She puts a finger to her lips and tilts her head to indicate we should enter a cave to our left. We do, though not without some hesitation.

She closes the door behind us and immediately casts a sound-dampening spell. The stern expression fades and is replaced by concern.

"We must make this quick. I'd hoped to have more time with you before you left, but Isaiah is furious. I'm lucky I was even able to escort you out." She puts a hand on my and Zandria's shoulders. "Tell me, did your parents explain what the Alchemist Alliance is before they passed away?"

"You mean before Darian murdered them?" I say.

Masia's face pales. "It was him, was it?" She sighs. "He has long been ambitious, but I never imagined he'd take such a dramatic turn."

"You believe us?" Remy says. "But the council just voted to kick us out."

"Not *all* of the council, just a majority. I voted in favor of taking your advice and preparing for a fight."

"And my father did not," Remy says.

She nods her assent. "But back to the matter at hand. Did they tell you about the Alliance?"

"Yes, sort of," I say. "They left us a letter hidden in the floor and directed me to it as they were dying. They never trusted Darian. The letter outlined the basics of what the Alchemist Alliance was and its purpose."

"Yes." Masia's eyes are lit with a strange fire. "Now that purpose falls to you."

"You're part of the Alliance?" Zandria asks.

"I am," Masia says. "I knew your parents well. They were good people, excellent Magi, and dedicated Alchemists. They would want you to continue their work."

"But how?" Zandria asks. "We found what was left of the Magi library. It wasn't much."

"Just a small room with a map and journal." I intentionally omit the spell book that hides in Zandria's pack. The last thing I wish to do is turn it over, especially if we can't ever return.

"May I see them?" I hand Masia the map and journal and she examines them eagerly.

"We're still trying to figure out what they mean," I say.

"I can help you with that," she says.

"You're really part of the Alchemist Alliance?" I can hardly believe our good luck that such a renowned Magi is one of us.

She smiles. "I am." She points to the map. "This is directing you to go west." She chews her lip as she considers the last rune on the map. "'To find a sanctuary,' it says."

"That must be where all the spell books that should have been in the library are," I say.

"Very possibly. I cannot leave my post here, especially if the Technocrats are on their way to attack us. But you three must leave, and I strongly suggest you follow that map to the sanctuary."

"What does the inscription mean, do you think?" I ask, pointing out the words on the little note that had been folded into the map: *Follow the past to find the future.*

"It's the motto of the Alchemist Alliance. They believed that by studying and embracing our past, we could regain our lost glory. And especially that we could find the keys to our lost powers in the past as well. No one knows for certain why the schism happened, separating us into two peoples: one with magic and one without. Nor why those with magic could no longer affect inanimate objects. But the Alchemists were convinced if they could figure that out, they could reverse it. We've been trying with the alchemicals every new generation. Maybe someday it will work, and some of us will be born with full powers."

A jolt runs through Zandria and me. Part of me wants to tell this woman that it *has* happened, but it's been too well drummed into me not to tell a soul, especially someone well-placed in the Armory. I can tell my sister feels the same.

"So no one has yet?" I ask. If she knew, would she tell us? Or hide the truth like we do?

She shakes her head. "Regrettably, no. But the recipe to create the alchemicals has been passed down to every generation."

Zandria and I exchange a look. "We don't have a recipe. Our parents must have died before giving it to us."

Masia frowns. "That can't be right. You said they wrote you a letter telling you about the Alchemist Alliance, yes?"

"They did," I say.

"It must be included in invisible ink. You can reveal it with a simple spell or try lemon juice."

A thrill rolls through me and Zandy. Our parents may have left us more than we realized.

"Thank you," I say. "We'll try that."

Masia glances down the hall behind her. "Now you must leave, and quickly too. Before Isaiah decides to dole out a more extreme punishment."

I shiver. I have no doubt Isaiah wanted to do more and was only thwarted by the compassion of the other councilors like Masia.

"What will you do? We're deadly serious about the Technocrat threat from Darian," Zandria says, her face taking on a wild look. "You can't let him back into the Chambers. Not ever."

Masia's expression hardens. "I'll be doing everything I can to block him and change the rest of the council's mind."

Remy's hands ball into fists. "We should stay and fight. I can't believe my father is doing this to us."

Masia pats his arm. "He's angry right now. But he loves you. He'll come around eventually."

I have my doubts. Isaiah isn't the forgiving sort. But perhaps he'll make an exception for Remy.

She ushers us through a hidden route in the Chambers, one that bypasses the gawking crowds that are probably assembling in the main thoroughfare we took to get here. For that, I'm grateful. I ran that gauntlet the last time Isaiah and the council dismissed me, and I'm not eager to do it again.

Soon, we reach the exit tunnels, and Masia bids us goodbye. We ascend via the staircase, Zandria and I crafting the spell to form it while Remy casts a shield spell just to be safe. Then we reach the deserted top of the ravine. Everything is still and seems so normal.

A far cry from what Remy and I encountered the last time. The sun shines over our heads, and birds sing in the trees. The hum of insects floats on the late summer breeze. For a moment, I wonder if perhaps we're overreacting. If Darian's threat was an empty one.

But then I remember who we're talking about. The man who put my sister in irons, who killed my parents, and who has been playing both sides for years.

No, the threat isn't empty. The Technocrats will come for the Chambers. The only question is when.

AFTER THE CHILLY RECEPTION OUR NEWS

received from the Armory councilors, all of
us are on edge. The fact the Technocrat encampment seems to have vanished into thin air only makes
our discomfort worse.

I don't trust this for a second. Every muscle in my body
is taut and ready for a fight.

Remy barely notices. He fumes behind me and Zandria as we
head into the forest, taking the path laid out by the map we found
in the secret room beneath Palinor.

"I can't believe my own father won't listen to me. Just
because . . . because . . ." he sputters but doesn't finish his sentence.

"Just because you've aligned yourself with me—the Magi who
saved a Technocrat," I say for him.

Zandria snaps. "Can you blame him, Aissa? You abandoned
your mission for the very person you were supposed to assassinate.
If any other Magi had done that, you'd condemn them too."

She isn't wrong. Until a couple weeks ago, I would've done
precisely that. But Aro upended my life. Turned my own heart
against itself. However foolhardy it may be, I wouldn't have it any
other way.

"Love made fools of us all," I retort—and instantly wish I
hadn't.

My sister's sharp, wounded look makes me regret alluding to
the feelings she once had for Darian.

Worse, he led her on because, more than his desire to raise
an army of loyal Heartless warriors, Darian wants to use us. Our
unique magic allows us to control the machines but also marks
us as the end result of the Alchemist Alliance's final experiment.

The alliance of Technos and Magi believed we could surmount our differences if everyone were restored to their original, magical state, and I'm doubtless Darian wishes to use that power to unite his own twisted kingdom.

"Darian must've gotten to him before us somehow," Remy mutters. "That lying traitor. My father trusts him more than me."

"Isaiah is thoroughly committed to the idea that installing Darian on the Techno throne is the only way to victory," I say.

Zandria *tsks*. "More like the idea he could be wrong is utterly unthinkable to him."

"I just don't—" Remy's voice cuts off as the ground beneath our feet trembles.

We halt, magic at the ready, and examine the woods around us. The trees quiver. The trembling increases, then stops as suddenly as it began. At first, all we hear is silence—not even the sound of small trundling animals or birds—then a whistle whines in the distance, slowly growing louder.

My chest tightens. I don't know what's happening, but I'm certain it's nothing good.

The earth rattles again, hard enough to knock us off our feet. A horrible noise booms behind us—in the direction of the Chambers.

Horror claws at my throat.

Technocrats.

Remy's face turns an ashen shade. He leaps to his feet and sprints back the way we came.

"Wait!" Zandria cries. "It's too late!"

My shock at my sister attempting to be the voice of reason and not run after danger is enough to make me pause, lagging behind them both by a few seconds. So much has changed.

We race after Remy, hoping to catch up to him before he gives us away to whatever caused that noise. We reach him just inside the tree line. My brain freezes, unable to process the enormity of what lies before us.

Nothing is left of the Chambers save a huge, smoking crater filled with rubble.

Zandria makes a choking noise beside me. Remy falls to his knees. My heart sinks through the earth, joining the broken bodies of my fellow Magi buried in the wreckage of the only place that ever felt like home.

Another whistle breaks the silence, along with the all-too-familiar sound of skittering metal legs.

A blast pummels the remains of the ravine, and moments later hundreds of seekers swarm through the rubble and dust, blanketing the ground. Behind them is a sight that makes my blood spike with magic and fear.

War machines.

My breath rasps. It's suddenly harder to breathe. I never imagined I'd see machines like these. I've only read about them in the Technocrat history books. The illustrations didn't do them justice. They're gigantic, even larger than the mechanimals that prance through Palinor in the annual Victory Parade.

These don't pretend at life like those do. They're built purely for the purpose of destruction. Some are boxy with arms that pound the earth, both to destroy everything in their path and propel themselves forward. Others have huge circular openings from which bombs spew toward my former home. Still others have drills that dig into the ground. Like they know the last of the Magi hid under the earth.

A hot flush of pure hatred rushes over me. All I want to do is rip apart every machine here. And every Technocrat too. Beside me, Zandy's hands ball into fists and her nostrils flare. I know she feels the same.

But that won't bring our friends, our people, back to life. It will only expose us and leave us to suffer the same—or an even worse—fate.

Zandria's face twists into an expression I've never seen her wear before. "I'll kill him," she whispers hoarsely.

Magi or not, Darian must be stopped. Permanently. And we'll do it together.

But not today.

I yank Remy to his feet and shake him. "We need to leave. Now."

Together, Zandria and I drag Remy away until his shock fades enough for him to keep pace with us while we run. The whistles of heavy artillery resound behind us, churning my stomach.

We must put as much distance as possible between us and those terrible machines.

The Chambers, the last refuge of the Magi, is now a tomb.

I choke back the sob that begs to be released and push forward. The Technocrats haven't seen us yet, but they will if we don't move quickly. We're fortunate this area still has an actual forest to hide in.

I shudder to think what would've happened had we been out in the open when those machines arrived.

Behind us, a new sound groans and cracks. We stop for just a moment to glance behind—only to see trees crashing to the ground.

"They're destroying the forest," Zandria says, her mouth slack with disbelief.

My stomach clenches. "In case any Magi stragglers try to flee," I say.

"Yeah, like us," Remy says. "*Rapide.*"

While Remy's speed spell pushes us faster, Zandria casts a silencing spell, and I cover us with the shield. We take no chances today.

By nightfall, we've pushed our bodies to the breaking point. It's dangerous to use the speed spell for too long, and we've exceeded the recommended time by two hours. Every inch of my body aches, a thousand pricks of pain. The sound of the machines is far in the distance now. They destroyed a vast section of the forest, and we mourn for the trees. Someday, when this is over, we'll return and help the forest regrow, like Magi have done for centuries.

We stop to rest by a small lake that interrupts the forest. I settle onto a log by the bank and split some food with Zandria and Remy. We eat silently. The weight of what we witnessed rests uncomfortably on our shoulders.

All hope of the Magi reclaiming their place has vanished. I don't know how many Magi languish in the Technocrats' dungeons or retain their cover in Palinor, but the number can't be large. Certainly not enough to replace the nearly thousand lives we just lost.

We're it. The three of us, and likely a handful of stragglers. If we don't survive, the Magi are truly extinct.

All we can hope to do now is thwart Darian's plans, and even that's ambitious. Overthrowing the Technocrat regime without our spy network feels like a lost cause.

Everything we've worked for, everything we've known and counted on our whole lives, is gone.

Except each other.

Zandria's hands clench and unclench as she sits next to me on the log, staring out at the placid lake. The world feels strangely calm after the upheaval that took place a few hours ago.

"Do you think . . . do you think any of them survived?" Zandria says quietly.

"No," Remy answers immediately, sitting on her other side.

"Our magic can do many things, but my father failed to warn anyone. They'd have been crushed before they even had the chance to ready a spell." There's a pain in his voice I've never heard before.

I put my head in my hands. "Remy's probably right. Though maybe a few survivors managed to get out one of the back tunnels."

Remy scoffs. "Then they'd have been picked off by the Technocrats and their machines." He shakes his head. "No, we shouldn't waste an ounce of hope on any of them surviving. It's a miracle we escaped when we did."

Zandria's chin trembles, but she manages to steel her jaw. She's been through so much these last few weeks that I want nothing more than to wrap her in a hug. But she's been standoffish since her rescue and has made clear that she's angry with me about Aro. She doesn't understand why I did what I did.

Sometimes, even I don't understand. It wasn't rational to fall in love with a Technocrat. It wasn't rational to save him. But I did both anyway.

Ripples. That's what I always used to remind myself of whenever I considered a move. If I do this, what will the fallout be? How will it impact everything else?

My heart didn't—and still doesn't—care about those ripples. Even if love will only lead us both to death and destruction.

Remy finishes eating and stands. "We need to keep moving. We're clear enough of the Technocrats that we could head back to Palinor now." A fierceness lights his face. "Then we can kill Darian. That's all I want to do."

"Not yet," I say. "Trying now would be a fool's errand. He's been hoarding spell books. He's more knowledgeable than we are about magic. We need our lost spells. Those will give us the edge to take him by surprise. If Masia was right, we may find the answers we need to defeat him at the end of that map, as well as learn more about Zandria's and my powers."

Zandria nods her agreement, but Remy paces. "You want to go chasing a myth? Right now? After what we just witnessed?" The edge in his voice sharpens with every word.

I rise, putting my hands on his shoulders to stop his pacing. "It is not a myth. It's our only real chance."

He shrugs me off. "What if it doesn't even exist? What if the Technos caught whoever was transporting the books before they reached this supposed sanctuary and burned them all? Why should we put our faith in something we have no way of knowing is real?" He throws up his hands. "Everyone believed the library was still somewhere in the city, but that didn't pan out. What makes you think this map will?"

I swallow hard. His points are sharp and cutting, and I can't deny he might be right. "Because we have to. We have to believe in something. Otherwise, we have nothing."

WE SPEND SEVERAL DAYS WINDING

through the far reaches of the continent as we
follow the map. We knew the country was vast,
but none of us has ever explored it before. It's sparsely
populated. That shouldn't surprise me, considering the
Technocrats wiped out half the population who lived here
one hundred years ago. Still, I expected more people. Instead
we find the crumbled remnants of several bombed villages, with
only a few stone walls standing, now overgrown with vines and
young trees. Twice, we've come upon a village or outpost where
Technocrats live a simpler life than those in the capital city.

But they're still Technocrats, and we're careful to give them
and their villages a wide berth.

The map led us over mountains and through a region of deep
forest. Then yesterday we entered a huge swath of swamp and
marshland. We had no choice but to trudge through it as carefully as possible. According to the map, our destination lies on
the other side.

We walked all day, then when night fell, we slept in shifts on
a crop of massive driftwood trees. There are dangerous animals
out here, alligators and birds of prey with wingspans as large as
my own arms spread wide. And those are just the ones we've seen
and warded off.

But the swamp isn't a comfortable place to sleep, and I wake
up strangely sore and grumpy.

When we finally break free of the swamp in the late morning,
a new, startling sight greets us in fits and starts through the thick
fog. The terrain ahead is hilly but desolate. Skeletal petrified trees,
no doubt the result of Technocrat bombs, still stand like a silent

army. Few people live in the western regions of the country anymore, and the Technos haven't bothered to populate it with their fake metal trees. Nothing grows in the soil but the hardiest weeds, ferns, and moss. The hills are covered with them, at least what we can see through gaps in the fog as it rolls by.

Zandria frowns. "Are you sure this is where we're supposed to go? I don't see anything that could be a library around here."

I check the map again. Our path is true. "Definitely. Even the hills are noted here."

Remy sighs, then weaves a spell to dry our wet feet and trousers after the journey through the swamp. "Then let's see what we can find. I doubt it will be much."

Remy's attitude has become fatalistic since we left the Chambers. The initial shock has faded, leaving behind only bitterness and grief. It weighs on all of us, an invisible hand constricting around our chests.

But unlike Remy, I can't afford to assume defeat. I still have too much to lose.

I miss Aro like I'd miss one of my limbs. I never expected to feel like this once I performed the Binding rite, but there's a constant ache, a need to be near him, in every breath I take. He grew on me so slowly, so stealthily. I didn't fully realize he had my heart until it was far too late. I miss working with him, oddly enough, even though what I was doing was supposed to be in service to the Technocrats. But his relentless determination to help other Heartless who weren't fortunate enough to be royalty was infectious. He helped them for the same reason he helped us escape.

Because it was the right thing to do.

Aro's moral compass is more finely tuned than that of some Magi. He opened my eyes in so many ways, and it's impossible to close them again. No matter how safe he believes himself to be in Palinor, I know he's at risk. And that terrifies me. Remy and Zandria may feel like they've lost everything and that the only way to ease the pain is to throw themselves deeper into darkness and revenge. But I still have light worth fighting for. I won't give up on it easily.

We begin to hear a strange noise. A mournful keening that echoes through the air. At first, it's disconcerting, but then I realize what it is: the wind howling through the leafless, petrified forest. I shudder and reach for Zandria's hand, but it isn't there. Her arms are folded over her chest and she stares straight ahead.

She hasn't forgiven me yet.

But she will. Eventually. I hope.

"It's just the wind," Remy says. Zandria shrugs and we continue into the hills. The pits and valleys between them are sharper than I expected. Almost like giant ants built these mounds dotting the landscape, ranging in size from small to enormous. The largest rises above the fog in the center of the hills. There's a solemnity about it that makes me shiver.

I look to the map, then point to that hill. "There. The tallest one is marked for some reason. If we head that way, it should give us a better idea of why we were led here."

"Or maybe there's nothing left of what was once here," Zandria says sourly. "This place is just a strange, hilly wasteland with bad weather." She may have originally sided with my plan to go after the lost library, but in the days since she's become more and more disillusioned with the idea. Remy's influence isn't helping. I miss the lighthearted Zandria who used to go tunnel diving with me every night. Who enjoyed an adventure for the sake of the journey.

Remy shrugs. "Why not? I have no better ideas."

We make our way cautiously through the fog, ever conscious of the fact we can't see everything that may be out here with us.

In spite of the fog, I feel exposed. I don't like that one bit. Even our shield spell is little help—if we used it, a large blank spot moving through the fog would be all too noticeable. If we manipulate the fog with our magic, we'll immediately give away our position to anyone or anything out here. No, the best course is to let the fog wrap around us and walk maddeningly slow and steady.

We pick our way through the mist as it clings to our cloaks and curls around our legs like a welcoming pet, heading for the largest hill in the center. Every now and then I glance behind, but all I can see is the fog and the grasping tree skeletons. Sometimes I swear I hear the sound of metal skittering, but neither Zandria nor Remy notices it. The keening of the wind is all that reaches their ears. If I wasn't casting the silencing spell, I'd cast the one that amplifies sounds for the caster instead just to be sure. But I don't dare drop one of the few things preventing us from being completely exposed.

Those same noises have haunted my nightmares all week. I'm probably imagining them.

It takes us about an hour to reach the central hill. Zandria puts her hands on her hips and stares up at the giant mound before us. "What does the map say we're supposed to do now?"

I turn it over in my hands, trying to make sense of it. "It doesn't specify. It just leads here."

"That's not helpful," Remy says.

"Maybe we won't know until we get to the top?" I say. "Maybe there's something we can only see from that vantage point."

"Worth a try," Zandria says and starts her ascent without waiting for us. That part of Zandria appears to be making a return—the constant desire to run ahead.

Remy and I hike up the hill after her. When we reach the summit, I recognize the sensation tingling in my toes—magic. Something the Magi created is waiting for us to find it.

We survey the foggy hills on all sides with matching scowls. The landscape is strange in a way that I can't quite put my finger on . . .

It's symmetrical. *Too* symmetrical.

The realization jolts through me, but I don't say anything to my companions yet. I examine the softly rolling hills, whose tips peek through the fog.

They're laid out in concentric circles, spreading out from this center peak like a drop of water rippling outward in a lake.

This is not a natural formation. The ancient Magi must've designed this, crafted the landscape in this whole area. Our legends make it clear this isn't unusual, but it's the first time I've seen something the Magi built in its entirety that wasn't the Chambers. While I have no doubt the Magi made this place, I can't help wondering why. What did they use these strange hills for? They're aesthetically pleasing, certainly, but their purpose is a mystery. Just like so much of the Magi's true history.

"It's beautiful," I whisper, a sudden emotion filling me up until I can't breathe. Awe? Joy? Anguish? I hardly know what to call it.

"It is," Zandria agrees.

Remy is silent. I'd bet anything he's thinking of his father and the Chambers again. We've lost so much. But at least we found this.

"Nothing's here," Zandria says, clearly frustrated. The cold and damp from the fog seeps into our hair and skin; we're all feeling more irritable than usual.

"That can't be right," I say, consulting the parchment map yet again. "This hill is marked on the map. It has to be the right place."

"Maybe whatever was here was blown to smithereens. Destroyed like the trees," Remy suggests. I stare daggers at him.

"We're not giving up yet." I close my eyes, letting my magic explore. Something tugs back.

There's powerful magic here, somewhere very close.

Sending a spell beneath my feet, I test the soil to determine where the magic is coming from. To my surprise, it seems to be directly below us.

I quickly cast a digging spell, sending dirt flying in all directions.

"What are you doing, Aissa?" Remy frowns, but I wave him off.

"Give me a minute," I say. Zandria appears at my elbow. Her curiosity always does have a way of winning out.

A couple feet down, something glints under the soil. My heart races. It can't be . . .

Zandria gasps. "Is that . . . is that the same black stone as the door we found under Palinor?"

I suck my breath in sharply. "Yes. Can't you feel it?"

She kneels down, holding her hand over the exposed stone. It shines even through the dirt. "I'd recognize that sensation anywhere."

A heady feeling sweeps over me. "This can't be solid stone. There must be a door into the hill somewhere. That must be what the map was trying to tell us."

We keep digging, this time with our hands so we can keep our protective spells in place. Now that we're above the fog, Remy casts the shield spell while we work, and Zandria takes on the silencing one. We reveal a few runes carved into the stone, but nothing that clearly indicates what the material is doing here. Only that it was made by Magi hands and isn't just another vein of rock.

I stand up straighter, wiping dirt from my face. This is even more difficult to open than that door in the Palinor tunnels. We don't have the luxury of time like we did then either, or a key, which makes this all the more frustrating.

I sigh and stretch, taking in the view again. It's strangely lovely. The fog swirls through the hills like a river. I wonder if the sun ever shines here. Looking down, this whole expanse seems like an elaborate labyrinth.

I look back the way we came—and my breath strangles in my throat.

Something just glinted through the fog. Only for a moment, but unmistakably metallic.

My blood pounds in my ears, and I yank Zandria and Remy down into a crouch. We're above the fog, and I'm not taking any chances right now, even with a shield spell in place.

"What is it?" Zandria whispers.

"Something followed us." I can barely choke the words out. We've been careful the whole way here. How did this thing find us?

Just when I'm beginning to think I imagined it, a long metal leg reaches through the fog. Then another, and another as the mech climbs up one of the shorter hills. My breath stutters in my chest.

It's a seeker.

"I *hate* seekers," Zandria mutters.

This is one of the larger ones—smaller than a wolf but bigger than a rabbit, with all the speed and nimbleness of a spider. Technos use them for reconnaissance over distances or to trap larger prey. Or, as in this case, both. It's the same kind that caught Zandria when we were searching Palinor's underground tunnels. I squeeze her hand tightly. It's cold and clammy, and I can feel her pulse racing through her palms. Our connection only lasts for a moment before she shrugs me off, frowning.

"It's probably just a scout," Remy says. "Looking for any stragglers that fled the massacre at the ravine."

My breathing only calms slightly. They may not be after us specifically. But they'd be happy to catch us just the same.

"Let's make sure it's alone," Zandria says. We wait, crouched on top of the hill, for another ten minutes while the spiderlike machine skitters over the mounds below, occasionally dipping back under the fog. Every step that brings it closer makes my fury grow. This thing would kill us, hunt down every last survivor, and wipe us out. Magic pools in my hands, stinging my fingertips and begging to be released.

I'm not just ready for a fight; I *want* one.

"I've seen enough. We can't let it report back on anything it sees here." I get to my feet. My entire body hums to the tune of pent-up revenge.

I begin a spell, halting the spider's progress as it reaches the base of the central hill. I send my magic deep into the metal beast. Prying and ripping. Shattering the mirrors and crushing the recorder buried inside it. Yanking each of its spindly legs off one by one and tossing them aside.

Then one final word of the spell—*explosi*—and the whole thing bursts apart, pieces of shimmering metal raining down through the fog.

Remy gapes at me and Zandria wraps her arms around her middle.

"We need to find a way in before more of those seekers arrive to investigate why one went dark," I say, urgency filling my limbs.

Zandria dusts the dirt off her trousers. "I'm done with digging." She lifts up her arms, working the motions of a handspell. At my sister's command, the soil rises from the top of the hill, revealing the black stone hiding beneath. Then she tosses the rocks and dirt down the slope.

Left exposed is a wide slab of black, shimmering rock embedded with runes and two circular hollows in the center. We kneel down, trying to decipher the runes. A few are familiar, but others are more difficult to understand, part of an ancient dialect our people lost in the wars, along with so much more.

Remy frowns at a rune just above one of the depressions. "I think . . . I think this one means *life*. Or the *living*, maybe?"

It does resemble the more modern runes we know for life. "Maybe we need to put something living in the depression to unlock the entrance?" I suggest.

"Good idea," Remy says. He plucks a small patch of moss and places it in the indented space. Something inside the hill rumbles.

We exchange an excited glance. "Sounds like we're onto something," I say. "But what about this one?" I point to the other indentation. I'm not sure I've seen that rune before, or anything like it.

"Death," Zandria says immediately, and both Remy and I look at her, surprised.

"What makes you say that?" I ask.

"They're opposites. They balance each other out, but both are necessary."

"How are we supposed to put a piece of death in this?" I say.

"Maybe this?" Remy rummages through his pack, then holds up a piece of jerky. "It's technically a dead animal." He places it in the depression, and we hold our breaths expectantly.

Nothing happens.

I frown. "Maybe it didn't die recently enough?"

We catch a beetle crawling in the dirt we disturbed and crush it quickly. Still nothing, other than a small twinge of guilt.

Suddenly Zandria's eyes widen. "This is the Alchemist Alliance we're talking about. Death could just mean not living."

"Machines," we say at the same time.

Zandria calls a piece of torn metal over to us and rests it in the chamber. More gears rumble beneath our feet, making the entire hill tremble. The two hollows begin to spin around each other, and a circle connecting them sinks into the hilltop, then slides to the right, revealing a ladder leading down into the darkness.

MY BREATH QUICKENS AND SO DOES

Zandria's. Remy holds up his hands. "Now that I've seen what you two can do to machines, I'm going to let you go first this time."

I laugh in spite of Zandria's grave demeanor. If we'd discovered this a couple of months ago, Zandria would already be down there exploring without a backward glance.

But I suppose we've all learned our lessons well.

"I'll go first." I start down the ladder into the black. Strangely, it isn't as cold as I expected. It's almost warm, in fact. Perhaps the Alchemist Alliance had some geothermal venting set up here long ago, or a warming spell that was strong enough to continue for a hundred years or more.

Either way, it's almost unsettling, but also oddly welcoming. Like this place was waiting for us.

When my feet hit the floor, lights blaze on, and I put my hand up to shield my eyes.

"What was that?" Zandria calls down from the top of the ladder.

"Lights," I say. "The torches on the walls must be spelled." I examine one more closely and realize I've seen this design before—it's similar to the torches in the secret passage Darian used to get in and out of the city. Perhaps they're not magic after all but contain a mechanism that ignites when weight is put on the floor.

Zandria joins me, with Remy close behind. "Interesting," she says, examining the torches. She grabs one from the wall, just as the circular slab we unlocked slides back into place over our heads.

Remy clears his throat. "I hope there's another way out."

"I'm sure the Alliance has a back door. Or a means to reopen that panel," Zandria says, though she doesn't look as sure as she sounds.

We get our bearings. We're in a long corridor made from the black marble that stretches out before us; the wall with the ladder attached to it is at our backs. Forward is the only way to go.

We move cautiously, Remy casting the silencing spell and me the cloaking spell. Zandria leads the way with the mechanical torch. No noises greet us, not even the skittering of small animals one might expect to infest a long-abandoned place like this. Just silence and the black walls emanating magic. And us.

My blood sings in my veins. I'm convinced that this, at last, is indeed the location of our lost library. This is what we've been searching for. This is what we were meant to find.

The tunnel continues for a long time, almost imperceptibly spiraling downward, until we finally round a corner and a large, cavernous room opens up before us. This time there are no mechanical lights on the walls; only our torch shows the way forward.

"Fiero," I say, and light bursts in my palms. I send the light floating upward to illuminate the space better.

What we see leaves us all speechless.

The ceiling is very high—did we really circle downward for that long?—and before us a stone bridge crosses an immense black gulf. On the other side a huge gate rises. Moss and vines cling to the unusual red stone of the gate's columns, draping like curtains. It's granite of some type, but in a hue I've never seen before. The columns flank a black door.

Zandria and I gape at the sight before us.

Remy eyes the bridge and the dark void beneath it nervously. "Could this be a trap?" he says.

"Not a trap," I say slowly. "But probably a test of some kind. Be on your guard."

Those words have barely left my lips when a terrible screeching echoes throughout the cavern.

Zandria tenses next to me. "It's coming from down there." She points to the gorge.

Metal creaks alongside another screech, gradually growing louder. I shiver. I've never encountered a machine that makes a noise quite like that before.

Then the sound bursts from the black void, quickly followed by the thing that made it: an enormous mechanical beast. It flies out of the gorge on wide steel wings that nearly knock us over with the force of the wind they command. Its head and body remind me of a serpent's, but its spine is crowned with sharp triangular ridges. Its maw gapes wide, but this time no screech comes out. Instead, it almost looks as if it's taking in gulps of air . . .

"Forges!" Zandria exclaims, shoving me and Remy back toward the corridor. Seconds later, heat blasts into the tunnel and bright flames scorch the edges of the wall.

"It breathes fire," I say, shocked. I shouldn't be, after having seen the Technocrats' war machines. This is definitely not what I'd hoped would greet us at the library.

"It must be a guardian," Remy says, getting to his feet and brushing the dirt off his pants. "Put here by the Alchemist Alliance."

"Of course, because Magi alone would have difficulty getting by it. A Technocrat would have a better understanding of the machine's weakness and could overcome it more easily," I say.

"But a Magi could do something against those flames," Zandria says.

"So, in order to defeat it, you must have knowledge of both the machines and magic," I say.

"Or just magic like ours," Zandria says.

The truth shivers through me. "This test is specifically for us."

"How could they know?" Remy says.

"Their experiments. They must have hidden whatever is down here to be found by the result of a successful experiment, or by no one at all. They wanted to keep it out of everyone's hands, even regular Magi," I say.

"But why?" Zandy asks.

I shake my head. I have no answer. But we have more pressing matters at hand.

"Maybe we'll find out once we get past that mechdragon and through the door," I say. "Remy, can you cast a water spell at the flames? Zandy and I can take care of the rest."

An odd expression crosses Zandria's face. "Should we . . . should we really destroy it?" She scuffs the toe of her boot in the dirt. "It was left here by the Alliance. If someone were to follow us . . ."

Like Darian. With the mechdragon gone, nothing would stop him from walking right in. And it's safe to bet the Alchemist Alliance didn't want their secrets to fall into the hands of someone as power hungry as he is.

"Good point. We won't destroy it. We'll only disable it. If you can keep it frozen, I can locate the power source and remove it. I've worked with havani before and I know what it feels like."

We cautiously edge closer to the tunnel's exit. Another blast of heat sends us skittering back. We press forward again, this time with Remy in the lead and a water spell at the ready. Before the mechdragon can try to roast us, Remy sends a pillar of water right into its gaping maw. The beast staggers back as we rush toward it, a spell on my lips and magic spinning from Zandria's fingertips. It tries to move, but Zandria's spell holds its metal pieces firmly in place. My magic probes the innerworkings of the machine, searching for that familiar sickly feeling of havani, the fuel that runs the

Technocrats' creations. But I find no hint of it. The surprise nearly causes me to drop my spell.

But then I remember: this wasn't made by Technocrats; it was made by the Alliance. Havani isn't the only thing that could power this. I begin the hunt again, but this time I'm searching for something different, something with a hint of magic.

My persistence is rewarded. Deep in the belly of the beast I find it: the magic-infused black marble. There's so much of it here that I didn't notice at first. But it isn't exactly like the others we've encountered. The large orb of black marble inside the mechdragon contains much more magic than the marble vein Remy and I found underground near the Chambers. And more than that strange door that stymied me and Zandy and set us on this path.

This marble contains more than enough magic to power the beast for a very, very long time.

I don't understand how that is possible, as it flies in the face of all we've been taught about magic, but clearly it is. With any luck, our answers will be behind the guarded door.

"I've found it," I say, a little short of breath. Extracting the marble orb from this beast without damaging it takes more effort than I expected. I pull a side panel off the creature and remove some of the clockwork from its guts, creating a hole large enough for the orb to move through. Then I rest it on the other side of the bridge.

"We'll put it back together later, after we've discovered what's inside," I say to my companions.

Together, we cross the bridge, feeling a little giddy. There's something about defeating a monster that raises one's spirits.

Zandria marches right up to the door in the gate—but before she can open it, she's yanked off her feet.

The moss and vines we thought were just overgrowth writhe,

slithering off the pillars and onto the ground, holding my sister aloft.

"Help!" she screams as an appendage made from moss covers her mouth.

Two tests. One for machines, one for magic. We should've anticipated that.

Remy uses his magic to slice off the arm suspending Zandria, and she drops to the ground, landing on all fours, then bounds toward us. Meanwhile, I hum a spell to make the moss freeze in place. "*Glacio!*"

The moss stops writhing, and we duck under it cautiously as we approach the door again. This time, we're more on guard. Fortunately, no other challenges present themselves as we push through the gates.

The door creaks open. Beyond is a sight to behold: a library, grand and gorgeous, extending for what feels like miles in all directions. It is at least five stories high, and every row is crammed with books and scrolls and wonders. Exquisitely carved red stone columns hold up each level.

A dizzy thrill overcomes me. I grin so wide it almost hurts.

The Magi's lost library, found at last.

"We really did it," Remy says. "I always thought it was just a legend, a false hope."

Zandria scoffs. "I'd think we deserve more faith from you now."

Remy grins—the first he's given since we left the Chambers. "You both have it in spades, I swear."

We stand on a midlevel balcony overlooking the entire expanse. Zandria lets out a whoop and leaps down the stairs two at a time until she reaches the bottom. I laugh and run after her. No one, not even the machines, could've followed us all the way down here. We're safe, surrounded by our past, our history, everything we have longed to find.

I haven't felt a lightness like this since that night in the garden with Aro. Happiness. Joy, even. We've lost so much, but it was all to gain this. I only wish Aro was here to see it. I'm sure he'd be enthralled as well.

Worry twinges in my chest. I hope he's safe and making progress toward thwarting Darian. I have no way of knowing until it's too late. My parents' deaths made it clear: when one half of a bonded pair dies, so does the other.

When we reach the bottom, I stand by Zandria in the center of the room and crane my neck to take in the full scope of what we've uncovered. Another laugh escapes my lips. Then another. Until I can't stop.

I can hardly believe we did it.

Zandria laughs too, unable to help herself, her coldness temporarily warming. At first Remy looks at us as if we've lost our minds, but soon he joins in.

I've never felt this free in my life.

I never want to leave. I want to remain here and read every book in this library from cover to cover and perfect every single spell. One glance and I know Zandria wishes the same.

Remy's laughter chokes off in a gasp.

"Remy, what's—" My own voice vanishes when I see what he sees. Zandria grabs his arm, and a hint of jealousy washes over me along with the surprise.

A woman stands in an archway just below the stairs. She has brown skin and silver hair pulled back into several long braids. Her clothes are white and wispy enough that I'm almost ready to believe she's a ghost.

She glides toward us, a curious expression on her face.

She stops a few feet away and holds out her hands in a welcoming gesture. "Greetings. Welcome to the Sanctuary."

"THE SANCTUARY," I SAY, EYES WIDENING.

"Just like it said on the map."

The ghostly woman laughs. "Ah, you found the map. Good. Only those indoctrinated into the Alchemist Alliance know of the Sanctuary's existence, and even then, only a handful ever knew the location. I assume they have long died off by now."

Zandria frowns. "I'm sorry, but who are you?" She glances behind us, as if she doesn't trust that there aren't more people here. "And how did you get in here?"

The woman holds up a finger, indicating silence. All three of us stand stock-still while the woman hums and weaves a spell we've never heard before. I suck my breath in sharply as my own magic rises to the surface, making my skin glow for a moment. Zandria's skin glows too. Remy's, however, does not.

The woman smiles. "Wonderful, two of you are just what I'd hoped you'd be." She gives a quick sidelong glance at Remy. "My name is Catoria. I'm the Sanctuary's guardian, and I've been here a long time."

"How old are you?" Zandria asks. I kick her ankle, but she rolls her eyes at me.

Catoria raises an eyebrow.

"Sorry," Zandria says sheepishly.

"I'm old enough to have lived through the great wars. Old enough to have watched the Technocrats rise to power and then thoroughly abuse it. You have much to learn if you hope to overthrow them."

Zandria and I exchange a look with Remy. There's nothing we want more. Even if we already know it's a futile effort. The mere hope of something that can put the Technocrats in their place, and raise up the Magi again, is worth fighting for.

"We're eager to learn," Zandria says.

A slow smile spreads across the old woman's face. "Good. I've been waiting for you. I will be your teacher. Come, let me show you the Sanctuary."

She motions for us to follow, then heads for the archway under the stairs that leads out of the library. I take a lingering glance behind—I hate to leave all these fascinating books when we just found them. But hopefully we'll return to this sector soon.

Catoria opens a door in the archway, and another tunnel presents itself. Like the columns in the library, this one is built from red granite, and a flowering moss clings to these walls. There's no sun since we are deep underground, but a soft light emanates through everything, not unlike the Magi-made sunlight that once lit the Chambers.

How I wish we had found this sooner. We could've brought all of the Magi here to hide, safely away from Darian, the Technocrats, and their infernal machines.

But we were too slow, too late. And now they're gone.

"How have you survived down here for so long?" Remy asks.

Catoria glances over her shoulder at him, an inscrutable expression on her face. "The magic of this place keeps the Guardian alive for as long as needed."

"What do you mean?" Zandria presses. I reach out to restrain my sister but quickly draw my hand back. She wouldn't appreciate it. Besides, I've missed Zandria's inquisitiveness, even if it is often unwise.

"These ruins were built by our ancestors long, long ago. Once, this was all aboveground. As the Magi grew in number, they spread out across the continent. A new dynasty was installed on the throne, and they made the city of Palinor their capital.

This place fell out of use and grew untamed. Its original name is lost to time. The wilderness swallowed it up, but there were those in the Alchemist Alliance who had heard the legends of a place where magic was still wild and whole, not split like it had become with the rise of the Technocrats. A handful of us led an expedition. It took years, but eventually we uncovered this place and preserved it."

She pauses as we reach a break in the tunnel and enter a new expanse. This is a large hall, filled with shimmering black marble columns amid statues carved from the red granite. The walls are lined with strange instruments I can only assume are weapons. Some I recognize—like swords, daggers, maces, and spears—but many others are unfamiliar.

I want nothing more than to learn how to wield each and every one.

Catoria places a hand on one of the black marble columns. "This was how we preserved it."

"With that strange marble?" Zandria laughs. "How on earth did you manage *that*?"

"Alchemy, of course. The combined knowledge of the Technocrats and the Magi is a powerful thing. We found a means of infusing the marble still living in the earth throughout the country with a spell we found here, in fact. One that would allow it to maintain its magical, protective properties long after the spell-caster had turned to dust."

"But that's impossible," Remy says, arms folded across his chest.

Catoria chuckles. "Are your friends here impossible too?" She glances between us. "I assume you know about their magic, yes?"

Remy's eyes narrow. "I do, though I'm having a hard time understanding it."

"I assure you it is quite possible for a normal Magi with the proper spell to keep the marble alive even after it's removed from the earth and crafted into other, useful things."

My mouth drops open. "So that's how you did it." I reel from the implications. There must be many powerful spells here, just waiting to be uncovered. "And you used it in Palinor too."

"We did. Some of our members had access to the Great Library. We were fearful that Technocrats were planning an attack and secreted out as many of the important books and scrolls as we could. And we reinforced the basement library level with the marble."

"And the hidden room even deeper than that."

"Indeed."

Zandria examines one of the statues. It's of a woman with a grave expression and a hunting cloak. Her hand extends into the hall, just like the rest of the statues, toward the center of the room.

"That's all well and good," Zandria says. "But it doesn't explain how you're still here."

The old woman's eyes flash. "Doesn't it though?" She sighs. "You have much to learn. Come."

Catoria marches us through the hall filled with silent stone sentinels from a time long past. If this was once the capital of the ancient Magi world, perhaps this was the throne room. Maybe the statues are kings and queens of long-lost legends. She leads us into another connecting tunnel similar to the last, and I begin to realize we're going from hill to hill to hill. Every one must contain a room or building of some sort, all of which are connected by these corridors.

When she reaches a doorway, Catoria pauses.

"I have been waiting for you for many years. I was tasked with guarding this place, armed with the most powerful spells ever known. And no one else to keep me company. Everyone I knew and loved has long perished. They're only vague memories and ghosts that haunt me now. Sometimes, I'm not even certain they were real." Catoria pulls her robes around her, even though there is not the slightest hint of a chill in the air. "There is a spell that can pull the life force from one living thing into another. It is a slow-working spell, otherwise the caster will go into shock. That is what has kept me living for so long. The earth itself has kept me alive."

I suck my breath in sharply. The rocky landscape where nothing seems to grow anymore. The petrified trees. I assumed this all had been caused by Technocrat bombs. But Catoria has slowly been stealing the life from her surroundings for more than a century.

"The landscape above—that's because of you?"

Catoria hangs her head. "I am not proud of this. It goes against Magi doctrine of revering all life. But I had no choice. I had to wait until our experiment succeeded. If it failed, then eventually all magic would be extinguished."

It was a terrible choice to make, with quite a price. "When you . . . if you die, will the land return to normal?"

She shrugs. "I do not know. Eventually, I hope so." Then she opens the door and lets us into another huge, cavernous chamber, filled with all sorts of strange contraptions. I've been in the Technocrats' workshops, but I've never seen the likes of these. The space reminds me of a research area, though larger than I've seen before. The tables are filled with glass tubes connected to small metal boxes and orbs. Most are gathering dust, but some look like they've seen recent use. This room has a rounded ceiling as well.

"What exactly is all this?" Zandria says, frowning.

"A laboratory," Catoria says. "The place where alchemicals were first discovered and where the ancient Magi manipulated them. And later on, the Alchemist Alliance."

A strange sort of awe fills me, followed by confusion. "But where are the alchemicals themselves?" I ask.

Catoria gestures at the air. "They're all around you. They're a part of everything. Magic, life, death. The trick is to pull just the right ones with our magic and tools and combine them to make new things."

"I don't understand," I say.

"You will. Some of our oldest, most potent spells use alchemicals," she says. "Come, there's one more thing I wish to show you. Then we can return to the library and I will answer more of your questions. I know you have many."

"That's for sure," Zandria mutters under her breath.

Catoria brings us to yet another room, this one full of flowering plants and trees bearing leaves in a multitude of unexpected colors. An underground river slices through the room, cutting it almost in half. On one side magical sunlight illuminates a dais, on which rests a shallow basin held up by three carved marble legs. Catoria takes us directly to the basin.

"This is a scrying pool." She presses one of the clear stones inlaid on the edge of the basin. Gears shift and a drawer slides out of the base. Resting inside are two rows of ten amulets, all made from the magic-infused black marble. Each is inscribed with a name. I immediately recognize our family name—Donovan—as well as Darian's *Azul*. Catoria selects *Donovan* and dips it into the basin. Then she murmurs a spell and waves her hands over the water.

The water shimmers and swirls, then stops in a strange, sudden manner. At first, I think I'm staring at our reflection, but the angle is all wrong. It's a vision of Zandria and me standing in this cave with Remy and Catoria in real time. I can see my shocked face as I realize what I see. Zandria's mouth goes slack as well.

"You can spy on people with this," Remy says. "That's quite useful."

"Indeed, it has been. You need something of the person you wish to see to put into the pool, and you must know the correct spell, of course." She places her hand on the drawer containing the amulets. "These amulets are infused with blood from each family committed to the Alchemist Alliance who also underwent the experiments. If blood from one of these families flows in your veins, the scrying pool will track you when the spell is cast."

"So you knew who we were ahead of time? Even what we looked like?" I say.

"I've been watching you two and your parents since you were both younglings." She frowns. "I was saddened to discover your parents had been killed. One day they stopped showing in the pool. I watched them grow up, fall in love. They seemed like kind people." She waves her hand. "But I have seen many killed over the years. It is always sad, but never surprising."

My fingers whisper over the other amulets. "What about the rest of them?"

"Are there any others like us?" Zandria asks. That would surely be something, if there were more Magi with our unique magic.

But Catoria shakes her head while wearing a grim expression. "I'm afraid only you have evolved to the final stage of progression. Yours is one of the few families left."

A chill sweeps over me. "How many are left?"

Catoria picks up three amulets, her hand hesitating over a fourth, obscuring the name. I wonder if that last one was my mother's line or that of Masia Harkness, and she's not accustomed to it no longer being active. My stomach flips.

"There are three bloodlines remaining: Donovan, Azul, and Heldreth. Though through you, your mother's line lives on. Hers was the Moss family." She picks up that fourth amulet and holds it in her hand for a moment before setting it back down. My suspicion is confirmed.

"Only three?" Remy says, surprised. "What happened?"

"The Technocrats, mostly. The first two were discovered by

the Magi at the start of the First Techno-Magi War and executed for treason. But more than half of those who died since perished in the Technocrats' dungeons."

I shudder and so does Zandria. We're both thinking of the same thing: those terrible metal suits.

"Do you know what the Technocrats do to the Magi?" she asks us.

"We do." I wish we didn't.

Catoria nods. "It is a terrible, cruel punishment. For merely existing. They fear what they don't understand. This is why we must heal the rift between our peoples. We must become one again, or this strife will never end."

Silence falls over us for a moment. The Alliance's aim has always been to bridge the divide between Technocrat and Magi. But the Armory's goal was to destroy the Technocrats' stranglehold on these lands. To destabilize our adversary and take back the power for ourselves. The Alliance never saw the relationship between our peoples as adversarial; they saw it as diverging. And something that could possibly be merged again, whether through science or diplomacy.

I can't deny that there's something strangely appealing about the idea, though my gut instinct is to revolt at the notion. We all know what happened to the Alliance and the Magi in the end.

Catoria clears her throat. "There were a handful of others in the Alliance bloodlines who didn't survive the experiment. Once pregnant, the mother had to ingest alchemicals to further the mutation process for the next generation. But they were poisonous, which is why each couple had to be bonded with the Binding rite to ensure the mother's and baby's survival. Unfortunately, two of those bloodlines were not strong enough."

"Wasn't there any other way?" I ask. It seems an awful thing to ask of someone. To risk their lives on a hunch.

"No, this was the only way." She glances up at us and our horrified faces, then—to our surprise—laughs. "You seem shocked. Have you never felt so certain of the righteousness of a cause that you would give your own life for it?"

Her words are a slap. Of course we have. We're all Magi spies. We risked our lives every day just by living in Palinor. But we did it to save our people . . . and I suppose that's exactly what the Alchemist Alliance believed. Just in a different way.

"I know what you're thinking, but please understand. No one was forced into this. Every one of these families volunteered and had the option to back out at any time. They were all informed of the risks, and they decided the reward was worth it." Now she smiles warmly and stretches her arms out toward us. "Their risks made your existence possible."

I shiver. I'm not sure how I feel about that. Until recently, I never had any idea what caused our magic to be different. Our parents told us they didn't know, but that we must have evolved. I suppose in their minds they were only telling us as much truth as we could handle at such a young age. But now that we know, we bear the responsibility of being the only Alliance bloodline to evolve and survive. A thought strikes me.

"You said there is a third Alliance bloodline remaining—what is it called again? How many are left? And where are they?"

"The Heldreth line. There is one left, a boy around your age, I think. His name is Owen."

Zandria's eyes widen. "But he isn't . . . evolved . . . like us?" My sister is struggling to accept this concept. I know it isn't easy to swallow.

Catoria shakes her head. "Sadly, no."

"Where can we find him?" I say. If we're not all that's left of the free Magi, that feels like a minor miracle. And if this person happens to be part of the Alliance as well, that can only work in our favor.

She grimaces. "He is a little more difficult to reach. His parents were nearly caught by the Technocrats years ago but managed to escape. They decided it wasn't worth the risk of raising their son on this continent, so they set sail across the ocean in search of rumored lands. But they didn't reach them. Instead, they used their magic to raise a massive island, uncharted on any map, to make their home. They coaxed trees and vegetables from the soil, fished in the sea, and raised their son there. From time to time, they'd go ashore for certain supplies but never stayed long. Sometimes they took Owen with them, but once he was old enough, they insisted he remain on the island. The last time his parents made the voyage, they never returned. They were caught and thrown in the dungeons and died soon after."

I swallow the lump in my throat. "That's horrible." Just like us, this poor boy lost his parents much too soon. His due to the Technocrats' cruelty, ours because our parents dared to defy Darian and his schemes. All of them died to keep their children safe. To ensure that one day, an evolved Magi would walk these lands with the full power of their ancestors. That they'd usher in a new age where we could live in peace.

A weight settles on my shoulders. I don't know how Zandria and I will match their expectations. We only barely escaped Palinor and failed to save the Magi in the Chambers. Though while our setbacks may have shaken my confidence, that doesn't mean we won't try.

We have to. We need to save our people. Apparently, that also means we must save the Technocrats from themselves.

That is a very tall order.

"Can you show him to us?" Remy asks.

Catoria picks up one of the amulets and dips it into the water, then recasts the spell. The water reacts as before: shimmering, swirling, then suddenly becoming as still as glass. It shows a boy with brown hair worn long and a bit wild. He stands on a dock; behind him lies a forest. He's fishing with his magic, weaving his hands over the water and bringing the fish up onto the wooden planks of the dock. He only takes as much as he needs for himself, then cleans them deftly and returns to the woods.

"So he lives on that island all alone now?" Zandria says.

"Yes," Catoria says.

"Well, that's terrible. We can't just leave him there," she says.

"Indeed, he would be useful," Catoria says. "Anyone indoctrinated into the Alliance is a boon to our cause. And he might have useful information as well. Every Alliance family had spell books they handed down and kept secret even after the Magi fell. The ones he inherited might contain spells we need."

"Then we should definitely go after him when we're done here," Remy says. "We need all the Magi we can get, and if they have new spells too, all the better."

Our new mentor nods her approval. "Bring him here, and I will teach him."

"Darian," I say suddenly. "Show us Darian." It wouldn't hurt to keep an eye on him and learn what he's up to.

Catoria frowns. "Darian is a disappointment. He was promising. He even fell in love with a Technocrat. I've watched him for a long time. Once I believed he would be dedicated to our cause. But he has turned on his own kind, and that is unacceptable."

"We need to stop him," Zandria says. "He's doing terrible things to other Magi." She spits out the words as if they taste as foul as they sound.

"Yes, you must. I have seen what he's done. It goes against everything the Magi and the Alchemist Alliance stand for."

She recasts the spell using the Azul amulet and the water soon shows us a scene in Palinor's Palace. Darian is in the throne room—I'd recognize that blood-red marble anywhere—meeting with the king and queen. We can't hear what they're saying, but Darian appears livid, while the king and queen seem to be brushing him off. I don't think I've ever seen him rattled like this. I hope it has something to do with Aro's efforts to thwart Darian's plans.

How I wish I had an amulet with Aro's blood so I could see him again, even just for a moment. More than anything, I need to know he's safe. But if Darian isn't happy and Aro's parents are still alive, perhaps that bodes well for his safety. I hope so.

Zandria hovers near Catoria, her curiosity finally appearing to win out over the sight of the man who inflicted so much damage to her in the dungeons.

"What exactly were the experiments those Alliance members underwent?" Zandria asks.

Remy is still examining the pool, watching Darian's activities, but I join their conversation. "Our parents died before they could tell us about the Alchemist Alliance. We only found out because they wrote us a letter that covered the basics."

"First things first then, I suppose. The Alliance's experiments used alchemicals, which are building blocks of magic from the old world. They are crafted through secret recipes that only a few know. This library contains the most complete record of them. They were used by the ancient Magi until the schism, where they lost the ability to impact inanimate matter with their magic. They believed the alchemicals had become useless, and using them fell out of practice, then out of memory. They were only an ancient legend when the Alliance made their expedition here to the Sanctuary. But we were rewarded greatly, more than we had imagined possible."

My mind reels. "Sorry, are you saying alchemicals are what made the ancient Magi powers possible?"

"Sort of. It's what they used when they needed to combine magic and man-made things. Like the marble in this place."

"So only people with those full powers could use alchemicals." Zandria tilts her head.

"Not exactly. Anyone could use alchemicals, but only those with full powers could use them for their original intended purpose. They're what runs in your veins, what inspired your magic to mutate in the womb and turn back the clock to become what it had the potential to be." She walks to the other side of the scrying pool and places her hands on the edge. "Alchemicals are change agents. And when we found the recipes, we decided to use them."

I remember something that Darian told me. "But it didn't always go as you expected, did it?"

She shakes her head and sighs. "No, nothing ever does, does it? Some of us were too hasty, too determined to implement new solutions before we'd fully tested them. One, I'll never quite forgive myself for." She takes a deep breath. "I crafted a particular alchemical blend I was sure would help restore powers to those without any magic. The leader of our alliance insisted we do more tests with volunteers first. And there were some promising results. But my apprentice was impatient. He stole the recipe from me and began making his own batch. Then he snuck into the Technocrats' main city and released it into their water supply. He was terribly disappointed when the change wasn't instantaneous."

"But the change happened later," I say, knowing what's coming next. Zandria gives me a strange look. I haven't told her about this yet. I'd nearly forgotten about it, actually.

"Yes. It had no impact on the Magi or adult Technocrats. But for some who were pregnant . . . it impacted their babies. Just a small amount. But when I heard reports of a rash of children being born without beating hearts, I knew exactly what had happened. The alchemical was supposed to start a chain reaction to ignite the magic in their genes at the epicenter—their hearts. Instead, it burned it up."

Zandria stiffens beside me and Remy gasps. "That's how the Heartless were created?" he says.

Catoria nods. "Yes, it was an accident. My greatest failure."

"It's gotten worse," I say. "Especially since Darian began adding those alchemicals into the water supply again."

"No!" Catoria says. "He wouldn't."

"He would, and he did. He told me himself. Bragged about it, even. He wants to create more Heartless and power their mechanical hearts with a magic-infused source to ensure their loyalty to him. He wants to build an army."

Catoria regards me with horror. She recovers herself and swallows hard. "I knew he wasn't up to anything good based on what I saw in the scrying pool," she says. "Stealing power from the captured Magi was proof enough if I'd had any doubts. But this . . . this is beyond the pale. He must be stopped."

"We couldn't agree more," I say.

Catoria holds up a hand. "I think I know how to help with the water supply issue, at least." She heads back to the library. "Come along," she calls behind her. "I'm sure you're dying to dig into some of the spell books in the library anyway, aren't you?"

The image of Darian in the scrying pool fades. We follow our new teacher back to the library.

She's right about one thing: we're eager to learn everything we can, absorb anything that can bring magic back to these lands in full force.

ONCE WE REACH THE LIBRARY AGAIN,

Catoria wastes no time heading directly for
whatever alchemical text she requires, leaving
us to our own devices for a while. I want to begin
perusing the nearest stack of books immediately, but first
I regroup with my sister and Remy.

"What do you think of her?" I whisper.

Zandria glances past me to where Catoria climbs the stairs to
the next level of stacks. The stairs are more solid than I would've
expected, despite being worn with age. "She's . . . something,
that's for sure."

Remy is more thoughtful. "I think she has a lot to teach us. But
I can't help wondering if she's hiding an awful lot too."

"She probably is," I say. "We only just met, after all. Though I
must admit, I find her fascinating."

Zandria harrumphs. "I agree she can teach us a lot, and I'm
inclined to like her. But I don't know that I agree with the Alliance's
mission to 'heal the rift' like Catoria said."

I frown at my sister, feeling colder than before. "What do
you mean?"

"I don't want to heal any rifts with Technocrats. I want to
destroy them. Decimate them like they did us." My jaw drops, but
she folds her arms across her chest. "Mama and Papa agreed. They
said so in that letter they left us."

If my sister had said this to me two months ago, I would've
wholeheartedly concurred. Forges, I probably even would have
said it first. But now, I can't. Do I still loathe the Technocrats? In
general, yes, but there are a specific few I don't mind. Some I even
like and love. Which means it's possible I'd like other Technos if

I got to know them. I can't reconcile that with the idea of wiping them all out.

My love for Aro has dulled the edge of my teeth, but not my rage. Only my desire for revenge.

"No, sister," I say. "There's something to what she says. Now that I know our history better, it's changed everything. Hasn't it impacted your opinion at all?"

"No," she says flatly. "My stay in their dungeon cured me of any possible sympathy I might feel."

"I'm with Zandria," Remy says. He runs a hand through his dark hair. "They just obliterated the Chambers. They murdered women and children, even those who weren't spies. They don't deserve our sympathy."

My heart sinks. Their argument is undeniably tempting. The wrath that swells within me every time I think about what happened to the Chambers rushes back to the surface. Yes, I do hate them. But if they're only fighting because they're misinformed, don't we have a responsibility to try to make them understand the truth? Our numbers have dwindled to their lowest point ever. I don't see how we could possibly destroy them as our people had been planning for decades.

"Can't we at least attempt to bring some Technos over to our side first?" I plead. "They're not all bad." Zandria glowers. "I know that sounds bizarre coming from my lips, but I've seen it."

My sister scoffs. "You've done exactly what you were forbidden to do: you let them in. You fell in love with one of our mortal enemies. That's treason. You've betrayed your own people, and now you're not thinking clearly." She straightens up and a new, strange light shines in her eyes. "We'll use this place for our own ends. The spells here must be ancient and powerful, and some are just for you and me to wield, sister. We can topple the Technocrats' terrible regime and make them pay for what they've done to the Magi."

Remy nods at her words.

"We'll make the regime pay dearly—on that we are of one mind, always," I say. Zandria smiles, a wild, terrible smile.

Catoria appears carrying a thin book that looks like it might crumble to dust if one of us were to sneeze within five feet of it. "I'm going to work on finding the right sort of alchemical recipe that will neutralize the ones Darian put into the water. The next time you journey near Palinor, you can add it to the water supply." She heads toward the laboratory, leaving us alone once again.

"Time to explore," Zandria says. I can't help grinning, even though her motives unsettle me. This is what we've been waiting for ever since we first learned about the Magi's lost library.

Remy starts on the main floor, but Zandria and I go straight to the top level. The shelves here are filled with scrolls in varying states of decay. Some are remarkably well preserved while others are crumbling and visibly missing pieces. I run a hand over one pile, almost willing my magic to pick the scroll with the most useful spells for me. Zandria takes the other side of the room.

We pore over the information, testing spells here and there for hours. Periodically, we call down to Remy or across to each other to share what we've discovered. Soon all the spells begin to blend together. Some have more mundane purposes, such as growing plants quickly, while others are alternate versions of spells we already know, like the light spell or water spell. But scattered throughout are spells that could unleash powerful magic on the lands. Of these, most don't have any relevance to our cause—we don't need to realign the stars in the heavens to defeat the Technocrats—but others have great promise.

One ancient scroll I find is in terrible condition, but I manage to hold the pieces together using a spell. A thrill trickles over me when I realize the ancient Magi definitely recorded spells for magic like Zandria's and mine on this parchment. I uncover two incantations I'm determined to master. The first is a means of bottling up a spell to release it at a later time. We could plant these spell bombs in the Palace and other strategic locations. Depending on how the spell is crafted, they could be released at a specific moment or detonated when disturbed. Imagine all the spells we might need, painstakingly set in place over the course of a few days or weeks, all erupting at once. We'd have to plan carefully and deliberately, but it might give us a real edge.

And a real chance at success.

The second spell should also prove useful—allowing us to infuse magic into something without the need for a binding spell. Zandria will be furious when she hears this exists, and will no doubt use it as another reason to claim I wasn't thinking clearly about Aro at the time I performed the Binding rite. But the truth is, I don't regret binding myself irrevocably to Aro; I only regret leaving him behind. Though I'm not fool enough to tell my sister that at the moment.

This spell is tricky and time consuming. Like many of the other spells from the ancient Magi, it requires the caster to use a combined hand and song spell, something that until now I'd never known was possible. We were always taught hand spells and incantations were simply variations on a theme. But once upon a time, the Magi used them in conjunction to sharpen their ability to manipulate matter and accomplish incredible feats of magic.

Now so can we.

I'm so engrossed in practice that Catoria manages to sneak up on me—something no one has done in a long time. I startle when she clears her throat, then summons Zandria and Remy over as well.

She gently spreads out an ancient piece of parchment on the reading table in front of her. "I must show you something. This parchment, a city record from the time when the Sanctuary was in its heyday, mentions a spell I've always wished I could find."

Zandria peers over her shoulder, curiously. "What does it do?"

Catoria sighs. "It's called the Heartsong. It can heal a heart."

The weight of her words presses in on my chest. "I thought that wasn't possible. That the heart is the limit of magic because that's where it resides in our body."

"There are many things I thought were impossible until recently," Remy says.

"There is much the ancients could do that hasn't survived. But you two give me new hope." Catoria glances at me and Zandy meaningfully.

My head spins. If we can heal hearts, then I could heal Aro—permanently. "Where's the spell?"

Catoria fiddles with the crumbling edge of the parchment. "This is the only mention of it I've found thus far. I've searched for it for years, but with no luck. But I'll keep searching. It must be here somewhere. If we can find it, you could use this spell to set right what the Alchemist Alliance accidentally wronged."

I turn the idea over in my mind. "That could go a long way to earning trust and gaining allies," I muse.

Zandria's face is blank. I can't tell what she's thinking, but she isn't as excited about this as I am. Though she hasn't seen the Heartless children for herself. Until I did, I never gave them much thought. But the day I visited the Heartless hospital changed me. I hope when Zandria sees them, it will change her too.

"That's fascinating, but as you said, that spell is long lost," Zandria says. "If this is the only hint of it you've uncovered in all your time here, that isn't very promising."

Catoria stares at the parchment. "Once it was all that consumed my thoughts, but it has been a long time since I searched. With your arrival, I am renewing my efforts."

"If it can be found, we will learn it," I assure Catoria. Then I pull out the little book I've been carrying in my pack since we found it hidden beneath Palinor. "Now, I wonder if you might be able to shed some light on this." I place it in front of her as she rolls up the ancient parchment and sets it aside. "We found it in the hidden room inside the old library. I assume the Alliance left it there for us to find, but we don't know the runes well enough to make out what it says. I believe it might be a journal of some sort."

Catoria examines it, running a hand over the first page. "Yes, it is a journal. From one of the founding members of the Alchemist Alliance. Anassa Viscuso. It was her idea to seek out the Sanctuary, and she led the expedition. She and her wife, Lela, a Technocrat, invented the challenges to access this place." A cloud passes over her face. "Later, after they safeguarded the Sanctuary, they were tasked with getting as many books as possible out of Palinor before the Technocrat army attacked. They succeeded in that, but when the Magi discovered Anassa was wedded to a Technocrat, they cast her out, erased her bloodline from the official histories. Anassa's family went underground and survived to see another generation of their line. Regrettably, when their child grew up, he was captured by the Technocrats and . . . well, you can intuit the rest."

"Anassa must have left it behind when they got the last of the books out of the original library," I say.

"Yes, and I doubt it was a mistake. Perhaps there is information in there that will help you."

Zandria snorts. "Sure, if we could read it."

"I can help you learn the runes, if you're interested," Catoria says.

"Definitely," I say, and Zandria nods too.

"Once you've finished spell practice, we can start on languages. Dinner will be down the western corridor in two hours. I trust you can find it easily enough."

"Yes, thank you," I say.

Catoria gathers her scrolls and places them carefully back on the shelves, then glides off to another section of the library. I place a hand over the journal. Its leather cover has a few cracks along the edges and spine, but it's otherwise in decent condition. It feels mysterious and old under my palm. There are secrets inside.

I can't wait to uncover them.

THOUGH TIME IS HARD TO TRACK ON OUR
own down here, an old clock that still works
is located on each level of the library. Clearly, getting lost in books is a time-honored problem. When
it's nearly time for dinner, we close our books and head
down the western corridor as instructed.

The passages all look very similar, and I can imagine it would
be easy to get lost if you didn't know where you were going. But
I'm beginning to form a mental map of the place, as I'm eager to
explore everything.

I suspect we've only just begun to uncover the Alchemist
Alliance's secrets.

The western passage leads us to the most surprising room
we've seen yet. Half of it is divided into sectors, each one burst-
ing with plants. Some are heavy with fruits and vegetables, while
others hint at tubers and the like beneath the ground.

The other half of the room is a kitchen area, complete with
several cold boxes and a baking box. The Technocrats call them
ovens, but the Magi have been using them for far longer, only with
a spell inside a concentrated area to cook things like bread. In the
very center of the room are several long tables, one of which is
laid out with enough food to fill us for days. My stomach rumbles.
We haven't eaten like this since we lived undercover in Palinor.

"Come, sit," Catoria says. "I usually only cook for myself. I
hope this is enough."

Remy laughs. "I should think so."

"Thank you," I say as we take our seats. Remy and Zandy
murmur their thanks as well.

There is everything we could wish to eat. Freshly baked bread and butter, a roasted chicken, steamed vegetables, and more. Cooking is not as labor intensive a thing as it is for the Technocrats. With our magic, all we need are fresh ingredients and the right spell. It is a craft Catoria has clearly perfected over the years.

"Are there animals here?" Zandria asks, glancing around.

Catoria nods. "A few. Enough to provide food for the Alliance while we used this as our headquarters, and now only a handful. I imagine you've deduced that each of these large rooms is a hill on the outside?"

We nod.

"There are a few cows and goats, and some chickens that live under one just through that door." She points to a door behind the garden area. "In the heyday of the Magi, the animals and crops were not indoors. It is only secrecy that has made us create spaces inside to mimic outside conditions for the animals."

"They did the same thing in the Chambers," Remy says. "Though not with the animals."

"I saw," Catoria says with a smile.

We eat quickly, eager to learn more about the ancient runes as our new teacher promised. Catoria takes us back to the library and one of the small study rooms that branch out from it on the lowest level. Three small leatherbound books sit in front of a few of the chairs.

"Have a seat," she says.

"What are these?" I ask as I gingerly pick up the little book before me.

"Primers. Long ago, the ancient Magi taught their children to read using these. I'm sure you were taught the more modern dialect with something similar."

"We were," I say, then frown, thinking again of Anassa's journal. "Was this older dialect in common use in Anassa's day?"

Catoria shakes her head. "No. But the Alliance had been

working on reviving it for years. She must have written her journal that way to keep it safe in case it was stolen."

"Almost like a code."

"Precisely. Shall we begin?"

For the next two hours, we do our best to follow Catoria as she teaches us what the runes mean. Some are similar to the modern runes, others are very different. I quickly see that subtle variations and combinations can change the meaning dramatically. It is complex yet fascinating, and when she finally decides we're done for the evening, our heads spin.

"We'll continue these lessons tomorrow," she says. "It's nighttime now, on the outside. I suggest we all retire."

She leads us to the dormitory wings, where there are separate structures built for men and women. Apparently, there are still other rooms under these hills with more private quarters, one of which Catoria long ago adopted as her own, so for now, these are all ours. Zandria and I settle in on our beds, and I can't help but be a little hurt when she chooses a bed on the other side of the room from mine. All our lives, we've shared a room and slept with no more than a couple feet between us. Sometimes it feels as if the forced separation of the dungeons sliced the bond between us in two.

I don't object or say a word about it. She's healing, and she'll have to do it in her own way. As much as I may like to, I can't force her to talk to me. She knows I'm here when she needs me, and that will have to be enough.

Zandria drifts off to sleep faster than me. I can tell by her slight snoring. But my mind will not stop whirring with questions and replaying all the day's surprises.

Suddenly, alone in the darkness, I remember something Masia Harkness said to us. The letter our parents left us must have our line's alchemical recipe hidden in it. Their recipe is the only one that worked so far; we must preserve it. I sit up and dig through my satchel until I find the letter. Then I tiptoe back to the kitchen area.

I really hope Catoria has lemons here somewhere.

I examine the produce she has stored and smile when I find a lemon. Then I cut it open and hold it over the letter.

I pause before squeezing out the juice. This shouldn't ruin the letter, but it's all we have left of our parents. If the juice does harm the letter instead of revealing a hidden message, I should be able to pull the liquid out with a spell. If I can't, Zandria will be furious.

I hold my breath and squeeze.

Juice sprinkles over the back of the letter and I use a quick spell to distribute it evenly across the page. The wait still feels interminable.

Then, little by little, words begin to appear.

It looks like a list of ingredients, followed by a spell that must combine them. And another spell for when the alchemicals are ingested. I shudder. My parents and grandparents were all so committed to the cause that they took this risk willingly. They knew what it meant, and they defied the Magi decree against using the Binding rite to do it.

And now this recipe is ours.

My hands tremble as I hold the paper. This is what created us. Made our powers possible.

Will we have to ingest this too in order to ensure our special magic continues? Assuming Zandria or I even survive to have children at some future point?

I don't have those answers. I just know this is important and worth protecting.

WHEN WE ARRIVED AT THE SANCTUARY

several days ago, I thought it would mean a
new opportunity for my sister and me to re-form
our bond. To right our alignment and find the same
path again.

I'm beginning to fear I was wrong.

Each morning we eat breakfast together with Catoria and
Remy. Zandria is always up before me so she doesn't have to speak
to me while we dress. She talks to the others, and only occasionally glances my way to argue about something. When we go to the
library to study spells, she and Remy work near each other, leaving
me to my own devices. I don't mind being alone. But I do mind
that my sister is avoiding me.

So this morning, I'm determined to at least begin breaking
down her walls. I went to bed earlier than usual last night so I
could be sure I woke before her. That meant I didn't get a chance
to explore the Sanctuary's network of caverns as I have done every
evening after everyone else falls asleep. But it will be worth it if I
can fix things between me and my sister.

I'm almost dressed when Zandria rolls over and stretches. She
frowns when she sees me.

"Good morning," I say.

"I suppose," Zandria says as she pulls on her clothes as quickly
as possible.

"Look," I say as we head for the kitchen area, my sister walking a little faster than me. "I know you're upset about everything
that happened. So am I. Don't shut me out. Please."

She scoffs. "I'm not shutting you out. I'm being studious. We
have a lot to learn, and I don't need to talk about anything with you."

"Zandy!" I call as she practically runs ahead. I trail her into the kitchen. Remy is already seated with Catoria, and he gives us a surprised glance.

Our new teacher smiles in greeting. "After breakfast, you will have time to study more of the spells. Then we will resume our studies of the runes."

The last few days have made me feel as though I were back in primary school. The ancient runes are taking longer than I expected to master.

"I'm eager to learn to read Anassa's journal and uncover what secrets she may have recorded in it," I say.

Across the table, Zandria snorts. Catoria raises an eyebrow at her. "Are you no longer interested in learning the ancient runes?"

"No, they're fascinating. It's been very helpful with some of the older scrolls," she says, giving me a long, meaningful look I can't decipher.

"What was that look for?" I ask her, beginning to feel a bit annoyed.

She shakes her head. "Just that my reasons for wanting to learn the runes are quite different from yours, sister." There's an edge to her words, but I'm at a loss as to why.

"What are you talking about?"

Catoria holds out her hands. "Girls, there is no need to argue—"

"You just want to read the journal because you feel a kinship with Anassa," Zandria says.

My brow furrows. "I mean, I suppose . . ." Suddenly I understand her meaning. My face heats. "Because of who she married. That's what you mean."

Catoria glances between us, confused, while Remy groans and sets his toast down.

"Is there something I should know? Anything that would

impact your allegiance to the Alliance?" Catoria asks us more sternly than I've heard her speak before. No wonder, since my sister is acting very childish this morning.

"Yes, I think there is," Zandria says. "Aissa also fell in love with a Technocrat. One she was supposed to assassinate."

"That sounds like quite a story," Catoria says.

I sigh, but at Catoria's unyielding expression, I relent. "The Armory Council assigned me and Zandria to find the Heartless heir to the Technocrat throne. We were told to look for a young girl, but the heir turned out to be the Palace researcher I thought I was using for information."

"And then she fell in love with him anyway," Zandria says, rolling her eyes.

I grimace. "That happened before I knew he was the heir. Knowing just . . . complicated things."

Zandria harrumphs. "Clearly."

"His name is Aro. He caught on to the fact I'm Magi, but he didn't turn me in. Then Darian betrayed me and Remy while we were trying to rescue Zandria from the Technocrats' dungeons, and Aro was the one who helped us escape."

Catoria holds up a hand. "Hold on a moment. Zandria, you were captured by the Technocrats? I knew one of you had been—I saw it in the scrying pool—but I wasn't sure which of you it was. I'm so sorry."

Zandria stares daggers at me. She must've intended to hide that fact, just as I'd hoped to hide my relationship with Aro for a while longer. Both those truths paint us in the eyes of others in ways we cannot control. Our vulnerabilities exposed for all to see.

Catoria examines us for a long moment, then finally speaks. "Well, that was right foolish of you, Aissa. Spies are not supposed to fall in love."

Though it's addressed to me, Zandria blanches at this remark as much as I do. We both unwittingly fell victim to that fatal mistake.

We eat the rest of our meal in silence. Before long, Remy and Zandria escape to the stacks, and Catoria excuses herself to her laboratory, leaving me alone yet again.

By the time we finish our daily lesson on runes, my head is filled to the brim and spinning with new information. I'm not even sure I could retain another spell right now, so instead I decide to explore while Remy and Zandria go off to do some weapons training.

I've only explored at night thus far, but I'm becoming more comfortable here. Catoria has been open and forthright about everything we've asked her, largely putting to rest any suspicions she might be hiding something. True, she still has information to share, but all we need to do is ask for it and it's ours.

Given that my sister will barely speak to me, I'm not sure what Zandria's opinion—or Remy's, for that matter—of Catoria is now, but they too act like the Sanctuary is beginning to feel like a new home.

I head into the northern corridor. Even though I don't believe I'm doing anything wrong, the spy in me is cautious. No one sees me duck into the tunnel or cast the silencing spell so my feet make no sound as I run headlong through the cavernous hills I've already explored. Some of these hills appear to have housed what look like small villages, round stone houses grouped together. They offer a peek into how our ancestors lived. Others seem like apartments, honeycombs of small rooms carved out of the bedrock, reaching toward the ceiling. Walking through here feels like walking into our past.

Finally, I reach where my explorations last stopped. A door that leads me into a tunnel, one so old it crumbles in places here and there. If a holding spell had been cast on it once, it was long enough ago that it's finally worn off. The tunnel starts to angle downward, then suddenly turns into steep, winding stairs. I can't help wondering where this could be taking me. I've created a mental map in my head of each hill and the tunnels that circle through the entire site. If I'm right, this tunnel first circled back toward the hill that houses what I've taken to calling the throne room—the one with the grand statues. But the downward slant means this leads to something beneath that room.

Until this moment, I hadn't questioned how many levels the Sanctuary concealed. Now my curiosity is on fire.

I begin to take the stairs two at a time. Soon I reach a landing—and a dead end. It's a small, circular room, and every inch of the walls is covered in ancient runes, creating a pattern both mysterious and lovely. No hint of any door or exit presents itself. I examine the walls closely, hoping to find some sort of rent or seam.

Nothing.

But if this is truly a dead end, why would the Ancient Magi have carved all these runes here? Did they use this small space, deep underground even then, for some long-forgotten ritual? A few of the runes I recognize from our lessons, but the order they're in is still incomprehensible to me.

"What are you doing down here?" Catoria's voice echoes from the stairs, startling me out of my reverie.

"I—I was just wandering. What is this place? What does it all mean?" I ask.

My mentor frowns. "You're here for new beginnings." She gestures in a manner that makes it clear she expects me to go back up the stairs.

I do as she indicates, and she follows silently a few feet behind me.

I like Catoria. I respect Catoria. But now I'm convinced Remy's speculation was right: she's definitely keeping things from us. Perhaps she'll reveal them all in good time. Perhaps she won't.

But if she thinks I'll simply forget all about this place and not delve further, she's sorely mistaken.

WE ARRIVED AT THE SANCTUARY TWO

weeks ago, but time has passed quickly
enough that it only feels like we've been here a
few days. Catoria is an excellent teacher; I understand
why she was selected to wait here for us for so long.
We've mastered several new spells and now have a rudimen-
tary understanding of the ancient Magi runes. We've even begun
to practice with some of the strange weapons in the Sanctuary's
training room.

Yet despite all we've learned, the library is massive. We could
spend years here and barely scrape the surface of all the knowledge
it holds.

There's too much to learn with so much depending on it.
And our only link to the outside world is Catoria's scrying pool.
We've checked on Darian a handful of times, but mostly he's been
skulking around the Palace unhappily.

Which is a relief. If he were happy . . . that would be
concerning.

My worry for Aro has increased. I miss him every second.
Through what I can translate of Anassa's journal, I've learned a
little more about the Binding rite. The bond is always strong,
but when a bonded couple is separated, they may begin to feel it
physically. Sometimes as an ache in the gut or head. Sometimes a
tightness in the chest. Nothing crippling, but a constant reminder
of their other half's absence.

I feel this keenly. At first, I thought I was simply being foolish,
but now I understand what is happening. Aro must feel it too.

We're always connected, no matter how much distance sepa-
rates us.

While I've been dealing with these emotions over the past few weeks, Zandria and Remy have grown closer and often train together. They both still feel betrayed by my choice to bind myself to a Technocrat. We tiptoe around each other, but at least they're not full-on ignoring me. I just hope someday they come around. If they don't, it doesn't bode well for pursuing the Alchemist Alliance's mission.

Tonight, I study Anassa's journal while Zandy and Remy cross staves. I watch them spar for a while, a strange twinge in my chest. It's been a long time since I sparred with my sister. Remy, I could take down easily. But my sister is my true match. She makes things challenging. I've missed that more than I realized.

I set the journal aside and get to my feet.

"Remy—can I take a round?"

He raises an eyebrow, then tosses me the staff. I catch it deftly in one hand.

Zandria tilts her head at me. "Think you can do better against me than Remy, sister?" she says.

I laugh. "Obviously."

"Hey!" Remy calls from the side of the room, frowning.

Zandria and I regard each other for a moment. Then she lunges. I twist to the side and out of range, striking her staff with my own. We circle each other, carrying on in a familiar dance: strike, block, duck, strike, duck, strike, block. After several minutes, I finally manage to score a hit and knock her off her feet—a rare occurrence. She's a little better than me with a staff, whereas daggers and close range is more my style.

I help her to her feet and she immediately strikes at me. I barely manage to block her. There's something angry and vicious brewing deep within her. Sadness stings my heart. My feisty, bold sister who found joy in her training is no more. It isn't something that can be fixed with a spell; her time in captivity broke her. I need to help, but I'm not sure how. Otherwise, like a bone not set right before it heals, this part of her might be twisted forever.

"Zandy, what happened in the dungeons?" I ask her in a voice low enough that Remy won't hear.

Her eyes flare and she strikes out again, harder this time. "I don't want to talk about it."

"You *need* to. You're bottling it up. If you don't let it out, you'll explode."

"Maybe I *want* to explode."

I shudder involuntarily, then block another strike. "I'm your sister. You can tell me anything. Why can't you tell me this?"

Her face turns an ashen color, then her expression hardens. "You won't understand."

Our staves cross, and we circle, each trying to push the other off balance. "I'm your twin—who could understand better?"

With a sudden spurt of energy, she shoves me back across the training room floor. "Someone who hates the Technocrats as much as I do."

Then she spits to the side and hurls her staff at me, catching me off guard. I dive out of its path and roll back up to my feet just in time to see Zandria stomping through the doorway.

I shout after her, "If you don't confront these demons, they'll devour you. Let me help!"

But she doesn't answer.

Remy gapes for a moment, then peels off the wall where he was watching us spar. He puts a hand on my shoulder when I try to follow Zandy.

"She needs space."

"How would you know? Until a few weeks ago, you hadn't seen her in years. She's my sister."

"She's hurt. And confused."

I brush him off and step through the doorway. "So are we all."

Remy catches my arm. "Did you ever stop to consider that maybe she's simply angry with you?"

I yank my arm back like I've been burned. Then I hurry away.

As much as I hate to admit it, Remy might be right. Not everything is the Technocrats' fault. To my sister, I committed the ultimate betrayal. Before the dungeons, she might have found a way to forgive me, laugh at me for it, even.

But now my entanglement with Aro has altered our relationship in ways I'm only beginning to understand.

By the time I find her in the girls' dormitory sector, she's asleep. Or maybe pretending to be asleep, but I'll give her the benefit of the doubt. I curl up on the cot beside her and watch her chest rise and fall under the blanket until I drift off myself.

In my dream, I'm held fast by chains. Spiked metal gauntlets pound against my flesh, bruising my ribs and breaking my nose. It is the most vivid, torturous nightmare I've ever experienced. I jolt awake, gasping.

Confusion pierces me. I'm choking on my own blood. Every single part of my body hurts.

I try to get to my feet and wind up on the floor instead. Zandria flutters at the edges of my vision.

"Stay awake!" she orders me. I try to obey, but the pain is excruciating. I'm on fire, my body feels crushed.

And I don't know how or why.

"Catoria!" Zandy yells. In a few minutes—or a few hours?—a soothing warmth begins to fill me. Soon I recover my voice and can focus my eyes again.

Catoria sits next to me, her hands holding mine as her healing spell shimmers under my skin. Shock becomes curiosity as the pain lessens.

I glance at Zandria. "I can't feel my legs," I say. Or move my neck. Panic buzzes in my ears.

"What happened to you?" she whispers.

"I was . . . I was dreaming. A man with metal gauntlets was beating me. I couldn't fight back because I was chained." I stare at the blood coating my night clothes. "How did this become real?"

Catoria tsks. "Dream magic, perhaps? Though that was a thing only the most powerful Magi were rumored to be able to do. I've never even seen those spells, so I don't know for certain if they exist." She narrows her eyes at the shadows in the corner of the room. "You've said that Darian betrayed you. Could you have been followed here?"

Zandria shakes her head, then her eyes widen . . . and quickly harden again. "What about a Binding rite? Could that cause injuries like this?"

My mouth drops open. I hadn't been planning to relay that particular fact to Catoria.

But it would make perfect sense.

Aro must have been attacked. And I suffered the consequences alongside him. My heart twists for him. I know exactly what pain he must be in right now.

Catoria raises her eyebrows. "It could." She sits back on her heels as the last of her magic works its way through my body. I can wiggle my toes again, which is a relief. "Is there something you wish to tell me, Aissa?"

Zandria's mouth is a hard line, and I give her a baleful look.

"I performed the Binding rite with someone. I had no choice. He would've died."

"Which would've been fine, considering you were supposed

to assassinate him," Zandria says. She folds her arms over her chest. Now that it's clear I'm not dying, only her anger remains.

Catoria frowns. "You're talking about that Heartless Technocrat, Aro, yes?"

"Yes," I say. "While he was helping us escape the dungeons, we ran into Darian and his guards, and Aro got stabbed in the heart during the fight. It ruined the clockwork and perforated the power source." I stare at my still-bloody hands. I know how silly these words must sound to them, but they make me choke up just thinking of all Aro has sacrificed for me, for us. "I couldn't leave him there to die. Not after all he'd risked."

Catoria stands suddenly, wrapping her long robes more closely around her frame. "This makes things much more dangerous for that boy. Do you even understand how the Binding rite works?"

Flashes of the terrible vision of my parents' bodies bleeding out on the floor of our living room return to me, and I flinch.

"I think so," I say, frowning.

"When he was hurt, you were too. In exactly the same ways. Now that you've been healed . . " She holds her hands up as she trails off.

I gape. "He's been healed too."

"Which will look mighty strange and suspicious to whoever did this to him."

My head falls into my hands. "Oh no. Darian must have him. He'll have no doubt why Aro's mysteriously healed."

"And from what you've told me about Darian, he will surely use it against the boy."

A weight presses in on my chest. If anything happens to Aro, it's my fault. I thought I was doing something good by saving him, but the reality finally hits home. Instead, I made everything exponentially more dangerous for us both.

If I die, so does he. If he dies, I die. Unless I'm strong enough to survive or have someone nearby to heal me quickly enough. And that will make the Technocrats ask questions. *Lots* of questions. Especially the king and queen.

Fierce horror hits me. I was counting on his parents protecting him, but if they realize he's been touched by magic . . . all bets are off.

I clench my hands into fists, biting back the lump in my throat. "How do I fix this?"

Catoria laughs wryly and heads for the dormitory door. "There is no fixing it. The Binding rite is one of the few permanent spells. It cannot be broken."

"Then what do I do?" I call after her. She stops at the doorway.

"The only thing you can. Get him out of Palinor and keep him close."

THE NEXT MORNING, WE SAY OUR GOODBYES

to Catoria with heavy hearts. There's so much
more to learn here that it's painful to leave. But
fear needles at me. Aro is Darian's prisoner now, of
that I'm certain.

When the roles were reversed, Aro came for me. Now
it's my turn to rescue him.

Remy and Zandria are not eager to return to Palinor, but they
see the necessity. While they bear no love for Aro, they don't want
to see me dead because the king and queen tired of their own
heir—a thing none of us would put past them.

We cover ourselves in the fog that haunts the Sanctuary's hilly
terrain above. It's hard to believe that such an extraordinary, vast
place hides beneath our feet.

We move slowly, keeping our eyes and ears as alert as possible.
When we hear the clank of metal, we halt immediately.

"Something's out there," Zandria whispers.

"A machine," I say.

"I hope it's not another seeker," Remy grumbles. Zandria
shivers.

We stay low in the fog, and soon our patience is rewarded.
From the swamp edging this area, a mechanical beast prowls out
of the tall grasses and trees. This one is a tiger mechanimal, long
and catlike. They have strong jaws that can take off a leg or arm
or head with ease, and run with all the grace and speed of the
animals they were modeled after.

In other words, this is one machine you don't want to
mess with.

It's too far away for Zandria and me to touch at the moment, but the ringing of its metal body carries over the hills. These sorts of machines don't usually come alone. Not like the scouts. They have handlers, which means soldiers won't be too far behind.

Our best bet is to sit still, hidden by the fog, and wait them out.

Our bodies are tense, magic flowing freely and ready to deploy at a moment's notice. The mechtiger approaches the foggy hills slowly, its ears—no doubt outfitted with listening devices—perk. No soldiers materialize yet, but someone on the other end of those ears is eavesdropping. And they'll come running in full force if they hear anything amiss.

"We should rip it apart as soon as it comes close," Zandria says.

"No," I say. "The second that mech stops transmitting what it hears, this place will be swarming with soldiers. We'd have an even more difficult time getting away. We need to wait this out and only destroy it if necessary."

Remy says something that steals my breath. "No wonder Darian wants a power source that won't fade. He could power mechs like these and worse for ages with it—similar to that dragon at the Sanctuary."

I shudder. I hadn't even thought of that, but that's likely part of his plans too. Anything Darian can do to claim more power, he'll most certainly try.

The mechtiger pauses at the edge of the rolling fog and tilts its ears to better capture the strange whistling noise the wind makes as it goes through the petrified trees. Then it presses on, stepping into the fog. We hold our breaths, waiting for it to find us. Here and there, we catch a glimpse of steel undulating through the fog. Zandria stiffens next to me like she's ready to bolt. I grab her hand and squeeze. For the first time in weeks, she lets me. She breathes out and closes her eyes for a moment to center herself again. When the mechtiger ranges near our hill, we press ourselves flat against the ground as best we can.

And then it keeps going.

It didn't hear us breathing over the whistling wind. It didn't rip us limb from limb, and we didn't have to expose ourselves. But it's still prowling through the hills and fog. A little of the tension eases, but we don't take our eyes off the mechtiger until it has completed its circuit of the area and returns to the swamp to report back to its masters. By the time we can stand normally again, our legs are cramped and sore.

"That was closer than I'd like," Zandria mutters as she rubs her legs and stretches before we head out again.

"What I don't like is that we have to go in the same direction that mech went in order to return to Palinor," Remy says. "We should stay here where it's safe."

I give him a dark look. "Safe for you. Nowhere is safe for me as long as Aro's in danger. Or have you already forgotten?"

Remy scowls but doesn't say more. We hurry out of the fog, then cast our cloaking and silencing spells for the journey through the swamp. I hate swamps. And I'm not looking forward to retracing our steps through it, especially with mechtigers on the prowl.

Once we clear the swamp, we search for a place to set up camp for the night. We've reached the forest proper now, one relatively untouched. We grow weary as night draws near. We'll have to stop soon.

We're tired enough that we almost stumble into a camp of Technocrat soldiers. Luckily our shield and silencing spells prevent them from seeing us, and we're able to tiptoe a safe distance away.

"At least a dozen of them, all the way out here," Remy muses. "Darian must be desperate to find us."

"And we're about to walk right back into Palinor," Zandria says. "He'll love that."

"At least their mechtigers are powered down for the evening," I say.

"We should ambush them while they sleep," Zandria says. "Then we won't have to worry about them anymore."

I shake my head. My sister has become preoccupied with revenge. While I don't blame her, three of us against a dozen isn't a risk we should take, even with our magic.

"They'll just send more when these soldiers don't check in with their commander," I say. "Let's find somewhere else to set up our camp."

Zandria growls. "Stupid Technos. My feet hurt."

I almost laugh. She sounds like her old self. I miss that Zandria so much. A hollow spot aches in my chest. "Sorry, Zandy, you'll have to make do for now."

She rolls her eyes at me and we backtread until we're far enough away to feel safe. No good spots present themselves, and I can't deny my feet hurt too. Suddenly, Remy stops us.

"Look at these trees," he says.

I frown. "What about them?" They seem like normal, natural trees to me.

"They're quite large, aren't they?"

"Yes, so what?" Zandria says.

"We can each make a nest inside one of these trees with a spell," Remy says. "Even a Technocrat walking by would have no idea we were there. And we can get a good night's rest too."

"Not bad, Remy," Zandria says approvingly.

I hum the words to a spell to make the nearest tree obey my commands. The bark peels away in the middle, and the insides shift to form a hollow big enough for me to curl up in. I crawl inside while Zandria and Remy do the same with their own trees.

I close the bark just enough that passersby won't notice any difference, but I can still breathe. Then, exhausted, I finally settle down to sleep.

When we wake in the morning, we cautiously leave our tree camps and eat a hasty, cold breakfast on the road. We may have been a safe distance from the Technocrats last night, but they're surely moving again this morning, and we need to get farther ahead for safety's sake.

It's always been a risk, being around Technocrats. But it's a whole different world now that they're actively hunting us.

We've only walked for one hour before Zandria stops us. "Something's strange about that bit of forest up ahead."

I stare where she points but don't see anything out of place. "What do you mean?"

"Well, for starters, see the bird in that tree?" She indicates a little bird with a red chest and black-and-silver wings. I've seen them before in the woods near the Chambers. They sing a sweet little song.

"Yes, I see it. What about it?"

"It's singing. But I can't hear anything."

She's right. A sudden flutter of hope rises in my chest.

"Someone's cast a silencing spell over that whole area," Remy says.

"Which means some of the Magi must've survived," Zandria says.

"Let's find out who it is," I say.

We've barely set foot in the grove before we're surrounded by a small band of Magi.

The tall man leading them is none other than Isaiah.

SHOCK ROOTS US TO THE SPOT. THEN JOY

takes over.

"Father!" Remy cries, leaping forward to embrace Isaiah in an awkward but surprisingly warm hug.

"Remy," Isaiah says. "I was certain they'd captured you. You left just before the Technocrats destroyed our home."

Remy straightens up, releasing his father. "We were already deep in the forest. We felt the ground shake and . . . and by the time we reached the ravine . . . it was too late."

Zandria steps forward. "How did you survive? We didn't think anyone had." More faces appear in the trees behind Isaiah as shield spells are dropped now that they know we're Magi.

"There was an escape route behind the Council Room. We got as many as possible out, but only about a hundred of us are left now. We've been evading the machines ever since." He frowns, and I can tell the gears in his head are already turning. A dangerous thing. "Where have you been hiding?"

"We found a . . . sanctuary . . . of sorts," I say. "To the west."

"But it became unsafe, so we're on the road again," Zandria quickly adds. I can't tell what Remy thinks of this, but neither Zandria nor I trust Isaiah with the secrets the Sanctuary holds. Not yet, at least.

"We're headed back to Palinor," I say. "We're going to get the rest of the Magi out of the dungeons." While that isn't the real impetus for our return, it is a thing we'd like to do, so it feels like less of a lie.

Remy folds his arms across his chest, suddenly standoffish. "Do you believe us now, Father? About Darian?"

Isaiah scoffs. "Darian had nothing to do with this, I assure you."

My hands ball into fists. "Please, tell me he doesn't know where you are. If you've contacted him, you've put the last remaining Magi in jeopardy."

For a moment, Isaiah almost seems uncertain, but it passes quickly. "He hasn't responded to my messages yet."

Zandria throws up her hands. "He captured us, tried to kill us. He attempted to persuade Aissa to join his side. To help him use Magi as a power source for the machines."

"Which is impossible," Isaiah says. Despite his words, several of the gathered Magi behind him exchange concerned looks. The Armory Council may have heard our case, but the rest of the Magi wouldn't have learned the details.

"Aissa and I both saw it with our own eyes," Remy pleads. "You must listen to reason. How do you think the Technocrats knew exactly where to send their bombs and war machines?"

"For all I know, you three led them right to our doorstep," Isaiah says. His gray eyes flare but then quickly calm. Even seeming a bit . . . smug. "But that doesn't matter," he continues. "We're going to take down the Technocrats. Our plan is still in action, just a little different now."

I frown. I don't like his tone one bit. "What are you talking about?"

"Come, I'll show you." He gestures for us to follow, and we do. My trepidation grows with every step. Isaiah finally stops in a clearing. With a wave of his hand, a shield spell vanishes, revealing a group of prisoners pinned to the ground by the living roots of a nearby tree. The roots, branches, and vines wrap around each prisoner—all Technocrats, I assume—from their feet to their chests to their necks. "We've been capturing their scouts. None of them will be able to report back."

"What do you intend to do with them?" Zandria asks, her face stony. I may find this troubling, but my sister definitely does not.

"We're bound for Palinor as well. Once we get there, we will surround their city with the bodies of their own."

I shiver, even though I know the Magi had little choice but to take these prisoners or kill them outright. These Technos are scouts; their job is to find our people with the aid of their machines and report on any hiding places they uncover. What else could the Magi do?

My eyes rove over the prisoners—about a dozen. Then my heart nearly stops. I know that blond hair. I know those pale blue eyes like half-moons.

Aro.

My thoughts scatter as heat radiates through my limbs. Aro is here. But how did he escape? How did he run afoul of Isaiah and the Magi?

Our eyes meet, and Aro's light up. His face, like mine, is still a bit bruised. Hopefully Isaiah doesn't catch on to that little detail.

"Not all of these people are scouts." I point toward Aro. I can't say exactly who he is, or Isaiah would be even more determined to kill him. In this case, a little white lie won't hurt. "That one. His name is Aro. I met him in Palinor while working for the Master Mechanic. If he left the city, he must've been fleeing retribution from the king and queen."

Isaiah's expression betrays no emotion. "He's a Technocrat," he says flatly.

"But one who's willing to help us. Who has proved his worth."

"It makes no difference. He knows our location and our faces. The only reason he's alive is so we can use him to prove a point later."

Anger rises within me, but I shove it down. An outburst won't aid my cause here. I glance over my shoulder at my sister and

Remy. They're biting their tongues for now. Aro is nothing more than another Technocrat to them, even if he did help us.

But he's everything to me.

Isaiah turns away, but I grab his arm. "Why don't you release him to our custody, and we'll be on our way. You won't have to trouble with him or worry about feeding him. It's just one lowly Technocrat."

Isaiah's expression turns grim as he shakes me off.

"You've spent too long in Palinor among the enemy. Do not forget yourself. Sympathy for the enemy is treason."

My breath hitches in my chest. His threat hits home.

"Don't worry," Zandria says. "We'll set her straight." She offers Isaiah her best smile. "She's still reeling from all we've been through the last few weeks, with our parents and all."

Isaiah's face softens slightly. "Of course. Just see that weakness doesn't show itself again."

"It won't," Zandria says. I clamp my mouth shut but send a long, desperate look to Aro. Something shines in his eyes. Love or tears, I can hardly tell. But being this close to him and not being able to touch him, talk to him, is pure torture.

Especially knowing Isaiah could kill him whenever he feels the time is right.

And then one of two things will happen: he'll kill me too, or if by some luck and the right magic I manage to keep myself and Aro alive through our connection, Isaiah will discover what I've done. That I performed the Binding rite—on its own a treasonable offense—with a Technocrat.

He'll murder us both for it. Isaiah is not the forgiving sort.

He leads us to where the remaining Magi have made camp nearby in a cave carved from the bedrock. It's surrounded by thick trees, and the terrain is rough and rocky. Perfect for dissuading machines and people from traversing it. Not the most comfortable to sleep on, either, but our magic can fix that by using the earth to form beds and pillows and anything else we need.

And of course, all of it is hidden beneath a shield spell.

We duck inside the cave and find ourselves bathed in light. Almost like the Chambers. I swallow hard. While it's been years since I've lived in the Chambers, it was always Home, with a capital H. It's hard to believe it's really gone. But this is the survivors' attempt to bring home with them. Though they've only been here a short while, green ferns and an array of colorful flowers line the cavern and offshoot corridors, and moss coats the floor. Fewer than one hundred Magi hide in this cave. That plus who knows how many captured Magi languishing in the Technocrats' dungeon are all that remain of our people.

So few. I don't know how we're going to defeat Darian and the Technocrat royals. But we have to find a way. Maybe Catoria is right. Maybe trying to heal the rift by restoring magic to all is the only route to success.

But by the same token, how could we ever trust the Technocrats with magic? Wouldn't they just abuse it for their own ends? While I'm firmly on the side of the Alchemist Alliance and finding a path toward peace, I haven't decided how I feel about that yet.

But right now as we greet our fellow Magi survivors and find a place to settle in, I need to focus on one thing: freeing Aro.

"Absolutely not," Zandria hisses at me from across the small alcove cave we've claimed for the time being.

"I just need to talk to him. That's all."

"You're going to try to free him," she says, folding her arms across her chest and giving me an accusatory look.

I sigh. "Yes, I want to free him. But I'm not done pleading my case to Isaiah yet."

Zandria snorts. "So you say."

"I'm your twin. Look at me. Am I lying?"

She frowns, but gazes directly in my eyes. Finally she lets out a deep breath. "Fine. I'll help you talk to him, but that's it. I'm not risking my neck for a Technocrat. And I don't understand why you are."

I've confessed everything to my sister. She knows the whole story, everything that happened after she was captured until Aro helped me free her and Remy from their metal suits. She knows how I feel, and she knows what he risked for me, for us.

She knows we owe him.

But her hatred of the Technocrats is more violent than ever. And I'm worried she's beginning to hate me by association. I don't know how to fix this. But I have to keep trying.

"Thank you," I say, getting to my feet. "Let's go before Remy comes back." He went to see who else survived and chat more with his father.

"Ah, yes, one more thing to hide from our allies." She shakes her head.

"Don't forget," I whisper to her. "You and I are the only ones we can truly trust with everything." I glance out into the cave, searching for any sign of Remy. "I still worry Remy might spill our secret to Isaiah."

"He won't," she says quickly. We leave our alcove campsite and I weave a shield spell while she handles the silencing one.

"What makes you so sure?" I ask her.

"Trust me."

I do trust her, but not her assessment of Remy. He was sent to spy on us in Palinor and report back to his father. And he did until he finally tired of it. But could his loyalty shift again now that he knows his father survived the massacre at the Chambers? The first thing he did after we were showed where to make camp was run right back to his father, after all.

A small hint of a smile runs across Zandy's face so quickly I almost think I imagined it. She was always quick to smile and laugh. Now, she's still headstrong and wild, but in a different way. She's lost her joy. I wish I could help her get it back.

I worry it's lost forever. That the Technos crushed every ounce of it out of her.

We slip through the Magi who are still awake, between the few small fires and people chatting. We have no trouble leaving the cave and disappearing into the darkness beyond.

I must know how Aro ended up here, of all places. More than ever, I wish he'd chosen to come with us. I could've protected him from Darian and Isaiah. But now it might be too late.

No, I refuse to accept that.

We pick our way between the thick trees and boulders until we find the spot where the prisoners are held. A handful of night creatures rustle in the branches and bushes, and the hum of insects welcomes us. I've missed these sounds, the ones of the natural world. I suppose Isaiah is right about one thing: we spent too much time stuck in Palinor. It's rejuvenating to be out in the world where things are living again. My thoughts stray to the Sanctuary. It's a fantastic place, but there's something unsettling about it too. Yet I'm eager to return, to continue to study until Zandria and I master every single spell in those books.

But first we must rescue Aro; I won't rest until that goal is achieved.

Isaiah ought to know better. The Armory's Twin Daggers are nothing if not stubborn and resourceful.

The vines and branches holding each prisoner down form a strange, viselike cage around them. It's almost like a living version of the metal suits the Technos use to contain us. Right now the prisoners appear to be sleeping. I spy Aro toward the far side and my heart ignites. It feels like ages since the last time I kissed him. Since I held his heart in my hands and made it whole again.

"Hurry up," Zandria hisses.

"Just keep watch," I tell her. She raises an eyebrow. "Please?"

She moves off a little ways to give me some privacy and keep a lookout for anyone making the rounds to check on the prisoners. There are no guards here. Instead, the Magi are relying on their spells to keep the Technos bound. Their strategy is very effective.

Only another Magi could free them. And what Magi would want to release a captured Technocrat?

They forgot about me.

I KNEEL NEXT TO ARO AND REACH THROUGH

the root-bars of his prison, gently brushing
my fingers across his cheek. His pale hair shines
silver in the moonlight. I shiver at the softness of
his skin.

"Aro," I whisper firmly. "Wake up."

He yawns, then startles. When he realizes it's me, relief
breaks over his face. He tries to adjust to a sitting position, but it's
hard to manage in the cage.

"Aissa," he says. "I can't believe you're here." He reaches a
hand through the roots and I catch it in mine.

"I can't believe *you're* here," I say. "How did this happen? I
thought you were determined to remain in Palinor."

"I was," he says. "Until that became impossible."

"Tell me everything." My heart pounds in my chest. I can't
help wondering what his presence here means for us, and for
Darian and his terrible plot.

"Where to start?" He lets out a small laugh. "The beginning,
I suppose. After I left you, I found my way into the root cellars
of the Palace. I hardly knew what to do, honestly. I had to stop
Darian, but what was I going to tell my parents? Darian is their
most trusted advisor. I couldn't go to them without real proof."

"What about what he was doing to the Magi prisoners?"

Aro shakes his head. "I have no delusions about my parents'
opinion of the Magi. My relationship with them is . . . complex.
They wouldn't have cared what he did with the prisoners." He bites
his lip. "For all I know, they gave him permission in the first place."

I suck my breath in between my teeth. He's right. That
wouldn't be surprising. In fact, it seems rather likely.

"I returned to my quarters as if nothing had happened. I was determined to dig up proof Darian is a Magi. He also acted as though nothing was wrong. But every now and then, I'd walk down a hall and feel cold creep up my back, and there was Darian, glowering at me. Sometimes he'd be moving his hands slightly or his lips." Aro frowns. "Do you think he was trying to cast some kind of spell on me?"

"Probably. If he was trying to hurt you, the only reason he didn't succeed is because we're bonded. We increase each other's strength. He doesn't know about that."

Aro's eyes light up. "We increase each other's strength? Now that is fascinating."

I can almost see the wheels in his brain turning over that tidbit and getting distracted. "Then what happened?"

"I confess, my attempts at gathering intel didn't go well. I tried eavesdropping on Darian's meetings with other researchers and questioning the guards a little more than was wise. All I learned from the latter was how annoyed they were that someone—I assume you—created a giant staircase in the middle of the night in the city that took half the guards two days straight to fill in. I don't think I'm quite cut out for the spy life."

I laugh softly. So that's what happened to our escape route after we left. "Research and the creative field are more your style. But that's a good thing."

"Not this time, I'm afraid. One evening, I was attacked. I'd snuck out of the Palace to visit Leon and get more minerals from the miner's stall. I was still trying to find a better alternative to the hearts than . . . than what Darian has in mind for them."

I swallow the tacks in my throat. What Darian has in mind for them is dangerous indeed.

"I wasn't hurt badly, just enough to bang me up a bit. Leon saw it happen through the window and he scared the attackers off.

When Leon helped me back to the Palace, Darian used the incident to convince my parents to keep me locked in my quarters under guard. Darian told them he had intelligence that an assassin had uncovered my identity and was coming to kill me."

I snort. "A very convenient half-truth."

"It certainly was," Aro agrees, shaking his head. "They wouldn't listen to me. Nothing I said could sway them. Not even when I took my mother aside and told her outright that Darian was a Magi and he was playing both sides. She laughed at me. They can't fathom that Darian would betray them, and they were already overprotective about me and my safety. They immediately put me under house arrest. For my own good, as my father told me."

"Let me guess, Darian offered to oversee your protection himself?"

"Of course. Despite my objections, they insisted. My mother told me I was being a fool and letting my imagination run away with me. As if I were a child." He scoffs, his hands balling into fists. "Darian had me at his mercy"—I stifle my laugh when he says mercy—"and it wasn't long before he made his move. A few days into house arrest, someone broke into my room early one morning and tried to kill me."

My hand tightens around his. "I know," I whisper. "Because I woke up one morning, safe in my bed, but beaten and bloody." I tremble at the memory. That level of vulnerability and confusion . . . with no idea what was happening . . . I didn't like how it felt one bit.

"So that was how I was healed," Aro says, his eyes twinkling. "I wondered, but I hadn't known how strong the bond really was."

"It was my mentor and Zandria, actually. They found me and healed me, which in turn healed you."

He brings my hand to his lips through the bars. "Thank you," he says. "Now that's twice you've saved my life."

"Does that make up for the fact I only met you because I was trying to kill you?"

He laughs. "Perhaps a little. The Anvil was definitely on my side that day. Before you healed me through the bond, Leon arrived. He's one of the few people my parents trust aside from Darian, so they'd allowed him to visit while I was under house arrest. He opened the door to my quarters and found me . . . and then watched me heal right before his eyes. If he hadn't known me since the day I was born, I'm certain he would've accused me of being Magi right then and there."

"What did he do if he didn't tell on you?"

"He helped me into the nearest chair and insisted I explain what was going on. I . . . I confessed everything. I told him I'd fallen in love with a Magi accidentally. And that she fell in love with me too, even though she was sent to kill me." At my concerned expression, he adds, "I didn't tell him it was you. I swear. I told him about Darian playing both sides for his own ends and what he's doing to the Magi prisoners to power the hearts of the Heartless."

"What did he think?"

Aro's face twists strangely. "He was more intrigued than I liked, but he is the Master Mechanic; machines are his specialty, after all. But he was most intrigued when I told him about how I helped the Magi girl escape and ran afoul of Darian. I told him about the Binding rite, how you healed my mechanical heart and that I'm alive because our hearts are intertwined. To be honest, it's still difficult for me to trust magic. I'd been terrified that the Binding rite hadn't fully worked. That Darian caught and killed you. I was so relieved to have some sign you were still alive."

"I was relieved about that too," I say, putting my hand against his cheek. He leans into it and kisses my palm.

"Leon promised he'd be back later to check on me. And he

insisted on taking Sparky with him. I was puzzled at first, but later realized he suspected my mechpet might be bugged by Darian."

He sees the look on my face and stops. "What?"

"Sparky was definitely bugged once. Remember when it stopped working normally and you asked me to fix it for you?"

Aro puts his head in his hands. "There was a listener inside."

"A broken one, thankfully, which caused the issue with Sparky's leg. I threw it into the incinerator, but it's possible you may have been bugged again."

"Clearly Leon had a good idea, then. I was on edge all day, terrified Darian would make another attempt. When Leon returned, he sat me down and gave me a key—the master key to the Palace. Only he and the queen have one like it. It unlocks any door."

"Leon helped you escape?" I say. Part of me is shocked and the rest . . . isn't. Leon always had a soft spot for the Heartless. Perhaps it was because of Aro. If so, then of course he'd want to help him escape.

"He practically forced me to. He told me I wasn't of use to anyone locked up in my rooms or dead. He insisted I run away. Leave Palinor before Darian killed me." He hangs his head. "I know I was determined to remain and fight him before, but this attack, and feeling thoroughly trapped, changed my mind. Leon was right. I couldn't fight Darian from my quarters. I needed to do something more, and for that I had to leave. That night, I escaped. I unlocked my rooms and snuck past the guards. Earlier, Leon had slipped some sleeping draught into their wine as he left. I made it out of the city and was resolved to find you, even though I had no idea where you might be. I figured the most likely place for Magi to hide and feel safe would be where there was the most wilderness. So I headed northwest. It wasn't long before I was caught by your Magi friends." Aro sighs. "I feel like a fool."

"You're not foolish. You were right. The wilderness is where we feel safest, and that's where you found us. Or rather, Isaiah found you. But I'm glad you're not in the Palace anymore. I hate to think what Darian might have had in store for you next once he discovered his assassination plot failed." I shiver. It would have been nothing pleasant, that much is certain.

"Very true. Though I'm worried my parents will send people after me. I don't want to put you in danger."

I glance at the other Technocrat prisoners. "The Magi seem to be doing just fine keeping the soldiers at bay, I think."

He gives me a sheepish look. "That they are," he says.

"How did Isaiah capture you?" I ask.

"I . . . I've never been outside the walls of the city before. I'd heard of what it was like, and I'd seen maps and drawings, of course—I even took one with me. But nothing prepared me for how vast everything is out here. It's not like the city, where there are people to ask directions and places to hide around every corner. I knew by the sun I was headed in the right direction, but other than that, I was flying blind." Aro hangs his head. "I walked directly into a trap. They must've heard me coming. I don't have silencing spells like your folk do."

"No, you don't." This time I sigh. The tables have turned. Now Aro's a captive, and my people are the captors.

I won't let him be executed. I just hope Zandria will forgive me.

"I missed you," I say.

Aro's eyes soften. "I missed you too. I'm glad we found each other, but I wish it was under different circumstances." He gestures to the cage holding him fast.

I grimace. "Me too." I lower my voice. "I'm not sure how yet, but I'm going to get you out of here. I won't let Isaiah kill you. He'll have to kill me too." I bite my lip. "I mean, he would, one way or the other. But he doesn't know that. Hopefully he never will." I lean closer to the bars and so does Aro, just enough for our lips to meet for a stolen moment.

"Thank you. I know it isn't easy to go against your own people."

"I've never been able to fully trust anyone but my sister my whole life. Except for you. I'm not about to lose that." A flicker of a smile crosses my face. "Besides, there's so much that must be done. We're working on a plan to free the rest of the Magi in the Palinor dungeons. You can help, once you're free."

His eyes widen. "What's the plan?"

I kiss him again, then put a finger to his lips. "I must go before someone finds me here. I've already stayed too long. Soon, I'll tell you everything."

I rise, feeling a little cooler now that we're not crouched near each other. The expression on Aro's face is one I wish I didn't have to see. He catches my hand once more before I fully straighten up.

"Everywhere you go, you take my heart with you."

"And mine with you." I pull away, blinking back the tears that suddenly flood my eyes.

I glance back once more, the ghostly vision of Aro's pale hair in the moonlight haunting me as Zandria tugs me away from the makeshift prison and back into the dark night.

THE NEXT MORNING, I WAKE RESOLVED TO

make a final appeal to Isaiah. Zandria isn't happy with me.

"What are you thinking?" she says. "He already made his decision."

"Which will kill me. Even if I didn't have feelings for Aro, what choice do I have?"

Zandria paces the small cave, while Remy leans back on his bedroll. He has yet to join our conversation, but I hope to get him on my side.

"His decision wouldn't affect you at all if you hadn't bonded with Aro in the first place!" Zandria hisses.

I place my hands on her shoulders, stopping her circuit. "But I did. I couldn't stand to see him die then, and I can't now either. Do you really want to watch *me* die?"

"No." Zandria's anger deflates. "I can't lose anyone else."

"Then I need your help." I glance at Remy. "Both of you."

"I think I'll stay out of this one, thank you," Remy says.

I shake my head. "Not an option. We're the only ones who know what Darian is up to. We must stick together."

"And study more of the spell books in the Sanctuary," Zandria says.

"All right, all right," Remy says, holding up his hands in defeat. He gets to his feet. "Yes, I'm with you. Of course, I am." He smirks. "Mostly because of all those spells."

A laugh escapes Zandria's lips, warm and sudden. Even she seems surprised.

"Thank you," I say. "Once we have Aro safely away, we should try to track down the last member of the Alchemist Alliance too.

The more Alliance members we have, the more likely we are to defeat Darian. Catoria said his family probably brought spell books with them. They might be old and have useful information. And maybe he knows things Catoria hasn't told us."

I can't help thinking of that strange landing deep under the Sanctuary and the wall covered entirely in runes that Catoria warned me away from. A new member of the Alliance would provide some perspective, especially if he were indoctrinated at an earlier age than us.

Zandria's eyes light up, her curiosity rearing its head. She's kept it under better control lately, likely because her impetuousness was part of what led to her capture. "That woman subsisted more on secrets than anything else, no matter what she says."

"It's our sacred duty to uncover them," I say, a wide grin on my face. "So, we rescue Aro, find Owen, and return to the Sanctuary to train."

Zandy rolls her eyes. "And so you can nest with your new beau. If Catoria doesn't strike him down the second he comes near the door."

"She wouldn't do that. We already explained my connection to Aro. Besides, the Alliance's end goal is to merge the two factions back into one people." While she wasn't thrilled I hid the fact I'd performed the Binding rite from her, Catoria is one of the few people who might be supportive of my relationship with Aro, however ill-advised it may have been to start. I'm confident she won't hurt him.

Light begins to fill the cave. "We should find my father," Remy says. "Try once more, then take our leave. If he won't free him, we'll circle back after nightfall. I know the spells my father uses—and what counterspells can dissolve them."

We pack our things quickly, with no intention of returning to the small cave we slept in last night. We find Isaiah having breakfast while he confers with some of his men not far from the cave entrance. I have no love for the Armory Council, but today, for the first time, I miss it. All members but Isaiah and Darian have been killed or captured. Thank the Anvil Darian isn't here. But if the rest of the Armory had survived, we might have a fighting chance of freeing Aro. As it is, I doubt Isaiah will listen to us. He's as stubborn as ever, and not one to change his mind. But if anyone can do that, it's Remy.

"Father," Remy calls out, and Isaiah lifts his head, surprised to see all three of us.

"Good morning," he says. The men with him look at us irritably.

"May we speak privately?" Remy asks, gesturing at all four of us.

Isaiah sighs. "Come with me." He quickly leads us to a small grove nearby that still provides a good view of the cave. "What can I do for you?" He eyes us wearily, his gaze lingering on my sister and me. He's still suspicious we're hiding something, even after everything that's transpired.

"We must beg you to reconsider the sentence for the Technocrat named Aro. He risked his life for our cause. That's no small thing," Remy says.

"Neither is the fact he's a Technocrat," Isaiah says.

"He could be useful," I say. "He works in the Palace. He'd continue providing intel for us, I'm certain of it."

"We already have spies inside Palinor, and they're higher up with better access. We have no use for him, other than to make him an example."

I shudder. The finality in Isaiah's words stings. He is singularly unable to even consider the suggestion that Technocrats are people deserving of mercy.

When I first realized the Alchemist Alliance's goal was to restore magic and balance to all people, not just the Magi, I was surprised. But the more I talk to people like Isaiah, the more I see that we must do something. Surely, it's possible to bridge the divide between the Technocrats and Magi. After all, Aro and I did it. Anassa and Lela did it. Even my classmate Vivienne fell in love with a Magi. I'd always written her off as frivolous and silly, like the rest of the Technos. She loved to talk about fashion and courtiers and the latest new inventions, but never any subject with real weight. But when her boyfriend was captured, she defended him to the king and queen and begged for mercy. She suffered greatly for it, to be sure. But those connections are real and worth fighting for.

"You won't even think about it? Please, Father," Remy says.

Isaiah face creases into a stern frown. "There is nothing to think about. With the council no more, my word goes. He will die after we reach the borders surrounding Palinor. He'll be hanged from one of their disgusting metal trees."

"But—"

Isaiah cuts off his son. "We're done. Do not broach this subject with me again. My decision is final."

"Then we're leaving. We can't stay and be a party to this abuse," I say.

Isaiah frowns deeply at his son. "We know who our enemy is. The massacre at the Chambers should have removed any doubts you may have had. I'd expected better of you all. Our people are stronger together, but you do what you must." With that he turns, leaving us gaping in his wake.

When night falls, we cloak ourselves carefully and hurry back to the Magi encampment. Aligning myself permanently to a Technocrat flies in the face of everything I was raised to believe, everything I cherished, even everything I intended. But there's no help for it. Hearts don't listen to reason. They don't comply with what you may insist is right. They choose their own path and drag you along for the ride whether you like it or not.

The truth is, I had little choice in the matter. Now Aro and I both are paying the price.

But once he's free, I will breathe a little easier. Keeping him close is keeping him safe, and right now that's all that matters. I can depend on Zandria and Remy protecting Aro too, however begrudgingly.

When we reach the tightly knit grove where the prisoners are kept, we keep close together and watch for guards. They didn't have any here last night, but there could be some hiding under a shield spell now. However, I learned something to help with that at the Sanctuary. I murmur the words just as Catoria taught us. Any people within range are suddenly lit up to my eyes only. There's one guard not far off, but he's facing away from the prisoners. That will work in our favor.

I motion to Zandria and Remy to keep watch, then carefully thread through the sleeping prisoners and their cages until I reach Aro. He's asleep as well, the moonlight again falling across his face and lighting his hair up like a candle. My heart beats faster and not just because we're taking such a huge risk by rescuing him. Because I can't help but thrill at the prospect of being near him again. Especially once he's out of danger.

I kneel next to the living cage and gently reach between the bars to wake Aro. He rouses slowly, but when he sees my face, his own lights up, breaking into a smile.

"You came back," he whispers. "I . . . I thought you left earlier."

I put a finger to his lips, indicating we can talk later. I use a handspell to make the living bars forming the lock on his cage unwind and recede. When I reach out my hand, Aro takes it gladly.

The world, which feels as if it has been tilted ever since we parted in the tunnels under Palinor, now rights itself.

I help him up and put the shield spell back in place. Hopefully no one will notice his cage is empty until morning. We walk briskly yet cautiously through the prison area. The last thing we wish to do is wake up the others and have them give us away.

Stealth is our greatest ally. We're stealing a prisoner from a camp full of spies.

Aro stumbles a few times, likely because his limbs are stiff from being stuck in that cage. He wouldn't even be in this mess if not for me.

He'd also be dead by now, and Darian would be installed on the throne. And neither the Magi nor the Technocrats would be any wiser that they'd been played for fools.

When we reach where Zandria waits for us in the bushes, she springs to her feet and whispers into my ear, "There are two guards now, chatting."

"Where's Remy?"

Zandria gestures up the path and we head there together . . . just as Aro steps on a branch, making it snap. My sister and I exchange a terrified look—we've both been casting shields, so the sound wasn't silenced.

"Go!" I hiss, dragging Aro along. Our shield covers all three, then four of us once we reach Remy. Zandria switches to casting the silencing spell so the guards can't tell where we are or which way we run. Aro trips more than once, but I help him back up and keep him going as quickly as we can. We don't stop until we're well outside the boundary of the Magi camp.

We keep moving at a slower pace, while Remy and Zandria split off to create a few false trails. That should throw anyone who tries to follow us off the scent. For a while anyway. It won't take long for Isaiah to figure out who set Aro free.

While we wait for Zandria and Remy to rejoin us, we stop to rest for a moment in a grove of trees where many low bushes with tiny white flowers grow. While last night it seemed almost normal to be chatting with Aro, now that he's free I'm dizzily aware of every inch of distance between us. Before Aro knew what I was, I was bolder around him because I'd convinced myself I was only acting.

But I'm not acting now, and this is no longer a game.

A flush creeps up Aro's neck, and he runs a hand through his pale hair. "Thank you," he says.

He holds out his hand to me, and I throw my arms around his neck, pressing my lips to his. Heat crawls over my skin as we kiss for the first time in what feels like forever. He kisses me back just as fiercely, his hands tightening on my hips. I never thought I'd see him again. Not really. I was sure we'd either have to live apart safely or die swiftly. Now, I never want to let him out of my sight.

A delicious heady feeling consumes me, then . . . something else. A tug, a pull from my heart. We break apart and stare at each other. The feeling isn't painful or pleasurable, but . . . necessary. Like there was a need unfulfilled for a long time that's been appeased.

"Look," he whispers. I gasp.

Thin, glowing threads spin between us, stemming from our hearts and twining together. The magic of the Binding rite connecting us.

I was definitely not expecting this.

My parents were bound, but I never saw anything like this between them when they embraced. Perhaps it's because we've been apart for a while? Or could it be due to my unique magic? Or the fact Aro is a Technocrat? Possibilities reel in my brain, but I have no answers.

Just the glow, and the tug, and the need.

"What's happening?" Aro asks.

"I'm not sure. Perhaps the spell didn't like the distance between us for so long."

Aro kisses my nose, his warm breath whispering over my face. "Smart spell." His hands slide to my waist. "Perhaps we just need to kiss more often."

I laugh and kiss him again for good measure, letting him fill up my senses. "It's worth a try." The magic's intensity ebbs and retreats back into our chests.

Remy clears his throat behind us, and I release Aro. I can feel my face burning, but I don't care. Remy can think what he wants. I already know he doesn't approve.

"We don't have time for this," Remy says.

"No, we definitely do not," Zandria says appearing out of the shadows. "They're already combing the woods."

I take Aro's hand and flash a quick, reassuring smile in his direction. Then we flee into the night.

WITH THE HELP OF A SPEED SPELL, WE

make excellent time, passing the hilly and foggy area where the Sanctuary hides and cutting through the lake lands just to the south of it in a single day.

We stop to make camp for the evening, and Remy sets up spells around the perimeter, preparing to take the first watch, while the rest of us settle down. We're camping under an overhang hidden largely by rocks, and Zandria lays down as far from me and Aro as possible. Aro and I curl up next to each other and whisper softly for a few minutes, but it isn't long before he is asleep too.

However, I can't seem to sleep. Worry plagues me. What if someone finds us while we sleep—Techno or Magi—and steals Aro back?

I know what I must do to ease my mind.

There's a spell I learned at the Sanctuary—a tracking spell. If I cast it on Aro and we're separated again, I could find him more easily. I sit up, humming the spell in the back of my throat. My magic responds, but it encounters resistance when I try to attach the spell.

At first, I'm puzzled, then it hits me: someone else must have already cast a tracking spell on him. I shiver. It could be Darian. Or Isaiah. Maybe that's why it was so easy to escape.

Unsettled, I cast a cancelling spell, untying the threads of foreign magic. Then I cast my own tracking spell again, this time with success. A little bit of the tightness in my chest unwinds, but worry still gnaws at me.

If someone put a tracking spell on Aro first, how long have they been pursuing him, and how close are they to reaching us?

Sleep eventually finds me, but tonight its hold is light and fitful and uneasy.

The next morning, we head west to the coast at a normal pace, avoiding the mountain range on the other side of the Sanctuary.

Aro holds my hand, which lifts my spirits. He tried to thank Zandria and Remy yesterday, but they wouldn't even look at him. If they can't get past the fact he's a Technocrat, it's going to cause us to make a mistake.

And that could be fatal.

As we make the trek, I fill Aro in on the details he doesn't know yet, and he tells me more about his time in Palinor after I left.

"The Alchemist Alliance made you and your sister the way you are? No wonder Darian was so desperate to have you join his cause." His eyes are alight with a curious glow. "I must meet this Catoria. I have many questions."

I grimace. "Look, you should know . . . we're not the only ones made by the Alliance. But we are the only ones made on purpose."

He tilts his head with a small frown as he ducks under a low branch. He's been gawking at the greenery all morning. He's never seen this many living trees in one place his whole life, and the deep forest is a revelation to him. "What do you mean?"

I swallow hard. I have no idea how he'll react to this news, but he has a right to know. "The Heartless weren't made by a curse. It was an accident. The Alchemist Alliance was trying to heal the rift between our peoples by putting a particular blend of alchemicals in the water supply . . . but it went horribly, unexpectedly wrong."

He stops and takes me by the elbow. "How did it go wrong? Do you know?" His expression is inscrutable. I can't imagine what he must be feeling right now.

"The alchemicals were intended to reignite the Magi gene in Technocrats while in the womb so they'd be born Magi." I take his hand and place it over my heart. We're close together now, our breath mingling. "Our magic is seated in our hearts. It runs through our veins. But Technocrat physiology must be a little different because when the gene reignited, the magic burned up their hearts, hence they—and you—were born Heartless. I'm sorry."

I hang my head, but he tilts my chin up and kisses me softly. "Thank you for telling me. It's terrible, but no worse than what I've been told all my life." He takes my hand, and we start walking again, faster now to catch up to Remy and Zandria who, unsurprisingly, haven't waited for us. "If anything, this is better. The intentions were good, even though the results were not as expected. As a scientist, I understand that. I've done that. Just not on that scale, of course. This Alliance sounds remarkable," he says.

"They certainly are," I agree. "We still have a lot to learn about them and what they knew. Each family had their own alchemical recipes and secret spell books to hand down to their descendants. If we're going to take on Darian, we need more Alliance members in order to pool our knowledge and defeat him."

The one thing giving me hope is that we have something Darian doesn't: the Sanctuary, with all the Magi's lost spells and even more we never knew existed from our ancestors. We must leverage that advantage at every opportunity.

"I'll help in whatever way I can," Aro says.

Zandria and Remy are certain Aro will only be dead weight that slows us down, but I think he may give us an advantage too.

"What do you know about the Technocrat patrols? Their search patterns? Do you think they'd range this far to the northwest?"

"It's unlikely. Any patrols we encounter here would've been assigned recently and probably aren't familiar with the landscape or where they are going. They won't have an edge on us."

"That's good news," I say.

"It's unlikely they'd take their larger mechs this far, either. Only if they had good reason to think they'd need some serious firepower."

I sober immediately. "Yes, like they did when they destroyed the Chambers."

Aro's eyes soften. "I can't begin to imagine the loss you've had to bear these past few weeks." His face darkens after a beat. "We still need to be on our guard. This is just the sort of place they'd send their smaller, nimbler mechs."

"Like the seekers." I shudder.

Zandria glowers, but Remy smirks at us over his shoulder. "We don't need to worry too much about those either. The other day, Aissa ripped one to shreds like it was nothing. They're no match for our twins."

"When it's just one or two, yes. But if there are enough to overpower us, that will be a problem," I correct Remy. Zandria pulls her cloak closer and keeps walking.

Aro laughs, running a hand through his blond hair. It's longer than before, but it still curls at the ends against his neck. "I just realized something. Why didn't I see this sooner? My mechs down in the tunnels that were mysteriously taken to pieces—that was you two, wasn't it?"

I can't help smirking. "It was. Sorry about that."

My sister snorts. "Not sorry at all. We couldn't let you find the Magi room hidden in the tunnels. We had to do something."

"Why were you down there?" I ask Aro, something I've wondered for a long time.

"Darian, actually. He told me he'd heard the Magi had a

power source that had been buried beneath the Palace. He thought it might be accessible through the drainage tunnels and gave me just enough to push me in the right direction. When I realized someone else was down there, I felt certain I was on the right path. I had no idea it wasn't a power source at all, but your library."

"Yes, I suppose a Technocrat wouldn't know that particular rumor. Darian really was playing all of us like his own personal orchestra." I squeeze my free hand into a fist, then release my breath slowly, letting my rising magic ebb back into my core.

"Yes, he played us all for fools once. But he never will again," Aro says. He kisses my knuckles, sending shivers up and down my spine.

If only we weren't on the run and we were traveling alone . . .

Soon we reach a place where the trees break and we can see all the way to the horizon. The beach is far below us, and the way down is almost vertical. We'll have to double back and find a safer path.

"This way looks quickest," Zandria says, and leads us down a steep pathway to the beach. We reach the sands, and I can't help but marvel at the expanse before us. We've heard of the ocean before and seen drawings and paintings, but this is the first time Zandria or I have ever set eyes on it. It's immense. Deep and vast.

But something is missing.

"Where's the island?" I say. "This is where Catoria said it would be."

"Maybe it's hidden?" Aro suggests.

Remy's eyes light up. "If that's the case, we can find it with an elemental spell." He wades into the water up to his ankles and then begins to cast. I know just what he's doing. He's using his magic to look for spikes in the earth element out over the water. A sizable spike could mean an island.

Remy drifts down the beach, testing with his magic, until he suddenly stops. "Here!" he cries.

My pulse speeds up as we join him. We may have just found Owen's home. Now we need to find Owen himself.

"We need a boat," Zandria says, voicing all of our thoughts.

"Owen's parents were captured by the Technocrats not long after they came ashore the last time," I say. "Maybe their boat is stowed somewhere nearby?"

"Good thinking," Zandria says. We start our search, roving up and down the beach, hunting for any hiding spots. If they used a cloaking spell on the boat, it should've worn off long ago. We regroup after scouring the beach and nearby woods for an hour, all of us empty-handed and frustrated.

Zandria puts her hands on her hips. "This doesn't make any sense. They must've come ashore somewhere around here."

A sudden, sickening thought occurs to me. "They might have destroyed the boat to prevent the Technocrats from discovering Owen."

My stomach sinks. Another family the Technos destroyed with their festering hatred. I glance at Aro. He doesn't seem as uncomfortable as I would've thought. Instead, he looks rather sad. His people are not quite as good and righteous as he was raised to believe. That has to be disheartening. I know it was when I realized not all Magi are good too.

Zandria groans, and so does Remy. "That would explain it," she says.

"We can always make a new one, can't we?" Aro asks.

"We'll have to," Remy says. Together, Remy, Zandria, and I cast a series of spells to cut down a thick tree from the woods and hollow out the insides. Then we smear tree sap on the outside to make it watertight and seaworthy. Aro marvels while we work, his analytical brain taking in every move we make and how it impacts the tree until it becomes a boat. He spent his whole life hating the Magi, but in truth he's fascinated by the unknown, even magic, despite his conditioning.

He's more at war with himself than he lets on. But the truth, I've begun to realize, is we don't have to choose between loyalty to our faction or each other—because we're really the same people. The trouble is that those factions don't know this yet.

"I'm sorry my people—my parents—have been cruel to yours," Aro says, surprising us all. "Your magic is a magnificent thing to behold. I want to set this right."

Remy and Zandria are taken aback, but still only a little swayed by his words. "Thanks," Remy says. Zandria shrugs.

We set the boat in the water, testing its seaworthiness, then board. "Wait, we don't have any oars," Aro says.

I smile. "We don't need them."

Zandria casts a spell to make the wind blow and push the boat along. Remy's handspell calms the waters in spite of the increased wind. Soon, we glide across the unnaturally placid water, speeding toward the little island that finally comes into view.

As we approach, I marvel at the Heldreths' craftsmanship. The island has a perfect white, sandy beach, abutted by a thick forest wild with green. Many of the trees are of the fruit-bearing variety, and fruit of various shapes and colors hang from the branches invitingly.

We slow the boat's speed and release the wind and water-calming spells. No sooner have we dragged the boat ashore than a face appears between the trees.

"Who are you and what are you doing here?"

THE BOY APPEARS TO BE ABOUT OUR AGE,
maybe a little older. Just as when we saw him
in the scrying pool, his skin is light brown and so
is his chin-length hair, though now his mouth gapes
at the four of us standing on the shoreline. His lips begin
to move in an incantation, but Zandria is faster. In seconds,
she's cast a handspell to freeze Owen's limbs in place.

Not exactly the best way to introduce ourselves, but certainly
the safest.

"We mean you no harm." I step forward with my hands out
in what I hope is a calming gesture.

"Then why did you freeze me?" Owen says, his eyes bright
with suspicion. Clearly, his parents taught him well.

"Because it looked like you were about to attack us with your
magic," I say. "We only came here to talk."

He frowns. "How did you even find me? No one is supposed
to know about this place."

"They don't," Zandria says, appearing at my side. "We
wouldn't either if not for the assistance of a powerful Magi elder."

His eyes widen. "So you're Magi too?"

"Yes, as only the Magi have magic." I decide, for the moment,
to hold off on explaining Aro until we get on firmer ground with
this person.

"Do you think you can behave more hospitably toward us?"
Zandria asks.

He laughs. "Yes, I've seen proof enough to know you're my
kind." Zandria releases the spell, and Owen stretches his hands
and fingers. "Thanks. Now, why are you here?"

We all exchange a look. "We're part of the Alchemist Alliance, like you and your parents before you," I say. "My sister and I were spies in the Technocrat city of Palinor and fled to warn the rest of the Magi when one of our own betrayed us. But catastrophe befell them, and now our numbers have been decimated. Between us, the survivors, and any Magi the Technocrats hold prisoner, there's maybe one hundred left, at best. We came here to find you because the two of us"—I gesture to me and my sister—"and you are all that's left of the Alchemist Alliance bloodlines, aside from the traitor. We need your help to stop his plan."

Owen's expressions go through a range of emotions. He sits atop a piece of driftwood on the beach. "You're telling me there are a hundred other Magi out there?" he says.

I raise an eyebrow. "Yes, but there was closer to a thousand before the Chambers—"

"What is the Chambers?"

Did his parents not educate him? Or had they been so cut off from society that they weren't sure about the other Magi anymore? Either way, this boy may not be as helpful as we hoped. But regardless, we could use more warm bodies on our side.

Zandria sits next to him on the driftwood log. "First, why don't you tell us what you know about the Magi and the country of Palinor, and we can fill in the gaps." She puts a hand on his shoulder. "We know you've been here for a long time."

"My whole life, actually," Owen says, running a hand through his hair. "My parents taught me about the great wars with the Technocrats, and about the Alchemist Alliance and how they sought to mend the divisions between us to no avail. And they told me about the Alliance's long-term mission to restore full magic powers to our people. But they told me that there were no other Magi left. That the mainland was overrun by the Technocrats and we were all who'd survived. That's why they created this island and we moved here. To raise me, train me in safety and seclusion."

Zandria speaks my thoughts before I can. "Seclusion is certainly right," she says.

Aro, who has been hovering behind us with Remy, breaks into the conversation. "Do you know what happened to your parents?"

Owen's eyes get a faraway sheen to them. "They went to the mainland occasionally for things we needed but couldn't produce on our own. Clothes and the like. One day, they never came back. I had no choice but to assume they were caught by the Technos. They always said it was too dangerous for me to go with them, that I was the last hope of the Alliance and had to remain here." He jams his walking stick into the sand. "It always chafed, but even more now that I know there are other Magi."

"I'm sure they meant well," Zandria says. "They obviously wanted to protect you."

"Instead they prevented me from learning the truth," Owen says. "I miss them terribly, but I'm angry at them too. If I'd been with them, maybe three would've been enough to fight back and escape together."

"They taught you magic, yes?" Remy says.

"They did. We have a primer spell book from the Great Academy, plus my parents passed along a few other spells they knew. But they hadn't finished teaching me everything . . ." His eyes get that faraway look again, and it makes my stomach twist.

"We lost our parents too," I say. "But not to the Technocrats. To Darian Azul, the traitor to the Magi and the Alchemist Alliance. He killed them."

Zandria stands and brushes off her trousers. "Yes, he did. Because he wanted to get to us."

"Zandy . . ." I say, with a warning tone.

She shrugs. "He's part of the Alliance. He deserves to know."

I grab her by the elbow to pull her aside, but she resists. "Maybe we should wait until—"

"No. If you can tell your Techno boyfriend, I can tell a member of the Alliance!"

"Techno?" Owen says warily as he rises to his feet.

I let go of my sister and automatically position myself in front of Aro. "It's a long story. But suffice to say, Aro is on our side. He believes in the Alliance's mission as well. Darian wants to kill him, and he's here under my protection."

"Truly," Aro says. "I want to help. I want to fix things just like the Alchemist Alliance did."

Owen regards him for a moment, looking back and forth and between him and me several times before relaxing. "All right, but Technocrats killed my parents. If he goes astray, I can't be held responsible."

"You will control yourself; if Zandria and Remy can, so can you," I say.

"Perhaps this will help," Aro says. "Have you heard of the Heartless, Owen?"

"Aro, you don't have to do that," I say.

"It's fine," he says.

"I think my parents mentioned it in passing, but I don't know much," Owen says.

"The Heartless are Technocrats who are born without working hearts. They're given clockwork hearts instead, which must be replaced every year. As the hearts wear out, they release a poison from the fuel cell inside them. Because of the poisoning and yearly surgeries, most Heartless don't live past twenty years, if that."

"That's terrible, but what does that have to do with us?"

"All my life I've hated the Magi because the Technocrats believe the condition is the result of lingering curse magic wrought in a last-gasp attempt by Magi elders as we crushed their final stronghold with our machines."

Owen's hands ball into fists, and I'd bet anything magic is

brewing in his veins right now. I'm ready to defend Aro if necessary, my own magic rising to the surface in response.

"But that was a lie. It was an accident, caused by the Alchemist Alliance. They thought that releasing certain alchemicals into the water supply would lead to Techno children with restored magical powers, but that attempt burned up the unborns' hearts instead." He pulls the collar of his shirt aside to show the dark spot on his chest that thumps with a clockwork beat. Owen gasps.

"You're one of the Heartless?" he says. "And the Alliance caused it?" He frowns. "My parents didn't tell me that."

"They may not have known," I say. "We didn't, and I doubt our parents did either. We only learned of it recently."

"And yet you're not angry with the Alliance?" Owen asks Aro.

Aro shakes his head. "I should be, I suppose. But the intent wasn't malicious like I'd always imagined. They were trying to heal, not harm. It went horribly awry, but if their desire was to heal our peoples and stop the war . . ." He smiles at me. "After meeting Aissa, how could I not want that too? We're not that different after all."

Owen looks at all of us, confused. "So then why does this Darian want to kill all of you?"

"That's what I was trying to tell you. He wants to use Aissa and me," Zandria says. "For our magic."

I grimace. My sister is getting far too lax about who she shares this information with, and it's beginning to worry me.

"Your magic? But can't he use any Magi?"

"No," Zandria says. "Our magic is special. You see, the Alchemist Alliance's experiments . . . they finally worked for our parents. Their children were born evolved."

"You mean you two can control anything with your magic? Not just organic matter?" His jaw is slack with surprise.

"It's true," Zandria says. "We had no idea until recently why we were special, and our parents were murdered before we could grill them about it. It's made us excellent spies, though we've had to hide the nature of our magic from Magi and Technocrat alike, hence my sister's hesitation in telling you."

"That's extraordinary!" he says. "The Alliance's experiments have been realized after all. My parents would've loved to see that. Can you . . . can you show me?"

"Gladly," Zandy says. She twists her fingers in the motions of a spell and my knife rises out of the sheath on my belt, startling even me.

"Incredible . . ." Owen breathes, and Aro laughs too. "If you can do that, what do you need me for?" he asks.

"We need allies," I say. "Isaiah, the leader of the remaining Magi, doesn't see eye to eye with us. He wants revenge, and while I don't blame him for that, he's more likely to lead the rest of our people to their deaths than anything else. He also still foolishly trusts Darian because Darian is the Magi spymaster. Isaiah can't believe he might betray his own kind. We're hoping you can help us stop Darian so we can reach some sort of peace between the Magi and the Technocrats."

"Which seems pretty impossible given who the king and queen are," Zandria says.

"They're not very open to negotiation, it's true," Aro says, and Zandria glances away.

"Then I suppose my choice is clear." Owen surprises us all when he gets to one knee and bows to me and Zandria. "I pledge myself to the Alliance and the heirs of Alchemy. I will do what I can to aid you, even if it means giving my life."

OWEN, WE QUICKLY DISCOVER, IS A HIGHLY inquisitive traveling companion. Having lived on an island his entire life, everything is new to him. From huge swathes of forest to mountains to lakes—all of it meets with amazement through his eyes. Plants and bushes and animals that seem normal to us are a revelation to Owen.

Last night, Zandria and Remy caught wild rabbits for dinner. Owen was both horrified and fascinated by it. Apparently, he has only eaten fish and the vegetables that grow on the island.

He couldn't bring himself to eat his portion. Zandria ate it for him.

"What?" she said to me when I raised my eyebrows as she took the meat. "I had nothing to eat but broth for weeks. No way am I letting perfectly good food go to waste."

This led to an uncomfortable conversation about why Zandria only had broth for weeks. Which ended abruptly when my sister stalked off into the nearby woods after Owen asked what had happened in the dungeons. The rest of us were left to explain that she suffered considerably. Owen has been trying to make it up to her ever since, much to Zandria's irritation.

We're not far from the Sanctuary when Aro suddenly hisses, "Stop!"

"What is it?" I ask. His face is drawn and serious enough to make even Zandria bite her tongue.

He takes a few steps forward and picks up a stick. Then he pokes at the ground and leaps backward.

The ground where he was standing moments ago shifts and

swoops up into the air. Decaying leaves and a few ferns now hang from a nearby tree in a net made of thin metal wire. I shudder.

It was meant for us.

"That," Aro says, "is not something we want to get caught in. The larger seekers can weave these and leave them behind to capture enemies. They work especially well in places with good cover, like these woods."

Zandria approaches Aro with arms folded across her chest. "How did you know it was there? What gave it away?"

Aro points to the netting. "Two things. First, I saw the glimmer of the wires running down that tree. Second, there's a mechanical fern by the base that contains the trip mechanism. Technocrats don't normally replace the ferns this far from the main city. There are plenty of trees and plants here already. It was out of place."

For a moment Zandria looks as if she might be ill, but she composes herself quickly. "We'll keep an eye out for that moving forward."

"We should probably slow our pace," I say. "We'll reach the Sanctuary this evening one way or another."

The others nod their agreement, and we set off again. Aro in particular is on guard for more traps. It isn't long, however, before a new problem presents itself: the sound of skittering metal legs.

A chill runs down my spine and I grip Aro's arm. "Those traps . . . do the seekers that make them usually stay close by?"

"Sometimes yes, they can be programmed to do that."

"Why didn't you say so before?" Zandria says from the front of our party.

Before Aro can reply, the seeker crashes through the trees, knocking Zandria off her feet. It towers over her, all six of its metal legs surrounding her body. Wires protrude from its mouth, hurtling toward my frozen sister.

"*Teneree!*" I send my spell at the mech looming over Zandria.

Fear has her in its grasp. But now the mech is in mine. The wires halt, held still by my spell. But the seeker struggles. I can't hold it for too long. Owen leaps forward to grab Zandria's arms and drag her out from under the mech. Moments later, a shield spell conceals them as he helps her hide behind a nearby tree.

Behind me Remy and Aro watch the forest for any other mechs that might be lying in wait. With my spell, I slam the mech against the nearest tree, but it barely makes a dent in the hard metal shell on its back. My incantation rises higher and I flip the metal beast upside down. Its legs writhe as it tries to turn over to no avail. Then my next spell rips off the metal underbelly, which makes a terrible screech. When the wires and internal clockwork are finally exposed, I remove the havani capsule and make short work of disassembling the rest.

Exhausted, I hurry to my sister. She's sitting up now, chatting excitedly with Owen.

"Are you all right?" I ask.

"Yes, I'm fine now. But Aissa, you have to see this." She nods at Owen. "Do it again."

He shrugs, strangely amused. Then he whispers a spell to make a nearby flower blossom. For a moment I seriously wonder if Zandria hit her head harder than I thought.

That's when I realize the same thing she did: Owen's shield is still up. Yet he's casting an incantation too.

That's supposed to be impossible.

Then again, so are we.

A thrill ripples over me. Owen might be a better ally than we thought.

"You're casting a handspell and a songspell at the same time," I say, hardly believing the words despite the proof in front of my own eyes. I wonder if Catoria had any inkling. Maybe this was the real reason she encouraged us to find him.

Owen tilts his head. "Yes, can't you?"

Zandy's eyes are full of light. "No, we've always been told it's impossible."

Remy and Aro approach to see what we're gawking at.

"Really? Another impossible Magi?" Remy laughs.

Aro, on the other hand, immediately puts on his researcher hat. "Aissa, didn't you tell me that each family line had their own recipe for the alchemicals they hoped would eventually produce Magi like you and your sister?"

"Yes, that's true."

"If each recipe was a little different, perhaps the end results are too. Your family's recipe managed to produce the desired effect, but the Heldreths' must have instigated a different mutation."

"That does make sense," Owen says.

Remy frowns. "You had no idea that wasn't normal? Could your parents do the same?"

Owen considers, his forehead knitting together in a deep *V*. "I don't know. We didn't need to use spells at the same time like that often—our daily life didn't usually require that sort of urgency—but I've done it before while fishing. I can't recall my parents ever doing the same, now that I think about it."

"You must be right, Aro," I say. "Owen has a different mutation." I exchange a glance with Zandy. "Catoria will be very interested to hear about this."

After we conceal the wreckage of the destroyed seeker, we head out again. By the time night falls, the strange, foggy hills that house the underground Sanctuary come into view.

The fog is thick and eerie, illuminated by the full moon and the otherwise clear night. The same skeletal trees reach out from the fog at odd intervals. Unlike the last time we were here, there's no wind whatsoever. Everything is still. Unnervingly so.

Aro and Owen are as struck by the surroundings as we were the first time.

"I've never seen anything like this," Aro says. "We have fog in Palinor, to be sure, but this is so thick it looks like . . . like soup."

I almost laugh. "I suppose it does."

Owen's eyes are wide. "You say there's a whole network of buildings beneath those hills?"

"Yes," Zandria says, standing next to him. "The hills are made of a special stone, and it protects the city that lies beneath."

He shakes his head and stares at the hills. "I always thought my parents trained me well. Now I find I know hardly anything at all."

"Don't worry," Remy says, walking by Owen and patting his shoulder. "We'll get you up to speed."

"As will Catoria," I add.

Once we've ascertained the coast is clear, we make a beeline for the tallest hill in the center and begin the descent through the top into the Sanctuary. This time, we avoid the mechdragon and vine kraken by using a secret passage Catoria showed us that can only be revealed with magic like mine and Zandria's or unlocked from the inside. Owen is disappointed; he was curious about the challenges. Perhaps Catoria will see fit to show him how they work once we've made introductions.

For now, it's certainly easier—and more expedient—for us to avoid them.

We find Catoria in the library. Owen greets her with the same deference he showed to Zandria and me when we first met.

She clasps his hand. "I'm glad you've found your way off that island at last."

The corner of Owen's lip twitches. "So am I."

Zandria pushes forward. "Catoria. Owen has unique magic as

well. He can cast two spells at once. One with his hands, the other as an incantation."

Catoria appraises Owen with new eyes. "Interesting. And useful. I'm glad you've pledged yourself to the Alliance. You will be an excellent addition to our cause."

"We should give you a name," Zandria says suddenly. She seems to have warmed considerably to Owen since she learned of his dual magic.

"But I already have a name," Owen says.

"No, a code name. The Magi spy network is—was—" She frowns. "Was called the Armory. And every spy had a weapon-based code name. We were the Twin Daggers. You should be the Poleaxe. It has two bladed sides, just like you can cast two spells simultaneously."

Owen grins, looking rather boyish. "I like the sound of that."

Catoria gestures to Aro. "Aissa? Are you going to make introductions?"

I wipe my sweaty hands on my tunic. "Catoria, this is Aro. Aro, meet Catoria."

While I'm sure Aro is exploding with questions about the Sanctuary, he was still born a prince. He approaches Catoria solemnly, bowing deeply before her.

"Thank you for allowing me to enter these premises. It's an extraordinary place. I'm very pleased to make your acquaintance."

Catoria eyes him up and down, then laughs. The sound echoes through the library. "Well said. And what do you know of the Alchemist Alliance?"

Aro straightens up. "All that Aissa has told me, but I'm eager to learn more. I'm a researcher—a scientist—in Palinor. Or I was." A frown briefly flits over his face. "I'm particularly fascinated by these alchemicals she's told me about. Especially the ones that created the Heartless."

Catoria's expression softens. "I nearly forgot. You're one of them."

Aro flashes me a quick smile. "Sort of. After what Aissa did, I'm not sure I count anymore. But perhaps there's a means of curing the Heartless with those alchemicals?"

Off to the side, I hear Owen whisper to Zandria, "What did Aissa do?" My sister rolls her eyes.

Catoria's face darkens. "I doubt they could cure those who are already afflicted. The creation of the Heartless was a grave mistake. But I've been working on something that might at least prevent more from being born."

"If I can be of any assistance . . ." Aro says eagerly.

"Perhaps you can," Catoria muses. "Come, I'll show you my lab."

She leads him through the door and into the labyrinth of tunnels beyond, leaving the rest of us behind in the library. I take a deep breath, inhaling the scent of old manuscripts and scrolls.

It's good to be back.

THE NEXT DAY, WE'RE AWAKENED BY THE

sound of Catoria rapping on the wall of the
girls' dormitory.

"We have much to do today," she says as we wipe
the sleep from our eyes. "You must eat, then I have something important to share with you."

She seems oddly excited. Curiosity fills us as we dress
quickly, then head for the dining hall. The boys are already there
when we arrive, but Catoria is nowhere in sight. Puzzled, we help
ourselves to the oatmeal and fruit waiting for us.

"Catoria woke you two as well?" Owen asks.

"She did," Zandria says. "Though Anvil knows why."

"She said she had something to share with us. Did she give
you any other hints?" I ask.

Remy shakes his head. "She said the same thing to us."

I smile. "Maybe she's finally ready to let us in on some of her
secrets."

Zandria frowns across the table from me, but Remy laughs.
"Maybe she is. That would be something."

Aro looks confused, so I explain. "Catoria is our mentor, but
we haven't been able to shake the feeling she holds as much back
as she teaches."

"I see," he says. "Too much too soon could be overwhelming.
If she's withholding something, it isn't necessarily for nefarious
reasons."

I laugh. "I agree. Remy and Zandria here, however, have
floated other ideas."

Zandria looks as if she's about to make a snide retort when her
mouth snaps shut instead.

"Are we ready?" Catoria says from the doorway.

She leads us into the throne room and then the stone corridor beyond. It isn't long before the tunnel becomes much older and I realize where we're going: the same place Catoria caught me exploring before we had to leave to save Aro.

When we reach the dead-end landing and the stone walls completely covered with ancient runes, everyone gapes but me. My sister gives me the side-eye.

"You've seen this before, haven't you?" she says.

I shrug. "I wanted to tell you about it, but you made it clear you didn't want to speak to me any more than necessary."

She stiffens, then turns away. I already regret my words. We need to talk, to air everything out between us and resolve things so we can be the team we once were. Shaming her isn't going to help.

"What is this place, Catoria?" Remy asks, giving me a pointed look.

"The end of the road." She places a hand reverently on the wall. "These are not just any runes. The ancient Magi could infuse magic into carvings, embedding the spell into the stone or parchment it was written on. Their magic lasts to this day."

Zandria examines the runes, as surprised as I was when I first saw them. "But why? What purpose does this place serve?"

Catoria smiles. "That is a good question, and one I can only partially answer. We're standing in an antechamber. The walls are the lock on a door. It can only be opened using the blood of four Magi houses and the magic of the ancient Magi to activate the opening spell embedded in the walls."

My eyes widen. "The Alchemist Alliance couldn't open it when they found the Sanctuary. You needed us."

Zandria snorts. "That's why you suggested we bring Owen back here. You needed a fourth bloodline."

Catoria tilts her head. "Both are true. This place stymied the Alliance when we used it for our base. But I've studied it and found several references to what lies beneath the throne room—indeed, under much of this complex."

"Well? What is it?" Remy says impatiently.

"Our past."

Zandria scoffs. "Stop speaking in riddles."

"It's a tomb," Aro guesses.

"I believe it to be the Tomb of Regents," Catoria says. "Legends say the great Magi rulers of long ago were all entombed in a grand underworld, buried with riches and magic talismans, the likes of which we've never seen. The Magi of my day called it a fairy tale. Impossible, but lovely to imagine."

"Then why do you believe this might be it?" Owen asks.

Catoria smiles broadly. "Because they said the same thing about the Sanctuary."

"What do all these runes mean? Is every one of them a spell?" I ask.

"Only some of them are. Most of them are here to obscure."

"You mean they're just random runes?" I say, frowning. This isn't quite what I was expecting.

"Many of them are random. Buried between them are the runes for the opening spell. The rest are family names."

"And that's why you need four bloodlines. It will activate the runes for the spell?" Zandria says, glancing up from where she was tracing a rune with a fingernail.

"Precisely."

Owen steps forward in the small space. "When can we cast it? We should open this up and find out what lies behind it. If it's full of treasure and magic, that could help us against the Technocrats."

"If you're all willing, we can try to open it right now."

We all agree—there is no reason to wait. Not if there's

something inside that could help our cause. Catoria pulls a knife from within her cloak and pricks each of our fingers, then her own, and instructs us to place our hands on the wall. Every Magi but Zandria, who hangs back with Aro; we only need one from each bloodline.

The stone warms under my palm and my fingers begin to tingle. Then the magic seems to reach out of the stone, pulling a very thin stream of blood from my hand. It winds around the runes, almost like it's searching for something, until the stream stops, and the magic and blood pool in one particular rune. It glows. Surprise trickles over me as I realize the others are having the same experience. Now four unique runes are illuminated on the wall—one for each of our bloodlines.

"Zandria," Catoria says. "Use your magic to access the opening runes. They look like this." She points at a rune. "There are four of them as well."

My sister steps forward and begins working a spell to open locked things. She does as Catoria instructs and sends the magic into the stone wall. Suddenly, four more runes glow, this time marking the four corners of a doorway.

Inside the wall, something begins to grind, then shift. A rectangular entrance moves backward a couple inches, then a seam appears in the middle, expanding as the slab splits in half and slides into the wall on either side.

A dark, shadowed entrance stands before us, taunting us with its secrets.

With eager expressions we walk single file through a dark corridor. Catoria goes first, and she gasps softly as the corridor turns, letting us out into an enormous underground cavern. Whether the cavern is natural or made by Magi hands is hard to say, but it's stunning either way. Bioluminescent moss coats the walls, the floor, and the high ceiling, filling the space with a soft glowing light. As far as we can see, the cavern floor is filled with beautifully carved stone tombs. Some of them are made from the black marble we know well, others from red, white, or gray stone—all of it positively fizzing with magic. We walk down the center aisle of the cavern, marveling at each exquisitely crafted monument. Every tomb bears the likeness of its owner, and embedded into the base are objects, each of them unique to the ruler. Swords, spears, knives, amulets, and all sorts of strange things I cannot name adorn them, along with many runes.

"Are those protective runes?" I ask Catoria, pointing to the nearest tomb.

She peers closer at them. Then she laughs. "In a sense," she says. "It's a similar mechanism to the lock on this place, but it looks like you need the right bloodline to open the tomb. They kept it safe in case looters ever found their way down here."

"That seems unlikely," Remy says.

"This place could be older than the Sanctuary," Owen muses. "And you said the Magi created the landscape here, right? Maybe it once looked very different and didn't have that locking mechanism until later. Then it just became a part of the burial ritual."

Catoria eyes Owen approvingly. "You may very well be correct."

Aro is close by my side, keeping a respectful silence. The full weight of the history of our lands, unknown to us all until very recently, bears down on us. Neither the Magi nor the Technocrats know the real truth. But soon their eyes must be opened too.

Zandria has wandered ahead, running her fingers over the edges of tombs as she goes. Halfway into this cavern I can see that the hall turns up ahead, possibly into a similar space. There are easily hundreds of tombs down here. Suddenly my sister pauses by one crafted from the red marble we've seen frequently in the Sanctuary. She glances back at us.

"There's a statue of this woman in one of the other halls," she says.

I move closer and realize she's right. The face is the same as the statue in hunting garb that we saw the day we arrived. "Who is she?" I say to Catoria as I run a finger across the rune of her name.

"Queen Egeria. A ruler with a true heart, true aim, whom no spell could harm," she reads. "The name is familiar, but I don't recall the details precisely. I'm sure I've read her tale somewhere here in the library." Catoria continues to examine the tomb, as does Zandria.

"If she warranted a statue in that hall, she must have been special," Zandria says. Then she gasps. We gather closer to see what she's looking at. Two short swords are embedded at the back of the tomb. The hilts are crafted from red marble brimming with magic, and the blades are carved with runes.

"They almost look like daggers," I say. "Just a bit too long."

"They're perfect," Zandria says, unable to take her eyes off the weapons.

Catoria examines them. "This one"—she points to the one on the left—"can pierce any armor and never misses, and the other can counter any offensive spell." She steps back. "But it takes Magi with full magic to use them. To anyone else, they would be just like normal swords. And only Aissa or Zandria will be able to remove them from the tombstone since they're magically embedded into it."

"Then we must have them," Zandria says, eyes shining.

"Yes," Catoria agrees. "These will serve the two of you well."

Before anyone can say another word, Zandy begins a hand-spell to release the short swords from the stone. Her magic molds the stone around them, turning it flat and smooth. The swords fall to the ground. She immediately grabs the one that never misses.

"I choose this one," she says, almost like a challenge to me.

But I'd have chosen the other one anyway. She almost looks disappointed when I let her have it.

"I'll gladly take the other," I say. When I retrieve the short sword, a tingling sensation ripples up my arm. The weapon feels almost like it's alive. Like it is saying hello.

"What about the rest?" Zandria looks longingly at the other tombs. Many others have weapons embedded in them as well. "Are they all magical too?"

"I believe so," Catoria says, wandering over to another nearby tomb with a rune-covered axe lodged in the side. "Yes, this one has a blade that never dulls." She turns back to us. "But we mustn't be greedy. Only Aissa and Zandria can wield these artifacts. We shouldn't take more than we need. We must leave the rest of the cache here to ensure it remains safe and hidden."

Zandria pouts but doesn't object. We explore for a while longer through the dizzying array of past kings and queens and discover there are two more enormous caverns just like this under the Sanctuary complex, each one older than the last. We tire before we can explore it all and decide to return to the upper levels for lunch and our continued studies.

We may leave the tombs behind for now, but someday this place and its artifacts will be opened again for Magi like us to use. It was the Alliance's goal, and now it is ours as well.

WE'VE BEEN AT THE SANCTUARY FOR SEV-

eral days, sharing more about the Alchemist
Alliance with Owen and Aro, practicing spells,
and doing our weapons training. And every day, Aro
and Catoria have disappeared into the laboratory to work
on their new recipe.

But despite the new skills we're learning, my mind keeps
wandering back to Palinor. Darian is still there, plotting to take
the throne. Working toward building his own army by stealing
magic from our people.

We must stop him.

Which means we must return. It is only a question of when.
As idyllic as this underground haven may be, our time here is
fleeting.

Every day we remain is a day Darian gains to advance his
machinations. And while we can spy on him in the scrying pool,
we can't hear his words. For all we know, he could be on the verge
of enacting his plan.

The only thing he still needs is my sister and me. We're going
to have to face him. And soon.

This afternoon, I've been studying old scrolls with Zandria,
Owen, and Remy on the third level of the library. But I've lost my
concentration. I replace the scroll I was reading on the shelf and
capture the others' attention.

"I can't take this waiting much longer," I say.

"Oh, thank the Anvil," Zandria says. "As much as I enjoy these
new spells, I'm beginning to feel cooped up."

"Same," Remy says. "I know our original plan was to learn all
we could so we can use our newfound knowledge to take down

Darian, but that could take years." He gestures to the vast expanse of the library. "We don't have the luxury."

"I couldn't agree more," I say. "Darian knows we're free and that we know his plans. I'd bet anything he's moved up the timeline."

"Then we're going to have to make do with what we've already learned," Zandria says.

"We need a plan. Concrete steps we can take once we're back in the city," I say.

"I can help with that," a voice from behind us says, startling me. Aro gives me his best lopsided grin. "But first, we have news. We've succeeded—we've created a batch of alchemicals that will counteract the ones Darian put in the water. No more Heartless will be born once we add it to the city's main water supply."

"That's wonderful," I say, beaming back at him. It may not cure those who are already Heartless, but to stop the plague . . . Aro is floating at the prospect.

Owen has a thoughtful expression on his face. "Can we use that to our advantage somehow? I mean, it sounds like if we want to defeat Darian and the Technocrat king and queen, we should start with what keeps them in power: the people of the city. As long as they fear and respect their rulers, they will defend their way of life. But what if we can show them there's another way? With the Alliance?"

I watch Zandria's face go through several emotions in quick succession. I already know she wants nothing more than to raze Palinor to the ground. But since we lack the means to accomplish that successfully, a guerrilla campaign against the Technocrat way of life, showing the people of the city that working together is a better way . . .

"That might actually work," I say. "It would undermine Darian's work and the people's confidence in the royals. That can only be in our favor."

"I have a few ideas of where we could start," Aro says.

"Aissa, Zandria!" Catoria calls from the bottom floor of the library. "Come to the scrying room immediately."

We waste no time following her. Once we're circled around the pool, she dips the Azul amulet into the placid waters and casts the spell. Darian appears. He's leaving the throne room and seems to be headed to the lower, research-based levels. The waters follow him down the stairs until he gets to the level where Remy and I were captured almost a month ago. He opens the door to the room where we hid, and I suck my breath in sharply.

The last time I saw this room, there were three containers to hold the Magi prisoners and siphon off their powers.

Now there are at least twenty. Their hulking glass-and-steel forms line every wall in the room. With the mechlights on, it's easier to see the glass panes and the metal tubes and wires connecting the cases. It's easier to tell they're monstrous devices, a new form of torture for the Magi.

Darian is ramping up his efforts. In a big way.

Aro and Owen gasp, but the rest of us are already familiar with this grim scene.

"So many already," Aro whispers as if he's afraid Darian might hear us.

"He's been busy," Catoria says. "Especially lately. He's had several meetings with the royals and many others I do not know. Moments ago, he met with the king and queen and looked far too happy for my liking. That's when I called for you. He's up to something. Something big and imminent."

A frisson of terror and tension shivers over me. "We must leave."

"Yes, you must," Catoria says. "Aro and I will finish making enough of the alchemicals needed to reverse the Heartless curse by tomorrow night. Between that and what you've learned here, you'll be fit to set things right."

When the following night falls, we eat a quick dinner, then return to the dormitory areas to pack our belongings. Catoria has been quite clear that the girls are to stay in the girls' dormitory and the boys in theirs. In fact, between all the traveling and separate rooms, Aro and I have hardly spent more than a handful of minutes alone together since his rescue.

But this is our last night in the Sanctuary. I don't know what will happen in Palinor. I don't know if we'll survive. As it is, we're living on stolen time. All I know is that I want a few more precious moments with Aro before that clock runs out. And there's something here I want to show him.

After Zandria finally falls asleep, I tiptoe out of the dormitory toward the boys' room down the hall. With a spell, I listen for any sounds coming from within. Once satisfied, I slip open the door and find where Aro lays on a cot. It's a far cry from his fancy rooms in the Palace, but he hasn't complained. He's almost peaceful while he sleeps, except for a tiny hint of a frown at the corner of his lips. Like something in his dream makes him sad.

I kneel next to him and place a hand on his shoulder. "Aro," I whisper. "Wake up."

He stirs, and I place a finger over my lips, indicating he should be quiet. He gives me a curious—and slightly groggy—glance.

"Come with me," I say, offering my hand. He takes it, and I pull him into the hallway. The spell that created the lights in the Sanctuary also dims them when night falls so anyone staying here doesn't completely lose track of time. Tonight, the hallway is aglow with a soft light. Just enough to illuminate our path.

"Where are we going?" Aro whispers, amused.

"You'll see," I say.

"That's quite cryptic of you."

I give him an arch look. "Not as fun when you're on the receiving end, is it?"

He laughs softly. "On the contrary." He pulls me close. The kiss is sweet, and for a moment I can feel the bond between us tugging at my heart approvingly. I wish I could revel in this forever.

I step back, cool air filling the space between us. "Let's go."

On the bottom floor of the dormitory sector is a circular room with doors that each lead to a different tunnel. I ventured down all of them the last time we were here, though I wasn't able to follow every path to their end. But one in particular stuck with me.

"Here." I open the door to a tunnel and red granite splashed with vinelike moss greets us. It takes us down an incline for what feels longer than I remember. For a moment, I worry I chose the wrong door, but then we reach the end of the tunnel, and beyond that door is what I seek.

This place is more of a cave than a room. Slicing through it is a small river I believe is connected to the one in the scrying pool room. It winds lazily, and part of its current is caught up in a shallow pool on one side of the cave. The water is clear and crisp, and here and there are flashes of little blue fish swimming. Everywhere we look, there's moss and ferns and black rocks. The air is filled with tiny bursts of flickering light—glow beetles. In the daytime, everything is lit in green and gold; but at night, the magic lights mimic moonlight, bathing everything in silver.

Catoria wasn't certain when I asked about it, but I suspect the river widens and deepens farther along, and that the ancient Magi may have used this place for traveling. Some parts of the bank appear to have once been underwater; the stones are piled in such a way that they could've formed part of a dock long, long ago. But those answers are lost to time.

Aro gapes. "Your ancestors truly crafted some stunning

things." He shakes his head. "And here I thought the garden hidden in the Palace was extraordinary, when you have all this."

"It is extraordinary. Just in a different way," I say. "It's almost like the reverse of your garden, actually."

He dips his head, the moonlight capturing his pale hair. "So it is."

We wander slowly, hand in hand, following the curve of the river. He's delighted when one of the glow beetles lands on his shoulder.

"Is it magic?" he asks.

"No, nature."

"These are real creatures?" His eyes widen. "Surely some spell gave them the ability to cast this light."

I laugh. "I promise you, no. You can find them in the woods sometimes too. Usually on warm summer nights, though not in these quantities."

He marvels at the tiny creature until it finally flits off.

"All my life, I've been told the greatest creations were born from the minds of Technocrats. My parents used it to justify any destruction they or their forebears wrought. They'd plow down an entire forest or hunt animals until they were nearly gone. Mine the same shafts until they were stripped bare of their resources. It was all for a greater good. To clear the path for Technocrat ingenuity. For most of my life, I believed it earnestly." He stops and faces me. "I was wrong. We all were. Traveling with you, seeing more of the world, I know now that there were already many incredible things around us. But we ignored them. Our own foolish egos have thrown the whole world off-kilter."

He grips my hands tightly. "It needs to be righted. I know your sister and your friends have doubts about my allegiances. That's understandable. My parents are the king and queen, after all. My interest may have started with my connection to you, but

I hope that you, at least, believe me when I say I'm as devoted to the Alchemist Alliance's cause as any of you."

The fire in his eyes is one I've seen before—in the labs when he spoke of wanting to cure the Heartless. He's well on his way to achieving that goal thanks to the Alliance.

"Aro, when you get that gleam in your eye, I believe every word you say. I know your allegiance is true."

He lifts me off my feet and swings me around, laughing. Even when my feet touch the mossy ground again, I still float. Aro's kisses leave me feeling both weak and powerful at the same time.

Our love may not be one we chose. It may not be sensible. And it will likely get us both killed.

Yet, somehow, this spark between us, the magic that binds us together, a love that defies all reason—that is our resistance. And we'll fight tooth and nail to preserve it.

Finally we decide we must return to the dormitories and get a little sleep. As we leave the river sector, a strange sinking feeling descends on me. Like I've just closed the door on an old friend I may never see again.

I can't help feeling that this night was the calm before the storm. The deadly pause before everything explodes.

IT TAKES US TWO AND A HALF DAYS TO

journey back to Palinor. We're careful to steer
clear of the place where the Magi set up their
makeshift camp. While my sister and Remy still don't
welcome Aro's presence, his insight into the machines
and how they're used by the Technocrat soldiers has proved
invaluable. He prevented us from falling into no less than half a
dozen traps on the way to the city. Remy seems to be forming a
begrudging sort of respect for him, but my sister has yet to follow
his lead. Owen, however, gets along with everyone.

We've decided to make the hidden Magi library room our base
of operations inside the city. It's well concealed in the labyrinth
beyond the drainage tunnels, and only Aro was investigating that
sector before. We can brick up the entrance he pulled down and
make a hidden door instead. If by some unlucky chance we're
found out, we will have a whole labyrinth of tunnels and escape
routes to flee into.

But first we need to get back into the city. No small task for
five fugitives. If my parents were here, they'd think what we're
planning is suicide. While Zandria and Remy are not yet convinced
Technocrats are worthy of the consideration the Alliance would
give them, we all agree we'd rather die trying than hide in safety
while our friends and foes destroy each other. And as far as I'm
concerned, if we're going to mend the divide between Magi and
Technocrats, the time is now, or never.

Aro has proven most helpful in this regard as well. Since he
regularly snuck out of his rooms in the Palace, he knows the secret
ways into the city. And he knows which ones are the least used.

We hide in the woods, just out of range of the Technocrat

scouts, and make our plans. We're surrounded primarily by mechanical trees, which Owen is somewhat disturbed by. It's one thing to know what the Technocrats did to the lands surrounding the city; it's another to see it firsthand. The metal trees are oddly pretty, but they smell and sound and feel bizarre to most Magi.

"Several of the mechtrees are tunnel entrances," Aro says. "The ones that hide tunnels have a specific pattern to their lower branches." He draws a tree in the sand with a cluster of three branches on its right side. "The middle of the cluster is the lever that opens the portal. Some of the older ones have a root lever instead, if I recall, but not most."

Zandria's arms are folded across her chest, but even she seems impressed. I nudge her. "See? I told you he could be useful."

A faint hint of a smile crosses her lips. She knows I'm right, even if she won't admit it.

"But which one of the portal trees is safest to use?" Remy asks.

Aro considers, then draws a circle in the dirt. "This is the city," he says, placing an X on the side closest to us. "This is where we are right now. Here and here"—he draws an X on the eastern side of the city and another on the southern side—"are where the most travel happens, so those are heavily manned. The north side, where we are now, is the next heaviest manned, and the least is the west. That's where we'll enter."

"And if you're wrong?" Zandria asks.

Aro shrugs. "Then we'd better be ready for a fight."

"See that you are," she says, then stalks off with Remy and Owen close at her heels.

Aro frowns. "Did that not go well?" he asks.

I laugh. "It went very well, actually. Zandy just doesn't want to admit having you around could be a good thing. But keep up the good work and she might eventually."

"I'll do my best." He catches my hand and tugs me toward him. My breath catches in my throat.

"We should get ready," I say.

"Yes, we should," he agrees, then he kisses me and the forest disappears for a few precious moments.

"Excuse me?" Owen says, startling us apart. "Sorry to intrude, but it's getting dark and Zandria asked me to fetch you."

I shake my head. Of course she did.

We rejoin the others and prepare to sneak back into Palinor. We cast our protective spells—cloaking and silencing—and work our way toward the mechtree Aro recommended we use. There are more patrols in the woods surrounding Palinor than usual, and several times we are forced to stop and hunker down behind a tree until they pass. Owen and Aro are particularly nervous, but for different reasons. For Owen, this is the first time he's really seen Technocrats. He was raised to believe they're monsters, so realizing their uniforms are all that distinguish them from us has to be a strange feeling, to say the least. And Aro . . . these are people he may have been friends with. Now, they'd kill him or deliver him to Darian and his whims. Both have every right to be frightened.

We all do.

To our relief, we reach the tunnels without incident. When we finally turn the corner where the magic-infused marble begins, Aro and Owen both gasp. They've glimpsed it at the Sanctuary, but there it's ubiquitous enough to be hardly noticeable. Here, it's wildly out of place.

"So this is what Darian was after. I've seen smaller pieces like it in his lab. He's been experimenting with it."

"We know," I say. He's betrayed the Magi in so many ways

that sometimes it's hard to keep track. I almost forgot about this component.

"You said the ancient Magi made this?" Owen asks. He reaches out a hand to touch the arch over our heads and smiles when he feels the magic tingle in his fingertips. "And it keeps its magic, even here."

"They did. Like with the Sanctuary, where they hid the whole complex underground, they preserved the library in a case of marble kept alive by some of the rescued spells. And when they got word the Technocrats were coming, they secreted out the books that once resided here to the Sanctuary."

"And then my grandfather's father built his Palace on top of the rubble," Aro says, sadly. "I wish all this destruction hadn't taken place. We were fighting over foolish things. Fear of those who are different. Greed, a desire for more power. When we could have made peace and shared that knowledge and power instead."

"Especially if the Alliance had gotten their way," Remy says. He hasn't said much about how he feels about the Alliance. He's here because of his dedication to me and Zandria—though he has little choice now that his father has all but disowned him. And I know he's bitter about that.

When we reach the door that once bewitched us, I pull the key out of my pack and open it. The room is just the way we left it—with one issue Zandria and I should address.

"What is that?" Aro says, pointing to the strangely shaped ceiling on one side of the room. It cuts low enough to block off a significant chunk of the room. Space we need back.

"Remember when I told you how we escaped?"

"That's the staircase?" He gapes.

I smirk. "This is the underside of it, yes. We crafted it from the secret room below us and made sure the walls and the floor cut off any means of entering this place. From the outside it seemed like a staircase leading nowhere. But we need to fix it if we want to use this place as our base of operations."

Owen frowns. "Won't they know exactly where we are then?"

"No, they filled it in. The surface is at least three stories above us, so the ground might tremble as we shift things around, but they won't know it's us. Even if they do figure it out, they're not getting past that marble with their machines. They'd need the key. Only I have that," I say.

"You three"—Zandria points to the boys—"should stay back in the tunnel while we do this."

Zandy weaves her hands and I hum the words to a spell. Our magic builds and mingles and worms its way into the wood and steel and stone of the staircase. Then it begins to lift, pushing and pulling, setting supports and beams back where they belong.

Then it's done.

"It's safe," I call over my shoulder, and Remy, Owen, and Aro enter the room again.

"Incredible," Aro says.

Owen gasps. "I almost didn't believe you'd really made that until now."

Zandy laughs. "Give us some credit."

Owen grins back and tilts his head at her. Remy, however, scowls at their exchange.

"Let's get this place cleaned up if we're going to stay here," Remy says, pushing farther into the room.

He's right; the hall is a disaster. Gray dust coats everything except the handful of things we disturbed the last time we were here. Broken marble pillars, the shattered, charred remnants of shelves and cases—the Alchemist Alliance took no chances when they left.

We fan out, picking up debris and piling it in the center of the room. Then Zandria and I take stock of the pieces we have left.

"We could put up a few walls so we each have some privacy and a place to sleep," I suggest, casting a glance at Aro.

Zandria gives me a withering look. "Don't get distracted, sister. We have too much important work still to do."

I can feel my cheeks redden. "Never. Don't worry about that," I say. "We could set up another area for eating and strategizing?"

"And a jail. Just in case we take any prisoners and need to interrogate them. You know . . ." Zandy taps her chin with a finger. "The hidden room the Alchemist Alliance used would be perfect for that. We'll just need to install something to restrain the prisoners."

"Are we planning on taking many prisoners?" I ask, frowning. This isn't tied to anything we've discussed, and I'm not sure it's in our best interest.

She shrugs. "Better to have and not need, than need and not have."

"I suppose," I say.

We continue to map out the space, my sister and I using our magic to make dividers out of the larger pieces of debris until we're exhausted. We sit in the makeshift war room to eat a quick meal.

"So," Owen begins, glancing around the table. "Where should we start in overthrowing these royals I hear so much about?"

Zandria smirks at him, but Aro speaks first. "I think we need to get the alchemicals into the water supply as soon as possible. Every day that poisons more people, and we must stop it."

I nod my agreement. "Let's plan to do that tomorrow night."

"Freeing our fellow Magi from the dungeons," Zandria says. "There's nothing more important we can do than save them."

"And persuade them to pledge their loyalty to the Alchemist Alliance," I add, though Zandria doesn't seem as vehement about that part. "Maybe we can steal weapons from the guards. Deplete their stores," I say, hoping to bring a light to my sister's eyes, but instead she frowns.

"What, and alert them to the fact we're here?"

"They'll find out the moment we begin freeing Magi prisoners. We may as well put them on edge and literally disarm them in the process." I've been considering this idea for a while. "They won't know the difference between us and simple thieves."

"Someone will," she says darkly.

"Let him know. Let him be afraid," Remy says suddenly. "It would serve Darian right to feel nervous for once. I like the idea."

Zandy rolls her eyes. "We need to focus on freeing Magi."

Aro smiles. "Darian will know that's us too."

"But it's still our number one priority," I say quickly. "Remy, do you know where the weapons storehouses are from your stint in the palace guard?"

"Most of them, yes."

"Excellent. We'll add that to the list."

We plot until our meal is over and we're all tired enough to heed the call of slumber. Aro and I place our bedrolls side by side in our makeshift room, but he's already snoring when I'm finally ready to sleep. I settle on my bedroll, exhausted but strangely giddy. Then I curl into him and his warmth and quickly give over to my dreams.

The next night, as darkness falls, Aro, Owen, and I slip away, headed toward the southern part of the city. On the plains outside the walls, a system of aqueducts runs from the lake lands beyond the mountains to the south. The northern territories are more sparsely populated, so the aqueducts don't extend all the way into those woods, but the running water in the city depends on them.

Hidden in my pocket are several vials of alchemicals Aro and Catoria swear will neutralize the ones put in the waters by that rogue Alliance member, and more recently Darian. All I know of the contents of these vials is what they've told me. I only hope they're right and that this will prevent more Heartless from being born—as well as not make the whole matter even worse.

Aro is certain it will work. I suspect it's partly because he was fascinated by Catoria and her wisdom. Our time in the Sanctuary revealed they have a lot in common too. And she's the first Magi aside from me to treat him as an equal.

Owen casts the cloaking spell while I work the silencing spell. Aro leads us to the building that houses the castellum, a central water tank that feeds water to the whole city. It's taller than the buildings around it, a hulking construction of stone fortified by metal columns and supports. Owen picks up the silencing spell too so I can cast an opening spell on the lock to the back doors. Then we slip inside. We follow the hall as it circles inward, directing us to two doors. A quick check reveals the one to our right leads into a room filled with levers and gears to control the water coming in and out of the castellum. The other, straight ahead, has a square window in the center and leads to a catwalk above the water tank. I unlock the door with a spell, and we step onto the walkway.

The basin is massive—more than double the size of the Palace's throne room and at least three stories deep, if not more. This, like many other things, was made by the Technocrats when they took over Palinor by force. Back in Catoria's time, the alchemicals would've needed to be added to the actual water source—the lakes to the south—or maybe just the aqueducts. Yet their impact rippled throughout an entire century. I palm one of the vials weighing down my pocket. How long do these things last?

Owen keeps watch while Aro and I walk single file along the catwalk that crisscrosses the top of the basin. When we stop in the middle, the walkway sways under our feet, but the Technos take great pride in their craft. It will hold.

At least I hope so.

I pull the vials from my pocket. "Are you ready?" I hand a couple to Aro.

For the first time, he seems slightly nervous about what we're about to do. "I suppose I have to be, don't I?"

"Or we don't do it. But you and Catoria are experts on how to neutralize what contaminated the waters in the first place. If anyone could find a solution, it would be the two of you."

Aro pauses for a moment. "You really believe that?"

"Absolutely."

He opens the stoppers to his vials. "Then let's get this over with."

I mirror his actions and we each pour our vials over the railing. The alchemicals shimmer and swirl. Then the water begins turning black. I suck my breath in sharply between my teeth as Aro pulls me to his side.

"What's happening?" I ask.

"Magic, I assume. The darkness must be part of the process to neutralize the old alchemicals. The new ones are destroying whatever is left in there. Look." He points to the walls of the basin. "See how it's concentrated around the edges? Whatever Darian put in here must have latched on to the walls to continuously infect the waters."

Even as he says the words, the edges of the basin grow darker and more shadowed.

"What about the darkness in the middle?" I ask.

He frowns. "Maybe that's the last vestiges of the first dose of alchemicals, run here through the aqueduct from the south. Catoria wasn't sure how much her assistant had put in the waters. Perhaps it's concentrated in a lake like it is here in the basin."

"We should hurry," Owen calls over to us, a worried expression on his face. "I heard something in the hall."

We quickly pocket the empty vials. At the other end of the basin there's another door. Owen pushes us through it. As we leave, I glance at the water once more—it shimmers again and all the darkness vanishes, as if it had never been there. Whatever those alchemicals did, they changed *something* in the water.

The sound of boots on the catwalk's metal echoes behind us, and we waste no time casting our protective spells. When the door bursts open, we all flatten ourselves against the wall, letting the men run by us on a wild-goose chase. With our shield spell in place, they have no idea we're there.

As soon as they're a safe distance away, we peel off the wall. This hallway winds in much the same way as the first one we took. After two more encounters with the guards, in which we sneak out under their noses, we find a side door and slip into the darkness. It was more humid in the castellum than I realized, and the cool night air is a welcome change. Aro's steps seem lighter than usual, as if a weight has finally been lifted from his shoulders.

Tonight, we did something good. We took the first step toward uniting the Magi and Technocrats. I only hope we don't stumble during the next.

WE'VE ONLY BEEN BACK IN THE CITY FOR

one full day, but my sister and I, armed with
Aro's insider knowledge of the Palace halls and
secret passages, are ready to launch our new mission:
recruit more allies.

Starting with the Magi prisoners.

We can't free them all at once. We'll rescue one tonight, then return tomorrow for another, maybe two if the first night goes smoothly. And every night we can after that, we'll steal another from under their noses. It may not be an army strong in numbers like the Technocrats or even a small army like the Magi still loyal to Isaiah, but it will be strong in magic.

And that counts for quite a lot.

With luck, it will be enough to prevent Darian from carrying out his plans. Then we'll have to figure out how to deal with the king and queen.

I pocket the black marble key, only mildly concerned about leaving all three boys behind together. Owen should be all right, but Remy is highly suspicious of Aro, and Aro is certainly wary of him.

But if they lay a finger on him, I'll know immediately.

When we reach the section of the tunnels not protected by the magic-infused marble, we cast our spells to keep us concealed. Darian sent Aro down here searching for exactly what we found; he may have conned someone else into searching for it too, for all we know. We must be extremely cautious.

Zandy is quieter and more careful than I have ever seen her in these tunnels. She whispers *fiero* and light sparks in her palm. She holds it up to illuminate our path. Aro's instructions take us farther down the main tunnel area than we've explored before. Once we sought that which was hidden; now we're looking for a way into the Palace itself.

The tunnels are just as I remember them: cool and damp, with a stench I wish I could forget. But I still had some of the ointment that lessens the smell in my pack, and we rubbed it under our noses before we left, which helps. We pass the remnants of Aro's demolition project—a couple of powered-down excavator mechs and rubble, rubble everywhere. Everything we see and the nothing we hear indicates this tunnel is now abandoned. Zandria begins to relax, but I remain strung tight as a wire.

Appearances aside, I don't think it's possible to be too careful around the Technocrats, especially in or under the Palace.

"Just like old times, isn't it?" Zandria remarks.

"It feels that way, doesn't it?"

"I've missed this," she says quietly, and my heart pinches.

"Me too," I agree.

I wasn't sure how she'd react to being back in this place, so close to where she was captured. She's taking it much better than I expected, and that gives me hope. I reach out and squeeze her hand. She squeezes back, a little piece of solidarity in the darkness.

It gives me the courage to finally broach a topic with her that I've been considering as we traveled here. "When we free the Magi in the dungeons, many of them may need help acclimating to freedom again. What do you think about being in charge of helping them do that? I know it hasn't been easy for you, but you know exactly what they're dealing with. I think you'd be best for the job."

Surprise flits over her face for a moment, then settles into consideration. "I think I'd like that," she says.

What I don't tell my sister is that I hope this will help her too. She's made it clear she doesn't want to talk to me about her time in the dungeons. But she needs to work through it somehow. Helping others who've been through the same trauma might do the trick.

When we approach the access point, I keep an eye out for the signs Aro told us about. We enter what seems like a dead-end tunnel, but upon closer examination, the far wall doesn't quite look right.

"There it is!" Zandria whispers.

On the wall is an emblem—three concentric circles with a diagonal line striking through them. It's the Technocrats' sigil, small enough that it's easy to miss, and the key to entering the Palace.

"Would you like to do the honors?" I ask my sister.

She presses the emblem. The brick slides into the wall and we stand back as a door swings outward. We step into the darkness, Zandy's light held aloft. After ascertaining that we are indeed alone, we close the door behind us. Compared to the tunnels we used to get into the city proper last night, these have not been maintained and thus are rarely, if ever, used. The walls are thickly coated in dust and cobwebs. The only hint of someone passing recently are the faint marks of boot prints on the dusty floor. Maybe Aro's from months ago.

"We should cover our tracks," I say. Zandria works a hand-spell, bringing up a light wind that whips behind us as we go, obscuring all trace of our having passed by.

And throwing dust into the air, but we breathe through our cloaks as a makeshift filter. The tunnel takes a steep turn up, then levels out not long after. According to Aro, we're nearing the dungeons. After continuing upward for a few more levels, we see the sigil on the wall and know another door must lie behind it.

First, we wait to make sure there aren't guards nearby.

"*Ampleo*," I whisper, and the sounds beyond the wall increase.

We hear the echoing of boots, but they fade quickly. Someone was just walking away from this wall. That's good news for us.

Zandria weaves her hands in a spell that makes a small circle in the brick turn translucent, about eye level and only a couple inches wide. She peers through to determine whether the coast is clear.

She shakes her head. "No one that I can see. Should be safe."

A strange heaviness falls over me. The faint memory of the times we searched for entries like this as we crawled beneath the city, reveling in the idea of being the monsters under every Technocrats' bed. Now I know we're all a little monstrous, some more than others. And it's up to us little monsters to defeat the biggest of all. The ones who would destroy Magi and Technocrats alike.

Our campaign against them begins tonight.

I cast the cloaking spell again as I press the sigil, and the door slides open to let us pass through. It whispers closed behind us as we scan the corridor in each direction. This time, Zandria casts the amplifying spell, and we determine we can hear more feet coming from the left side of the tunnel than the right.

Right it is.

We creep down the hall, invisible to the guards. When footsteps approach rapidly, we flatten ourselves against the wall and hold our breaths. A pair of elite guards march down the corridor, marked by their black cloaks with a silver metal band just above the hem. Their faces are grim and expressionless, as cold as the metal swords at their sides.

I pity the person they're going to retrieve.

When they're out of hearing distance, Zandria leans over. "We should find Darian's lab. Destroy whatever equipment he's created to drain the Magi." Her body vibrates with rage. I wonder how many times she was dragged away by the elite guard for questioning or torture. For all I know, she could've been alone the entire ordeal, or tortured multiple times a day. But I can't blame her for not wanting to relive it. I wouldn't want to either.

"Another night, definitely. Aro can give us specific directions. I'm not sure how to get there from here."

"We shouldn't wait. We're in the Palace. We can't let him use it on another Magi if we can help it."

I place a hand on her arm. "We're here to rescue more allies tonight. We'll have a better chance of success if we know exactly where we're going first."

Her eyes flash with frustration, and for a moment I fear she's going to take off like she used to do. But instead she inhales deeply and shoves that pent-up frustration down.

Sooner or later, she must confront that boiling rage within her or she'll explode. It just can't be tonight.

"All right, all right," she says. "I just hate being this close and letting it stand."

I squeeze her hand. "I feel the same. But we have to play the long game. We must survive."

We continue down the hall. Before we rescue a prisoner, we'll require a layout of the dungeon. Remy and I saw part of it when Aro rescued us, but we need a map of the entire thing so we know which cells we've rescued people from and if there's anything different about the area where they hold the Magi. Then, we can rescue someone and get the forges out of here.

The going is slow, as we're avoiding guards and still trying to get the lay of the land, which is difficult due to many offshoots and dead-end corridors. But once we're confident we've made a full circuit and entered notations of the dungeon, we have to pick a cell to open. Zandria gravitates to one around the corner from our escape route. "I have a good feeling about this one," she says, and I have no objection. Zandria quietly casts a handspell to pull the gears inside the lock into just the right position to unlatch. A soft plink rings out in the hall and we hold our breaths. There isn't anywhere to hide here other than under our shield spell. We're much more exposed now than we ever were in the drainage tunnels.

Magic courses through my veins, but I keep it in check. If I were to cast any kind of attack spell, I'd have to drop the shield first, and there's no way I'm risking that right now. We should've brought Owen tonight too. His dual casting ability would've come in handy.

Instead of kicking myself for not thinking about Owen sooner, I focus on the now. My sister and I are the key to eking out some semblance of peace between the Technos and the Magi; we have to make it out of here alive.

When no one appears to arrest us, we creak open the door and slip inside the cell, closing it gently behind us. In the middle of the room, a person is suspended in a metal suit. I can barely hear the faintness of their breathing. I glance at my sister—she's gone stock-still.

I shake her arm. "Zandy! Snap out of it. I know this is difficult, but we don't have time for you to freeze up. Let's get them out of this suit, back in walking condition, and then get out of here."

She blinks. "We must hurry," she says, then immediately begins working her magic. One by one the bolts holding the suit together fall to the floor. I've dropped our shield for now and help pull pieces of the suit off as I begin humming the notes of a healing spell. If this Magi's condition is anything like Zandria's was, they'll be in bad shape. We need them to be able to at least walk so we can escape.

When I take the helmet off, I see that it's a girl. Her long dark hair is matted with blood and knots. She wears pants and a tunic that were probably finely made but are now fraying and stained with blood and dirt, making the original color impossible to determine. My stomach turns. This one wasn't just sentenced to imprisonment; she's been tortured too. Her eyes are swollen shut, and her face is bruised beyond recognition. Blood drips from her mouth, but I can't tell whether that's because her tongue became infected after the Technos burned it to stop her from incanting or she's been beaten recently.

The one thing I do know is she's not conscious. That needs to change. Fast.

We rest her on the floor of the cell, and I get to work healing her while Zandria removes the rest of the bonds from her hands and legs.

"Her hands . . ." Zandria says, a quiver sneaking into her voice.

"I know. It's awful," I say. "Just try not to look." The spell I sing softly over the girl rises in pitch, soothing her bruises, knitting the broken bones in her hands back together, and sealing new pink skin over the wounds and burns on her feet and legs. In a few minutes, she coughs. Her eyes open as the swelling in her face subsides and it returns to its normal shape. She gasps when she sees us, and so do we.

Vivienne.

"FORGES!" ZANDRIA MOANS. "WE JUST

wasted all that time on a Technocrat!"

"Aissa?" Vivienne says, then glances to her right. "Zandria? What are you . . . how . . . ?" She bursts into tears.

"It's not wasted," I say quietly. "She loved Paul, the baker's son. When she vouched for him after the queen discovered he was a Magi, she endured terrible torture." I shudder, remembering the day I accidentally witnessed the queen take out her "mercy" on Vivienne. I wouldn't wish that on anyone. "She didn't deserve that, and she doesn't deserve to be here."

"But we're here to rescue our own kind," Zandy hisses.

"And yet we've rescued her." I get to my feet and help Vivienne to hers.

"What's going on?" she whispers. "I don't know how you found me, I don't know how I'm even alive, but please get me out of here."

"Why?" Zandria demands of me, refusing to acknowledge Vivienne.

"Because we need allies. From both sides of the war. Just like the original Alchemist Alliance."

Zandria bristles for a moment longer, likely recalling how we used to dream about destroying everything to do with the Technocrats back when we were in school with Vivienne. Finally, she relents. "Fine. We don't have time to free anyone else tonight anyway. But if this goes south, it's on you."

I smile. "We're leaving, Viv. Stay close, and remain as quiet as possible, all right?" She nods, visibly too scared to speak. We move toward the door and crack it open. Zandria has set our shield in place, and I work the silencing spell. We've hardly left the cell before the click of metal heels on the floor echoes down the hall, making our adrenaline spike.

I've heard that sound a few times before: when Queen Cyrene walked the halls of the Palace.

"Move!" I hiss, and we hurry down the hall with Vivienne between us, racing around the corner. Several guards stand nearby, and we halt. Vivienne squeaks, but the guards don't hear thanks to our silencing spell.

Behind us, we hear the sound of a cell door unlatching. Moments later, an icy voice rings out down the hall. "Guards!"

Vivienne cringes, wrapping her arms around her middle.

We freeze. We're stuck between the guards and the queen. In my head, I run through several possible scenarios and outcomes. None of them sound good. But one way or another, we're going to have to make a break for it. I see no other way out.

Behind me, Zandria pulls out the short sword she chose in the Tomb of Regents from her belt, gripping the hilt tightly. We may very soon see whether these swords really do have magical properties.

The queen rounds the corner, her face scowling with ice-cold rage. "Where is the prisoner in that cell?" She points angrily down the hall. "She was there less than an hour ago."

The guards immediately stand at attention, alarm on their faces. No one wants to get on Queen Cyrene's bad side. Not if they want to keep all their limbs and live to see another day.

One of the guards speaks up. "We haven't seen or heard anything, Your Majesty."

The queen approaches him, moving faster than I would've thought possible. I can feel the breeze as she glides by us while we flatten ourselves against the hallway wall. She stops inches from the guard's face.

"Why not?" She waves her hand back down the hall. "Clearly she's gone. How do you explain that?"

"I . . . I can't, Your Majesty." This is the first time I've ever seen a Technocrat guard look nervous. I'd relish it if we weren't in as much danger of encountering the queen's ire.

"And what about you?" She addresses another guard. He shakes his head.

"No, Your Majesty."

He barely finishes saying "Your Majesty" before the queen lurches forward and grabs him by the throat. He gurgles as his feet leave the ground. A bead of blood swells on his neck where she digs her razor-sharp nail into his throat. Zandria and Vivienne both recoil, leaning close to me.

"Use your head if you wish to keep it," Queen Cyrene growls at the guard, then she releases him before he passes out. "That goes for all of you." She points to the other guards and they straighten their spines. "Now, if a girl was here an hour ago and suddenly isn't, but no one heard a thing, what might have happened?"

She waits for an answer, but the guards stare dumbly back. Finally, one tentatively speaks up. "The Magi, Your Majesty?"

She smiles horribly. "One of you does have half a brain after all. Now go, find them. If a Magi made it into the Palace, she may not be the only thing they came for. They could be anywhere."

One of the younger guards asks, "But how can we find someone who helped a prisoner escape without any trace at all?"

The queen edges toward him, and he takes a step back. "They're canny folk. Their magic can mask sounds, even make them invisible. But they still take up space. Do a full sweep of every hallway in the dungeon. Then go floor by floor until you've found them. Enlist the whole guard."

Even though I know our spells will hold, I'm terrified of making a sound. We need to move—and soon—but if they're sweeping the halls in a four-deep formation, we'll be caught. Unless we duck into a cell first. But with the Technos on high alert, that would attract attention too.

Sweat begins to bead on my forehead. I don't see any safe way out of this. We'll have to make a break for it while one of us causes a distraction. I glance at my companions. I can't allow either Vivienne or my sister to be recaptured. They've already suffered in these dungeons for far too long. Going back would break them.

If anyone has to risk getting caught, it's going to be me.

I motion to Zandria to remain where she is and that I'll head back down the hall in the direction of Vivienne's cell. At first she frowns, then her eyes widen. She shakes her head vigorously.

It's the only way, I mouth at her, and her free hand balls into a fist at her side. She doesn't like it, but she knows that I'm right. We've trained together enough; she understands she and Vivienne will need to run for the door behind the Techno sigil once I cause the distraction. I glance quickly at the map in my hands. I should be able to double back and get through the door too, if I play my cards right.

Regardless, this is a risky plan. But so was breaking into the Palace tonight.

The main problem is we'll each have one spell less—meaning Zandy and Vivienne will remain under the shield, but without a silencing spell. And for the distraction, I won't have any spells protecting me for a few minutes, until I can replace the shield again.

How foolish we were sneaking around below the city, believing ourselves invincible.

I pause at the corner, while the queen continues to chastise the guards as they assume a four-fold formation, just like I feared.

Then I drop my shield spell.

One of the guards gasps, and the whole group—including the dread queen—turns toward my end of the hall. To my relief,

Zandria and Vivienne dash forward under their cloaking spell and make it past the guards without being detected. Now they only have to reach that door and open it without anyone noticing. Zandy's right about one thing; this would've been easier if Vivienne were a Magi. But there's no help for it now.

"Apprehend her!" the queen screams. The guards waste no time heeding her command. I bolt down the corridor, grateful for the circuit Zandria and I took before. I know where to go, and which halls lead to dead ends. I hum the shield spell under my breath as I run. An electric thrill fills my limbs. My sister and I trained daily for maneuvers exactly like this.

Tonight, we'd better make our parents proud. Otherwise, we'll end up dead as well.

I need to escape with Zandria and Vivienne, for my people, my sister, and the boy I'm bound to. They're all depending on me.

The weight of this understanding is heavy, but in a strange way it lifts me up. Buoys me. Lights a fire under my feet hotter than any forge.

Heavy boots stomp behind me, but the guards no longer see where I run. Though if they stopped, they'd hear me. While my shoes are leather and better for sneaking than the guards' boots, my breathing could definitely become a problem.

I skate around the next corner. Then I duck down one hallway and momentarily drop my shield, intentionally letting them see me. I double back and race down another corridor toward the secret door. Hopefully, Zandria and Vivienne are already running down the passage.

But when I reach the area from the opposite angle with my shield back in place, I find exactly what I'd hoped to avoid: guards. Even more of them. My breath hitches in my chest when I see the queen.

She's still here.

I can't let her see me open the sigil wall and enter that secret door. I don't know how much she knows about the Palace tunnels—Aro told me he discovered them by accident one day—but we can't risk her realizing it's there. She'll send every machine she's got to scour the tunnels, then drag us before her throne to suffer her mercy.

The moment I register the queen's presence, she frowns in my direction.

Queen Cyrene holds up a fist. "Silence!" she barks. Every guard obeys instantly.

I try to calm my breathing, but between that and my racing heart, I fear I've given myself away.

She steps forward ahead of the guards, a sinister gleam in her frosty blue eyes. "They're here."

Suddenly, I know what I must do. I run back down the hall, not even trying to conceal my footsteps this time.

The Technocrats take the bait and charge after the noise I make. It takes a moment for me to realize someone is gaining on me faster than I expected. I glance behind and realize it's the queen. My pulse spikes. She *is* fast. There must be some mechanical enhancement that isn't visible on the outside allowing her to move like that.

Under no circumstances can I let her get ahold of me.

If she does, I'll have no choice but to kill her. That wouldn't have given me a moment's pause a few weeks ago, but it does now. Killing someone steals a little piece of your soul. And while she may deserve a taste of her own mercy, she's still Aro's mother. Their relationship is complicated. If I kill her, even if it's the only option, Aro might never forgive me.

Something tugs on the end of my favorite cloak. I whirl around, nearly knocking the queen off her feet as her nails slice through the fabric's edge. A corner flutters to the ground, and she grins wickedly.

"Almost got you," she says.

"*Ventus*," I whisper, letting go of my shield to cast another spell. The magic blasts her back with an enormous gust of wind. She tumbles, knocking her head on the metal wall in the process, then slumps to the floor in a mess of silk and pale blond curls. My hands shake. That was much too close.

But I don't have time to dwell on that now. More shouts resound behind me. Guards. I relinquished my shield to cast the wind spell, making me a much easier target.

I face them, keeping a keen ear out for any hint the queen has regained consciousness.

The guards hesitate when they see me. One of them even laughs. I must seem insignificant. A mere girl against four armed guards. But then they see their ruthless queen in a heap on the floor behind me.

That changes the expression on their faces in an instant.

"Step away from the queen, Magi," the closest one shouts at me. They're keeping their distance. Good. "Where's the prisoner you stole?"

"Don't worry, she's safe," I say. My magic brews inside my veins, filling me with a heady rush. "*Ventus*," I intone again, directing the gale of wind toward the guards and blasting them back against the metal walls. Two of them are knocked out like the queen, but the other two struggle back to their feet, brandishing their weapons despite the disoriented glaze in their eyes.

"*Ascensio*," I murmur, and my magic sweeps them up, suspending them in the hall a few feet over the floor. They struggle and kick, but it's no match for my magic. I walk by them and wave, then my magic smashes their helmets together and tosses them aside.

This time, no one gets up.

MY LEGS FEEL WEAK AND SHAKY, BUT I RUN

back down the corridor to where the door
hides. I slam my palm against the sigil and it
slides open. When it closes behind me, I decide not
to take any chances. I call my magic back up, muttering
the spell: "*Cincin.*"

Even if the Technocrats do know about these hidden tunnels,
that will keep them out until I or Zandria undoes the locking spell.
Hopefully Darian won't catch on. I'll have to ask Aro whether he
knows about these particular tunnels. I know he's aware of the
ones that lead out of Palinor, at least.

I've barely gone three feet down the tunnel when Zandria
appears before me and wraps her arms around me in a bear hug.

"Worried, sister?" I say, surprised by the unexpected show
of affection. I hug her back just as fiercely. This is the most affection she's shown me since we rescued her. It gives me hope that
despite her surliness, family does still come first. And that eventually she might be more like her old self again. "You shouldn't
have waited."

She releases me and gives me a look. "I wasn't about to leave
here without you. If you hadn't come out soon, I was ready to go
back in after you."

"I'm glad you didn't. I barely escaped the queen." I show her
my cloak. "She took a piece out of my cloak and everything."

She raises an eyebrow. "Sounds like she doesn't approve of
you and Aro."

"Apparently not. Though I never expected a warm welcome."

Vivienne peeks around the corner. "Are you all right, Aissa?"
she asks.

"I'm fine." Then to Zandria, I ask, "How's she taking the fact we're Magi?"

She shrugs. "A lot better than I expected, actually." She studies our old schoolmate for a moment. Then, low enough so only I can hear, she says, "I might even be all right with letting her live. Provided she agrees to keep our secrets."

"Good. Because I'm not about to let you kill her after all we just went through," I say. Vivienne stares at us wide-eyed. "Don't worry, we're not going to hurt you. But we will have to keep you in our home base until we can trust you."

Vivienne straightens her spine. "You're Magi. So was Paul. I didn't know, but I still loved him. The queen tortured me because of it. I owe the royals nothing." She practically spits the last word. "If you're working against them, I'm in. One hundred percent."

I'm taken aback by her forceful words. Vivienne was always a good little Techno. But then again, Zandria and I were too, as far as our classmates knew. You never know what bravery might be simmering underneath a placid exterior.

"Then you should earn our trust quickly," I say. "But we need to leave here before anyone discovers us."

With Vivienne between Zandria and me, we retrace our steps back through the tunnels, silent as mice. Vivienne appears lost in her own head; I'm not about to question her yet. It will be a different story, though, when we reach our hideout.

The going is quicker now that we know the route, and it isn't long before we're back in front of the strange black, shimmering door. Vivienne gawks at it, tentatively placing a hand on the stone.

"I've never seen anything like this," she says.

"Neither had we when we first saw it," I say. "In a lot of ways, it represents our goals."

She raises an eyebrow at me, and Zandria hisses in a warning tone, "Aissa . . ."

"Don't worry, I won't tell her everything yet," I say. Vivienne's less nervous now. In fact, she seems to grow stronger with every step we take away from those dungeons.

I unlock the door, and we enter the old library. Now that it's been cleaned up—the boys have been busy while we've been away—we could almost make a home here. For a while, anyway.

Remy is the first to greet us. "Who's this?" he asks, eying Vivienne.

Zandria brushes by him. "A new prisoner." He frowns, and I shake my head.

"She isn't a prisoner. Not really. But she is a Technocrat. She was being tortured by the queen."

"So why did you rescue her?" Remy asks, and I can see the irritation building inside him. "And why did you bring her here?"

"Her name is Vivienne," she says while holding a hand out to Remy. He regards it as if she were handing him a block of cheese filled with maggots. But Vivienne stands there, determined.

Remy does his best to ignore her.

I sigh. "She was held in one of the Magi suits. We didn't know who it was until it was too late." Vivienne folds her arms across her chest as she takes in the dusty, ruined majesty of the library. "She was arrested and tortured because she fell in love with a Magi and defended him when he was captured."

Understanding lights Remy's face. "Wait a minute. Is she the girl you saw that day in the Palace?"

Aro appears at my elbow, surprise crossing his face when he recognizes Vivienne. "Yes, she is," he answers for me. "I remember her. You were upset she'd been caught up too."

I nod curtly, a strange hollowness expanding in my chest at the memory of that day. It was then that I learned exactly what the Technocrats do to the Magi they capture. And the full width of the gap between Aro and me. Yet somehow, we managed to bridge it.

"I should've come with you tonight," Aro says.

Remy rolls his eyes. "Don't be ridiculous. You would've just gotten in the way."

I cringe, though he's not wrong. I place a hand on Aro's arm. "It's better that you didn't."

"Yeah, we saw your mom tonight, Aro," Zandria says snidely from the other side of the room. "I'm sure she would've loved to see you."

"Which is another reason I'm glad you didn't come with us," I say.

"She almost took a piece out of Aissa here too." Zandria laughs, but it has an odd ring to it. Sometimes it feels like the old Zandy, who could laugh and find amusement in anything, is channeling that mirth into her rage.

"What? Are you all right?"

I brush off his concern but kiss his cheek. "I'm fine." I show him my cloak. "My cloak, however, has seen better days." In addition to the missing corner, a jagged slash rips down the back of it.

Aro frowns at my cloak while Zandria smirks and walks over to where we're keeping our food stores. Remy and Owen set up cold spells last night to keep things preserved longer.

Vivienne approaches me, Remy, and Aro at the same time Owen joins us. "I won't be your prisoner," she says defiantly. "But I will be your ally. Give me a chance to prove myself."

Remy scoffs. "You're a Techno. What can you do for us?"

Aro frowns deeper. "I am too. And I've managed to help."

Vivienne smiles slightly. "I know people. You want to overthrow the king and queen, yes?"

"Something like that," I say, not yet ready to share all the details of our plans.

"Then you need the people of the city on your side; otherwise, you'll have an all-out revolt on your hands."

"That's a good point," Owen admits. I agree—it's the same logic we were both in favor of days earlier.

"I can help you get the people on your side." Vivienne inches closer to our circle. "We just have to expose the royals for the awful despots they are, and the people will join you."

"Why should we trust you?" Remy says.

"Because I hate them with every fiber of my being," Vivienne says. She quivers with pent-up rage.

I place a hand on her shoulder. "I know the queen tortured you. They thought you had information about the Magi because of your involvement with Paul."

Vivienne looks at me, somewhat surprised. "Yes, but you have no idea what they did. The lengths the king and queen will go to . . . the atrocities they'll commit . . ." Her chest heaves, but she swallows down the emotion threatening to overwhelm her. "Their depravity knows no bounds. They must be stopped. Their reign must end."

Aro winces, but Remy eyes her appraisingly. "What could they have done to you that's so terrible? You're a Technocrat. Do you have any idea what they've done to the Magi? What they do when they capture them?"

Vivienne's eyes burn daggers into Remy. "Yes," she hisses. "I had to suffer just like a Magi would. That was my punishment for loving one, for defending one. But that was only the beginning." She crosses her arms over her chest. "The queen took particular delight in torturing me personally. Every day for the last . . . well, I don't know how long. Few weeks? Few years? It felt endless. Interminable. Thank you for getting me out of there. If nothing else, my gratitude for that alone binds me to your cause."

"I'm glad to have you on our side," I say.

"But that doesn't change anything," Remy says. "Not yet. You can't leave here until all of us trust you."

"I don't want to leave," Vivienne says. "I want to help."

Owen speaks up. "You said the queen's torture was just the beginning. What do you mean?" His expression is inscrutable. I haven't been able to get a full read on him yet. It's hard to tell what he's thinking on matters of importance. He may be a Magi, but his point of view is often more innocent than ours.

They study each other for a moment. "Their cruelty . . . they revel in it." Vivienne shudders and stares at her feet.

Owen steps closer. "What did they do?" Her eyes lift to meet his, then her expression hardens.

"One night, they brought me outside onto the Palace grounds. A park I'd never seen before. There was only a small audience—the king and queen, a few of the highest-born courtiers, and a few others I didn't recognize. They dragged me there in that awful metal suit. I couldn't move or see what was happening until they removed the helmet. There were two other captives in metal suits. One was standing to the side, and the other was held up between two guards. The king and queen sat on a dais and the guests formed a semicircle around me, the two captives, and a bonfire. I was terrified but also a little relieved. It's so cold in those dungeons, and this was the first hint of warmth I'd felt in weeks."

An awful feeling shivers in my gut. I'm not sure where this is headed, but I'm willing to bet that fire wasn't there to keep anyone warm.

"I was dragged right in front of the royals, and then the queen began asking me—for the millionth time—to confess what I knew about the Magi."

Zandria interrupts her. "What did she want to know, exactly?"

Vivienne waves a hand. "How many are left. Where they hide. Who else is a pretender here in Palinor. That sort of thing."

My heart sinks. "The sort of thing you know nothing about."

"Exactly," Vivienne says. "But the king and queen didn't

believe me. Not the first time I swore to it, and not any of the many, many other times since. Especially not that night." She swallows hard and her eyes glisten. "I pleaded with them to believe me. But they called me a liar. A traitor. Then they took the helmet off of one of the other captives. The one who was standing. It was Paul's father. He was terrified. They asked the same questions of him. Then they announced that this was the last chance for us to come clean or we'd suffer the consequences." She wraps her arms around her middle protectively. "I was sure they were going to kill me, both of us, really. But it was far worse."

Aro grips my hand. As hard as this is for Vivienne, I know it's hard for Aro too. Confronting the atrocities his family has carried out and the real impact that has had on people isn't something he's dealt with until recently. He spent his life obsessed with trying to buy more time for himself and the other Heartless destined to die young. In the process, he overlooked other people who needed saving.

"What did they do?" Aro asks Vivienne, and she glances up as if realizing for the first time he's there. Aro's voice is thick with regret.

"I didn't realize until it was too late, but the suit of the third captive, the one who was standing with only the help of two guards, was attached to a pulley. When the royals issued their decree, the king pulled a lever and the captive was hoisted up . . ." Her voice chokes off. Her hands clench and unclench at her sides, and her skin turns a blotchy red.

No one says a word. I want to ask what happened, but I'm too terrified to know the truth.

Vivienne finds her voice again. "He was hoisted up and over the fire. And then dropped into it."

My entire body turns to ice.

"By the Anvil," Zandria whispers. I didn't even notice she'd drawn near again while Vivienne told her story. Remy and Owen look like they're going to be ill, and Aro clenches my hands tightly.

"He . . . he must've been unconscious before. That's why the guards were holding him up. It wasn't long before he woke. The fire . . . with heat like that . . . there was no way he couldn't have." She takes a deep breath to compose herself. "He began screaming. I begged them to stop but . . . but . . . the queen just smiled and told me this was a mercy and I should be grateful for it." She gags. "That sound . . . his screams . . . and the . . . the smell . . . They will haunt me forever."

Tears burn my eyes. "It was Paul in that suit, wasn't it?"

Vivienne can only nod.

A deafening silence descends on us all. This is what we're up against. Cruelty that knows no bounds.

I glance up at Aro. His cheeks are wet. The stark reality of his parents' reign is almost too much for him to comprehend.

The flesh-and-blood stakes stand in front of us. There's no doubt in any of our minds: this must end.

"I'm so sorry, Vivienne," I say, taking her hands in mine. "I believe you'll make an excellent addition to our rebellion."

A wicked gleam shines through the tears in her eyes. "I can't wait to tear that Palace down and destroy them. Promise me something, Aissa."

"What is it?"

"When we destroy everything they love, I want to be there. I want to see the look on their faces."

"You will be. I promise." We shake on it. "Now, let's show you our base of operations."

"I AM NOT ALLOWING YOU TO GO OUT THERE

alone with her!" Zandria throws her hands up as she paces the area we've designated the war room. We've transformed a large piece of wood that was once part of the walls into a long, makeshift table that we can use to plan and plot against the Technocrats, and right now it acts as a barrier between us.

"You don't get a choice," I say, hands on my hips. While I appreciate Zandria watching out for me, I'm not the one who's prone to taking foolish risks. And Vivienne is not a risk. She's scarred by her time in the dungeons. She won't betray us.

But Zandria isn't convinced.

"Vivienne wants to help. This is a test to see if she really can. Of course I'm going with her, Zandria." I put a hand on my sister's arm. "It'll be fine, I promise."

"It will be fine," Remy says as he enters the room. "Because I'm coming with you."

I sigh. "I think we've proved beyond a shadow of a doubt that I don't need you to be my babysitter. I'm more than equipped to handle myself and any obstacles we encounter up there."

Remy sits at the table and bites into an apple he took from the cold storage. "You don't know what we'll encounter up there. But you do need someone to cover your back. And it isn't going to be that Technocrat girl."

Zandria has a pained expression on her face. "I should be the one to go with you," she says.

"No, you shouldn't. We agreed after last night: we won't go to the surface at the same time. It's too risky. If one of us gets caught, we need the other to be free to get us out again."

Our agreement was purely logical. We're the only Magi like us, who can use our magic on the machines.

We're going to need it if we want to win this war.

One of us at a time topside, and always with our appearance at least slightly altered by a spell. I can't deny, though, it's strange to see Zandria in her disguise. She may be my twin, but we've grown to be so different that we don't even wear the same face anymore when we're out in the city. It makes the distance between us feel greater than ever.

"It's too risky for you to go anywhere with her," she tosses back.

Remy steps between us. "I'll be there with Aissa, all right? She may tell a good story, but I don't trust this Vivienne any more than you do. Probably less." He incinerates the apple core in his palm with a quick spell, then shakes the ash away. "If the Techno girl tries anything suspicious, I'll kill her. Plain and simple."

Fantastic. Now I've got Remy to contend with too. All just to keep our first real ally alive.

"I won't do anything suspicious, I can promise you that," Vivienne says from the doorway, causing us all to turn around. I wince.

"Sorry, Vivienne," I say, but she waves me off. We raided a clothing shop early this morning before it opened, since we've all been traveling and wearing the same few changes of clothes for far too long. Vivienne's clothes were in even worse condition. But now, free of the dungeons, after a Magi-made bath, in clothes that aren't bloody, and rested, she's almost back to the girl I remember. But with a sharper edge.

"I spent weeks in the Technocrats' dungeon; believe me when I say I understand your caution, Remy. If I were you, I wouldn't trust me yet either." She moves into the room. "But know this: I'm in your debt, Aissa, Zandria. I swear, I won't betray you. I feel greater allegiance to you than I ever did to the royals. We have the same goals."

Something swells in my chest I don't think I've ever felt toward Vivienne before: respect. I underestimated her. In school, I wrote her off as another foolish, shallow Techno girl. But she has hidden depths.

"See?" I say to Zandria and Remy. "I'll be perfectly safe."

"She can't even fight," Remy says.

Vivienne steps right up to Remy. "Then teach me. I want to learn. There's nothing I want more than to know how to fight."

Remy is taken aback. "You want to fight?" he scoffs. "You don't look like you've ever even held a sword."

She shrugs. "I haven't. But that doesn't mean I can't."

I can't hold back my smile. One even cracks Zandria's lips. "All right," I say. "We'll teach you. We only have a handful of weapons, but after our raid tonight, we'll have more to practice with."

A new light shines in Vivienne's eyes. "I can't wait."

"Then let's start now," Remy says. "Come on." He motions for her to follow him, and I trail him too, curious.

"Well, this I have to see," Zandria says.

He leads her out to the main part of the library under the dome and hands her a long pole that strongly resembles a staff, taking up another one for himself. She accepts it without batting an eye. This attracts Aro's and Owen's attention as well. Soon Aro's arm wraps around my waist, his breath whispering over my ear. Sometimes, I swear I can feel his presence before I see him. I wonder if that's an effect of the Binding rite too.

"They aren't going to hurt each other, are they?" I hear the frown in his voice.

"No. Vivienne wants to learn how to defend herself and to fight. Remy has offered to show her."

"Right now?" Aro lifts his brows in surprise. "Aren't you going out for a raid in a couple hours?"

"Hopefully she'll still be coming with me."

"If not, I could—"

"Absolutely not," I say, more sternly than I intend. "Someone might recognize you. Vivienne is only well known by her friends. The queen may know her face, but she rarely leaves the Palace, so that's not a big concern. We can't risk losing you."

He hears the words left unsaid. Our lives are inextricably intertwined, for better or worse.

He places a hand on my cheek and draws me in for a brief kiss that sends magic tiptoeing up my spine. Zandria groans from a few feet away.

I rest my forehead against his. "It's better for you to stay here, helping Zandy and Owen plan our next raid, our next move. You're the best ally we have in that department. You know the city better than any of us. Even my sister can't deny that."

She tosses me a sharp look over her shoulder, and I laugh.

"I'll do my best to be useful. But eventually, I'm going to have to face my mother and father again."

"I know. It may be sooner than I'd like."

We go quiet, leaning into each other while we watch Remy show Vivienne the basics of using a staff. She drops it the first few times—and to be fair, Remy is definitely not cutting her the slack he normally would a trainee—but she begins to pick it up faster than I expected.

"Maybe I should start training too," Aro says. "Remy seems to be a good teacher."

All I can see in that scenario is Remy having an excuse to hurt Aro. Though he's agreed to leave Aro alone since harming him means harming me, if Remy got worked up enough, I don't trust that he wouldn't forget a little.

"If anyone trains you, it will be me," I say. "We can start tomorrow."

He grins, the same sort of charming, lopsided smile he used to give me back when we were just getting to know each other. A foolish flirtation that became something much, much more. That smile still makes butterflies shimmy in my stomach.

"I can't wait," he says.

Later that night, as dusk falls over the city with a hush, Remy, Vivienne, and I leave the lair. Remy insists on taking more precautions than necessary. He's adamant Vivienne cannot know about the nature of my and Zandy's magic yet. When it comes time to move the drainage tunnel cover so we can get to the streets, he insists on enveloping her in darkness so she can't see me cast the spell.

"You're a little too suspicious, Remy," I tell him.

He scowls at me. "You can never be too suspicious when it comes to the Technos."

I shake my head and let the tunnel cover rise up and settle next to the opening. Remy drops the darkening spell over Vivienne's eyes, and we climb out. I go first, casting a cloaking spell over all of us and the opening. Anyone who passes by the alley won't notice anything amiss.

We remain cloaked in magic as we hit the streets. Remy and I have changed our faces, and I've changed my hair color too, to ensure we won't be recognized if we have to drop the shield to cast other spells. Vivienne keeps her cloak about her face, just to be safe.

Remy leads us to where Technocrat guards keep extra stores of weapons for the gates. The building is normally locked but not guarded, which makes it the perfect target for our purposes.

Vivienne offered to come along and be a distraction if we need one. She's always been as much of a flirt as Zandria, and bantering with the gate guards seems right up her alley. According to Aro, the gate guards don't overlap with the dungeon guards—the latter are on a higher tier because of the greater importance of the prisoners—so no one ought to recognize her.

We may not need her as a lookout, but it's good to have her with us if necessary. At the very least, she provides another set of arms to carry weapons back to our hideout.

We tread carefully, winding through back alleys and making false paths to ensure we're not being followed. I've seen no sign of Darian since we returned to Palinor, a thing I'm rather grateful for. But I'm sure it won't be long until we're on his radar again. Tonight's raid might be the thing that puts us there, if Vivienne's rescue didn't already.

Finally the guards' storehouse comes into view: a nondescript brick building with metal window casings and a thick metal door. We hide around the corner from the building, watching it for a good ten minutes before making our move.

"All right," Remy says. "There shouldn't be anyone inside, and there's no sign of anyone coming by soon, which all works in our favor. Vivienne, you will be posted here"—Remy draws a diagram of the guard building in the dirt—"to keep watch, just in case. Aissa and I will break into the storeroom and take as much as we can."

Vivienne gives a curt nod, and within minutes we're all in position. Remy specifically posted Vivienne facing away from the door so she can't see me unlock it with my magic. Not that she'd be likely to anyway, since Remy is casting his shield spell over me while I work.

We slip into the storeroom, closing the door behind us. "*Fiero,*" I whisper, and light bursts in my palm. I flick my other wrist and the light floats up to hover in front of us. The room is packed wall to wall with swords, spears, and crossbows. We immediately begin picking out weapons and a few pieces of armor that might come in handy too. I pause when I hear the sound of voices outside. Vivienne's laughter echoes back to my ears. She's already working her wiles.

We need to hurry.

I'm almost done piling up as many weapons as I can carry when I notice that a high shelf in the back has more than just weapons on it. The glint of a little machine winks back at me, and I shudder.

My first terrified thought is that it's a listening device, but it isn't like any of the others I've seen. I wave a hand, casting a handspell to bring one toward me for closer examination. I pull the cover off the top of the square-shaped device and examine it in more detail. Inside is a mess of wires and a round metal-and-glass chamber filled with black powder.

My breath catches.

While I've never seen it before, I know what that powder means. This is an explosive device. A bomb. We didn't delve deeply into that particular subject in school, but our parents once got hold of the blueprints for a bomb and made us memorize how they worked in case we ever needed to defuse one with our magic.

My skin crawls, and I resist the urge to toss the thing away; that would spell nothing good for us. I swallow hard instead and examine it. There are definitely no listening devices in here. This machine has one, sole function: to obliterate everything in its path.

"Remy," I whisper. "Come here."

He frowns at the device in my hands. "Is that . . . is that what I think it is?" He takes a step back.

"It's a bomb. But it's smaller than the ones they used to destroy the Magi cities. Though it can still do a lot of damage. We should take some of these."

Remy recoils. "You can't be serious."

"Of course I'm serious. They won't expect us to have these, to use them against them. It can work in our favor."

"You want to bring one of their machines into our hideout?" Remy looks alarmed.

"It isn't a listener. I checked. And there's no timer on the bomb either. You set it by pressing this button here." I point to the detonator. "I don't know how many ticks it will give before exploding, but likely it's between ten to twenty to give you time to get away."

"I'm not getting anywhere near that thing. If you want to bring it back, that's on you. But I'm telling you it's a bad idea."

"It's coming with me. In fact, two of them are." I weave my hands and lift a second device down off the high shelf. Then I gently set them both in my pack.

"What is—" The voice from behind us startles us, and we whirl around just in time to see a surprised guard's face twist into anger.

And to then see Vivienne smash a brick across the back of his head.

The guard's eyes roll back, and he crumples to the storeroom floor. My hands shake. I was too intrigued by the bomb. I didn't even hear the guard open the door.

It's a good thing Vivienne came with us after all.

She tosses the brick aside and brushes her hands on her trousers. "Sorry, I could only flirt with him for so long. He was determined to get a new sword. Kept saying his was dull."

Remy gapes at her.

"Thanks for that," I say.

She shrugs, then tugs at the guard's arms to pull him away

from the door. I shake off my shock and help her hide his uncon-scious form behind a row of lances.

"We should leave," I say. We have three leather sacks for the weapons, and we quickly finish filling them, then slip back out of the storeroom. We're as careful as possible, but I have a nagging feeling that eyes watch us every step of the way. For all they can see, it's just Vivienne, a lone girl walking through the alleyways of Palinor while Remy, me, and our new stash of weapons are safe under the cloaking spell.

Remy barely says a word as we head back to the tunnel entrance and descend into the darkness. I'm not sure if he's angry with me for bringing back the bombs or just surprised Vivienne turned out to be useful.

Regardless, the darkness feels more welcoming to me than ever. We've always been safer here than in the light.

AS PROMISED, ARO AND I BEGIN OUR SPAR-

ring sessions the next day. We sift through the
newly acquired stash to select our weapons. I'm
both excited to train with Aro and a little nervous.
I'm so used to sparring with people whose limits I know
well, like Zandria and Remy—what if I push him too far?
What if I accidentally hurt him? What if he hurts me?

He's already wearing some Technocrat armor we took along
with the weapons, a metal breastplate and guards for his shoulders
and arms. I insisted he wear it, just to be safe. And so I don't have
an excuse to cut him any slack.

I've opted not to use any armor. The thought of encasing
myself in metal again, even briefly and partially, is enough to
make panic rise in my chest.

"Ready?" I ask.

His hand hovers over a finely crafted sword, then he picks it
up, weighing it in his hand. "Yes, I believe I am."

"Then let's begin," I say, picking up an identical sword. While
I've practiced a bit on my own with my new short sword from
the Sanctuary, I'm wary about using it with others. We're still
learning about the ancient Magi's magic, and it might be more
unpredictable than I expect.

We cross blades and begin to feint and parry around the room.
He's a much better swordsman than I expected.

"Who taught you to use a sword?" I know Aro was mentored
by Leon and Darian when it came to machines, but he's never
spoken about this part of his life before.

An odd expression crosses his face. "My mother, actually."

Our swords clang together as we strike, rattling my teeth.

"Your mother? The queen bothered to learn how to fence?" I scoff. "That's surprising, given she has the entire army at her disposal, not to mention her mech enhancements."

"She wasn't always the queen, you know." Aro blocks my next attack. "But she's always been ruthless. I suspect that's why my father married her. She taught me, but mostly I trained with her guards. She knew the Heartless were considered weak. And she was determined no son of hers ever would be."

I duck under his swinging sword, then spin around again to face him. "I'm loathe to admit it, but she trained you well."

Aro laughs. "A fair concession. I'll take that as a compliment."

"Just don't get too full of yourself."

This time, I attack more aggressively, putting him on the defensive. He evades well and tumbles out of the way. But mid-tumble, I trip him, then pin him to the floor, my knee on his chest and blade at his throat.

We both breathe heavily, a shared laugh bubbling in our chests.

"Well played," he whispers.

Then, without warning, Aro disarms me. Quick as a blink, he has me pinned to the floor instead. Our faces are so close together that his hair brushes over my cheek.

"My turn," he says.

I kiss him softly, all the while weaving my fingers at my side. He rises into the air, limbs frozen, gasping with surprise. I scramble to my feet, then set him back on his.

"Now that's cheating," Aro says, laughing.

"No, that's called an advantage." I release him from the spell and he rubs his arms. "Shall we call it a draw?"

He moves closer and places his hands on my hips. "I think we're quite evenly matched." He smiles wryly. "Until you began cheating, of course."

"I make no apology for using every weapon in my arsenal," I say, looping my arms around his neck. This time our kisses are not so soft, but warm and urgent and deep. Magic tugs in my chest— the bond again—making me feel as if my whole body glows.

"Ahem," Zandria coughs from the doorway, arms folded across her chest. "I thought you were training in here."

Aro and I disentangle, but our hands remain entwined.

"We were," I say, beaming at Aro. "He held his own."

"I'm sure he did," Zandria says, rolling her eyes. Owen appears behind her.

"Is the room taken?" he says. "We were going to work with some of the newer weapons. Including my code namesake." He grins.

"We just finished," I say, leading Aro away. I pause in the doorway, watching my sister with Owen for a few moments. He makes her laugh as she chooses her weapon, and she smiles with him in a way that feels warm and genuine.

It has been a very long time since I've seen a smile like that from her.

"Everything all right?" Aro asks.

"Yes, I think it is," I say. My sister may have issues with me, and a history with Remy, but Owen is new. Literally so, in how cut off from the world his upbringing was. And while sometimes he seems much younger than us, he's very rational, and capable of viewing scenarios objectively. Spending time with him might do my sister good in more ways than one.

Tonight it's my turn to guard our base of operations while Zandria and Remy rescue another Magi from the Palace dungeons. I've spent most of the evening in the war room, hunched over Anassa's journal. Deciphering it has become a fascinating trip into the past—and into a long-ago Alliance leader's mind.

Anassa was smart and cunning, yet also compassionate enough to lead the Alchemist Alliance with a steady hand through very tumultuous times. She was funny too, and dearly loved her family. I've learned more about the Binding rite from her journal as well. She performed the rite with Lela; even then that was a taboo, though it was normal between Magi spouses. They didn't tell anyone, including other Alliance members. But Anassa mentioned something I found interesting: the separation between partners. Lela hadn't been able to join her on the first expedition to find the Sanctuary. They were apart for months, long enough that it became a physically painful thing for them both.

And when they were finally reunited, the bond's magic ignited in much the same way it did for me and Aro.

The Binding rite is no joke. It makes each person one half of a whole, and prolonged separation can weaken them both. Once they realized this, they vowed to never be apart again.

For almost my entire life, I've considered my twin my other half. But now Aro is too. Another part of me I cannot live without.

I glance at Aro, on the other side of the table from me, hunched over a book about alchemicals Catoria lent him in much the same way I've been over the diary. A deep V forms over the bridge of his nose as he concentrates on the text. His long fingers drum a light rhythm on the table beside him, but he doesn't seem to notice he's doing it.

Something inside me swells, catching me off guard.

I don't ever want to be separated from him again.

He notices me staring at him. "Is something wrong?" he asks, wiping his cheek distractedly, then considering his hand. "Is there ink on my face? These older books fade so easily."

I smile. "No. You're perfect."

He ducks his head as Owen walks into the room. "Either of you up for some sparring?" he asks hopefully. "Being cooped up inside has me needing something more to take off the edge."

"Weren't you cooped up on a small island for years?" Aro says.

"I was free to roam wherever I wanted on it. Actively hiding and without nature around me is . . . stressful." Owen shrugs. "Sparring helps."

"I see," Aro says. "I'm afraid I'm still recovering from my session with Aissa earlier today." His pale blue eyes twinkle in my direction.

"And I'm rather engrossed in this journal," I say. "But it would be nice to spar another time."

Owen sighs. "I understand. I wish Zandria were here. She always seems to be up for sparring no matter the time of day."

I snort. "That does sound like my sister."

Owen looks as if he's about to leave the room, but then he stops and steps closer to me, puzzling at the book in my hands.

"Did you know the cover is coming off that book?" he says.

"What?" I say, turning the book over.

"Here," he says. "In the corner. It's worn thin and beginning to peel away. Maybe you can fix it with a spell? It's clearly important; I'd hate to see it fall apart."

I run a finger gently over the edge. "I guess I shouldn't be surprised after it was jostled in my pack for days on end while we traveled." It might've withstood all the travel Anassa did, but that was back when it was newly made. Now it's much older and more brittle.

Owen peers closer. "Wait a moment. Is that something tucked inside?"

I follow his gaze and suck my breath in sharply. I can just see the edge of a different, older parchment hidden between the leather cover and the board. Gingerly, I pull the leather back, revealing an ancient sheet of paper. Aro hurries to my other side. I spread the paper carefully on the table so as not to damage it. The page is covered in faded ancient runes. In some places, it's so faded that I can't make out the words at all. The bottom left-hand corner is missing, but when I double check the inside of the journal's cover, I find no trace of it. It must have crumbled away long before it was hidden in this book.

"What do you think it is?" Owen breathes.

"Something important," Aro says. "It must be to have been hidden away so carefully."

I do my best to make out the runes at the top of the page. In the top right are runes in a different hand—Anassa's. They're more legible than the others.

"*For when the past is present*," I read aloud. A shiver runs over my arms.

"What could that mean?" Aro wonders, peering over my shoulder. "Look." He points to one of the runes about halfway down the page. "That rune is for an alchemical. Could this be a recipe?"

I hold up a hand to quiet the boys while I concentrate on translating. "No," I say slowly. "I think this is a spell of some sort. A very old one that utilizes alchemicals too."

I puzzle for a long moment over the first rune in what appears to be the title.

Then a heady, dizzying rush whispers over me.

"Anvil save us, I think this is the Heartsong."

"I don't believe it," Zandria says once she and Remy return with a rescued Magi. The newest Alliance recruit, Evyn, is sleeping in one of the rooms. To my surprise, Remy spent more time getting her settled and calmed than Zandria did. My sister told me she wanted to take the lead with the new recruits, but her actions say otherwise.

"It's true." I point to the runes at the top of the page. "This looks like the rune for *heart* and the other for *song*. What else could it be?"

She shakes her head with disbelief. "Even if it is the Heartsong, what does it matter? You can hardly make out half the runes, and a whole piece is missing here at the bottom. If anything, it's just a tease."

I've been worried over the same details, but I've already come up with a solution. Well, part of a solution.

"We can use a spell to bond more ink to the faded parts, which should make this more legible." I sigh. "Though there isn't much we can do about the missing piece."

If Catoria were here, she might be able to puzzle it out. But as it is, I'm stumped. Aro was right earlier—this spell uses magic and alchemicals, various ones at different times in the spell. It is highly complex, more so than any other spell I've seen before.

"Well, it is certainly the strangest spell I've ever seen, if it is one," Zandria says. "But I hope you aren't getting your hopes up over this when we can't even use it." She gives me a significant look.

My sister knows me too well. Of course my hopes are up. If anything, after we're finished in Palinor (assuming we survive), we'll take this to our mentor and see if her knowledge can help us solve the puzzle.

"Only a little," I say, and she shakes her head. I decide to appeal to her more practical side. "Zandria, a spell that could cure the Heartless could also thwart Darian's plans. That is something worth pursuing, even though it may take us some time."

"Well, I disagree. We don't have time to waste worrying about it," she says, standing up from the table. "We have more pressing things to consider, like rescuing the Magi in the dungeons and destroying the Technocrats."

Before I can say another word, she hurries from the room. While I knew my sister wouldn't be eager to heal Technocrats, I did hope she'd be more open to it. I can't help worrying her brushing this off has more to do with her personal dislike than the challenge of deciphering the spell in full.

Aro puts his arm over my shoulder and I lean into him. "What do you think?" I ask. We hardly had time to discuss it earlier. Zandria and Remy arrived moments after I discovered what the paper really was.

"It's worth pursuing. If we can figure out the spell, then we have an obligation to use it. It's the right thing to do."

"I agree. And it could go a long way to helping win over the people of the city too."

He smiles and kisses my forehead. "Always plotting."

"What about you, though? I thought you'd be more excited about what it could mean." I rest a hand over his chest and the machine ticks off beneath my fingers.

Aro runs a hand through his hair, considering. "You know, it's funny. Worry about my heart used to consume me. I'd dream of a day, foolish as I knew it was, that I could have a human heart. But ever since we were bonded, I think of it less and less. I'm no longer being poisoned. It doesn't cause me pain anymore. The urgency just isn't there. But it might be nice not to have a machine in my chest anymore." He tugs my hand. "What I am sure of is that we must pursue it. Not for me, but for all the Heartless who haven't been so fortunate as to have a Magi to bond with. They're still very much at risk, both from poisoning and from Darian's machinations. He cannot be allowed to take advantage of their desperation."

His pale half-moon eyes gaze into mine, filling me with certainty. "Then we'll just have to figure it out," I say.

"I'll make sure we do," Aro says, an eager grin spreading over his face. "We've all learned the basics of the runes from Catoria, and I've been studying alchemicals. We can solve this riddle. And then no one will ever need another mechanical heart."

There he is, Aro the researcher who stole my heart with his passion for his work. Little did I know then it really was a love for his people and a deep-seated desire to help others. This time we're on the same side. If there's a way to recreate the Heartsong, we'll find it together.

OVER THE LAST WEEK, WE'VE GONE ON A

new raid every day. Sometimes at night, other times during the day, depending on what we're after. Our food and weapon stores have increased exponentially. Zandria and I take turns raiding the dungeons in pairs with either Remy or Owen, and we've saved several more Magi. Some have been in those suits for months, but thus far no one has been there longer than a year.

I assume because they simply don't survive that long in such a torturous state.

The freed Magi have all sworn their allegiance to the Alchemist Alliance and know how to return to our base of operations. But most have family in safehouses here in the city and have chosen to find them instead of remaining at our hideout. I can't blame them, even though we've tried to convince them our underground bunker is safer. We've taught them the appearance-changing spell; they can conceal who they are when they need to.

We've also decided on a signal, one we can give out in the event we need everyone to convene. The letters *AA* carved into the trunk of the great willow tree on the square.

Remy has stepped up and taken the lead on helping the former prisoners reach their safehouses and ensuring they have what they need. And he's planning to check on them each week to ensure they're still safe and up to speed on the Alliance's progress. Zandria was supposed to do this, but in the end, she balked at it. It seems it was too soon for her to be so near all that pain again.

Vivienne and Remy train regularly now, as do Aro and I. And of course, I still spar with my sister when she's willing, to keep myself in the best form possible.

Remy no longer complains when we bring Vivienne on the raids, but he's still unwilling to let her wander aboveground on her own. Personally, I feel she's earned our trust.

But gradually, she's winning him over.

An hour ago, we returned from an early morning raid of a bakery. Vivienne clued us in to the fact it's the best time to swipe nearly everything we need for the week. While the bakers display a fair amount of their wares in cases, they keep the bulk of their daily stores in the back room as they cool. In the morning hours, they're distracted by setting up the front and chatting with the first customers.

All we had to do was climb in the open window and steal a few loaves of bread, a basket of rolls, even a pie—I haven't eaten a pie in what feels like years—and slink back out the door. We only take what we need so we're not leaving the stores destitute.

I've also been discussing some ideas with Aro about how to handle his parents. The people of the city are key. We need them on our side.

The trick will be getting them there.

We've finished distributing the rolls for our breakfast and are storing away the rest when Zandria strides into the war room and doesn't stop until she's toe to toe with me.

"Someone followed you," Zandria says, scowling. She and Owen have been on guard duty in the tunnels outside our hideout this morning.

The blood drains from my face. I'm always cautious. I even change my red hair to a jet black whenever I'm in the city to ensure I don't stand out. Who on earth could've followed us here?

"Where did you find them?" I ask, my entire body humming with nerves. We've only just settled into this hideout. I'd hate to have to abandon it already.

"Skulking around the tunnels. He couldn't get in, of course, but he seemed to know where the entrance was. He must've seen you come in here."

"That's impossible."

She folds her arms across her chest and stares daggers at me. "He's even asking for you. By name."

My blood runs cold. "What?"

"I was inclined to simply kill him but thought you might be mad if I didn't at least tell you about it first, since you have such a soft spot for our enemies now."

I roll my eyes at Zandria. "Trust me, killing them isn't all it's cracked up to be." A shiver runs through me. Even now, that fight with Caden haunts me.

Zandria raises an eyebrow. I've told her about the incident before, but it's the sort of thing she'll never fully understand until confronted with it. Unless I'm wrong, and her heart's simply frozen after being held in the Technocrats' dungeons.

"Take me to him," I say, and she leads the way to the cells we made from the Alliance's hidden room.

My shock is complete when I see a familiar face trapped behind the root bars of the cell.

"Leon?" I gasp.

Zandria raises her eyebrows. "This is Leon Salter? I thought he'd be . . . taller."

Leon isn't short, but he's not tall like Aro. His dark skin and grizzled white hair are the same as before, but the expression on his face is less surly than usual. He looks almost . . . desperate. Which isn't surprising considering where he is.

"I'll talk to him. Alone," I tell Zandria. Curiosity fills me, but I must be cautious around my former employer. I can't imagine why he'd follow me here unless the king and queen put him up to it. But why would they ask Leon when they have Darian? Nothing makes sense.

"You better fill me in on every word later," Zandria says.

"Definitely. Just like old times," I say. She smiles suddenly, almost like the sister she used to be, before climbing the stairs and leaving me with our prisoner.

I enter the small room, with its handful of cells in case we need them. Zandria was right; it's a good thing we took that precaution.

Leon stands when he sees me and shuffles forward on his mechanical foot and normal, flesh one. He squints, and I realize my hair is still black. I whisper the spell and it turns red again.

He sighs in relief. "Aissa, it's really you. I thought it was when I spied you topside."

I scoff. "I'm surprised you even know my name. You only showed me contempt when I worked for you."

"You had a lot to prove," he says. "I can't take just anyone." He grunts. "Usually they don't last more than a couple days. You lasted longer than any apprentice I've trained in years."

Part of me warms to hear that. Despite his grumpiness toward me, I did good work. I knew that, but it's still nice to have confirmation from the Master Mechanic himself.

"Who knows you're here? Why were you following me?" *How did you even know I was back in the city* is another question burning on my tongue, but I decide to let him answer the others first.

"No one knows," he says, taken aback. "The king and queen may pay me well for my work, but they don't control me or my movements."

"So they didn't send you?"

He scoffs.

"Then why were you following me?"

"I almost didn't recognize you at first with the dark hair, but your face is unmistakable."

I grit my teeth. I don't enjoy the part of that spell that changes features. It's painful, while changing my hair is not. And the latter has been just as effective—up until now. Of course, Leon would notice. He's rather annoying in that way.

"All right, that explains how you found me, but why?"

"Aro. He told me about a Magi girl who healed him. It wasn't hard to figure out that was you." Leon grips the bars tightly. He wears an expression I've never seen cross his face before. Hope, almost. "You saved him. You achieved what I've wanted to do for decades."

Shock roots me to the spot. I knew Aro had told Leon he fell in love with a Magi, but he was careful not to mention me by name.

"And what is that?"

"His machine heart was broken. You healed it . . . with magic. Yes, I know what you are. Trust me, it brings me no pleasure to be going to a Magi for help."

I snort. "Then why are you? And what exactly do you want help with?" Sometimes, Leon is a master of not getting to the point.

"Because the cause is greater than my pride."

I raise both my eyebrows. This is unexpected. "What cause?"

"Saving the Heartless. They don't deserve to suffer. You have the power to change that."

For a moment, I'm taken aback. I don't actually have that power—yet—but he'd have no way of knowing. If we can successfully decipher the Heartsong, we may be able to save them. But at the moment, the Binding rite is all I have, and I could only do that once.

"Did Aro explain how the spell worked?"

Leon shakes his head.

"In essence, his heart and mine are intertwined, permanently. It means that when he hurts, I hurt, literally. If he dies, I die. That's how he was healed right before your eyes. I experienced the same beating he'd gotten, but from miles away. I was healed by another Magi, and thereby so was Aro."

Disappointment slackens Leon's face. He grunts. "Then you wouldn't be able to bind like that with hundreds of children."

"Definitely not. You can only be bound to a single person."

"Is there nothing else you could do? No other spell you could try?" I'm surprised to see actual emotion aside from grumpiness in Leon. "I know the king and queen have been cruel to the Magi they've found. But the Heartless . . . they're innocents."

If we had the complete Heartsong, it could go a long way toward healing the rift between Technocrat and Magi. Though not with the king and queen. Their hatred, their fear of our power, is too great. The second they get wind of our reappearance in Palinor, they'll order us found and slaughtered. They probably already have. I'm sure Darian would be delighted to carry out those orders.

"There is one spell with some promise, but it will take time and research. Most of our spells were lost in the wars."

"If you can, please help them."

I frown. I've long wondered why Leon has such a soft spot for the Heartless. "Why do you care so much about the Heartless, anyway? You didn't charge the hospital for the hearts we delivered. That was unlike you."

Leon sinks onto the bench made from a stone slab in his cell. "I had a family once. A wife and daughter. The girl was born Heartless. I crafted her hearts personally. I made them as perfect as possible. But she was weak from the start . . ." His voice cracks. "She didn't live to see her third birthday."

Sympathy swells in my heart in just the way I shouldn't let it. This man is my enemy. Once, I couldn't wait to destroy this city just to see the look on his face. But now that he sits across from me, completely at my mercy, the fight has slipped out of me.

He risked his life, knowing full well we'd probably kill him, to plead for us to save the Heartless. To do the one thing he couldn't. The memory of the Heartless hospital, those sweet, sad faces tainted with the gray tint from the havani that powers their hearts, has never left me. He's right; they're innocent.

"Look," he says. "I don't care what you do to me. Kill me if you must. But please, just do what you can for them. That's all I want. For no parent to have to lose another child to that terrible curse."

"I'll think about it," I tell him. The backs of my eyes burn as I leave the room. Who would've ever imagined that Leon Salter's words would move me to tears?

"Absolutely not!" Zandria says. I've just explained to her I don't think we should kill Leon. "We cannot let him go."

"We're letting Vivienne live," I point out.

"That's not necessarily a permanent thing," Zandria responds. "And it doesn't mean we need to keep making exceptions. He knows what we can do, Aissa!"

Remy holds up his hands to get our attention. "Fighting among ourselves will do us no good."

Zandria sighs, and Owen puts a hand on her shoulder. She begins to relax. He's been having that effect on her more often lately. I wonder if there's something brewing between them. I will have to ask her later.

"I don't see what good will come of killing him," Owen says. "Why don't we just keep him in the dungeon for now? He might be useful later on. You said he knows the king and queen well, doesn't he?"

"I'd rather let him go, but I can agree to that for now," I say, and Owen tilts his head at me. "Leon hasn't done anything to harm us. He's only here to beg for the lives of children. Killing him over that seems wrong."

"We wouldn't be killing him for that; we'd be doing it because he's one of them," Zandria says.

"We can always kill him later, if need be," Remy says, "as long as he's here under our watch."

That finally appeases Zandria. "Fine. We'll let him live, for now. But I make no promises once he's outlived his usefulness."

She huffs off, followed closely by Owen. I shudder, unable to help thinking how closely her words echo those of Isaiah about his own Technocrat captives. She's still thinking in terms of value to our cause and regaining power for the Magi. Revenge, even. But as we free Magi and bring Technocrats over to our side, I'm becoming more and more convinced that the Alchemist Alliance was right: the struggle itself for power and dominance is part of the problem. We need to find a way to become equals again.

Aro, drawn out by the argument, appears next to me, wrapping an arm around my waist.

Remy sighs. "I should be training Vivienne right about now," he says, and leaves the room.

"Don't worry too much about your sister," Aro says. "She has a good heart. But it's been broken by what happened to her. It will heal eventually."

I sigh and rub my hands over my face. "I hope so. I hate fighting with her." We always bickered; what siblings don't? But this is different. Before, we were always on the same side, just with different approaches to our end goal.

Now, we don't seem to have the same goal anymore.

I have no idea how I will achieve the peace that the Alchemist Alliance has sought for so long, especially with my twin fighting me for revenge every step of the way. But I'm starting with mercy.

Real mercy, not the terrible kind the king and queen dole out to their subjects.

Aro presses his lips to my temple. "We just need to keep on the right path, and eventually she'll see the light."

"I'm worried she might slit Leon's throat in the meantime."

"You can't focus on that. We need to bring more people to our side. Vivienne's working on that, isn't she?" Aro says.

"She is. And after the torture she went through at the hands of the queen, she's almost as determined as Zandria is to stage a coup."

Aro laughs. "She's got a fire in her, that's for certain." He bites his lip. "What will you do with Leon?"

"We're not going to kill him," I say.

"Oh, thank the Anvil," he says.

"For now, at least. I've managed to convince Zandria he might be useful to us." I sigh. "He followed us because he wanted to ask me to help the Heartless with magic if we can. I didn't make him any promises, but . . ."

His eyes light up. "The Heartsong might win over the Master Mechanic himself to the Alliance. I'll redouble my efforts at deciphering it." He embraces me and whispers in my ear, giving me chills. "Thank you for helping Leon. He's always known what and who I am. He's one of the few people I trust."

I snort. "Need I remind you, you also trusted Darian?"

Aro winces. "Please don't. I trusted you too. I suppose I have a knack for being taken in by spies."

"And people who want to kill you," I add.

"Yes, that has been quite an awkward trend, hasn't it?" A smile quirks at the edge of his lips. "But it's true, we must help the Heartless. I think that might be the key to winning the people over."

"First, let's start with their finances, shall we?"

Until recently, Aro had no idea how badly the Techno leaders tax their residents. With Darian ramping up his experiments, they've doubled the taxes in recent weeks. People are struggling. If we can return those funds to the public, it might undercut the loyalty the royals currently enjoy. And if we can attribute it to the Alchemist Alliance, it will only bolster our cause.

WHILE I'M LOATHE TO HAVE ARO
aboveground where Darian or any other of
the Palace spies might see him, tonight we need
him to break into the Treasury. He's never been
inside, but he knows where his parents keep it locked
and secure. And there's an excellent chance this insight will
be essential to our success.

Owen and I head out with Aro in the lead, all of us carefully hidden under the cloaking spell, to find the secret Royal Treasury. I would've expected the king and queen to keep the funds under lock and key inside the Palace, but according to Aro, they're too paranoid for even that. Instead they chose a secure, well-guarded facility.

One might think stealing from his parents would cause Aro some inner turmoil, but if it has, he's kept it well hidden. To be honest, he seemed eager, bordering on gleeful, as he plotted the logistics for taking their tax revenue out from under their noses.

Aro stops our group in front of an unassuming building. Without his assurances I never would've guessed it houses two-thirds of the Technocrats' wealth. The rest they keep on hand in the Palace as both a decoy and for easy access to spend as lavishly as they please.

Owen frowns at it. "Are you sure this is the right place?"

"I know, it could pass for a tenement house," Aro says. "But it's uninhabited. The only ones who go in or out are some of their most trusted guards."

And their most dangerous guards. But Aro doesn't need to remind us of that.

The building is square and plain and squat, only a single story tall. I silently weave a spell we learned at the Sanctuary, one to reveal life-forms within a certain radius, lighting them up to the caster's eyes well enough to detect them even through stone—or metal—walls. Within a few moments, I can see that there are at least twenty guards dispersed throughout the building and that many of them are underground.

Realization dawns. "They keep the money in a vault in the basement."

"Yes. And if I know my parents, it will be nearly impenetrable."

Owen raises an eyebrow. "Then why are we hitting this one and not the one in the Palace? It sounds like that would be easier to get to."

"It probably would. But liberating funds from this one will rattle the king and queen more." I consider the building's metal and brick configuration. "I wouldn't worry about it being impenetrable. That may be the case for a regular Technocrat or Magi. But not for me."

Aro laughs softly. "You're fearless, Aissa."

That isn't quite true. Plenty of things scare me. But I know my own worth. I know what I'm capable of, and I know I can do this. Getting past all those guards will be the real challenge. There's no vault, no matter how deeply buried, or lock so intricate it can withstand my magic. People, with their own will and creativity to govern them, can always surprise. Having Aro here creates a new challenge, but it's necessary in case our magic alone isn't enough.

"We should move in before the guards change," Aro says.

Our spells are in place, but I'll have to release the silencing one once we get inside to take out some of the guards. Owen will keep up the shield as long as he can, but if he needs to use both hand-spells and incantations to attack, we'll be exposed. The king and queen were quite careful to ensure no tunnel access was possible for the Royal Treasury, and there's only one door that goes in or out—the front. With Aro safely behind us, Owen and I head for the entrance.

"There are two guards posted at the door," I whisper. "Then four more interspersed down the hall. Once we get to the basement, the guards double. We may not be able to use the shield at all if we have to keep attacking. We must be sure to get them all, then bind them up. None can happen upon us as we open the vault—they'll raise the alarm."

Owen nods and Aro's hand fidgets with the sword on his belt. From our sparring practices, I know he can use it well, but that might not be enough tonight.

We pause under our shield, plastering ourselves to the side of the wall. Then I hum, casting a new spell that opens the lock and throws the door wide. We hold our breaths. We won't have to wait long to be discovered.

"Who's there?" calls one of the guards angrily.

When he gets no response, the first guard ventures through the door and looks around. He can't see us under our magic, but he drops like a stone at my sleeping spell. "*Somnis.*"

"What the forges is going on out here?" shouts the other guard as he barrels through the open doorway. But I'm ready and waiting.

"*Somnis,*" I say. And he too drops to the ground.

Without missing a beat, we drag the guards inside and close the door behind us. We lay them unceremoniously out on the floor, hands and feet bound and gagged, far enough out of the way that anyone glancing down the hall might not see them. The building is set up in such a way that there's only one direction to go, herding us through to either be caught or complete our mission. The walls are not mirrored like they are in the Palace but use brick and stone reinforced with metal supports at regular intervals.

It isn't long before we encounter the next batch of guards.

We crouch around the bend from where they're posted. My

spell shows they're spread out down a stretch of hall in such a way that once we ambush one, the others will notice and attack.

"That makes things tricky," Owen whispers.

I bite my lip. "I have an idea," I explain, and Owen and Aro nod in agreement. We edge closer to the bend, hearts in our throats. Then we turn the corner, arms raised in a violent wind spell that whips down the hall, blasting them off their feet within seconds. They don't have time to respond before we've knocked them out, tossing them against the walls like rag dolls.

Pulses racing, we survey the damage and tie them up before moving on. They'll all live but will have massive headaches when they wake, that's for sure.

"Remind me not to get on your bad side," Aro whispers, then kisses me softly behind the ear. Owen rolls his eyes, and I blush.

Now the only thing standing in our way is the challenge that awaits us in the basement. I cast the detection spell again to get a sense of where the guards are now, in case they've shifted positions. They're still in the same spots, and we take a moment to decide the best course of action.

I've never forgotten the first time I fought a Technocrat: Caden the guard. It didn't go at all like I'd expected it would. He surprised me, so I couldn't use the spells I might normally cast to incapacitate an enemy. I'm determined to never be caught off guard like that again. I've always favored having a plan, and now I want to be prepared for every possibility. Succeeding tonight is a key part of what we hope will swing the residents of Palinor in our favor.

"Owen, you and I should start with the wind spell again. See how many we can catch up in it, maybe toss them into each other to incapacitate them." I don't enjoy killing. There was a time I fantasized about murdering every Technocrat in the city in their beds while they slept, but the reality, I learned with Caden, is terrible and sickening. Now that I understand better that we're all really from the same people, not as different as I was told, I'd rather reserve killing as a last resort.

Zandria thinks I'm crazy. If I'd gone through the things she has, I might side with her. Our experiences have diverged, and eventually we'll have to reconcile them if we want our new Alchemist Alliance to get a real foothold. But tonight it's just me and Aro and Owen, and they're more willing to be guided by me than she is.

"After that, use a sleeping spell if you can on any who get close," I say.

"I'll be ready to fight if they break through," Aro says.

I nod. "Hopefully we can make short work of them, but you never know what surprises they might have in store."

"Understood," Owen says.

"Then let's go," Aro says.

Nerves kick up a frenzy in my gut. There are a lot of guards in the basement just below us. More than I've successfully taken on before. But I believe we can do this. We have to.

Failure has never been an option.

UNDER OWEN'S SHIELD SPELL, I USE MY
magic to unlock the basement door, and it
swings open. A short flight of stairs descends
before us, and we wait for a breath or two to ensure
no guards come racing up the stairs after hearing the door
open. No one appears, and we start down the stairs. I can
hear voices of guards and something else that sets me on edge.

The unmistakable metallic creak of machines prowling.

My heart stutters in my chest. Of course they have machines
guarding the Treasury.

I'm the only one in our party who can take them on magically.
While Aro and Owen can do their best to fight them off, I stand
the best chance of disabling them.

The muscles in my body are strung tight as wires. The gears
in my brain begin to turn, plotting out escape tactics if it becomes
clear we'll be overwhelmed.

For the first time tonight, I'm nervous.

But we press on, and now I'm sure my friends have heard
the machines. Owen looks queasy, but he does an admirable job
maintaining our shield spell nonetheless.

When we reach the bottom of the stairs, the sight before us
sends my adrenaline skyrocketing. A dozen guards are spread out
down a long, wide hall with shiny metal walls. In the center is the
door to the Treasury room. It's a monstrous, rectangular machine
built into the wall, with jumbled gears and wires entwined in
a manner that would be hopeless to untangle for someone who
didn't know the proper key.

But I don't need keys.

Roaming between the guards are six enormous spidermechs,

the kind that can pin a grown man down and wind wires around him in seconds. I shudder.

I *really* hate that kind of mech.

Owen's breath catches when he sees them. Aro, though, isn't surprised. He told us they'd likely have mechs patrolling here too. The only good news is that he's likely to have more insight into how these mechs are programmed and can avoid getting caught by one.

But it's still better if I can take them all out.

I use my hands to cast the wind spell, weaving my fingers in just the right motions to stir up the air around me with magic and power. When I nod at a nervous-looking Owen, we send the wind spinning down the hall, sweeping up five of the guards right off the bat. Their companions' shocked faces quickly harden, and they scatter as I try to knock them over by throwing the caught-up guards into them. I only knock out two, then a couple of the guards regain their feet. I catch them up a second time, knocking their heads together to finally render them unconscious.

That takes care of seven. We still have five left, plus those spidermechs. They skitter toward the stairs and my heart takes a seat in my throat.

"I've got these. Handle the rest of the guards, Owen," I say.

He drops his shield to cast the wind spell with his hands and another defensive incantation, revealing our position and numbers. While Owen incapacitates the nearest Techno guard with a sleeping spell, and the next with a burst of flame, the closest spidermech lunges at me.

"*Ascensio!*" I lift it off its wriggling metal legs with my magic. Then I slam it into the next mech coming for Owen, tangling them together in a mess of metal and wires. I hum, pushing my magic into their bodies, making the metal hot enough that the floor scorches. They make a strange, unexpected squeal as they begin to melt and twist together.

Owen grapples with three guards—a tricky task even with his dual casting ability. Aro launches himself into the fray to help, which distracts me more than I should let it. The next mech comes for me, long wires spitting in my direction. It catches me around the wrist, then yanks me forward. I stumble to my knees but never stop the words of my incantation.

"Explosi!" The machine bursts into pieces. I direct the sharpest of those pieces toward the remaining guards attacking Owen and Aro, slicing the hands off one and a foot off another with the razor-thin metal of the spidermech's body. The wire around my wrist loosens and slithers to my feet.

Half the machines down. Magic and blood thrum in my ears. The last three advance on me together. One crawls across the ceiling, another on the floor, and the third along the left wall. My palms are slick. This is more mechs—especially dangerous ones made specifically for capturing people—than I've ever taken on at once.

I take a deep breath and remind myself I was literally made to do this.

My spell winds around them, teasing their wires from their bodies at my command instead of their own. Once my magic has a good hold on the wire lassos from all three, I yank on them, pulling the two in front of me together. Keeping an eye on the one above me, I quickly use the wires to trap the pair of spidermechs in much the same way they trapped others: tied tightly enough they can't even wriggle.

That should hold for a while at least.

Before I can cast another spell, the one on the ceiling swings down, knocking me off my feet and the breath from my chest. My head swims, but I don't have time to be dazed. The mech's pincers click menacingly in front of my face, and I duck left just in time, so they pierce my shoulder instead. The pain is blinding; Aro grunts with surprise. I grit my teeth and keep humming my incantation, the magic inside me winding up to strike.

"*Explosi*," I manage to whisper.

The mech bursts apart, sending shrapnel down the hall. I realize too late that might not have been wisest, though it seemed the best idea in the moment. My thigh stings where Aro has been hit with a small piece, and Owen has a scratch on his arm, but it could have been worse. While I've been fighting off the machine, my companions overpowered the remaining guards. They're all tied up and sleeping—thanks to a spell by Owen—at the far end of the hall.

Aro helps me up and Owen glances between us as if he can't decide which of us to heal first.

I can't help it. I laugh.

And then promptly regret it. It literally hurts to laugh right now.

"Can you heal my shoulder?" I ask Owen. "The wound originated with me. That will be the most effective way of helping both of us."

"So that's how it manifests," Owen says. "I know you've told me, but it's another thing to see firsthand."

Aro takes my hand, pressing my fingers to his lips and sending a shiver down my spine. I'm relieved neither of them is too badly injured.

We risk taking a few minutes for Owen to heal our wounds before entering the treasury itself. If we need to make a speedy getaway, we must be in top condition. He uses an incantation for my shoulder and a handspell for Aro's thigh to make the healing faster.

Once I'm able to move my shoulder again without pain, we start toward the door, but a metallic rattle stops me in my tracks. The two mechs I tied up are still trying to get out of their own wire bonds.

"Hold on," I say. Then I move my hands in a spell. The magic swells inside my chest, shooting down my arms as I clasp my hands together tightly. Then I rip them wide apart and the two mechs split down the middle, wires and all, with a resounding screech.

The legs on one of the mechs jerk a few more times, then still for good.

Owen clears his throat. "Are we ready now?"

I turn my attention to the locked treasury. A massive jumble of gears and wires thread through the thick metal door. There isn't even a place that's clearly a lock or a clue how one would go about unlocking it.

I catch Aro's eye. "Any suggestions of where to start?"

He shrugs helplessly. "I knew about this place, but this is the first time I've ever actually been here. Never had a reason to before."

"It doesn't even look like a door. Just . . . a machine stuck in the wall or something," Owen says.

There's one thing every machine must have: a power source. Some, like children's toys, are windup machines, but most are more complex and require havani to power them. I'm willing to bet havani is somewhere in this door. And if I can find it, trace it back, I might be able to untangle these parts and turn the lock. Better yet, I might even be able to ignite it and blow the whole thing apart. Maybe tear the door to shreds. But I suspect it will make more of an impact on the highly paranoid king and queen if someone steals from them and the lock has been left untampered.

If we're lucky they might even begin to turn on their closest allies, anyone who has knowledge of this secret financial hideaway, believing them to either be helping the Magi or Magi themselves.

But first I need to figure this out.

Aro and Owen keep watch in case any other guards or mechs

decide to join us. I call my magic up again, slipping it gently between the gears and wires, probing deeper into the door that's a veritable machine in its own right. Had I realized it was this intricate, I would've asked Leon about it before we left; he's probably the one who designed it.

The spell helps me understand how this thing works, gently pulling a wire out here and a few gears and metal plates there. Almost like it's untying a tangled knot. At the center, my magic brushes over the havani powering it. That sickly feeling is unmistakable. I pull the fuel out too, though even just touching it with my magic nauseates me. Once I settle the havani core on the floor I survey the mess I've made.

Underneath all those gears and wires is a small wheel, so well hidden I'd never have known it was there until now. With a wave of my hand, my magic spins the wheel, and more gears inside the doorframe groan. Something clicks, echoing in the ghostly quiet hallway.

And then the door slowly swings open.

I GRIN FROM EAR TO EAR AS WE CAUTIOUSLY

enter the treasury. Mechlights flicker on automatically. In two seconds flat my emotions swing
from elation to frustration.

There's gold here, massive amounts of it. Box after
box of coins line the walls and are stacked on low shelves,
joined by more stacks of shimmering gold bricks, just waiting to
be melted down and crafted into something precious.

Interspersed between them are the many, many arms of one
giant, sinuous machine.

When the lights turn on, the machine begins to move, metal
arms undulating like an enormous, lithe tree. Appendages at
the ends grasp at boxes of coins, shifting them closer to the
trunk of the metal beast. It's built into the wall in the far corner
of the room in much the same way the lock on the door was
constructed.

My mouth goes dry. "Aro, how do we shut this down?"

His face is drawn and pale, and he shakes his head. "I
don't know."

"Look for something," I say. "I need to fend this off." The
arms swing toward the door where we stand, and I send spell
after spell to buy Aro time to figure it out. First a blast of wind,
then I rip the appendage off another arm, only to get smacked in
the chest by the stump. I stumble into Owen, the air knocked out
of me for a moment.

"Look, there's a panel here in the wall," Aro says, then frowns.
"It's all letters."

"It must be a code. What would they use that no one else
would know?"

He glares at it, but I can't help. Another mecharm is headed our way. I pool my magic and send a spell so fierce, the arm splits into two pieces. I'd love to rip the entire thing to shreds, make it explode like those spidermechs, but with the machine being part of the actual wall, that might backfire in a big way. I don't want to bring the whole building down on our heads. The arms are moving too quickly and randomly for me to get close enough to unpack the wires and parts like I did with the door. It's one of the most impressive machines I've ever seen.

We need to figure out this code.

Suddenly, the giant, looming machine freezes in midair. Then it retracts its arms into the wall.

I breathe out in relief. "I knew you'd figure it out. What was it?"

Aro's wearing an odd expression, one I can't quite decipher. "My full first name. Arondel."

"You're their biggest secret. No one else would have any knowledge except for them. Good thinking."

"I almost didn't even try it," he admits. "I . . . I didn't think they thought of me that often. Let alone to secure something as important as this." A deep *V* forms on his forehead.

I rub his arm. "They're your parents. I'm sure in their own twisted way they care for you. Probably more than for anyone else but themselves. But they've done monstrous things they must answer for."

"I know." He squeezes my hand. "And I also know if they knew about you, they'd kill you in a heartbeat. Their love kept me locked up until Leon finally convinced them to allow me to work in the lower levels of the Palace." His eyes burn into mine. "I've learned more about family from you and your friends than I ever did from them."

Owen clears his throat. "Shouldn't we, uh . . . ?" He gestures to the piles of money before us.

"Yes, definitely," I say. "As much as we can possibly bring with us."

It's hard to decide where to begin. We each have several bags, and we fill them all to the brim. I plan to use a floating spell to carry them. Some we'll keep so we can pay for goods like food and clothing instead of having to resort to theft. But we have no intention of holding on to most of it for long.

We avoid the gold bars—they'd be too traceable, and if we want to give this back to the people of the city, coins that can be easily circulated are the best bet. I use a spell to fill my bags quickly and then help Aro and Owen with theirs. Coins jingle as they stream into the sacks. A heady thrill shoots through me.

King Damon and Queen Cyrene will be furious. I wish I could see their faces when they hear the news.

But for now we need to make a speedy exit.

I decide to mess with the mechs a little bit to confuse the royals. I use my magic to put the monster mech in the wall back together, fixing the handful of pieces I managed to take off. When I'm done, it looks almost as if it wasn't even touched.

The only noticeable difference is the missing coins.

We leave the vault behind, and I reassemble the lock on the door in the same manner. Then I turn my attention to the spider-mechs. There's no hope of putting them back together, nor do I have any desire to do so. I can respect the ingenuity behind the door lock and the tentacled machine protecting the royals' wealth, but not these. Instead, I pile them in the center of the hall, then cast a melting incantation. Soon, liquid metal crawls over the floor. I send a breath of frigid air over it, and within minutes it's hardened, as if it were an intentional decoration on the floor.

Then we flee into the night, Owen casting the shield and silencing spells and me floating our bags of coins.

When we reach the city square, memories fill me. Here's where I was assigned my apprenticeship to Leon. There's the massive willow tree where I ran and hid after Zandria was captured.

This is where we'll turn much of the Technos' money loose for their citizens to find once dawn breaks.

We intend to leave no doubt about who has given them this gift. Aro is certain his parents will try to cover and take credit for it, pretending to be generous while fuming privately, if we don't.

Owen works on the credit while I disperse the funds. This is the fun part.

With a spell, I toss the first bag into the air, then rip the cloth apart, sending the coins scattering everywhere. I do the same with all but one bag, making them burst apart in various places to cover as much ground as possible. When I'm done, the whole square glitters in the moonlight.

"It's a bit dramatic, but it will make the people happy," Aro says, wrapping an arm around my waist. A pleasant shiver runs through my belly.

Owen, meanwhile, has scorched the earth with the words, *Alchemist Alliance*. The first who happen on the square will see them, and even if the Technocrats try to scrub them out, rumors will spread like a wildfire nothing can extinguish.

I smile and kiss Aro. He swings me around, and I could swear I'm floating. When he sets me back down on the ground, I laugh and put an arm around each of my companions.

"I think our work here is done."

Aro and Owen return to our base of operations, but I have one last thing I need to do. I follow the directions Aro gave me to a part of town that's a bit more rundown than the one we just left. It isn't far from where Zandria and I used to live, actually. I look for the small brick building, number 127 according to Aro, and stop in front of the walk.

No one can see me under my shield spell, but I feel strangely exposed nonetheless.

I creep up to a window at the rear of the house, where the bedrooms most likely are located, and peer inside. It's dark, but the moonlight shines through the curtains when I part them with my magic, revealing a sleeping woman with her arms around a little girl sucking her thumb in her sleep. My heart aches more than I expected it would.

My guilt, my fault. My mistake.

This is Caden's wife and child. I took him away from them, let Aro cover up his death with convenient lies. I may not have liked Caden, but that didn't give me the right.

Satisfied that I have the correct house, I let the curtains fall back into place and tiptoe to the front door. There, I leave a purse of coins full enough to cover the money Caden would've brought home in an entire year. Then I disappear into the darkness.

WHEN I WAKE THE NEXT MORNING, I FIND

Aro in the war room after breakfast. He glances up from his book with an eager look on his face.

"You're in a good mood this morning," I say. "Did you uncover something new while studying the runes?" I take a seat next to him on the bench as I eat a croissant we swiped from the bakery the other day.

"Nothing you don't already know about," he says. "But I've been thinking a lot." His face seems to be trying to take on a full range of emotions all at once. His hands are warm, and they slide down my arms to pull me closer by my elbows.

"About what?" I ask.

"My parents." He shakes his head. "I can't stop thinking about our mission last night. The key to shutting the machine off was my full name. The last few weeks I've believed my parents to be indifferent to me. As unfeeling as you and the other Magi believe them to be. But this . . . this is forcing me to reexamine that."

"Aro," I say. "I know you want to believe your parents have some . . ." I pause, trying to find the right word. " . . . good in them. But all the evidence points to the contrary."

His eyes don't lose an ounce of that eager gleam. "Except what I learned last night. I think I can reach them."

Personally, I think he's grasping at straws. But I can appreciate why. It can't be easy to come to terms with your family being the source of so much suffering and pain.

"How are you going to do that? You already tried warning them about Darian, and that didn't go well."

Aro grimaces. "True. But I have so much more to tell them

now. They have no idea Magi and Technocrats were once the same people. No inkling about the genetic mutation that split us into two factions."

"But will they even listen to you if you do tell them?"

"I have proof now. I can show them the alchemicals, explain how the Heartless were created and how Darian made it worse. And that we fixed it." He catches my hand and places it on his heart. "How magic saved my life. How a *Magi* saved my life."

My breath shudders in my throat. "I'm not so sure we should be sharing the alchemicals with them. I don't know that we can trust them with that information. Look what Darian did with his knowledge of magic and machines." I swallow hard. "And if you tell them we're bonded, Darian will find out. He'll use that against us. That must remain a secret for the time being."

His enthusiasm dampens slightly. "All right, I can see the wisdom in that. But still, after seeing the Sanctuary and learning about the Alchemist Alliance, I have so much more ammunition to use to convince them."

A chill sweeps over me. "Aro, you can't mention the Sanctuary either. Darian . . . I'm sure he's heard of it. He probably has plans to look for it once he completes his coup here in Palinor. It must be protected."

Aro sighs. "I promise I won't say anything about the Sanctuary. But I must try. Darian is the real threat."

"I just don't know if that's a good idea." I shrug. "Perhaps that's the problem with the way of life I'm accustomed to. Everything we do must be kept a secret. Information can be dangerous."

"Who are we considering sharing information with?" Zandria's voice calls from the doorway. I stiffen in response. My sister leans against the wall, frowning with her arms folded.

"No one. Aro and I were just discussing ways we might be able to make King Damon and Queen Cyrene see reason."

Zandria makes a choking noise. "See reason? You can't be serious?" She moves closer to the table where we sit.

"I know they have cruel tendencies, but they're not wholly unreasonable people," Aro says.

I cringe. I can't agree with him. Cruelty is the point of nearly everything the king and queen do.

"Not unreasonable?" Zandria's voice launches an octave higher than usual, making Aro draw back. I remain firmly between them.

"Zandria, I don't think he meant—"

"Is it *reasonable* for them to lock Magi in metal suits until they wither and die?"

Aro turns pale. "Of course not, they don't—"

"Is it *reasonable* for them to torture anyone and everyone they please, just for sport? How about Vivienne's story? Was it reasonable for them to burn her boyfriend alive?" she sputters. "How is anyone who thinks those things are acceptable to be reasoned with?"

"None of those things are reasonable. They're horrifically misguided—"

"Misguided?" Zandria laughs, her anger turning manic. "No, there's nothing misguided or naive about their actions. They are cruel and calculating, the sort of plans only the worst people can dream up. They cannot be reasoned with. They can only be destroyed."

My sister quivers with rage. I place a hand tentatively on her shoulder, hoping to calm her, but instead she slaps it away. "And you? Do you agree with him?"

I glance between my sister and my boyfriend. Then I shake my head. "I don't believe they can be reasoned with. But killing them isn't the answer either. Stopping them, absolutely. Removing them from power and imprisoning them where they can do no more harm."

"Do no more harm?" Fire flashes in Zandy's eyes. "The only

thing that will ensure that is their deaths. Letting them live is the same as letting them go unpunished. I won't stand for it."

Aro rises. "I understand your anger. My parents have earned all your hatred and more. But we're not going to kill them. I won't stand for that."

"Who says you have any say in the decision?" Magic begins to simmer in Zandria's veins. I can sense it pooling in her palms.

"Zandy," I say with a sharp warning in my voice. She gives me a cutting glance.

"After everything we've been through, everything you and I and the Magi have suffered," Zandria says to me, "how can you even consider letting them live?"

A wild frustration burns within in my chest. She's right about one thing. I don't like the idea of letting them live. But I can't condone killing Aro's parents. Certainly not right in front of him.

I glance helplessly between the two most important people in my life, and for the first time, I'm at a complete loss for words.

"I can't believe you," Zandria hisses, then hurries out of the room. I want to run after her, comfort her, but I'm the last person who can do that right now.

My eyes sting, and I rub them before any tears can fall. Somehow, I keep making things worse with my sister. Aro places a hand on my shoulder.

"I didn't mean to put you in that position," he says, a miserable expression on his face. He knows as well as I do that there are no good choices when it comes to his parents, and definitely none that will make everyone happy.

"It was bound to happen eventually." I pull away slightly. "I know you want to reach out to your parents, but the risks of doing so are far greater than any possible reward. I just don't see a path to making that happen right now. If one presents itself, we can revisit. But bear in mind, everyone else here wants them dead.

And I can't blame them for that, even if I disagree it's the right course of action."

Aro's jaw twitches as his mouth settles into a hard line. "All right. We'll table that for now."

"Thank you," I say, then sink back onto the bench.

"What about you?" Aro says. "Are you all right?"

"I'm frustrated with my sister. And myself, I think. When I put her in charge of helping the freed Magi acclimate, I thought it would go a long way to bringing her some peace, some sense of direction. Maybe even a little closure. She won't talk to me about what happened to her, but those Magi understand. They've experienced the same thing. But all it seems to have done is fuel the fires of her rage, and she's avoided them while they're here." Aro puts an arm around my shoulders, and I lean into him. "It isn't at all as I expected."

He kisses the top of my head. "That's the problem with people. They're unpredictable. Especially when they're hurting. Your sister has some deep wounds. They may not ever fully heal."

"I wish I knew a spell that could just . . . fix her. I miss my partner. I miss how things used to be between us."

I can't see his face, but I can feel him smiling over me. "You were indeed a formidable team, as my many broken-down machines can attest."

I laugh in spite of myself, but quickly sober again. I want my sister back, but I have no idea how to help her. All I can do is keep trying.

THE NEXT FEW DAYS PASS IN A BLUR OF

raids and rumors. Vivienne reports back that many are talking about the Alchemist Alliance, wondering what it is and what it means. Our stunt definitely seems to have worked in our favor. She's been strategically dropping hints about the Alliance and its purpose, piquing interest in many Technocrats.

Remy and I are on our way to another storehouse to ensure as few weapons as possible stay in the hands of the Technocrats, with Vivienne again joining us to run interference. Not only has Remy not objected to her presence, but he almost seems happy she's with us. He speaks to her more than to me.

The evening is drenched with rain, making the going slow and shield spells impractical. Luckily there are always fewer spying eyes out and about in a downpour like this. Remy leads the way—he knows where most of these are from his time undercover in the palace guard. We've done this a few times and have a routine. Vivienne keeps watch out front, distracts anyone if necessary, while Remy and I take as many weapons as we can carry. Since it's raining, we won't be able to take as much as usual—we'll have to conceal them under our cloaks instead of a shield spell—but we still have three sets of hands.

Tonight's storehouse is a simple one-story building only a short walk from the eastern gate.

"The guard won't be changing for several hours, so it's unlikely we'll be interrupted," Remy says.

Vivienne takes her place, while I break the lock with my magic. Remy and I slip inside the dark room, leaving the door slightly ajar. I cast a light and send it floating toward the ceiling.

The place is filled top to bottom with swords, maces, staves, and even a few of those bombs we saw at one of the first storehouses we raided. I waste no time getting to work, but Remy pauses.

"Something's off," he says.

I frown, glancing around. "What do you mean?" To me, this storehouse looks the same as the others we've raided.

He shakes his head. "I'm not sure. Just . . . something doesn't feel right."

I quickly cast an amplification spell, but no unusual noises reach our ears. "Anything more specific than a gut feeling?"

"No. Sorry." He shrugs, but anxiety clouds his face.

I consider for a moment. All we have to go on is Remy's feeling, which could easily be nothing more than that. As far as we can see and hear, we're alone, and no guards or spidermechs lay in wait. Besides, we're already here; it would be a shame to waste the opportunity.

"Well, let's hurry and get out of here as soon as possible."

We gather as many weapons as we can manage between us and a pile for Vivienne in half our usual time. Remy gives the signal and she joins us, slipping through the doorway and shaking the rain off her cloak.

The door slams shut behind her, startling us all.

I move to open it, but the door doesn't budge.

"What just happened?" Vivienne asks, a quiver in her voice.

The storehouse trembles. Then the walls begin to move, closing in on us at an alarming rate.

If we don't do something, we'll be crushed or impaled by the weapons sweeping toward us.

"Aissa!" Remy cries. "Make it stop!"

My head whirls. "Get ready to run. Technos could be waiting for us outside."

I summon my magic with an incantation, sending it up and out into the walls. "*Explosi!*"

The first of the swords scratch against my arms as the walls burst apart. The ceiling rains down on us, a brick knocking me in the head before I can duck out of the way. My head throbs, and the world swims in front of me, but I don't lose consciousness. One of the others grabs my hand and yanks me out of the wreckage of the collapsing building.

"Run," Remy hisses in my ear. We sprint headlong down the street through the rain, abandoning the weapons we came for. I hear a grunt behind me. When I whirl around, Remy limps with a metal arrow sticking out of his calf. Another is lodged in one shoulder.

"Don't stop!" he yells. But Vivienne ignores him. She runs back to him, supporting him with her own shoulder.

"Get to the tunnel," I say. "I'll hold them off."

More metal arrows rain down on us. I'm still a little disoriented, but I'm fairly certain of the direction to cast my attack spell in. I wish I'd brought Owen too. His dual casting ability would really come in handy right now. I prevent the first few arrows from hitting me, then quickly glance behind to ensure Remy and Vivienne are getting away. They disappear down the alley that leads to our escape route. But before I have the chance to feel relief, a sharp pain bites into my arm.

An arrow has gone clean through my wrist.

Dizziness threatens me again as blood slides over my fingers. Bile rises in my throat. I look away and manage to keep it down as pain ratchets through my arm.

I have to focus and figure out where they're shooting these arrows from.

I deflect the bolts as best I can, all the while retreating down the street. Finally, I spy a glint of metallic movement on a rooftop opposite where the storehouse stood.

I send a new spell spinning through the wind and rain toward the Technocrat on the rooftop. "*Somnis.*"

Finally the arrows stop. It must've only been one guard, probably posted there by Darian. He had to be close to activate the machine and lock us in. We must have really gotten the royals' attention when we stole from their treasury.

The adrenaline begins to drain from my body, leaving only the shooting pain behind. Another arrow is embedded in my shoulder, but the pain in my wrist is particularly brutal. It ratchets all the way to my elbow like a white-hot flame. I grit my teeth. There's no way I could cast a handspell right now.

My head swims. I can't seem to breathe normally. The sick feeling in my stomach rises higher, but it's not just from the pain this time.

Poison. Those arrows were dipped in poison.

Poor Aro. He must be so worried, feeling everything I do.

But I refuse to let this be the way we end.

Part of me wants to pass out here in the street, but the pain keeps me alert. I move as quickly as I can, all too aware I'm leaving a trail of blood behind me, until I get to the escape tunnel. I'm just beginning to wonder how I'm going to get down when Vivienne climbs up the ladder.

"Let me help you," she says. I take her offer gratefully.

When we reach the floor, I hum the spell to put the lid back on the tunnel. It's much harder than usual. The arrows are weakening me in more ways than one. Remy begins to object. "Don't start," I say. "She just saw me blow up a machine. If she hasn't figured it out yet, she will soon enough."

Vivienne snorts. "That you can use magic on the machines?

Yeah, that's not a secret anymore. But you can trust me. I won't tell anyone."

"Thank you," I say, then stumble to my knees, landing next to Remy. Sweat beads on his forehead and he bleeds from several places, but Vivienne has bandaged him as best she can with pieces of cloth.

Vivienne hovers over us. "Can you heal yourselves?"

I try the healing incantation over my wrist. It manages to slow the bleeding but leaves me gasping for breath. If it were just a wound, I could do it. But with poison in the mix too . . .

Real fear prickles over me, turning my body cold. I don't think I've ever felt this frail in my life.

My vision begins to blur. "We're too weak. The arrows were poisoned."

"Then you're getting up and moving. Now," she orders. Vivienne pulls me to my feet and leans me against the wall, then does the same for Remy. We both lean on her, making a very awkward and slow trek through the tunnels.

I'm not so sure we're going to make it. Without another Magi to remove the poison, we're done for.

Halfway to our hideout, I hear a familiar cry. The world before my eyes is blurry, but the bright red hue of my sister's hair is unmistakable. A strong arm wraps around my waist and helps me the rest of the way.

My sister's healing spell moves around me as we walk, forcing out the poison, then healing my wounds. I choke back a cry and grit my teeth when her magic pulls the arrow from my back. But soon, that is healed over too.

We enter our hideout to find Aro standing near the door, a bit dazed and staring at his hands.

"You're all right," he says, pulling me into a tight embrace as

Owen and Vivienne help Remy to his room. He looks much better than he did a few minutes ago.

But Zandria faces me, her anger pulling me away from Aro.

"What were you thinking?" she cries. "We had plenty of weapons. I told you it was dangerous to keep pulling the same trick over and over again." She throws her hands up. "You and Remy could've been killed!"

Her words are a slap in the face, but it still doesn't escape my notice that she didn't mention Vivienne.

"You're right," I say. "Darian must've guessed where we'd strike next. Remy . . . he sensed something was off, but I decided to go ahead with the raid anyway."

"It was foolish," she says. "We need to diversify our strategy."

"I can help with that," Vivienne says. "I have lots of ideas of places we can raid to make the royals nervous." She grins wickedly.

"So can I," Aro says.

"We'll work on revamping our strategy in the morning," I say. "Now I think we all need some sleep. It's been a long night."

Zandria's fists are still balled at her side, but she gradually uncurls her fingers. "Fine. I'm going to go check on Remy," she says.

"He's much better now," Vivienne calls after her, but Zandria ignores her. She shrugs. "See you in the morning, Aissa."

As she leaves for the room we've designated for guests, I turn to Aro. I screwed up tonight, and I can't afford to do that. Aro can see the tension building within me as we enter our room.

"Aissa, it's all right. Everyone makes mistakes," Aro says, pulling me closer. I yank my arm away.

"But I don't. I *can't*," I say. I'm too angry with myself to let him comfort me now.

Aro frowns. "We all know the stakes are very high. Beating yourself up over it isn't going to help."

"I made the call on what to raid tonight; I'm responsible." I pace the tiny room. "I've wanted Zandria to lead with me, but her heart just doesn't seem to be in it."

Aro stops me by placing his hands on my shoulders. He leans down to press his lips to my cheek. It's not until that moment that I realize I'm crying. Then suddenly, I can't seem to stop. He wraps his arms around me, pulling me down with him onto the pillows. Then he kisses away every last tear until I finally fall asleep.

TONIGHT ZANDRIA AND REMY ARE RESCU-
ing another Magi from the dungeons, while
Owen and I are returning from another raid. This
time, at Vivienne's suggestion, we raided a mining
shop and stole as much havani as possible. I've sealed it
up in a metal box to carry because even just holding the stuff
in its glass containers nauseates me.

My sister is still angry at me. And this time, rightly so. If normal
arrows struck us, we could've healed our wounds with a healing
spell. But the poison . . . that was Darian's idea, I'm certain of it.
He knows our weaknesses. I've been so focused on needing to do
something that I wasn't willing to hear Zandria's warning in time.
I need to remember that my own ideas are not the only ones that
may have merit, and I've been discounting hers for weeks, writing
her off as too broken to think clearly. If I want things back the way
they once were, I need to start treating her as a real partner again.

We're halfway back to the alley with the tunnel entrance, our
spoils in our packs, when something halts me in my tracks. I signal to Owen to hold, narrowing my eyes at the darkness. It's been
raining for the last few days and everything is soaked. The rain
picked up a few minutes ago, hurtling to the ground, and through
it something down the street caught my eye.

It almost looked like the figure of a person, outlined by the
pouring rain.

"What do you see?" Owen whispers, staring at the darkness
over my shoulder.

"I'm not sure yet," I say.

Moments later, I blink, and suddenly a person walks onto
the street. They must've realized the rain would give them away

under a shield spell. In weather like this, a silencing spell is much more useful.

The big question is, who is this mysterious Magi? They wear a heavy cloak with the hood pulled up over their head, so we can't see their face. My heart leaps into my throat. The Magi we've rescued have all agreed to either help with our missions and raids or remain in hiding until they're called on. It's unlikely one of them would be taking a stroll through the city on a rainy evening. Could it be Darian, out doing something nefarious? Or someone else?

Owen whispers, "That's another Magi. No one else could've just appeared on the street like that."

"Yes, and we're going to follow them. If more Magi are here in the city, we need to know." Maybe it's simply a passing Magi, and we can recruit them to join the Alchemist Alliance. We can use all the help we can get.

The figure walks casually, like they know where they're headed. We keep a good distance behind, but still close enough that we can see the path they take. My curiosity rises with every step. Could there be another group of Magi hiding in Palinor like we are? Maybe they fled the destruction of the Chambers. Or were they posted here and didn't know what else to do once their home base was obliterated? Since we've never been explicitly told who else was stationed here in Palinor—and there must have been others besides us and the baker's family—that seems more and more possible.

Excitement worms its way through me in just the way I shouldn't let it. The figure may turn out to be Darian after all. Though it would be useful to know more about his movements and machinations. I can tell Owen is brimming over with curiosity too, but he's remained quiet. We've warned him about Darian; he understands the stakes and the risks we take returning to the city.

He also understands how necessary it is.

Magic fizzes in my blood, adrenaline sending it into over-drive. I know this city like the back of my hand. I own these streets. The stranger won't be able to lose me, even if it becomes clear I'm following them.

The figure finally stops at a small house in the north section of town, not far from where the miner's shop and a few other tradespeople of lower rank reside. They approach the back door, glancing back as they pass a lit window that bathes the drenched traveler in warm, buttery light for just a moment. My breath catches when I recognize the man's face.

Isaiah Gaville.

So he's finally returned to Palinor. That means the clock is now ticking on our mission for the Alchemist Alliance. It will be nearly impossible to build bridges between the Magi and Technocrats when all Isaiah wants to do is burn the world down.

The Anvil will crush me before I let him do that.

When we reach our hideout, I immediately call for my sister and Remy. Owen is hard at my heels, confused by why I feel this news is so urgent to deliver.

He has never met the Magi leader. He doesn't have a full understanding of what Isaiah wants to do. For all that Owen is as a good fighter and excellent spellcaster, he's sorely lacking in practical experience. But he will be able to view this development more objectively than I, my sister, and Remy can.

"What's wrong, Aissa?" Zandria comes out of the sparring room with Remy and Vivienne.

"Isaiah's in Palinor," I say.

Remy's expression goes through several stages. Surprise to happiness to dismay. "Did you speak to him?"

I scoff. "Of course not. We didn't exactly part under good terms." I glance at Aro as he ventures into the hall as well. "He has no doubt realized who freed one of his prisoners."

Zandria frowns. "We should speak with him together. We're safer in numbers."

"And Aro and Vivienne need to stay here. Safely away from him." I know our leader wouldn't hesitate to make an example of us—and especially them—if he felt it necessary. I'm not risking my life or Aro's life on that.

"Agreed," Remy says, glancing at Vivienne. The look he gives her makes me wonder fleetingly if he might actually be concerned for her safety. She was pivotal in saving our lives the other night during the botched raid, and he's clearly been warming up to her.

"If we leave now, we might be able to intercept him while he's still in the city," I say. "The rest of the Magi must be hidden somewhere in the woods, and no more than a day's travel away."

Zandria grabs her pack and the rune-carved short sword she got from the Sanctuary's royal tomb. She shrugs. "Just in case I need it," she says. My own short sword is already strapped to my leg. Remy shakes his head.

"I know we're at odds with him right now, but he's still my father. He won't attack us," he says.

Zandria and I exchange a significant look. "We're not convinced of that."

Remy doesn't answer and instead heads out of the base.

I turn to Aro. "Stay here, and even if you hear someone at the door, do not open it. We have the key. No one else will."

"Be safe," he says, pulling me to him and kissing me softly. Warmth fills me from head to toe as I lean into him.

Zandria groans, and I break off the kiss just in time to see her following Remy out the door. Vivienne laughs.

"She really isn't a fan, is she?" Vivienne says.

I release Aro's hand. "No, it's hard for her to see any Technocrat in a positive light. Aro most of all."

Vivienne's face quickly sobers. "I can understand that."

I follow Zandria and Remy, and we make our way to the surface quickly. With our cloaks up to ward off the rain, we hurry toward the sector of town where Owen and I last glimpsed Isaiah. We approach the house I saw him enter just in time to see Isaiah walking away from it.

"There he is," I hiss, and my companions suck their breath in sharply. We hurry to intercept him before he disappears down an alleyway. His eyes widen when he sees us approaching, then his expression quickly becomes a scowl.

Isaiah strides up to us purposely. "I see you found me." He gives us all a once-over, his eyes lingering on his son. "What is it you want? You've made it clear you're not working with the rest of your people."

"We want to know what you're doing in Palinor," I say through gritted teeth.

Isaiah smiles. "Advancing my plans, of course. To free our prisoners and unite all the Magi." He looks at Zandria and Remy. "You're welcome to join me."

"You're still planning to make examples out of the Technocrats you've captured outside the city walls?" I shiver but do my best not to let it show. Now more than ever, it's critical that Isaiah not believe me weak.

He tilts his head. "Minus one prisoner." He narrows his eyes at me. "One you took a particular interest in."

I shrug. "I can't imagine what you mean."

"That's it?" Remy says. "That's your whole plan? What if it doesn't work?"

"That's true," Zandria says. "The Technos are cruel. They won't care if a few of their people die."

"And Darian isn't just going to release the prize prisoners he needs for his own plans without a fight," I add.

"Darian doesn't have any prize prisoners. I don't know what you think you heard or saw, but you were gravely mistaken." Isaiah scowls deeper. "The negotiation is proving harder than I'd hoped. But I have a backup plan."

Zandria folds her arms over her chest, though the keen interest in her eyes is unmistakable. I worry that the only thing preventing her from joining in Isaiah's plans is fear of what Aro dying will mean for me.

It chills me more than I'm prepared for.

"What is this backup plan, Father?" Remy asks.

"We will sink the city."

Shock steals my voice for a few beats too long. Zandria recovers first. "How?"

Isaiah raises an eyebrow. "I have more than enough Magi survivors gathered. We'll combine our magics and create a massive earthquake. We may not be able to touch their walls or machines with our spells, but nothing can stop us from digging into the earth beneath their feet." The fervor in Isaiah's eyes is disturbing. He usually seems cold as ice, but in this moment he's running fever hot.

The destruction of the Chambers has scarred him in some deep way. Making him willing to go to lengths he never would've considered before. The spell he's speaking of must be powerful indeed, and to join all those Magi together in casting a single spell is a dangerous, risky move. For more than just the Technocrats. I've seen the Magi who are left. Many of them are injured. Many more were not trained to fight physically or magically. They're in no condition to cast a spell of that magnitude. He could do some of them permanent harm.

It's a desperate move. From a man desperate for revenge.

I remember not long ago Zandria compared me to him. My

drive to be a good spy, to bring glory and power to my people, blinded me to the truth for far too long. Now, between Aro and the Alchemist Alliance, my eyes have been opened.

But Isaiah is completely unwilling to hear the truth.

"That's crazy," I say at the same time Zandria says, "That's brilliant."

I give her a sharp glance, but she ignores me.

"As I said before, if you wish to join us and help ruin the Technocrats, I'd welcome you all. Despite your past transgressions." He glances at me. I can't help smirking. "With our numbers so few, it's more important than ever that all Magi band together against our common enemy."

Zandria and Remy exchange a look—one I do not like at all.

"We'll consider it," Remy says. "But I wish you'd heed what we've told you about Darian. We're not lying, and we're not mistaken." Remy lowers his voice. "You taught me well, Father. Do you really think I'd make a mistake like this? Falsely accuse one of our own if it were not wholly warranted?"

Isaiah doesn't waver in his determination. He really is made of steel and ice. Strange how he and the Technocrat king and queen have that in common.

Isaiah meets his son's gaze directly. "I know Darian. I've known him for his entire life. He is the most dedicated Magi I've ever met. Anything you may have mistaken for betrayal was simply a part of his cover with the Technocrats. A ruse. He's in a sensitive position there; this would not be the first time he's taken steps to preserve appearances."

My mouth drops open, but I quickly snap it shut. Of course this wouldn't be the first time Darian has "preserved appearances." I shouldn't be surprised. Who knows how long he's been experimenting on other Magi?

His betrayal is definitely not some ruse. It's the only true thing about the man. But judging by the expressions on Zandria's and Remy's faces, it almost seems as though they want to believe that could be the case. Alarm bells ring in the back of my brain. I need to get them away from Isaiah and remind them of all Darian has done to us before Isaiah convinces them I'm wrong. For Anvil's sake, Darian murdered our parents.

"That's an absurd lie, and you should know it," I say, clenching my fists hard enough that my nails dig into my palms. "And that plan is insane. You'll kill everyone if you sink the city. Including us."

Isaiah's eyes glow. "The plan is perfectly sound. It will ensure the reign of the Technocrats comes to a complete and unequivocal end. There will not be many survivors. And we can pick off any that do survive at the edges of the sunken city if they try to escape. The Magi will finally resume our rightful place. We can heal these lands and restore balance. This has always been our goal. Now we are on the verge of success."

His voice is frighteningly calm. I grab my sister by the arm. "We're leaving."

But Zandria doesn't budge just yet. My heart sinks into my boots.

"If we want to find you, where are you and the Magi?" Zandy asks.

Isaiah smiles. "In the woods, to the west and deep enough that the real trees still prevail."

She nods, and glances at Remy again. He stares at his father. I yank on Zandria's arm this time, and that manages to break Isaiah's hold. As we finally take our leave, Isaiah calls after us.

"Consider this seriously. Because I'm very serious about what we plan to do."

I shiver under my cloak, then practically drag Zandria and Remy away from Isaiah. It isn't long before my sister shrugs me off.

"Where are you going, Aissa?" she asks. "This isn't even the way back to—"

"I know," I hiss. "I don't want Isaiah to have any idea where our hideout is. He might get ideas about recapturing Aro. Then he'd discover Vivienne. And Leon." I throw my hands up. Zandria raises an eyebrow at me, but Remy scowls at the ground.

"He definitely wouldn't be thrilled with all the Technocrats you've befriended," Zandria says huffily. "It's unwise."

"Well, he is wrong about wanting to sink the city. That's ridiculous and dangerous," I retort, checking over my shoulder. Isaiah hasn't moved far from where we left him.

"I don't know. I think my father has a point, Aissa," Remy says.

"About what?" I bristle.

"What if this is the only way to end the Technos' rule? They have a stranglehold on these lands, and they bring destruction wherever they go. His plan may be a big move, but it would end them."

"I agree," Zandria says.

I gawk at them in horror. "What about the Alliance?

My sister shrugs. "All the Alliance has to offer besides the library of spells is a dream. Living in harmony with them is a nice thought, but it's not reasonable, Aissa. It never was."

"Not reasonable?" My voice takes on a higher pitch. I can't believe what I'm hearing. "I thought we agreed to undermine the Technocrats. Turn the people against them?"

"And how long will that take?" Zandria says. "The Armory already spent decades working a long game. Look where it got them."

Remy nods. "The same could happen to us. There isn't time for a long-term plan. We need to take quick, decisive, drastic action. Now."

"But we know the Technos aren't all bad! It's the ones in power who need to be taken out, not everyone else!" I try to keep my voice down, but it's getting harder. Beyond my sister and Remy, I can see Isaiah standing under an awning, watching us curiously. My entire body feels like it's on fire. "What about Vivienne? She just saved our lives the other night!"

Regret flickers over Remy's face for a fleeting moment, but then his expression hardens again.

Zandria folds her arms across her chest. "She's still one of them."

"She can leave the city before we attack," Remy says.

"How can you even consider this? He's working with Darian—the man who murdered our parents and tried to kill us too, for Anvil's sake!" Fury builds inside my chest.

"Yes, my father is wrong about Darian, we're not arguing that point," Remy says. He exchanges a glance with Zandria. "But I think his solution is what we need."

"You're seriously going to switch sides after talking to your daddy for five minutes?" I spit out.

Remy's face grows red. "Look—I'm going to the Magi camp. You and anyone else you want to live need to leave the city too. And soon."

Hot rage billows within me, but I hold it inside. "What about the Magi we've saved from the dungeons who've sworn loyalty to the Alchemist Alliance? Did what we learned at the Sanctuary have no impact on you? Mean nothing to you?"

His face softens. "Of course it did. But we still don't have enough Magi standing with us, and we're never going to be able to win all the Technos to our side. The royals will kill us as soon as listen to us."

"The only way we can reclaim this city for our own is to raze it to the ground," Zandria says.

The blood drains from my face. "Sister, we've been the Magi's Twin Daggers, to be directed by the Armory Council. We were almost forced to be Darian's Twin Daggers, to strike at both the Technocrats and our own people. Don't you see? Everyone else wants to use us. Even the Alliance created us for a purpose. This time *we* get to choose what we'll be. Please don't let Isaiah dictate the terms of your existence once again."

Zandria gives me the strangest look, and I don't know what to make of it. Part rage, part despair. All I know is that it means she's slipping away from me.

"You're right. I am deciding my own fate this time. No one—not Isaiah, Darian, or even you—gets to make that choice for me. I won't stand with the people who tortured me. Who would kill me as soon as look at me." She glances at Remy. "I'm going too. I hope you come to your senses soon, Aissa. Before it's too late."

Horror shudders through me. I can't quite wrap my head around what Zandy just said. "You can't be serious."

"Oh, I am. I get why Aro must live, though I still think the reason for it is crazy. But the rest of the Technos? They can burn in the forges for all I care."

She spins on her heel and marches toward where Isaiah waits before I can say another word. My whole body feels frozen, as if someone cast an ice spell over me.

"I should go with her," Remy says, not meeting my eyes. He hurries after my sister.

My legs feel weak, but I manage to stay upright. I knew Zandria was struggling to come to terms with what we are and how we came to be. With what the Alchemist Alliance created us to do. I've struggled with it myself. It's an enormous responsibility—if not an outright impossible one.

But those odds have never daunted us before.

I can only stare, close-lipped, as Isaiah welcomes my sister and my friend, then leads them out of the city.

I don't know if any of Isaiah's lackeys are out and about in

Palinor, so I take precautions to ensure I'm not followed back to the base. I duck down a few dark alleys and double back more than once until I'm satisfied that if anyone was following me, they'd be hopelessly lost by now. Then I finally head back toward the tunnel entrance.

Somehow I manage to keep my composure until I'm safely back underground, hidden away behind our magic-infused marble fortress. Then the dam breaks.

I slide down the wall, tears running down my face. My breath is so tight, I can't even make a sound while I cry.

But Aro senses my distress nonetheless. It feels as if my heart is breaking; perhaps our bond can share emotional pain as well as physical. He sits next to me on the floor, pulling me onto his lap. "What happened?" he whispers. "Where are Zandria and Remy?"

"They decided to join Isaiah."

I can feel Aro choke on his breath. He's as shocked as I am by the news. Then his arms wrap more tightly around me. For a moment, I let myself curl into him and the comfort there.

But comfort isn't what I need right now. It isn't going to change anything.

I disentangle myself when my tears stop flowing.

"I'm sorry, I need to be alone right now," I say. I rise and head into the makeshift room I share with Aro. He doesn't say anything, just gives me the space I requested. I know he'll be there when I need him. But right now, I have to think. Short of physically preventing her from leaving, there was nothing I could do to stop my sister from joining Isaiah's mob.

Now I understand that look she gave me. She may be covering it up with rage and sadness, but what really lies underneath is fear. It's driving her to save her own skin and cast off that unwanted—and until recently, entirely unknown—responsibility.

Opening my pack, I pull out the Alchemist Alliance journal I found in this same place so many weeks ago. Tucked inside is my parents' last letter to me and my sister, with our unique alchemical recipe on the back. I open it, smoothing it out on my knee. It's worn from being read over and over. The edges are beginning to fray.

Even our parents believed the Technocrats were beyond redemption, if this letter is any indication. But while the people who live in this city now may cheer at the Royal Victory Parade and dance at the ball, they weren't alive during the wars. They weren't the ones who wrought our destruction and devastated the world, driving us underground. They're the grandchildren and great-grandchildren of those who did. As far as they know, the Magi are little more than a myth now.

They have no idea we're still here, plotting to destroy everything they love.

To do to them what they did to us.

As much as I hate the Technocrats who are responsible for hurting us in the present—like the royals and those who aid them in their torture—the other thousands of people who live here are innocent. Sinking the city and killing them isn't justice. It isn't even revenge.

It's murder.

The Alchemist Alliance understood that. That's why they had both Technocrats and Magi in their numbers. They wanted to save their world. Prevent a tragedy from happening.

They failed. And now it falls to us to pick up the pieces and prevent a second one.

Neither the Magi nor the Technocrats are innocent, and both factions must be willing to come together. We've made some headway with the redistribution of money, but we need something more. Something bigger.

A sudden urgency fills me. I know better than to try to change

Zandy's mind again; she's as stubborn as I am. She'll have to see the truth in her own time and on her own terms. I hope it won't be too late by the time that happens.

But what worries me most is that she'll try to take more of our allies with her. This couldn't have been as spur of the moment as it seemed.

I leave my room, blowing right by Aro lingering nearby. I hurry to find Owen. He was on guard duty last I saw him before we left in search of Isaiah, and I'm relieved to find him in the tunnels still at his post. He frowns when he sees me.

"Your sister and Remy . . . they haven't returned yet," he says.

"I know." I put a hand on his shoulder. "They're letting their hatred rule them. They're abandoning the Alliance."

Owen's eyes widen. "They joined that man Isaiah?"

I sigh.

"I never thought your sister would leave you like that."

I give a sad half laugh. "Neither did I. But she has, and now we must do what we can to stop them from carrying out their plans. They're going to sink the city."

His eyes widen. He begins to say something, then stops. Then does it again. His face reddens.

"What is it?" I ask him, apprehension filling me.

"Are . . . are Zandria and Remy . . . betrothed?" Owen asks.

A surprised laugh bursts from my mouth before I can stop it. "No, not that either of them has told me, at least."

How did I not see this before? Owen has a crush on my sister. They've grown closer ever since we rescued him from his island. The poor boy. She must not return his feelings. If she did, I know my sister well enough to know she'd have said or done something to try to bring him with her.

"I'm sorry, she's a terrible flirt. And she loves to practice. I'm sure she had no idea that you have . . . feelings for her."

At this Owen's face reddens deeper, and he stares at his shoes. "I see."

Now I feel terrible. "Would you like something to take your mind off this?" He nods curtly.

"Excellent. I have a plan."

CHAPTER 34

NOW THAT ZANDRIA AND REMY ARE GONE,
I've freed Leon from his cell. I never thought
it was necessary to hold him, and the only people
who objected are no longer here. For the last few
days, he has been coming and going at will and helping
us strategize. Tonight, we've been solidifying our plan.

That plan is twofold: build an alliance with Technocrat allies
in the city and shore up the city's defenses—magically. The walls
won't stand if the Magi yank the earth out from under them, no
matter how strong the barriers are physically. But my magic can
help them withstand the onslaught of whatever the Magi may try.

There's only one catch: If the Magi cast their spell, strength-
ened a hundredfold with all those spellcasters joining their power
together, and the city still stands, Isaiah and the rest of the Magi
will know immediately magic is involved.

Impossible magic. My magic.

It will mean exposing the secret I've guarded closely ever since
I was a child, to the people I was ordered to keep it from. And
the only one who could undo my magic is Zandria. If she casts a
counterspell, she'll be outing both of us to Isaiah and risking his
wrath and retribution. If she doesn't, Isaiah's plan will fail. It's a
risky bet, but I have to believe her loyalty to her family will ultimately win out over vengeance.

I only hope my faith is not misplaced.

"I'll bolster the defenses at each section of the walls," I say,
indicating on the large diagram of the city we've rendered on the
table. "Then I'll use the drainage tunnels to shore up the underside
of the city as well. I'll have to work at night to avoid suspicion. I'll

only be able to cover so much ground each night too. A spell this large will take time and a lot of energy to cast."

Not to mention this will be the first time I've cast this spell. It was one I found in the Sanctuary, a semipermanent incantation that the user doesn't need to continuously cast in order to maintain, like our shield spells require. But it takes more out of a Magi in exchange. I lean into Aro, who stands behind me. His presence is steadying but can never make up for my sister's absence and betrayal. "I need to make it strong enough to withstand the magic of a hundred casters. That's no small task."

"There are people in the city who could help," Vivienne says. "Between the money the Alliance gave back to the people and the rumors I've been spreading, there are many who only need a little push to join us."

"It's true," Leon agrees. "Ever since you and your sister made a staircase appear in the center of the city, there have been rumors of the old legends coming back to life. There are those who are sympathetic to your cause, who don't necessarily agree the magic users should've been hunted down, and still more who wouldn't mind seeing the king and queen overthrown."

"We can rally them when needed," Vivienne says.

"We'll choose those we think would be most interested in joining a new Alchemist Alliance. We can test them to ensure loyalty," Leon says.

"That will be your assignment then. But whatever you do, be sure not to let on what the Magi numbers are and where our hideout is located. Always take precautions when coming here," I say.

"What can I do?" Aro asks.

He has asked me this many times since Isaiah returned to Palinor and is never satisfied with the answer. The truth is, I'm terrified for him. Being in the same city as Darian made me nervous before, but I saw the wisdom in occasionally bringing Aro on a mission. Now that Isaiah's back . . . two powerful Magi who want to kill Aro roaming the city is too many.

"You need to stay here out of sight and focus on deciphering the Heartsong. If we can complete it, that would be huge," I insist as he opens his mouth to argue once again. "You're my biggest weakness. If Isaiah captures and kills you, I'll die too. The city will sink, and everyone in it will be crushed to death. The stakes are too high. I know you don't like it, but it's too risky right now."

Frustration is clear in Aro's tense posture. "My parents tried to keep me under lock and key. It didn't work. Yes, of course, I'll keep working on the Heartsong. But this is as much my fight—more, even—and I won't stand by and let everyone else take all the risks."

I place a hand on his arm, but this time it doesn't calm him. "You must. I know it chafes, but it's for the best. When it comes time to confront your parents, we'll need you most. That will come after we stop Isaiah's plan."

His hands clench at his sides. "Stop acting as if I'm weak. I'm perfectly capable of protecting myself. We've trained together; you know full well I can fight."

I take a deep breath, trying to keep myself from getting angry with him. "All I'm saying is that there are people out there actively hunting you to kill you. *Multiple* people on both sides of this war. You're too recognizable."

"Then change my face like you change your own! Palinor is my kingdom too."

The blood drains from my face. I've considered changing his appearance before. But what makes him a risk is also one of the few things that might offer him protection if he were brought back to the Palace. The truth is, I'd be scared either way. And that would be a distraction. I'd be more likely to make a fatal mistake. "Aro . . . that's not . . . Look, can we talk about this later? I'm sorry, I didn't realize what this was doing to you."

He deflates when he sees the others staring at us. "Fine. I'll just go to sleep. You clearly don't need me for this."

"Aro, I—" He leaves the room before I can finish the sentence. The others give me pitying looks, and I clear my throat. Appearing weak is the last thing I need to do in front of the other Alliance members.

But before I can get back on track, I'm stunned to hear the magic-infused marble door to our hideout sliding open. I automatically put my hand in my pocket to make sure I still have the key.

"What in the forges . . ." I hurry into the main hall, and my heart leaps when I see a familiar cloaked form standing in front of the closing door. "Catoria!" I exclaim.

She lowers the hood of her cloak and glances around. "I see you've made good use of what the Alliance left behind. You've certainly made yourselves at home." I detect a tiny hint of disapproval at what we've done with the place, but I'm so relieved to see her that I don't care.

"Catoria, what brings you here? It's good to see you." I clasp her hands in greeting and lead her into the war room where the others peek out curiously. Owen recognizes her immediately, but Vivienne and Leon regard her warily. She's clearly not a Technocrat, and despite their recent commitment to the Alliance, they've long been told magic users are terrifying.

Her eyes skim over the newcomers like she's opening them up and peering at their insides. Then she breaks into a smile. "I see you've enlisted some Technocrats. Good, good. That's what the Alliance was aiming for. Bringing us all together."

"Catoria, this is Vivienne and Leon. We rescued Vivienne from the dungeons, and Leon is a friend of Aro's." The two greet Catoria and she tilts her head back.

"I'm heartened to see this," she says. "Now, where is your sister? And Remy?" She glances at the diagram of the city on the table.

"They're gone," I say quietly.

"Are they returning soon?"

I shake my head.

Concern flits across her face. "Aissa, where are they? We need them if we are to succeed and renew the Alchemist Alliance."

"I know. Isaiah . . . he persuaded them to join him in his plans. His negotiations with the Technocrats to ransom the prisoners he collected aren't going well. When they finally fail, he plans to use all the remaining Magi he's brought together to cast a spell to sink the city."

Catoria frowns deeply. "What would possess him to do that?"

"Hate," I say simply. "He hates the Technocrats with every fiber of his being. Just like Zandy and I used to."

"That's a fool's errand. He'd be destroying the very city he wishes to take over!"

"I tried reasoning with him; he won't listen. But the others listened to what he said. They've left to join him."

"Well, we must get them back." She bustles over to the table to examine the map we've been working with. "Good, good. I'm glad we still have you, Aissa. I'm afraid the protection of this entire city and its occupants now rests on your shoulders."

I glance down, and my chest constricts. As if I needed any more pressure than what I've already put on myself . . .

My eyes snap back up. "Why exactly are you here now, Catoria?"

"I'm ancient. I've lived much longer than any one person has a right to. My role was to teach you when you appeared. Now, you're here. I'm not needed at the Sanctuary anymore. It's safe underground."

"All right," I say, still not quite understanding.

She stands up straighter, taking a deep breath in. "I've been in hiding for decades. I want to live what's left of my life well. I need to taste the sun and feel the breeze, maybe die for my cause if it becomes necessary. Standing side by side with the new Alliance while we face our foes and bridge these divides is the only thing I wish to be doing."

I surprise everyone by throwing my arms around Catoria's neck. I didn't even expect to do it, but I'm so upset by the loss of Zandria and Remy that having Catoria as an ally is exactly what I needed. Even with all she's taught us, her knowledge of magic far exceeds ours. She's a formidable foe.

And I can't wait to fight by her side.

After making introductions, I show Catoria more of what we have planned. We've fashioned a makeshift workshop out of one section of the empty library. Leon and I have been working to construct Trojan horses that we will plant right under the Technocrats' noses. We were inspired by the Technocrats' cunning machine in the storehouse that nearly killed Remy, Vivienne, and me.

We learned many spells during our time at the Sanctuary. They've proved useful, but until recently I didn't know how I'd use one type in particular: bottling spells to deploy at a later date, when the bottle is broken to release what's inside. This was one of the long-lost spells, the kind the ancient Magi used when they could cast their magic on all things. The Technocrats—and Darian—will never see it coming.

"Here's where we've been working on," I tell Catoria, followed by Leon and Vivienne. I'm fairly certain Leon only accompanies us to be sure Catoria doesn't touch his work and break it. I doubt she would, but he's as overbearing and protective of his work as ever. Now, I understand why.

The worktable is strewn with all sorts of nuts and bolts and gears and parts Leon has secreted in here with him. He can't be seen working on this project in his own shop. I pluck one small machine off the table. It's not much bigger than the mechanical hearts Leon had me making back when I still maintained my cover as his apprentice. I hold it up for Catoria to see, and Leon grunts. He doesn't say anything out loud, but the look he gives me says quite clearly, *Be careful with that or I'm going to get angry.*

The little machine is small and flat and has six tiny retractable legs similar to the seekers.

Catoria peers at it. "Fascinating. And what does this do?"

I pick up a sword lying nearby on the table. "I can attach these little machines to swords and just about anything else with a touch of a button." I press one of two small buttons on the underside of the machine. Its legs shoot out and clamp around the blade. Setting the sword down on the table again, I pry open a chamber of the small machine to show her the inside. There's a tiny vial made of thin glass. "I'll bottle a spell inside the glass. Then when the machine is in place—such as affixed to a weapon—I'll press this button."

I press the second button on the open lid to demonstrate. At first nothing happens, but the second I move the sword, a tiny hammer smashes the air.

"If it had been closed, it would have broken the vial to pieces and released the spell. I'm planning to put freezing spells, dizzy spells, sleeping spells, and more in these and sneak them into their weapon stores around the city."

"Could you do a fire spell?" Owen suggests.

"We could," I say slowly. "But the point of these is to delay and prevent them from attacking. If we want to bring Technocrats to our side, we're better off using spells that won't kill them."

Owen considers. "Maybe we should have some prepared just in case?"

Leon huffs. "If you're going to start killing people with these, I won't make any more of them." He folds his arms across his chest and stares down Owen. Owen makes a valiant effort to meet the Master Mechanic's gaze but soon looks away.

Leon Salter is still not a man to be trifled with.

"Don't worry, Leon." I say. "Our goal is not to kill. The Alliance's mission is to heal."

"Well said," Catoria interjects. "May I see?" She points to the little machine. I remove it from the sword and pass it to her so she can examine it more closely. "Brilliant idea."

She gives it back and I place it on the table. "We thought so. But if Isaiah and the others are planning to sink the city, then we won't have much reason to use them. We'll be too busy fighting our own kind instead."

"Couldn't we use them on the Magi too, if we need to slow them without killing them?" Vivienne says.

"We can. They'll be able to cancel the spells and overcome them more easily than a Technocrat, but it would slow them down. Good idea, Viv." Then I frown. "We'll just need a better understanding of where they'll be gathering to cast the sinking spell—then we could set a bunch of these as a trap, maybe in the trees." I turn to Leon. "You can make trip wires, can't you?"

Leon unfolds his arms. "Give me two days and I can craft you an entire net of trip wires that will work with these machines."

"Perfect," I say. I'm about to move on, but Catoria draws near to Leon. He raises an eyebrow at her but doesn't move a muscle.

"You make the machines for the king and queen, don't you?" she asks him.

"I'm the Master Mechanic."

She tilts her head. "Why would you betray them like this? I'm sure Aissa has vetted you, but I'm curious. What brought you here?"

Leon swallows hard. "My daughter was born Heartless. She didn't live for more than a handful of years. But she was the most precious thing in the world to me." He gestures at me. "When I heard that she healed a Heartless, I had to know more. I came here to beg her to heal the rest of them. They're innocent. They deserve a real chance at life."

Catoria bows her head. "I'm truly saddened by your loss. I must apologize on behalf of the original Alchemist Alliance. It was the work of an overeager assistant that brought on the Heartless curse. I wish we could take it back."

Leon regards her with surprise. An apology from a Magi is probably one of the last things he ever expected he'd get.

Catoria reaches for his hand—the mechanical one. To my great surprise, Leon doesn't bite off her head. "What happened here? Did this also lead you to the Alliance?"

This time Leon's jaw clenches. "It was long ago."

But Catoria's inquisitive gaze manages to loosen his lips. Is this some tricky spell she's casting, or is he really feeling talkative tonight? I hardly know, but I'm glad to hear his story at last.

"I was a fool. I was a gifted mechanic, apprenticed to the best in the city. But I was not rich, and neither was my family. My daughter had been born earlier that year, and while we had managed to afford the mechanical heart that kept her alive, in only one month's time, she'd need another surgery to replace it. That was expensive enough to be out of reach. One day, an impressive order came into the shop. It was for an extravagant mechanimal for the Victory Parade. An elephant, enormous and studded with jewels. The then-Master Mechanic and I worked on it for two solid weeks before it was done. We brought it before the newly crowned king and queen, and they were delighted with the machine. The queen in particular examined it thoroughly. Then we brought it to the storage house on the palace grounds. My master only left me alone with it for a minute, but it was enough for temptation to take hold. I quickly pried off one, single diamond and slipped it into my pocket."

Leon clears his throat, breaking the spell for a moment.

"That diamond was more than enough to pay for the operation my daughter needed. I thought I had gotten away with it—why would they miss such a tiny little jewel on such a large machine? It could have easily fallen off. But the queen noticed. And she called the Master Mechanic before her to answer for it. At first, he was flabbergasted. His work was always done with care. It was not likely a jewel would merely fall out of one of his settings. Then he remembered those few fleeting moments I had been alone, polishing the mechanimal in the storage shed. He wasn't about to lose his best customer, or his head, for me. I was brought before the king and queen." Leon scoffs. "It was terrifying. I thought I'd gotten away with it and there I was, caught red-handed. I confessed, begging for leniency because of my daughter. Stealing from the royals is a capital crime, and the punishment is death. But the queen is merciful."

A sense of dread at his words shivers over me. My eyes meet Vivienne's. The pulse at the base of her throat visibly throbs.

We both know exactly how merciful Queen Cyrene actually is.

"The queen allowed me to keep my life, but she took my hand and foot as payment of the debt I owed." Leon stares at his mechanical hand and shrugs. "My Master Mechanic did the best he could crafting these for me, under orders he was not to use anything finer than plain steel. He forged and fitted them on me, and I've had them ever since."

Before anyone else can say a word, Catoria puts her hands on either side of Leon's face and kisses his forehead, despite his deep scowl. "You have suffered greatly. But it is not for nothing."

"I'm so sorry, Leon. I had no idea," I say. Then something else occurs to me. "Wait a moment. When . . . when did your daughter die, exactly?" When he first told me about her, I had assumed her death was because she could not take the repeated surgeries, but now . . .

He looks me right in the eyes. "The money from the diamond covered two surgeries. We saved as best we could, but I was still an apprentice mechanic and the pay was just enough to cover food and lodging. She didn't make it to her third birthday."

Vivienne gasps, and Owen is visibly distressed. Catoria doesn't seem surprised at all.

As for me, in that moment, as Leon's eyes burn into mine, I know the truth. He blames the queen. And he will happily watch her world burn.

After we've concluded our strategy session and the others have dispersed, I pull Catoria aside in the war room. I take the ancient parchment I believe to be the Heartsong out from its hiding place in the wall and gently spread it out on the table. "We found it."

Catoria's eyes widen as she examines the runes. "The Heartsong." Then she frowns. "Where?"

"Hidden in Anassa's journal. She must have found it and placed it there for safekeeping. As you can see, it's damaged. I did manage to darken some of the text temporarily with a spell and copied it here," I say, pulling out a second, newer sheet of paper. "Aro and I have been studying this, searching for some hint as to what the missing portion contains. It looks like it intermittently uses magic and then weaves in alchemicals. Based on the pattern of the top portion, we think it should be an alchemical rune, but we're not sure which one."

"And you were hoping I might know?" Catoria says.

"We were."

She sits at the table, considering the original and the copy, nodding her head. "Well done preserving this." She runs a finger over the missing corner. "I will need to examine this more thoroughly. Perhaps Aro can assist? He does have a knack for alchemicals."

"He'd be delighted, I'm certain of it."

"Do keep in mind that even if we decipher this, the spell will only work for you and your sister. Any Magi can heal skin and bone, but only those such as yourselves can do this." She presses her fingers to the old parchment reverently. "Healing the Heartless might finally close the rift between our people."

My magic aches to begin practicing this spell immediately. "Thank you for your help, Catoria."

It's late, and she heads for the makeshift room we assigned her earlier, taking the copy of the spell with her to study.

If we can complete the spell, we could use it to accomplish so much. But I can't deny that what excites me most about it is what I might be able to do for Aro. I could give him a real heart. And he could leave that terrible contraption behind for good.

With Catoria here, we just might be able to succeed. For the first time in days, there's a smile on my lips and hope in my heart.

CATORIA HAS BEEN HERE FOR SEVERAL
days now and has made herself right at home.
She and Aro have been thick as thieves night and
day, huddled over an old alchemical textbook.

Aro still isn't happy with me for refusing to give him
a mission topside, but having Catoria here and making some
forward progress on the Heartsong has lightened his mood.

Apparently, the spell must be performed by slowly adding certain alchemicals one by one and in a very specific order between casting each section of the spell. Once the last alchemical is added—the one that's missing—the combination will transform the damaged tissue back into a heart. Or in the case of the Heartless, regrow one.

Last night, Aro told me he believed they were close to determining which alchemical was the correct final one. He and Catoria have been hard at work all morning, while I've been sparring with Owen. He was already adept with a staff and sword when we found him, but he's been getting very good with his namesake, the poleaxe, too. Zandria's absence has been troubling for us both, and sparring together is giving us a much-needed outlet.

It doesn't hurt that Owen is funny and nowhere near as self-righteous as Remy, which makes him much more pleasant company.

We've been training together for the last hour, in many ways like Zandria and I used to do. I've created a makeshift obstacle course similar to what we once had in our secret basement room. We run, leap, tumble, all while casting spells, with the added challenge of evading attacks from the other. By the time Aro appears in the doorway with news, we're breathless and ragged.

Aro's excitement shifts almost imperceptibly to a frown before quickly returning to joy. Could he be a little jealous that I've been training with Owen?

"We did it," he says. "We've figured out the last alchemical in the Heartsong."

I step forward and take his hand. "You're certain?"

"Absolutely. We've tested many variations and none produce a restorative effect but this one. It needs the full spell to heal a heart, but Catoria used it to heal an injured rat we caught in the sewers. No other combination could achieve that."

My heart pounds in my ears. We've done it. At last. "Send Vivienne to tell Leon. He knows what to do."

Aro grins widely and ducks away.

Once we took Leon into our full confidence, we told him about the Heartsong. He was determined to help in any way he could. He's already identified a few families who'd be willing to have their Heartless children undergo the procedure. He didn't tell them it's a spell, but with their children only able to survive another surgery or two, they're desperate and will try anything.

I only hope Aro and Catoria are right and that we don't disappoint.

The rewards of success are many and mighty. If we fail, we risk unraveling all the goodwill the new Alchemist Alliance has been building in Palinor.

That evening, Vivienne returns with Leon and a boy of about ten in tow. Vivienne holds his hand and leads him into one of the makeshift bedrooms. When she removes his blindfold, his eyes widen as he glances around curiously.

Aro and Catoria have set up supplies with the correct

alchemicals lined up in the order I need to work them into the spell. My hands are suddenly slick. I'm really going to do this. I trust Catoria, but I also know she created the alchemical compound that led to the Heartless. What if she's wrong again?

"Are you going to fix me?" the boy asks. He has dark hair that's a little too long and shadows below his eyes. He doesn't yet have smoky lines snaking up his neck or down his arms, a telltale sign of havani poisoning, which is one less thing I need to worry about fixing.

"Yes," I say, more confidently than I feel.

"Thank you," he says. He fidgets, like he's not quite sure what to do with his hands.

"Can you lay down on the cot and remove your shirt, please?" I say as Catoria joins us. She's going to cast a sleeping spell on the child while I work the Heartsong.

The boy does as I ask, and within moments, he's fast asleep. Catoria remains, just in case the spell wears off before I'm finished. Aro is on my other side, ready to hand me alchemicals for each section of the Heartsong.

I should be elated, but instead my chest feels strange and tight. We finally can cast this spell that's eluded us for weeks. But it isn't the same without Zandria here. We should be doing this together.

I swallow my heartache down and begin to hum. Over the last few days, I committed the spell to memory. Still, I glance at the paper I've copied it onto just to be sure I don't make a mistake.

We're testing this on a real live person. Someone who wants, desperately, to live freely. There's no room for error here.

Magic swells inside my chest at the behest of the spell, spinning down my arms and pooling in my hands. The familiar warmth is energizing. I place my hands over the boy's chest, muttering the incantation all the while. In some ways, the Heartsong reminds me a little of the Binding rite, only much more complex. I reach the end of the first part of the spell and Aro hands me a dropper containing the first alchemical. One drop of each is all I should need. I keep humming and the magic takes hold of the droplet as it falls onto the boy's chest. It fizzes and sparks in a way I didn't expect, and I almost gasp and break the spell. But I keep my hold on my magic, and now I know what to expect with the next droplet.

The magic helps the alchemical absorb into the skin over the boy's mechanical heart as I begin the second part of the spell. We continue like this, spell and droplet, fizz and spark, spell and droplet, for nine verses. With every one, the boy remains placid and sleeping, and his skin shifts and moves. His mechanical heart seems to be pushing upward, stretching his skin taut. Then it's time for the final alchemical. The moment of truth.

I squeeze the dropper, my incantation keeping tight hold of the magic threads that now circle the prone child. This time the spark turns into a blue flame, and I use the last verse to manage it, mold it, shape it into the boy's chest. Through my magic, I can feel the alchemicals combining, transforming. Regrowing a new heart in place of the mechanical one. Something about the alchemicals woven into the fabric of the spell has heightened my awareness of them and the entire process. I can sense each new artery and piece of flesh, every new drop of blood called forth into being, with a headiness I hardly know how to describe. I don't stop the incantation for a moment, even though I can tell how much this spell takes out of me.

Then, as the boy's new flesh-and-blood heart begins to beat, the old mechanical one detaches, no longer needed, and bursts through the skin on his chest. It's startling how quickly it happens, but Catoria wastes no time in removing the machine and healing the skin over his new, whole heart. Because of the repeated surgeries, most Heartless have had the ribs removed over where the mechanical heart lies for easier access and shorter surgeries. Now, Catoria heals those ribs, regrowing them to protect the new organ the Heartsong has bestowed on him. I finish my spell moments after Catoria completes hers.

A strange panic surges within me, and I place my hand on the boy's chest. A steady beat—not a mechanical tick—presses back. The boy breathes normally as if nothing at all has happened while he sleeps.

"We did it," Aro breathes, as if he can hardly believe his eyes.

"Wake him up, Catoria," I say. She casts a quick handspell that sends the boy jolting upright on the cot.

His hand immediately flies to his chest. For a moment, his eyes are wide and panicked. But when he realizes the lack of the ticktock beat that has haunted him his whole life hasn't killed him, he relaxes slightly.

"Did it work?" he asks me.

I hold up his mechanical heart and smile. "It did. You'll never need one of these again."

He laughs, rubbing his hand on his chest, trying to adjust to not having a machine there.

"What's your name?" I ask him.

"Sol," he says.

"Well, Sol, you can rest here for a while, but once we send you home, tell your parents and anyone who asks that the Alchemist Alliance saved you. And we can save the rest of the Heartless too, if they'll let us."

Aro grips Sol's arm. "You were very brave," he says. "I'm so glad—" His throat closes with emotion for a moment. "I'm so glad."

When he rises, tears shine in his eyes. I can't even fathom how he must feel right now. Everything he ever dreamed of accomplishing, and had nearly lost all hope of doing, just happened this night.

We have a cure for the Heartless. A means of saving innocents, righting a hundred-year-old wrong, and ruining Darian's plans all in one.

WHEN THE MOON IS HIGH AND MY COMPAN-

ions sleep, I press my lips to Aro's forehead and slip out of the hideout. In no time, I'm snaking through the alleyways of Palinor.

It's been ten days since my sister left. I've done this every night. Someone has to patrol the city. Someone has to protect it and put the warding spells in place. I don't know when Isaiah plans to strike, but he won't keep us waiting long. He's successfully set Magi against Magi, sister against sister. I never dreamed I'd have to protect others from my own flesh and blood.

Zandria's betrayal is a sting, lodged deep in my gut. The point is sharp and biting, and I'll never be able to dig it out. I'm angry Remy joined his father too, but not as surprised. He's a fool, though I can't wholly blame him for siding with what's left of his family. But my sister . . . I'll never understand how she could do this. She knows better than anyone what's at stake. Her captivity twisted her reason beyond recognition. Poisoned it with hatred that's seeped into her core. Isaiah will never accept what she really is. She'll have to hide it for the rest of her life or suffer the consequences.

She has turned her back on the Alchemist Alliance. She's turned her back on me.

But that doesn't mean I'll abandon my mission. On the contrary, I'm more determined than ever to stop, or at least sabotage, Isaiah's plans. Vivienne has been hard at work spreading rumors about the miraculous healing of a Heartless child at the hands of the Alchemist Alliance. People are talking. They're curious and inclined to view us favorably. Soon, we'll need to take full advantage of that goodwill.

Tonight, I'll venture into the drainage tunnels and cast another warding spell on the underbelly of this city. Once I hated this place, but now I'm risking everything and defying my own people to protect it.

The night is cool and clear, and under my cloaking spell I can walk as freely as I please. I've been patrolling for over an hour when I pass the place where Darian once helped us enter the city through a secret passage. Out of the corner of my eye, I see the wall containing that passage move. I choke on my gasp and duck around a corner. A figure I know well emerges onto the street.

Isaiah.

He's always managed to sneak in and out of the city easily; Darian must've showed him the secret entrances years ago.

I mark the direction he takes and wait a few moments to ensure he's alone. When I'm finally satisfied no one else accompanies him, I hurry after the Magi leader.

He walks at a brisk pace, not bothering to hide himself under a cloaking spell tonight. I'm sure he isn't here regularly enough for the royals to know his face, but it's still a bold move. He wanders a path nearly identical to the one he took when I followed him a couple weeks ago. It's not the nicest part of town, but it is a great place to go incognito. He must be visiting a well-placed Magi masquerading as a courtier or someone rich who doesn't want to be seen in their normal setting.

The last time I saw Isaiah, I returned to the hideout to inform the others immediately. I made note of the house, of course, but I wasn't able to ascertain who lives there when I returned later on. In fact, it reminded me quite a lot of the house Darian keeps in the city for pretense, though not as fine.

Whoever they are, they're involved in Isaiah's machinations. I need to know exactly what his plans are if I'm going to stop him.

Isaiah approaches the house and pauses by a side door. I'm far enough away that he shouldn't be able to sense me under my spell like Darian did that awful night in the lower levels of the Palace. Isaiah moves his hands like he's casting a spell, making my breath hitch.

Maybe I'm wrong. Maybe he does know he's being followed.

Then he begins to change before my eyes. His body lengthens, growing taller. His hair shortens, and his neatly trimmed beard is replaced by a bare face.

A face that belongs to Darian Azul.

My heart gallops in my chest. My palms have turned ice cold as my brain tries to grasp what I just saw.

The horrible truth seeps into me, slowly at first, then all at once like fire rushing through my veins.

Darian is pretending to be Isaiah.

Or is it the other way around?

Confusion reigns in my head, but my feet begin to move the second he disappears into the house. I must get closer if I want to know the truth.

I creep toward the house. Mech-rosebushes line the side of it, and I duck into the small space between them and the brick exterior, stopping beneath a window. A light glows inside. I keep my cloaking spell in place as I pull myself up by the window ledge to peek into the room. Darian removes his cloak and addresses the people he's meeting. I can't see their faces from this vantage point, but as soon as I hear their voices, I drop my hold on the window ledge and crouch beneath it, shuddering.

I don't need to see them to know who they are. Darian—or Isaiah as Darian—is meeting with King Damon and Queen Cyrene. There is absolutely no mistaking the voices that haunt my worst nightmares.

I must know what they're talking about. I whisper the incantation that will allow me to hear them better—*Ampleo*—and try to keep my hands from shaking. I feel exposed without my shield to protect me.

"What news do you bring?" the king asks.

Darian's voice is unmistakable too. Is there a spell that can alter that?

"We're in position. We're ready when you are," Darian says. "How does the construction fare?"

The queen sighs, clearly frustrated. "Slower than we'd hoped. Apparently, it takes more than we thought to transform one of the storage levels into a prison block. But we can rely on Leon for the suits. He is dependable for good work done well and efficiently. He'll deliver by the deadline."

Understanding rocks me. Leon mentioned the other day that the royals had placed a large order for the metal suits. They order small quantities from time to time, but this order stood out. These aren't just mere stock replacements. They're constructing a larger prison space.

Because they're expecting a large influx of prisoners. *Magi* prisoners.

My pulse skyrockets. This must be Darian and not Isaiah. If it *were* Isaiah, I'd have expected him to kill the king and queen. The fact that he hasn't . . . something else is going on. And it isn't good.

"Glad to hear it," Darian grunts.

"What about your preparations? Is everything in place?" Queen Cyrene asks.

"Oh yes. I've rounded up all the remaining Magi. They believe unequivocally that I'm one of Isaiah's most trusted advisors and on their side. They suspect nothing." The smile in his voice and the half lie he tells make my stomach roil.

"At dawn the day after tomorrow, be sure to have them at the southeastern corner, near the plains. We'll be ready and waiting," the queen says.

"It will be done," Darian says.

"Then you're dismissed," the king says with a note of finality. I don't have to watch to know that Darian bows before them and puts his cloak back on before leaving the house. I quickly release the amplification spell and recast my shield to ensure he won't see me. I don't dare move until the royals leave the house too. I'm shocked they're out here at all. I always thought they remained in the Palace and never ventured into the city. To see them here . . . this is very serious indeed.

I wait for several long minutes, but I don't hear any noises. Finally, my curiosity gets the better of me, and I risk a peek—under my cloaking spell—through the window.

They're gone.

But they definitely didn't leave through any of the doors of the house. There must be a hidden entrance. Maybe this is a safe house they keep to meet with their spies. I shiver. I can hardly believe what I've just overheard, and yet the awful feeling in my gut leaves no doubt of the truth.

Darian is playing both sides, even more effectively than before.

Despite the cold sense of dread seeping into my bones, I hurry back to our base in the tunnels. I must alert the others. If my suspicion is right, I must find a way to warn the rest of the Magi as well.

Most importantly, my sister and Remy. I can't let them fall into another trap.

I watch my back, taking a roundabout route just in case Darian caught on that someone was eavesdropping. When I'm satisfied I've lost my imaginary pursuers, I finally return to the tunnels.

The first thing I do when I get there is wake Catoria.

She rubs the sleep from her eyes. Then frowns deeply at me. "What are you waking an old woman for?"

"Haven't you slept enough over the last hundred years?"

Catoria laughs, then gets to her feet, wrapping her cloak around her thin frame. "True enough. What do you need from me?"

I bite my lip. "Did you bring the scrying stones?"

She tilts her head, curious. "I did. Do you need to check on someone?"

"I need to know where Darian Azul is right now."

She gives me an odd look that says I'll have to explain this more fully later, while she opens her pack and pulls out a pouch that clinks as though stones rest inside. My anxiety rises, spooling and spinning and carving me hollow.

We move into the war room, where Catoria picks up a canteen from the table and pours water into a bowl. Then she drops one of the scrying stones into it and begins the spell. The water shimmers and swirls, and in a few moments settles into a placid state, just like glass. An image of a man walking in the woods appears. His cloak is pulled over his head, and we can't see his face. My body vibrates, frustrated with having to watch and wait. Catoria regards me curiously but doesn't ask questions yet.

If she sees what I fear we'll see eventually, she'll have more questions than I can answer.

The figure approaches an area that appears empty until he passes through it. Suddenly it's filled with people. The Magi camp. The hood lowers and the bottom drops out of my stomach.

The person the scrying stone follows for the Azul family line looks exactly like Isaiah.

Catoria grunts. "Strange. That's not Darian at all. That's never happened before . . ."

"No," I manage to croak out from a throat lined with knives. "It *is* Darian. Of that I'm absolutely positive." I sink into a chair at the table beside Catoria. This time the unspoken questions are clearly written across her face.

"While I was patrolling this evening, I saw someone sneaking around and realized it was Isaiah. Or, rather, I thought it was Isaiah. I followed him to a house in the city—the same place where I spied him before. That was when I saw him do it. At the time I couldn't tell whether he was casting a spell or undoing one, but now I understand. It's been Darian all along. He's only pretending to be Isaiah. He removed his disguise and entered the house. When I peeked inside . . ." My breath begins to rattle at the memory. "He was meeting with the Technocrat king and queen."

I grab a hold of her wrists. "Catoria, they're plotting to capture or kill all the remaining Magi. The royals are building a new wing of prisons just for Darian and his experiments." I shake my head. "I should've guessed something like this was happening when Leon told me he'd received a large order for more of the Magi suits."

I wrap my arms around my middle and shudder as Aro walks into the room.

"I thought I heard voices," he says. Then he takes one look at my face and immediately is at my side. "Aissa, what's wrong? What happened?"

I quickly fill him in on what Catoria's scrying pool confirmed: Darian has been pretending to be Isaiah, the Technocrat king and queen know all about it, and they plan to use it to their advantage to get rid of the Magi for good.

"I have no idea how long Darian has been keeping up this ruse," I say. "Though I wouldn't be surprised if Isaiah died in the bombing of the Chambers and Darian has been the pretender ever since." As soon as I say the words, I'm certain of their truth. "Yes, that must be it. Isaiah hasn't behaved as I'd expect from a man who's just seen what his son warned him about come to pass."

Aro sits back on his heels and runs his fingers through his pale hair. "No wonder he was determined to kill me," he says.

I give a half-hearted laugh. "He certainly was, wasn't he?"

Suddenly, I realize why Aro had a tracking spell on him when we rescued him from the Magi camp, and why it was so easy to free him. Darian was trying to use him as bait. As an Alliance member, he would've at least heard rumors of the Sanctuary. We thought we were being coy, but he must've realized what we'd discovered. And he hoped to use Aro to lead him to it.

"Poor Remy. He doesn't even know his father died." Aro shakes his head sadly. My heart begins to ache. I know what it's like to lose your parents. Remy may have had differences with his father from time to time, but he'll still be devastated.

Now Darian is making a play to control both sides of this war. He's killed the Magi leader and taken over the leadership of our faction under his disguise. And his plan to wrest control of Palinor from the royal line has been in the works—with the Magi's help—for a decade. All he needs to do is kill Aro and arrange the deaths of the king and queen. I'm sure he has something fittingly tragic in the works that will rally the Technocrat populace to his side and bolster his claim to the throne. Then he'll make a new army out of the Heartless to suppress any potential rebellion and ensure his reign lasts as long as he sees fit.

Catoria has been considering her scrying pool where Darian still masquerades as Isaiah for the Magi camp. "We have to stop him."

I get to my feet. "Yes, we must warn the others immediately."

Aro puts his hands on my shoulders. "Hold on," he says. "It's the wee hours of the morning. I assume you've been out all night?"

My cheeks redden. "Possibly."

"You need to rest before you can save the world."

"Right now I just want to save my sister and Remy. I can worry about the rest of the world later when they're safely back where they belong." I feel sick to my stomach knowing my sister is in that camp, under the sway of our enemy. The man who's determined to use us and our magic with or without our consent. The man who betrayed the Magi in every possible way. The man who murdered our parents.

I can't let her stay there another second.

But Aro holds me fast. He's insistent that I rest, at least for a couple of hours before taking off again.

"It's dangerous out there. You must be at your best. And you can't be without sleep."

Finally, I acquiesce. He's right, even though I don't like it.

I settle on the cushions laid out in our little room, and Aro lies down next to me.

"I need to talk to my parents," he says. "If I could just try to reason with them again, especially now that we've healed a Heartless—"

"They're fully aware of what Darian's doing. They approve of his work. And to be honest, I don't think they'll care that we healed a Heartless. The Heartless are useful to them as they provide a reason to hate Magi." My words are not as measured as usual. I'm exhausted and my head is too focused on my sister. They slip out before I can think better of speaking them. "I'm sorry, I can't have this argument again right now."

I turn on my side, avoiding the look on Aro's face. He sighs and then, to my relief, wraps his arms around me, a comforting warmth that soon lulls me off to sleep.

CHAPTER

37

WHEN I WAKE IN THE AFTERNOON, I'M

annoyed at Aro for letting me sleep so long, but he's insistent that I needed that more than anything.

"You've barely slept since Zandria and Remy left," he says, kissing the top of my head. "You've been burning yourself out and were in no condition to take on Darian and the entire Techno army without rest."

Begrudgingly, I have to admit that he's right. But now I waste no time assembling our allies. We meet in the war room that evening, and I share what I know.

Needless to say, they're as horrified and disturbed as I am.

"It'll be a massacre," Vivienne says, her face pale and drawn. "Remy and Zandria have no idea what they've walked into."

My stomach twists. "I'm heading out there tonight to ensure they do." The idea of Zandria being under Darian's control, obeying his orders, makes me want to vomit. And rip something apart.

I clench my hands into fists, then release them. "Vivienne, Leon—are the Heartless confined solely to their hospital, or are they elsewhere too?"

Leon frowns. "There's an orphanage here in the city, but some of the Heartless live at home with their parents." He glares at the ground. "Though not many, I'm afraid."

"I need you to warn the Heartless hospital and the orphanage and anyone else who cares for the Heartless to get out of Palinor now. Be sure they avoid the northwest sector and woods beyond the city. The Magi are in the forest there."

Leon raises an eyebrow. "There's another Heartless hospital near the seaport. They might be able to shelter them temporarily."

"Perfect," I say.

Confused, Vivienne glances between us. "Why do only the Heartless need to leave?"

I swallow hard. I haven't shared this with everyone yet. But now is the time. "Darian wants to use them. He's draining the Magi he captures with the end goal of powering hearts for the Heartless. He believes they'll be indebted to him and will become his own personal, nearly invincible army. He's plotting a coup. It starts with killing Aro and 'curing' the rest of the Heartless. We must get them out of Palinor before he can make his move."

Vivienne looks like she's about to be ill. But she nods. "I'll take the hospital, and you can take the orphanage," she says to Leon.

"Also, this would be a good time to bring the Technocrats you've been grooming on board—at least inform them of what we now know. We're going to need them soon," I say.

Vivienne and Leon quickly leave to set about their tasks.

I turn to Catoria. "I need your help."

She raises an eyebrow. "And my scrying stones?"

"Exactly."

She pours some water into a bowl and dips the Donovan stone inside, then casts the spell. In moments, two images appear, one of me staring at the bowl and the other of my sister. Catoria whispers a few more words I don't quite catch and only the image of Zandria remains, now filling the bowl. I startle when I realize she's no longer in the woods.

She's already in the city.

The brick-and-steel buildings are unmistakable. My heart slams into my throat. "What's she doing here?"

"Could Darian have moved up his schedule?" Owen asks.

"I must intercept her. Hold on . . ." I glance closer to see if I can determine which direction she's going and see she's heading for the square. I grab Catoria's arm. "If we leave right now, we can catch up to her."

"What about us?" Aro asks hopefully.

"You stay here. Owen, warn our Magi allies. If all goes well, we'll be back soon with my sister."

Aro's expression hardens. "So you have a task for everyone but me."

Frustration rises in my chest. "I'm not going to fight with you about this right now, Aro. There isn't time. I have to get to my sister before she makes a horrible mistake."

Before he can object further, I drag Catoria out of the room. Arguing is wasting precious time we don't have.

We hurry into the tunnels, then head for the square under our magically made disguises. The face-changing spell has come in handy on many occasions. It's the only thing I'm grateful to Darian for—he gave my sister the spell book that contained it. We don't need anyone to recognize us but her. I know the face she's wearing, and she'll recognize mine too. Catoria doesn't need to change hers, but for the sake of not attracting strange glances, she's made herself appear about thirty years younger, so she could pass for a mother rather than a grandmother.

When we reach the square, we split up to cover more ground. We agree to meet back at the southern corner in twenty minutes. When I pass by the center of the square, I spy my sister in disguise, headed in the direction I just came from. I rush to intercept her. When she sees me, surprise flits across her face, then, strangely, relief.

"Zandy," I say. "I have important news you must hear."

"Not as important as mine," she says. Every trace of the animosity she displayed the last time I saw her has melted away. I almost wonder if I imagined it. But no, her expression that night isn't one I'll ever forget.

She sits me down on a bench at the edge of the square with a grave air about her. "Aissa, Isaiah is almost ready to carry out his plan. The negotiations officially fell through as of last night. The Magi will strike and sink the city as the first rays of dawn appear."

"And they'll be at the southeastern corner, just inside the tree line, yes?" I say.

Zandria is taken aback. "Yes. How did you guess?"

"I didn't guess. I knew."

She frowns, then her eyes widen. "Were you spying on us?"

I shake my head. "Only to find you once we learned of the plan. When we discovered you were in the city, we came to intercept you."

"I don't understand," she says.

I squeeze my sister's hands. "Isaiah is not who you think he is."

Zandria is beginning to get annoyed with me. "What are you talking about, Aissa?"

"Last night I saw Isaiah enter the city through one of the hidden entrances. I followed him to learn more about what he was doing here." I swallow hard. "He went to the same house where I first spied him before. But this time, I saw who he was meeting."

"Well, who was it?" Zandria says impatiently.

"The king and queen. And just before he entered the house, he removed a face-changing spell."

Zandria's breath hisses sharply between her teeth. "What?" she whispers.

"Zandy, Darian has been parading around wearing Isaiah's face. The Isaiah we knew is either dead or captured, which is as good as dead right now."

My sister recoils, then glances up as Catoria joins us. The old woman sighs sadly. "I'm afraid she's correct. We verified it with the scrying stones. The Azul stone brought up a man with Isaiah's face in a camp of Magi. There is no mistaking it."

"I'd be willing to bet that Isaiah died in the Chambers catastrophe. And that Darian was there to swoop in to gather up any survivors and use them for his own ends," I say. My sister's hands quiver in mine, but I hold them fast.

"That explains so much," she says. "Isaiah—Darian—has gone too far. He has the entire camp in a frenzy. Everyone has been practicing the spell all the time. He's wearing them ragged. He even has children who've barely learned to control their magic preparing to cast it. If he isn't stopped, he's going to destroy them all. We thought something had broken in Isaiah after the Chambers, but now . . ." She shudders. "What's Darian planning? Did you hear?"

Zandria's description of the Magi camp gives me chills. "He has no intention of sinking the city. He's bringing all the Magi to one central location to make it easy for the Technocrats to capture them. His behavior in the camp must be to purposely weaken the Magi. The king and queen are turning one of the Palace storage levels into prison cells, and Leon recently received a large order for the mechanical suits. He's delivering them, of course, to avoid arousing suspicion. But he isn't happy about it, now that he knows more about how they've been used."

Horror twists Zandy's face. "Darian will drain them of their magic, one by one, to build the Heartless army he's been dreaming of." She leaps to her feet. "Remy! He's still in the camp. He has no idea."

"I know, that's why I was coming to warn you."

"You don't understand." Desperation crosses her face. "He's not working with Isaiah. Nor was I. We left to *sabotage* Isaiah's plan. That's why we had the confrontation with you out in the open, and why we didn't tell you first. We needed Isaiah to believe we were sincere. Remy still believes his father is in charge and that even if everything goes awry, he'll forgive him eventually.

But if that's actually Darian, and he discovers what we've been up to . . ."

"He'll kill Remy," I finish for her.

"We can't allow that to happen," she says.

"We won't," Catoria says. "But right now finding Remy cannot be our first priority. We need more Magi on our side if we want to defeat Darian and the king and queen. We need assistance now. You two were doing quite well freeing Magi before from what I hear; now is the time to go all out. We know Darian is at the camp and likely will remain there to keep up appearances. That means we only have guards to worry about, and they're no match for our powers. We should get Owen, and then we can divide into pairs to free as many Magi as possible tonight."

While neither of us likes the idea of leaving Remy to the mercy of Darian, we understand the wisdom of Catoria's plan. We need more people who are loyal to the Alliance and have magic to use in this fight.

"All right," I say. "Let's get Owen."

I rise, but before we can leave, Zandria grabs my arm. "Aissa, wait." She regards Catoria nervously. "I know we haven't always seen eye to eye on what the new Alliance's goals should be. And I'm still not sure I'm entirely sold on the Technos and Magi being full equals. But after seeing the Magi camp and knowing what we do now about Darian . . . we're going to destroy each other if we don't stop this war. I don't see any other way to do that than somehow making peace."

Warmth blooms in my chest and I grip my sister's shoulders. "Zandria, we healed one of the Heartless. The Heartsong spell worked. Vivienne has been spreading rumors about it far and wide. More Technocrats may be ready for the Alliance than we expected."

Her face turns cloudy. "Now we just have to worry about own people."

"We'll find a way," I say. And with my sister back at my side, I wholeheartedly believe it.

WHEN WE REACH THE TUNNELS AND THE

black marble arches, I can't help but feel as
though something is off. I can't put my finger on
it, but my hackles are raised, and I'm more on my
guard than usual. We open the door—still locked, which
is a relief—and head into the main chamber.

Owen lays unconscious in the middle of the room. Zandria
rushes over to him, immediately verifying whether he's breathing.
She lets out a sigh of relief when he moans and puts a hand to his
temple. A bruise is forming there. "Someone knocked him out,"
Zandria says.

I stiffen immediately, then run toward my room, shouting,
"Aro!" I haven't felt anything, so he should be safe, but I won't feel
good about this until I see him with my own eyes. "Aro!"

But when I reach our room, no one is there. I check every
room in our hideout, and find the same thing: nothing, nothing,
nothing.

Aro is gone.

I clench my teeth as the truth hits me. Frustrated at being
left behind yet again, Aro must've knocked out Owen when he
returned from putting out the signal rune for the Magi we rescued.
He has his own plan to help us win this war.

I know exactly what it is.

And that it's doomed to fail.

"Forges!" I spit out, and Zandria gives me a surprised look.

"It's all right, Aissa, Owen will be fine." He's come around
and sits up as Zandria applies a healing spell to the cut and bruise
on his temple.

"It's Aro I'm worried about."

"I think he hit me with something," Owen mumbles.

"Yes, I think he did," I say. "He's been frustrated now that his work on the Heartsong is complete. But he's told me before what he wants to do to help. He's gone to the Palace to try to talk some sense into his parents."

Zandria barks out a laugh. "That's foolish of him."

"I've told him that over and over. But they're his parents. He doesn't believe he's in any danger."

"Do you think they'll hurt him?" Catoria asks.

I shudder. "I have no idea. But I'm positive Darian will the second he gets the chance. Getting rid of Aro is a critical part of his plans to take the throne."

"That means getting rid of you too, though I doubt Darian knows it yet," Zandria says.

Catoria puts a hand on my shoulder. "We'll be here to support the both of you with magic if it comes to that," she says.

But I only feel marginally better. Catoria and Zandria can't babysit me round the clock. Especially not when we have an entire city to defend on multiple fronts.

I steel my spine. I refuse to cower in fear over what Darian might do.

I found Aro once before when he was hidden under our noses. I can find him again. I just need to get into the Palace. Thanks to his directions about the tunnels, that's a simpler task than it was before.

Owen is on his feet again, much more stable than he was a few minutes ago. "Are you all right now?" I ask him.

"Practically perfect." He glances at Zandria and blushes. I raise my eyebrows when I realize my sister's cheeks are pink too.

"Then let's go rescue more Magi . . . and my prince."

Half an hour later, we're well into the tunnels that lead to the dungeons. Zandria has been arguing with me the entire way. She, Catoria, and Owen need to free as many Magi prisoners as possible while I go to the upper levels and hunt for Aro.

"I don't like this one bit, Aissa," Zandria grumbles. She knows she can't stop me from going. But that doesn't mean she won't complain about it.

"This will be quicker and more efficient. Besides, it's not like Aro will need assistance getting out of here aside from our shield spell." I hold my arms wide. "See? I'm fine physically, which means he is too."

Zandria rolls her eyes. "Whatever you say."

Catoria speaks up as we reach the secret door by the dungeons. "Aissa is correct. It's the most efficient way to achieve all our goals at once. She has a point about him being physically healthy too." She eyes me carefully. "But let me bolster you a little just in case."

She mutters the words to a spell so softly that I can't make them out, but I feel the fizz of her magic course over me, and then I feel fresher, stronger, more alive than moments ago.

"What was that?" I say, my voice full of wonder.

"An energizing spell," she says. "It takes a little of the caster's own energy with it, otherwise, I'd cast it on all of us. But I think you'll need it the most today."

"Thank you," I say. "And good luck."

The others enter the dungeons through the hidden door, and I wait for a moment to be sure they don't run into immediate trouble. When no sounds of guards or a fight come through the wall, I continue as the tunnel circles ever upward.

A knot tightens in my stomach. Aro's angry with me. But I'm afraid he's about to discover the hard way I'm right.

When I reach the secret door to the ground floor, I kneel before it, listening for any signs of life beyond. Feeling confident no one is there, I press the sigil, and the door slides open, quiet as a whisper. I tiptoe out into the hall under the safety of my cloaking spell and get my bearings. This isn't a hall I recognize, but given where we entered the tunnels, I know approximately where I am in the Palace. The east wing. Aro's quarters shouldn't be too far from here. The trick will be how well guarded those main doors leading to his quarters are.

I could be wrong, but knowing the king and queen, there's an excellent chance Aro was locked up in his rooms the second he set foot in the Palace. Good thing he gave me Leon's master key for safekeeping.

It's slightly unnerving to not see my reflection in the steel mirror-walled halls. But I'm struck by memories of when I was first here, searching for a little girl who was the heir to the throne, my head full of confusingly warm thoughts about the boy who would turn out to be the true heir. Now here I am, after him once again.

Tonight, no guard stands watch outside the door to the hallway leading to Aro's quarters. Perhaps they were reassigned and haven't yet resumed their post. I wait until there are no servants or courtiers coming and going through this area, then I slip through the door and creep down the hall. When I unlock the door to Aro's room, I swallow my surprise.

It's empty.

I quickly search Aro's room but find no trace of him. Wherever he went, his parents haven't locked him up in here again. Yet.

He must be with his parents. But where would they be? Either in their own quarters—which I never found when I was here before—or somewhere else in the Palace.

It's time to use my backup plan: the tracking spell I initially cast on Aro the night we rescued him from Isaiah/Darian's grasp while he slept. Just in case I ever needed it.

Right now, I'm glad I took that precaution. Aro might be even more furious with me when he realizes. But if it means keeping him safe, I'll gladly bear his wrath.

I weave my hand over a small stone cylinder made from that magic-infused black marble. A tracker is a spell that holds; I only need to cast it once to reactivate it, leaving me free to conceal myself under a shield. Until the Sanctuary, I didn't realize there were many spells like this and the Binding rite, ones that don't need to be released before the user can cast another spell. But it works, and the cylinder angles toward the door leading to the hallway. It's a strange feeling, a tug of magic in the right direction. I can feel it all the way in my heart, perhaps our bond reacting to the magic of this new spell.

I hold out the tracking stone, letting it guide my path. Cautious as always, I pause behind every door before opening it to determine what awaits me in the hallway beyond, then proceed with all the speed I can safely muster. The tracking stone takes me down a hall I once traveled more accidentally than anything not far from Aro's quarters. That was the day I witnessed the queen torturing Vivienne. A sight I'll never forget. Whenever I think I've seen the full fathom of the queen's mercy, there always seems to be deeper depths for her to sink to. I shudder but keep moving down the corridor.

The stone takes me to the same door I remember.

Aro's inside. No question.

How I will reach him without anyone else inside the room noticing that someone opened the door is, however, a big question.

I hear voices, but I can't make them out, nor do I dare relinquish my cloaking spell. Frustration fills me. I'm so close, yet stymied.

The door swings open, and a harried-looking serving girl rushes into the hall and down the corridor, tears streaming down her cheeks.

". . . and be quick about it!" the king calls after her.

A plan forms in my mind. I consider the layout of the hallway. There are several doors, and I quickly determine which are rooms and which are closets.

Then I wait.

When the serving girl returns holding a dustpan and brush, I pounce. My shield drops as I mutter a sleeping spell, "*Somnis.*"

The girl slumps in my arms, and I drag her into the nearest closet, quietly shutting the door on her slumbering form. I feel a pang of guilt. She's going to be confused when she wakes, and if one of her masters discovers her before that happens, there will be fires to burn. But it's necessary.

Before anyone else can wander down the hall, I cast the form-changing spell, grimacing as the magic works its way through my muscles and skin and bones. When it's done, I check my reflection in the hall.

I look exactly like the serving girl. I pick up the brush and dustpan from the floor, then hunch over slightly in the manner the girl carried herself and open the door.

"It's about time," the king says the moment I enter the room. "Clean up that mess you made, girl. Then get us more refreshments." King Damon smiles as he says this, and the sharp metal tips of his teeth catch the mechlights in an alarming manner.

"Yes, Your Majesty," I say as meekly as possible. Broken glass is scattered over the floor near a large metal cabinet; that must be the mess he's referring to. He probably frightened the poor girl enough that she dropped drinking glasses and they shattered. I waste no time cleaning it up as I scope out the room.

It's much the same as the first time I saw it—a regal drawing room—but this time the couches and chairs are arranged in a more normal fashion, and the curtains are open, letting moonlight filter into the room. The spurt of blood still streaks across one wall, and two more have joined it since. The king and queen lounge on one of the couches, seemingly at ease, though clearly annoyed with me, the serving girl.

My heart stutters and I nearly drop the dustpan when I spy Aro sitting on a chair in the corner. His pale hair glimmers in the mechlights, and his face is creased with irritation.

Judging by the scowl on Aro's face, his conversation with his parents is definitely not going the way he expected.

Once I've cleaned up the broken glass, I toss the debris down the garbage chute and then position myself at what I hope is an appropriately respectful distance in the corner. The king stares at me expectantly, and even the queen turns her head and frowns.

"If you're trying to get fired, say the word, and we can give you a whipping right away," King Damon says.

I do my best not to startle, realizing my fatal error. The serving girl must have been in the middle of a task when she broke the glass items. They looked like wine glasses. Since the king and queen aren't currently drinking anything, it's a fair bet they're waiting for me to pour them more. I take a step toward the wine cabinet when the queen tsks and gives a heavy sigh.

"Honestly. We haven't cut your ears off—yet—but perhaps we should for how well you listen." The queen scowls. Aro's forehead is creased by a deep *V* between his brows.

I bow low. "My apologies, Your Majesties. Please, may I beg you for a reminder so that I may do your bidding correctly?"

"Moth—" Aro begins, but the queen cuts him off before he can finish the word. *Mother.* They hide this secret even from the servants. He sighs. "For the Anvil's sake, just tell the poor girl what she's supposed to do. She's clearly terrified."

This elicits a smirk from the queen and a grunt from the king. The king gets to his feet and steps toward me. My heart throbs in my chest, pounding so loud I fear he might hear my Magi blood.

Or even smell it with some strange mechanical enhancement. Who knows what these people have dreamed up?

The king is tall with dark, peppered hair, the opposite of his queen. His robes are a deep purple, almost black, and his eyes glint strangely. When he gets closer, towering over me, I realize it's because there's something mechanical in them. I don't dare stare long enough to get a good look, but the rumors he can see keenly for long distances may not be fairy tales after all.

I duck my head and bow again. He sneers, sending skitters down my spine. When I glance up for a moment, his wickedly sharp teeth flash at me.

Rage rushes through me. The only thing preventing me from reaching out and stopping his heart is Aro.

Aro, who is right there, watching me. If I kill his parents—in front of him, no less—there's no world in which he'll forgive me. I know what it's like to lose your parents. As much as I hate his, I can't do that to him.

That's the only thing that saves them. And probably me.

King Damon reaches past me to open the door of the tall metal cabinet. I move to the side and it swings open. For a moment, I'm not sure what this contraption is, but he gestures at the spout and the nearby cabinet full of glass and metal goblets.

"Does this ring any bells?"

"Yes, Your Majesty. My apologies, Your Majesty."

"Then get to it." He sneers as he returns to the couch.

"Right away, Your Majesty," I say, automatically reaching for a goblet while I study the strange metal cabinet. The spout disappears into the metal box, as if this is some vintage they enjoy so much that they have it on tap here in this room. There are a few small holes around eye level and a seam down the center. I can't quite tell whether it's decorative or serves a purpose. At waist height is a lock. My breath catches.

What on earth is this contraption? Is this a trick?

Three sets of eyes burn into my back. I have no choice but to take the risk. I pull the lever on the spout and a thick, warm liquid spills into the goblet I hold beneath it. The unmistakable scent of iron hits my nose, turning my stomach, but it's mixed with something else.

Something fizzy. Something magic.

Inside the cabinet, something—*someone*—moans. Then something shifts and the cabinet shakes.

Horror shoots through me so fast it makes me dizzy. My vision floods red with rage.

The royals are drinking Magi blood.

They're *drinking* Magi blood.

They're not just murdering and torturing Magi. No, that's not enough for them. They're stealing our very essence—the thing that made them hate us when our lines diverged centuries ago—for themselves.

No wonder they seem to have barely aged in the years I've lived in Palinor. No wonder their strength and keen senses are legendary. Who knows what consuming unbridled magic might do to a Technocrat?

Suddenly everything is crystal clear. My breath calms and the ringing in my ears stops.

I turn slowly, and my eyes immediately go to the two empty, red-stained goblets on the table.

I squeeze the goblet in my hands hard enough that it shatters. A plume of red and silver bursts, then shivers to the floor. My hands are bloody and sting with cuts, but I don't even feel the pain. The blood isn't mine. At least not most of it.

The king stands again and strides toward me. "What on earth is wrong with you, g—"

Before he can finish the word, my spell catches him by the

throat, yanking him off his feet. His eyes widen as he chokes. His hands scrabble at the invisible strings holding him up.

Fury consumes me. I squeeze my fist and the magic tightens around his throat.

King Damon gasps. I hate him. I want him to die.

Him and the queen. They're the ones perpetuating the lies about the Magi. They're the ones bent on destroying my people.

The queen rises, a keen glimmer in her eyes. "A spy in our midst," she murmurs, showing little interest in her suffocating husband. "Poor thing. You just realized what we keep in that cabinet, didn't you?"

Aro—who has remained seated in shocked silence this whole time—gets to his feet. "Mother," he says in a low voice. "What *do* you keep in that cabinet?"

He doesn't know. For such a smart boy, he has long been blind to his parents' cruel mercy.

Now he's waking up to find he's been living with nightmares made of flesh and metal, gilded with gold and precious gems.

Both our worlds have been upended.

My bloodied hands catch my eyes and the memory of my first kill—Caden—shoves its way forward. Aro found me, protected me then. But if I kill the king, there will be no protecting me. Not here in the middle of the Palace.

The queen ignores her son's question. She isn't done talking to me yet. "How are you doing this?" she says, stepping forward, more out of curiosity than self-preservation. "Our best scientist has assured us that our augmentations around key areas of our bodies should protect us from Magi spells since they can't touch metal . . . but that has not stopped *you*." She takes another step toward me, and her cold blue eyes rake over me. "Fascinating creature."

Meanwhile, the king sputters, still desperately trying to

breathe. His legs kick and spasm, but he can't break free of my spell.

Aro's eyes plead with me, and something inside me shifts. I can't do it. Never mind how much I may want to, I can't kill his parents in front of him.

Instead I swing my arm toward the right side of the room and open my hand, sending the king careening into the queen. They tumble over the couch in a whirl of silk and limbs and surprise. I pull my hands back and cast one more spell: "*Somnis!*"

When they're rendered unconscious, I quickly cancel my face-changing spell. Pain shivers over me as my body resumes its true form.

Then it's just me and Aro, staring at each other over his parents' limp bodies.

"AISSA," ARO WHISPERS, BREAKING THE
silence first. He unclenches his hands, revealing tiny beads of blood on the palms—the same
location as the small cuts I got from the broken glass.

The awkwardness slips away, and before I know it, I've
thrown my arms around his neck, and his lips are on mine.

When we break apart, the first thing I say is, "I came here
to rescue you."

Aro laughs, part relief and part amusement. "I knew you
would."

I kiss him again, harder this time, curling my fingers in his
hair. "Don't run away on me again."

He frowns. "I had to do something. I can't stand being idle. It
isn't fair to ask of me."

"I know. I'm sorry. Nothing about this is fair."

"You're risking your life for this fight. You can't stop me from
doing the same. This is my home and my city."

I sigh. I haven't wanted to admit it, but he's right. "I won't. Not
anymore." The reason we came here in the first place thrusts itself
back to the forefront of my mind now that Aro is safe. "Darian is
making his move. Tonight."

Aro sucks his breath in sharply. "So soon?"

"I found Zandria and she told me everything. She and Remy
left so they could undermine Isaiah." I shake my head. "Only she
was shocked to hear it isn't Isaiah at all."

"What about Remy?" Aro asks.

An uncomfortable feeling swims in my gut. "He's still in the
Magi camp. He doesn't know the truth. He's still trying to reason
with the man he believes to be his father."

"He must be warned," Aro says.

"There's no time. The Magi will be congregating at dawn under the pretext of casting the spell together. That's when"—I jerk my head at Aro's sleeping parents—"they'll attack. The Magi won't stand a chance."

"We need to stop Darian."

I smile slightly. "We're already working on that." I glance down at our feet and his parents' unconscious forms. Rage ripples through me once more. If my sister were here, she'd probably be gloating at being proven correct. Now even Aro must admit his parents are beyond the point of being reasoned with. "I have to do one more thing here, then we should leave the Palace as soon as possible."

"What can I do?" he asks.

"Help me with this cabinet?"

Aro attempts to unlock it, but to no avail. Then he stands aside and waits while I weave my hands, casting a spell on the cabinet. At first my hands are close together, then I stretch them wide, and magic rips the metal cabinet straight down the middle. A man with sandy-colored hair, not much older than my father was when he died, slumps into Aro's waiting arms. We quickly detach the metal tubes connecting him to the cruel machine.

The man is weak from blood loss and lack of movement. I sing a rejuvenating spell over him to regrow his blood and heal any wounds we may not have noticed yet. In a few minutes he regains consciousness, and his eyes open. They're a shocking blue, not less so for the surprise in them.

"It's all right," I whisper. "We're here to help you. But you must be quiet. Can you do that? Nod if so." The man nods. "Good. What is your name?"

"Travers," the man whispers hoarsely.

"I'm Aissa, and this is Aro. I'm a Magi like you, and Aro is a Technocrat. We're part of an underground organization called the Alchemist Alliance. Would you like to help us save the last of the Magi and this city?"

Travers's eyes are wide as saucers, and it takes a moment for him to absorb what I've told him. He eyes Aro with mistrust, but finally settles.

"Yes."

"Excellent." I help Travers to his feet. There's one last thing I need to do before we leave. I hum, the words to the spell forming on my lips. The sashes of the fine damask curtains unwind from their ties and soar toward me. Under my direction, they wrap around the king and queen, tying them up on the floor like livestock for the slaughter.

Aro raises an eyebrow. I shrug. "I can't leave them here able to get help once they wake up. I need to slow them down, and this is the most humane way I can think of."

Travers spits on them, startling both me and Aro. "We should lock them both in their own metal suits," he says.

I put a restraining hand on his arm. "We don't have time for that right now. We have work to do, and that means we need to get out of the Palace with as many Magi prisoners as possible. Come on."

Travers doesn't argue. We pause by the door to listen for what might be outside but don't hear much of anything.

"Are you strong enough to cast?" I ask Travers.

"Yes."

"Good. If you can handle the silencing spell, I'll put up a shield."

"Even for him?" Travers gestures at Aro.

"Especially him. He's been a prisoner here too. In a way. We don't want him to be stopped as we leave."

Once our spells are in place, I crack the door and ensure no one is in sight. The way is clear, and we slip from the room, then hurry down the hall. The number of servants and guards seems to have swelled slightly. Hopefully that's just a coincidence. I can't help worrying about my sister and Owen and Catoria. I hope they're safely on their way back to our hideout with several freed Magi prisoners in tow.

Aro leads us toward a secret tunnel entrance that will take us on a shortcut down to the dungeons and into the drainage system beyond. It's what he used to sneak down there, hunting for his own buried treasure. The next corridor we take is secluded and more out of the way than the others. The number of onlookers has reduced considerably, much to my relief. And Travers's too. He's been tense the whole way, walking between me and Aro with his shoulders up to his ears.

Zandy and I may be able to heal the Magi physically, but no spell can undo the trauma inflicted by the king and queen.

If we can overthrow them, succeed with our coup, perhaps that will go a little ways toward healing for these people. My sister included.

But first we need to live through this night.

We enter the secret tunnels and break into a run all the way down to the dungeon level. At the secret entrance there, we do the same ritual we have every time: wait, listen, check, hurry. While I hope my sister and our companions are already safely away from the Palace, I need to be sure, and I want to free any Magi they might not have released yet.

We sneak by a few guards, all of whom seem untroubled. Hopefully that means my friends were successful. The first few rooms we try are already empty of their prisoners; they were in use the last time I was here. We've been stealing Magi away at random in the hopes that the guards won't find any pattern to our strikes, but tonight our mission is different. We're after as many as possible.

When we reach a cell with a Magi inside, I make short work of the lock, shocking Travers.

He gapes at me. "But that's . . . that's . . ."

"Impossible?" I say, my lips quirking at the edges. I'm not quite sure when I decided this, but I'm done hiding my powers. There's no more reason to. We've all—Magi and Technocrat— been lied to. The time for a reckoning with the truth is now.

"Yes," he says, still staring.

"Well, it's not. We've all been deceived about what we really are. There's much to explain, but it must wait until we've completed this task."

Travers swallows his surprise and picks up the cloaking spell. But the expression on his face as I rip the metal suit off the trapped Magi with a single spell is priceless.

Aro catches the woman as she collapses. She's older, probably my mother's age, with tangled, unwashed blond hair. She's ema- ciated; I can see her ribs through the thin shift she wears. For a moment, I worry she's dead, but quickly discern that's not the case. I weave my magic over her, teasing out any disease or infection left in her body, regrowing her torn-out tongue and healing her mangled hands.

When she regains consciousness, we help her to her feet and quickly make introductions. Her name is Fiona. I give her some of the jerky I always carry in my bag, and it renews her further.

We hurry back into the hall and repeat the process four more times. All the Magi we rescue are in varying states of muscular atrophy and depleted strength. Two of them—Neil and Mika— have only been here a few weeks. They were probably captured not long before Zandria. But like Fiona, Jedrick and Hanniel have been here so long they don't remember when they were captured. It could have been months, or even years. All three of them are more confused and addled than I'd hoped. I wonder if this is from something new Darian has been doing to his prisoners. We saved several before who had been here for a long time, but they weren't like this. Perhaps this is what happens to the Magi he drains. I shudder. I hadn't fully considered the ramifications of that process. The loss of some of their magic, that essence that makes us who we are, could cause untold damage.

Regardless, we must get these Magi safely away before we can rescue more. It's clear they'll be more hindrance than help should a fight arise. And trying to herd them quietly down the hall is becoming a challenge.

Still, it kills me to leave even a single Magi behind in this dungeon. But we have no choice.

We're almost at the secret entrance when guards' voices stop us in our tracks. The Magi we've rescued quiver between me and Aro. From under the safety of the cloaking spell, I peek around the corner and immediately draw back.

Darian stands in the hall, along with a very awake—and very angry—king and queen.

My heart leaps into my throat. Aro leans toward me. "What is it?"

"Your parents. And Darian," I whisper into his ear. We don't need the others to be more terrified than they already are.

Aro's eyes widen. "Already? I thought Darian would be with the Magi preparing to cast that spell."

"I thought so too," I say. Any change in Darian's plan is troubling. Did he realize Zandria and Remy were secretly working against Isaiah? Or is there something in the dungeons he wants to retrieve in case the spell actually works?

All I know is he's here, and that complicates everything.

The only positive thing is that there are fewer guards than usual. I assume they've been ordered to lie in wait somewhere for the signal to capture the Magi gathering outside the city just before dawn.

"What's happening?" Travers asks nervously. "Why have we stopped?"

"I need . . . to reevaluate our plans. A little hitch, that's all."

"Hitch? What hitch?" Fiona chimes in. The others cower behind her.

I face them. "We can't leave the way we planned. Not right now. We may need to hide in the dungeons a little longer than I'd hoped."

"I could cause a distraction," Aro says.

I grab his wrist. "Don't you dare. He'll kill you this time, and you know it."

"Not in front of my parents. I'm sure of it."

"Well, I'm not." I take a deep breath, dizziness filling up my chest. "No, if anyone is going to cause a distraction, it will be me."

Several shouts come from the hall behind us, spinning me back around. Darian and the royals have opened one of the cells, only to find the Magi they held there missing.

We're officially out of time.

"Wait here!" barks Darian. It takes a moment for me to realize he's speaking to the king and queen. He's going to reveal us, and he doesn't want them to know he's Magi. Not yet, anyway. I imagine he'll revel in it when he finally kills them.

"Go!" I hiss at my companions, shoving them down the hall. Darian's boots ring out on the metal floors as he marches in our direction. Judging by the clanking that accompanies him, several machines follow in his wake.

Those are for capturing us. Or some of us. Darian knows full well they'll be no match for me and my magic. But my companions . . . it would be too easy to force me into a stalemate if he captures everyone else. Especially when he discovers Aro here with me. He probably already suspects. He must've found the king and queen asleep and cancelled my spell to wake them up. They would've told him all that transpired. And with Aro missing again . . . well, there's only one reasonable explanation as to where he went.

The fear of my fellow Magi is thick enough that I could almost reach out and grab hold of it. We make it around the next corner before Darian, but I'm sure he's tracking our magic by now. If we can circle around and make it to the secret entrance before he reaches us, we might stand a chance of escaping. Otherwise, we may not make it out of this.

Cold fear begins to gnaw at me.

"This way," I whisper. "I know you're still weak, but you may need to fight. Be ready."

We round the corner and come out near the secret doorway. To my horror it's blocked—by a machine shaped like a wolf, metal hackles raised. Skittering metal clangs from a nearby cell, and out come two more machines just like it.

We back up, but when I whirl around, Darian is behind us, his hands discretely casting the cancellation spell. A tingling sensation runs over us as the cloaking and silencing spells vanish. When the other Magi realize Darian can see us, they cry out. The royals and their guards rush from the empty cell into the hall.

We're boxed in. Darian on one side, mechwolves on another, and the king and queen and their guards in front of us. We can't get through that door without casualties now.

We're left with no good choices. Every one of the freed prisoners senses this. Their magic comes to life in their blood, fizzing the air around us. Some at the ready to strike, some wild and weak and uncontained.

"Hello, Aissa," Darian says.

The king and queen gasp. "Aro!" Queen Cyrene says, an admonishing tone in her voice. The king's hands ball into fists at his sides.

A spell hums in my throat before I fully process what I'm about to do. But before I can make my move, the secret door slides open without warning.

Then the mechwolves are yanked off their feet.

The Technocrats gape as their own machines hover in the air before them for one long moment.

Then they're hurled into the guards, and the royals scatter to take cover.

BEFORE THE DUST SETTLES, ZANDRIA, OWEN,
and Catoria stand next to us, magic at the
ready. Zandria alters the spell she cast to knock
the mechwolves off their feet and rips them apart
with a terrible screech of metal on metal. Meanwhile,
Aro ushers the weaker Magi into the not-so-secret passage,
instructing them to keep running until they hit the drainage
tunnels, and not to stop even then.

Queen Cyrene's eyes widen, then freeze over with hatred.
"How did you do that to our machines?" She steps forward, guards
flanking her. "Capture them," she orders the guards and Darian.

"I'm so glad to see you," I say to Zandria as we cast defensive
spells.

I mumble an incantation that pulls the guards' weapons out
of their hands and turns the pointy ends on them. Two of the six
guards halt in their tracks, but the others duck under the swords
and keep marching toward us. Their cloaks mark them as the elite
guards: Darian's personally trained soldiers. The ones who are
supposed to be the most vicious, the most fearless. This is the first
time we've fought them.

Catoria weaves a sleeping spell on the guards who paused,
while the elite ones lunge at us. At close range, we have no option
but to fight them hand to hand while casting defensive spells as
quickly as possible. Zandy and I have trained for this for years, yet
in the moment everything is a hundred times more difficult than
in the training room.

I duck the first swing of an elite guard's fist. Zandria grabs
one of the swords that was poised in midair and feints at her own
adversary while she weaves an offensive spell with her free hand.

Owen defends himself with the poleaxe he gained from one of the weapons raids, but ends up knocked flat. Zandria, howling at the top of her lungs, throws off her own guard and whirls around to stab the one about to strike at Owen.

Owen weaves his hands, letting loose a spell that shoves back the guard Zandria was just fighting as he tries to take advantage of her distraction. Perhaps the feelings Owen has for my sister are mutual after all. But I only have a moment to consider this before the guards come at me again. This time I'm ready with a blinding spell. One of them is disoriented for a moment, but the other recovers quickly. I dodge out of the way as he grabs for me, then kick him headfirst into the metal wall. He slumps to the ground.

Behind me, metal clanks on metal. Aro, blocking an attack from the second guard as he tried to sneak up on me. He catches the guard in the stomach with the hilt of his sword and the man doubles over.

"*Somnis*," I incant, and the guard drops to the floor.

Automatically, I look for my twin. And find she's disarmed and incapacitated her opponent. She smiles wildly at first, then her expression turns to dismay as she sees something behind us in the hallway.

I whirl around. Darian now holds a blade to Aro's neck. Aro looks nervous.

Without thinking, I lurch toward them, but Darian presses the knife harder against Aro's skin. I can feel it against my own. He must be drawing a little bit of blood.

"Take another step, and he will bleed all over this floor."

I glance at King Damon and Queen Cyrene. While they're surprised, they make no move whatsoever to stop Darian.

They truly don't care. When I glance back at Aro, the pain in his eyes makes clear the same understanding is hurtling through him. The belief his parents would always protect him is the one thing he's been banking on this whole time. I tried to warn him, we all did, but it was something he had to learn for himself.

And that time is now, the worst possible moment.

"Mother? Father?" Aro manages to croak out. King Damon and Queen Cyrene just shrug.

"Do what you must, Darian. He's been consorting with Magi. He's no longer our son," the king says.

The expression on Aro's face slowly transforms from shock to grief-stricken horror. He looks as if the world were just yanked out from under his feet.

Cold shivers down my spine. The ice in the king's voice, the deadly seriousness. The same people who obsessively protected Aro his whole life have utterly abandoned him.

"We'll be leaving now," Darian says. Then he looks me in the eyes and smirks. "Thank you, Aissa. Bringing Aro couldn't have worked out better for me. And don't worry. I haven't forgotten my plans for you and your sister. Once I'm done with him, you'll be my main priority."

I shudder. Terror ripples off Zandria beside me.

"Leave him be," I say, trying to keep the desperation out of my voice.

Darian simply drags Aro down the hall away from us. Aro can barely walk, but I definitely feel no sense of injury. Darian must have him under a spell of some kind, one he cast without the royals noticing. The fiend gets bolder and bolder, becoming more confident now that his plans are close to fruition.

The only thing I can't understand is why he didn't kill Aro just now. What must he need him for?

Then it hits me. His heart. He knows I did something to it I won't tell him willingly. And by now I'm sure he's heard rumors of the Heartless child we healed. He must be planning to cast a spell of some sort on Aro to reveal my actions so he can mimic them when he "cures" the Heartless. I almost smile.

He'll be disappointed when he realizes the truth. He can't bind himself to every Heartless.

King Damon and Queen Cyrene stare aghast at Darian as it becomes clear he intends to leave them here.

"Where do you think you're going?" the king demands. "I thought you were going to kill him."

Darian looks between us and them. "I'm sure you'll be fine. I have more important things to take care of, remember? Our plans to capture the rest of the Magi cannot be delayed."

Queen Cyrene bristles. "You will remain here and kill these Magi first, Darian. That's an order."

But he keeps backing down the hall. Then he laughs. "I know you've believed yourselves to be in control all these years, but it's getting old. Everything you've achieved is thanks to me. I'll take my due now."

While the guards have not yet arisen, several more appear in the hall. The odds of us getting out of this alive slip away by the second. Zandria twines one hand through mine. The odds may be against us, but we'll still stand and fight, united once again.

We'll win or die trying. And hopefully give the others time to get out alive.

The king beckons to the new guards. "Arrest them. All of them. Even Darian."

The dungeon guards are clearly surprised but waste no time advancing. Catoria and Owen join me and Zandy, forming a line between them and our escape route to ensure the rescued Magi's safety.

Two thirds of the guards rush at us, and the other third advances on Darian. The king and queen edge closer to him. They're furious, and frankly look as though they're itching for a fight.

I'm sure they'd love to let their mercy loose on us and Darian.

We fend off our guards with weapons and magic, infuriating the royals even more. They're screaming at Darian now. He toys with the guards who are left standing.

He mutters under his breath. I can't tell which spell he casts, but magic swells in the hall, making the hair on the back of my neck stand on end. Within a few seconds, the guards fly back, nearly knocking the king and queen off their feet. The dazed guards struggle to regain their footing, but not before the king and queen shove forward to confront Darian.

"You're Magi?" Queen Cyrene accuses him.

Darian smirks.

"Mother, Father, please, leave here," Aro says. His eyes are wild with terror. He knows exactly how far Darian is willing to go.

"Tsk," Queen Cyrene responds.

"He can't hurt us. Not with all the metal in our bodies," King Damon says.

"Not when he knows the wrath of our mercy all too well." The queen points a long, metal-ridged finger in Darian's face. "If you—"

"Your machinations are small-minded and foolish," Darian says. "I've bored of you."

The royals are clearly affronted. "I beg your pardon?" the queen says.

"Who do you think you are?" the king demands.

Darian smiles as if he's never been happier, his free hand weaving under his cloak too fast for me to make out the movements. "I no longer have need of you."

He raises his hand in the air, fingers splayed. The king and queen are jerked off their feet in a whirl of silk and metal, sputtering incoherently. The guards grappling with us back away, gaping slack-jawed.

Darian closes his hand into a fist and squeezes.

The king and queen grab at their chests, unable to stop the spell at work. I know this one. I used to fantasize about casting it on one of the largest mechs during the Royal Victory Parade, bringing it down amid the crowds and causing chaos and destruction.

"No!" Aro shouts. But Darian squeezes his fingers even more tightly closed.

The king and queen go limp as the life slips out of them. Then Darian tosses their bodies to the side of the hall, as merciful to them as they were to their own prisoners.

ALL OF US—GUARDS INCLUDED—STAND

aghast at what Darian has done. A moan
escapes from Aro's lips, but before I can get a
handle on the situation, blinding light explodes from
Darian's fingers. Disorientation reigns.

When the light fades and we can see again, he and Aro
have vanished.

"No!" I cry out. Zandria grabs my arm. Catoria is already
at our side, casting a sleeping spell on the guards. Then she and
Owen examine the limp bodies of the king and queen.

"It's too late for them," she says.

Nausea claws at my throat. Zandria wraps her arms around
me. I lean into her, letting my sister's warmth comfort me.

"We'll get him back," she says. Tears stream down my face. I
didn't even realize I was crying. Yes, we will. It's only been a few
short months since I met Aro, but now I can't fathom life without
him. Regardless of what happens, we're in this together until the
bitter end.

I stiffen. "We have to get to the woods. As soon as possible.
That's where Darian is headed." Whether or not he'll take Aro
there alive, I can't say, but I hope with everything inside me.

Zandria's eyes flare. "He still needs to capture the rest of the
Magi. It's central to his plans."

"We must get them on our side before they make a fatal
mistake."

Owen speaks up. "We don't just need them on our side. We
need the Technos too." He glances between us. "This is what we've
been working toward this whole time, isn't it?"

We step over the guards' slumbering forms and head back into the secret tunnels, carefully securing the entry behind us. We haven't gone far before Travers and the other Magi we freed this evening appear before us.

"We thought the royals had captured you for sure," Travers says.

"Well, we're still standing and the royals aren't," Zandria says.

Fiona hisses. "King Damon and Queen Cyrene . . . they're dead?"

"Darian killed them. He's been playing both sides. We have much to fill you in on," I say.

"It sounds like it," Travers says.

"We have others, Technocrats, who are on our side too. Who've sworn allegiance to the Alchemist Alliance." I address my friends. "We need to bring Vivienne and Leon up to speed. We need their help."

"I'm the fastest," Zandria says. "Where are they supposed to meet us?"

"No." I shake my head. "You and I must remain together. We need both our magics to defeat Darian. And if he kills Aro. . . ."

I can't bear to finish that sentence. We both know what I don't say. Should I die, there will be no one left with power to rival Darian's if Zandria is chasing after Vivienne and Leon.

"I'll go," Owen says. "Just point me in the right direction."

Zandy frowns. "I don't know . . ."

"That's an excellent idea," Catoria says.

"Yes, but they're heading in a different direction than the one we're going in," I say. "They're bringing as many of the Heartless and their allies as possible out of the city to hide in the woods to the east. We're going to the south."

Owen's face grows serious. "Then I'd best be as fast as possible."

Catoria takes his hands. "You need the strength to do it." With that she weaves a speed spell so he can move faster than should be humanly possible.

When Catoria releases Owen, Zandy throws her arms around him, surprising all of us. Then—even more surprising, and yet somehow perfectly Zandria—she grabs his face and plants a kiss on his lips. The startled boy doesn't stand a chance. When she releases him, a dazed smile swims over his face.

"You'd better join us before dawn," she tells him.

"I definitely will," he says.

"Thank you," I say to Owen, raising an eyebrow at my sister that she deftly ignores.

Then he's off. Catoria casts a quickening spell on the rest of us too, but not full-powered like Owen's. There are more of us, and we can't afford to lose our energy that quickly.

But the boost helps, and soon we're out of the tunnels and back on the streets. The sky above our heads is still dark, but the edges are beginning to lighten. We waste no time seeking out the secret tunnels that go under the walls and let out in the forest.

It won't be long before dawn rises and the Magi attempt their terrible spell. If they succeed, it will destroy us all.

In the woods, a rough wind tangles through the metal trees, chiming the tinny branches together. It's eerie enough to set my teeth on edge.

We exited the tunnels at the southeastern corner. We need cover, and just south of the city are plains that stretch toward the southern mountains, lined by the steel aqueducts that bring water into the city. There aren't many places to hide outside the tree line. Plus, we need to locate the Technocrat guards and incapacitate them before a full-on battle breaks out.

Suddenly, I stagger backward. My chest aches fiercely. The breath is stolen from my lungs.

"Aissa, what's wrong?" Zandria grips my arms like I'm about to fly away.

When I catch my breath again it hurts to talk. "Aro was just punched in the chest. Very hard."

Zandria's eyes turn to steel. "I won't allow Darian to do this to you."

"You may not have a choice," Catoria reminds her, but it does nothing to douse the fire in my sister's eyes. She helps me to my feet, and the world stops spinning.

"I'm all right," I say, straightening my spine.

"I'm not," Zandria says. "Darian has already taken our parents. I'm not about to let him take you away from me too."

Catoria pulls Zandy aside. "Gives us a moment," she says to the rest of us. Curiosity fills me, but I release my sister's hand and the two of them walk a few yards away, speaking in hushed whispers.

Moments later, Zandria grins broadly, a wicked gleam in her eyes that gives me chills. Then she heads deeper into the woods without saying goodbye. Catoria rejoins us, an expression on her face that I can't quite decipher.

"Where's she going?" I ask. "We should be sticking together. That's why Owen went to find Vivienne and Leon. If I fall and Zandy's not here, we'll be crushed by the Technocrats." Annoyance brews in my chest. My sister has ever been impulsive, but this was one of those times I believed I could count on her. And I never expected Catoria would egg her on.

"She hasn't gone far. She's retrieving something for me," Catoria says cryptically.

"Which is?" I demand.

Catoria shakes her head. "You'll see soon enough."

I swallow the questions burning on my tongue. I'm not at all happy with my sister disappearing at such a critical moment, but I know how stubborn Catoria can be. Pressing her on this will only waste time we don't have. "Fine. Let's find those guards."

We reach a spot with good cover, then all stand in a circle, facing outward, as we each cast a locator spell that together searches in every direction.

"I think I found the Magi," Fiona says after a couple minutes. "They're deeper in the forest, and they feel different. I can sense their magic."

"Good work," I say. "We'll need to warn them once we know where the Technocrats are hiding."

I keep searching to the south, and that's when I find them: in the aqueducts. The metal structures stretch across the plains all the way into the mountains. I've never been in one myself, but we learned about them in school. The water flows through a conduit above the two-story-high aqueduct, which is supported by metal beams. An enclosed level is just below the conduit to allow for inspections and repairs. Below that is a pattern of archways and metal columns with doors in every third one. It should be wide enough for at least three or four of the guards to stand shoulder to shoulder as they wait inside the enclosed level. The entire city guard is there, packed inside, waiting for Darian to give them a signal. Then they'll pour out through the doors and overwhelm our Magi friends. I shudder.

"They're already here." I nudge Catoria and point in the direction of the aqueducts. "And they're sitting ducks."

"All you have to do is put the stopper on the bottle," she says.

My chest still aches, and I'm sure Aro's does too, but it doesn't stop me from casting a spell to melt the hinges and seal the edges of the first door in the aqueduct. It won't open if Darian manages to get a signal to them. He can't be far away. By now he must be with the Magi. Maybe even planning to reveal Aro's identity and execute him in front of them, all to whip them into a frenzy. Anything Darian believes he can leverage—no matter how small—he will.

While I work, Catoria and the others keep watch, weaving a magical net around our group that will alert her if anyone comes near. Once I'm confident I've sealed all the doors in the aqueduct within my range, we regroup. There are more doors farther away that they can get to, but now they'll have lost the element of surprise, and the Magi will see them coming.

"We need to warn Remy," I say, but before we can take a step in the direction of the Magi, a loud noise erupts from somewhere near the city. It sounds like something enormous and metal wakes. And it isn't happy about it. The pounding continues, starting small and then growing, when a new sight greets us from the east: Owen, carefully winding through the metal trees.

Behind him is a veritable army of Heartless children and their nurses. Some are sickly, the dark tendrils of poison weaving around their arms and necks, while others with newer transplants have a healthier glow. But all are weak. They've spent their lives either recovering from major surgery or slowly being poisoned. My heart aches at the sight of so many. The group Owen has brought stretches between the trees as far as I can see.

Catoria gasps softly, immediately understanding what she sees. Her eyes water with unshed tears. The guilt she feels must be tearing her up inside. I place a hand on her shoulder.

"This is Darian's doing, not yours. That's why there are so many now."

Catoria shakes her head. "No, it is my fault. I crafted the alchemical that did this. I made the tool, Darian only used it."

"Which is exactly why he's responsible," I insist, but her forlorn expression doesn't budge.

We greet Owen. "Where are Leon and Vivienne?" I ask.

An odd expression flashes over Owen's face. "They're with

your sister. They said they had something they needed to do. Something about waking everyone up?" He glances back and forth between us as if we might understand better.

Suddenly, I do. Sort of.

"That noise," I say. "Whatever is causing it must be their doing. They want to wake everyone in the city to either escape or witness the Alchemist Alliance."

Even as I say the words, the sound increases. It almost sounds like . . . metal feet. And voices. The hum of life stirring within the city walls is unmistakable.

"Was this what you were whispering to my sister about?" I ask Catoria. She just shrugs, but mischief sparkles in her eyes.

"Fine. Let's find the Magi and get these children safely away from the city," I say.

Our party heads into the woods toward where Fiona sensed the Magi were hiding with the locator spell, all while I keep an eye on our backs. My stomach tightens. Dawn creeps across the edges of the sky, every scrap of light bringing us closer to destruction. And something fizzes in the air—an accumulation of magic.

Then, we see them: the Magi march toward where the metal forest meets the plains, much closer to the walls than I expected. They're not bothering to hide under a shield now because they're preparing to cast their spell. They must reserve their magic for that.

It's going to get them killed.

Suddenly, a hot plume of rage bursts through me.

Darian, wearing Isaiah's face, stands in front of the gathered Magi not far from the city gates. The guard houses are abandoned, which of course he knows. All the soldiers are trapped in the aqueducts waiting for a cue they won't be able to heed now that they're sealed inside.

Aro is bound and gagged, propped up to Darian/Isaiah's right. I'm glad I'm not alone. It's no longer just me and my sister.

We've gained allies. True ones, not spies out to deceive. As I take in my gathered friends, pride swells within my chest. Each member of the Alchemist Alliance we've brought together has a unique talent, something necessary they bring to the table. And I'm grateful that every single one of them is here.

Because if I were facing down a hundred Magi—and who knows how many Technocrats who could find their way out of the aqueducts at any moment—on my own, I'd be done for. As special as my magic may be, it was never meant to be used alone.

Our real power lies in the mission that binds us together, stronger than any metal alloy.

The noise coming from the city reaches a fever pitch, drawing my attention. For a moment I see a flash of metal in the sky, illuminated by the breaking dawn. Then the southern gates crumble with an earsplitting roar as an enormous mechanical elephant barrels through, knocking over several Magi—including Darian/Isaiah—in the process.

More giant mechs follow the elephant—a horse with a mechanical whinny, a lion, and a bear. They halt next to the elephant, their bejeweled eyes boring down on the gathered Magi who've scattered back into the metal trees. Two small figures appear beside the mechs—Leon and Vivienne. Behind them, the hum of people grows louder, and curious faces peek out from around the corner of the now-destroyed city gates. Some are Technocrats, but many are Magi we freed. Leon and Vivienne must've raided the storehouse where the huge mechanimals from the annual Victory Parade are housed and released them, sending them clomping through the city streets to wake everyone up. And our Magi allies knew it had to be our doing.

Just as the shocked silence seems ready to break, a huge, shining form rises over the city, swooping up and over the tops of the buildings. Its wide steel wings flap, sending blasts of air across the rooftops along with a metallic roar. Here and there I catch a glimpse of a figure on its back—one with bright red hair. The mechdragon makes another circuit of the city, seemingly determined to wake every single person who lives in Palinor.

Owen lets out a whoop, and I almost burst out laughing. Instead I throw my arms around Catoria, nearly knocking the older woman over in the process. "You brought the mechdragon!"

She gives me a sly smile as she extricates herself from my surprise embrace. "It was the fastest way to travel. And I thought, given the circumstances, it might prove more useful here than guarding the Sanctuary."

"Where the Anvil did you hide such a thing?"

"When I arrived, I simply sunk it in the eastern forest. I knew either you or your sister could raise it later."

Darian regains his footing and shouts commands to the Magi. They're gearing up to attack Leon and Vivienne and any Technocrat bystanders. We need to put a stop to this right away.

I address the Magi we freed tonight. "Those Technocrats are not our enemies, despite what you may have been groomed to believe. Only people like Darian are, the ones who seek to hoard power and abuse it. You've all sworn allegiance to the Alchemist Alliance. If we ever want to be free from this cycle of cruelty, this is the time for us to stand."

While they're understandably wary of the enormous mechs, the freed Magi are brave. We lead them forward to form a small but steady line between the Magi and the Technocrats. The other Alliance Magi who were hiding in the city join us, increasing our ranks. But we're still vastly outnumbered.

"Friends!" I cry to the other Magi. "Don't be afraid. Please, just listen to what we have to say." Murmurs ripple through their ranks and the Technocrats behind us.

"Do not heed their words," Darian/Isaiah says over the

burgeoning whispers. "These are the traitors I warned you about. They've betrayed their own kind and now stand with our enemies." He points in my direction. "She even rescued the Technocrat prince, not once but twice!"

Horrified cries break out from the Magi. But then I see a familiar figure. Remy pushes his way through the crowd to stand with us, and I'm so relieved that tears burn behind my eyes.

He clasps my arm in greeting. "Glad you made it," he says. "I was beginning to worry."

I pull him closer and whisper into his ear. "Remy, I'm sorry to tell you like this, but . . . Isaiah is actually Darian. He's been masquerading as your father since the Chambers was destroyed." Remy's face darkens, reddening with rage for a moment before he swallows it down, shoving it away to deal with at the right time. First, we have to stop a war.

"Thank you for telling me."

The clomp of metal boots begins to echo across the plains. The guards have discovered a way out of the aqueducts. They may have had to use an exit farther away, but they're making faster progress toward our tense standoff than I anticipated. More and more stream out of the metal structures every second, forming the lines of war platoons and cutting the Magi off from escape.

Remy addresses the Magi. "These are our friends and fellow Magi. We must heed them."

As they begin to recognize their friends, some of the Magi shout the names of those we've rescued, tinged with surprise and dismay. Others glance between Remy and Darian/Isaiah, confused and unsure.

"Stay strong!" Darian/Isaiah cries. "Do not let their lies twist your resolve. Look!" He points to the quickly approaching Technocrat army. "They have us surrounded. It's us or them."

It's a lie, but a compelling one. To the Magi trapped between the plains, the metal trees, and the crushed city gates now swarming with curious bystanders, it seems like they've been cornered.

They lash out accordingly.

Some begin the sinking spell, making the earth tremble beneath our feet. The wards I set in place over the last week hold—for now. I don't know how long they'll last. I ran out of time to finish my work. Others throw up defensive spells, like shields.

But far more of them strike at the Technos on all sides. One lobs a blast of fire at Leon and Vivienne, but I cast a water spell quickly enough to head that off.

"Get behind the mechs!" I yell to our Technocrat allies, and Leon does. But not Vivienne. She pulls the staff off her back to defend herself. But her staff can't protect her from magical attacks. Remy sees this too and puts himself between her and the Magi, fending off any attack spells that come their way. But he needn't worry too much. Vials full of defensive spells sit in Vivienne's belt. The first Magi to get past Remy is hit with a sleeping spell.

The rest of the Alliance members do our best to hold the crumbled gates, counterspelling every blast of magic we can. I finally have an opportunity to use my shortsword. It does its job even better than I expected, negating every magical attack on me without fail. Soon, however, the Magi's full attention is drawn to the Technocrat guards still streaming from the aqueducts. There are at least four or five times as many guards as there are Magi. The threat is real and present. A group of Magi toward the center begin the sinking spell in earnest. The ground trembles forcefully enough to knock the first few rows of Technocrat soldiers off their feet.

"We can't let them destroy each other," Catoria says at my side.

Anxiety slides over my skin like ice freezing. We've lost control of this fight before it even began. Suddenly the screech of metal in the air grows louder. Zandria and the mechdragon soar over our heads, then swoop down, sending a huge blast of fire into the Technocrat ranks. Many of those Technos do not rise again.

"Zandy, what are you doing?" I scream up at her, but I doubt she can hear me. Killing Technocrats indiscriminately isn't going to help our cause. It only serves Darian. But at the same time, it did force them to retreat. The mechdragon perches on top of the aqueduct, its snout still smoking.

Catoria, who has been murmuring a spell beside me for some time now, spins the last words of the incantation: "*Verra bulle!*" The Magi under Darian's sway are encircled by a giant bubble, blocking them off from the Technocrats. Surprise halts everyone in their tracks for a moment, even Darian/Isaiah, who is stuck outside the dome with Aro.

I don't waste a second. "You've been misled. In more ways than one. First"—I point at Darian—"that man is not Isaiah." I move my hands, performing the cancelling spell we learned at the Sanctuary, and Darian is stripped of his disguise. He glares at us.

The Magi under the dome who've been following him, however, are even less amused. So are the Technocrat guards who've re-formed their lines on the plains.

Owen casts an amplification spell so everyone gathered in the woods and plains can hear what we say.

"You thought you were following Isaiah. But Isaiah is dead. Betrayed by Darian Azul, who's been playing both sides for years. He was leading you into a trap. Those guards? They were hiding in the aqueducts waiting to capture you, all so Darian could experiment on you."

Remy backs me up. "It's true. I've seen it myself. He's built a machine that can steal Magi power."

Our people sound angrier inside their dome.

"Don't listen to them," Darian says. He waves his hand and a violent blast of wind sends Catoria flying.

Then chaos breaks loose.

With Catoria down, her spell is interrupted. The Magi are no longer cut off from the Technocrat army, which immediately attacks. Most of the Magi, who seemed confused about who to trust a moment ago, fight back and defend themselves. Beside me, Owen and Remy help Catoria to her feet.

A sharp ache in my temple sends me staggering, knocking into Remy.

Then I double over, pain ricocheting through my gut.

"Aissa!" Vivienne shouts, joining us. "What's happening?" she asks Remy.

"It's Darian," he says, gritting his teeth. "He's hurting Aro. Because of their bond, it hurts Aissa too."

"We need to stop him," Owen says.

A sharp sting pierces my hands. Blood wells up in my palms. Catoria has regained her feet and begins a healing spell over me. But Darian is determined to harm Aro, cutting him up piece by piece. By now, Darian must realize that what he does to Aro impacts me too. And if he hasn't yet, he will soon.

Metal screeching against metal steals my attention away for the moment. Zandria and the mechdragon have taken off into the air, sending an orange column of flame into the Technos attacking the Magi. They fall back, but the Magi ramp up their magical attacks.

Pain explodes in my face and my nose begins to bleed. Through watering eyes, I can see Aro doubled over too, with Darian hovering over him.

And now he holds a knife.

He doesn't have to kill Aro in such a fashion. He could do it the way we were trained. The less bloody method with magic. But killing Aro is only half the point. Darian's angry that Aro isn't the fool he assumed he was. That he dared question him and ally with me. Darian doesn't just want Aro to die; he wants him to suffer.

My pulse throbs in my neck, the beat connecting me and Aro ticking off the seconds we have left.

With the entire Magi and Technocrat armies battling between us, there's no way I can reach him in time.

But someone else can.

Zandria circles the mechdragon around again, this time sending the dragon's flames toward Darian. I cringe when she does this; Aro could easily be caught in the fire as well, but my sister is nothing if not reckless. Darian sends a plume of water at the dragon, shoving back the flames. Rage and frustration burn over Zandria's face as she pulls the dragon up and circles over Darian and Aro.

Aro has crawled away as best he can with his hands and feet bound, but Darian stalks toward him again. My palms turn slick as the shadow of the mechdragon passes over us all.

With a sharp cry, the mechdragon speeds down toward Darian. If Zandria keeps up that pace, she's going to crash and possibly destroy the mech and herself.

Darian sends an attack spell at her—I can't tell which—but she counters with a spell of her own. Beside me, Owen mutters an incantation, sending his magic spinning across the plains toward Darian. Meanwhile, my sister and the mechdragon bear down on our enemy, her shortsword held aloft as they charge. Darian tries to dodge out of the way, but his movements are now slowed, as if he moves through quicksand, thanks to Owen's spell. Aro rolls on to his back and uses both feet to kick Darian in the legs, sending him careening toward Zandria and the mechdragon.

Zandria's shortsword whistles as it arcs through the air, then she banks the flying machine at the last possible moment, its steel wings spread wide, and soars back into the sky.

Darian's eyes are wide with shocked pain, but unseeing. Blood pours over his clothes from the deep gash in his neck. Then he crumples to the ground and doesn't rise again.

Everything stops.

Magi and Technocrat alike knew this man, trusted him, and were betrayed by him. Both considered him one of their leaders. Without him, all they have left is the fight and the hate. And maybe, like I realized weeks ago, that can be overcome.

My eyes meet Aro's across the plains. Cooling relief fills us both. Zandria lands the mechdragon not far from him and cuts the ropes on his wrists and ankles. Then he climbs onto the metal beast's back too, and they fly to our side of the battlefield to join the rest of the Alliance members.

I throw my arms around both of them—my heart and my family. Darian is gone. But when I look up, it's clear the problems he caused, the fires he stoked, remain.

"Owen?" I say. "Can you cast the amplification spell again?" He does as I ask.

I address the Technocrats first, both guards and bystanders. "You recognized your Head Scientist, didn't you? He was really the Magi spymaster. And the man the king and queen entrusted with their secrets. With being their successor . . . but only when their son died."

One of the guards shouts, "They don't have any children!"

Aro steps forward. "Yes, they do. I'm their son and the rightful heir. Darian has been trying to kill me for weeks. He murdered my parents earlier this evening. I was the only thing standing in his way to throne."

"Who can vouch for you?" another guard asks.

Leon comes forward and a hush falls over the Technocrats. Due to his role, a Master Mechanic commands respect. Leon may not have lived the life of a courtier, but that was because he chose not to. Every Technocrat knows who he is.

"He tells the truth. I've known him since he was a small boy. Aro was born Heartless, and I was enlisted to personally make his clockwork hearts."

Murmurs punctuated by shouts roll through the gathered crowd and the Technocrat army.

"He's Heartless? Then how can he take the throne?" a voice in the crowd calls out. Echoes quickly spread through the woods.

Aro stands up straighter and glances at me. We've discussed this moment many times, late at night. We've examined it from every angle. Either this will work, or everything will go horribly wrong because of it.

But our peoples have been kept in the dark for too long. It's time for the truth.

Aro addresses the crowd again. "While my heart may not be flesh and blood, I no longer require replacements." He takes my hand. "This woman, a Magi, saved my life. Removed the poisonous havani that once powered my heart and filled it with magic instead, all at great personal risk to herself. My heart will beat as long as she lives."

Shock descends on the crowd, Techno and Magi alike. Then voices erupt on all sides.

"Impossible!"

"We can't trust magic users!"

"Lies! Magi can't use magic on machines!"

Zandria appears at my side and twines her hand with my free one, giving it a quick squeeze. We've kept this secret for so long that exposing ourselves now, in front of all these people, is terrifying.

But it's the only thing that will convince them we speak the truth.

I hum while Zandria weaves her hands. For a moment, it's almost like we're back in the tunnels beneath the city, about to take apart the digger mechs to render them unusable. But now the stakes are much higher. My spell ensnares the mechanical elephant, throwing its trunk high, then stomping its feet. Zandria takes control of the metal horse, making it rear and toss its silver-threaded mane.

Leon startles, as do many of the Technos and Magi who surround us. "I swear to you all," he says. "Those machines are powered down."

"It's a trick!"

"Liar!"

The crowd isn't as impressed as they should be by this display, but we have another trick up our sleeves. The tune of my incantation shifts, and the elephant shivers, a horrible, metallic rattling. The bolts holding its pieces together unscrew in unison, then shoot into the air to hover over our heads. When the note spins higher, the sheets of metal that make up the elephant's body spread apart almost as if the mech momentarily expands, then fall the ground. Next to me, Zandria's hands weave continuously, then they stop and squeeze together. The horse folds in on itself, all that metal—some of the pieces very thick—responding in a most unnatural way. In a few minutes, all that's left is a giant ball of squished steel.

The hush that falls over the southern plains is so thick you could slice it like bread.

Catoria raises her own voice. "Darian spread his lies for too long. It's time for you all to hear the truth."

I grab Vivienne's arm and give her a meaningful look. "It's time," I say. "Bring them here." Her eyes light up, then she dashes into the tree line.

"I'm sure you're wondering to what end Darian betrayed all his allegiances," I say. Murmurs in the crowd quickly confirm my words. "He had been trying to create more of the Heartless, poisoning your waters with the same compound that was accidentally released a hundred years ago. He wanted an army, powered by magic-infused hearts that never need to be replaced. That's why he wanted to capture Magi. He perfected a technique of draining magic from us and infusing it into a particular sort of stone. His goal was to secure the loyalty of those who relied on him and magic to live so he could use them to rule everything."

Footfalls and rustling branches come from the woods. "Technocrats, you've been told only a tiny percentage of your population is born Heartless, but the truth is the number increases every year thanks to Darian and his poison. The ones from the hospitals in the city are here, behind me."

Children and their nurses stream through the metal trees to the edge of the grassy plains. There are almost as many of them as there are Magi and Technocrats combined.

The enemy factions are floored. The murmurs become shouts of horror and rage.

Zandria holds up a hand, commanding attention. "We have a proposition. Magi, by accident or not, we are responsible for this blight. All these children born without hearts. Before the great wars, our ancestors tried to heal the breach between our people by finding a way to restore magic to the Technocrats."

The anxiety in the crowds on both sides spikes, but I pick up my sister's thread. "Long ago, we weren't Magi and Technocrats. We were just . . . people. People who had magic and could use it on anything and everything. Then some were born without magic. And those with magic could only impact the natural, living world. We divided into two factions, but we're all from the same family tree. Before the wars, some of the Magi and Technocrats banded together and formed the Alchemist Alliance, whose mission was to return us to our original, normal state. The Heartless are the result of a rogue attempt to do that gone horribly awry."

I glance at my sister, hoping she'll go along with this part of my plan. "My sister and I have the power to fix this. Our magic is the old magic restored. All Magi have long been taught that the one thing we can't heal is the heart, because that's where our magic resides. But that isn't true. The ancient Magi had a spell, the Heartsong, that could do exactly that." I smile at my sister. "We can heal the Heartless. All of them, given some time. You may have heard rumors of a boy healed, given a new flesh-and-blood heart. We did that, and we can produce him and his testimony as proof. Technocrats, if you lay down your weapons and agree to let the Magi live in peace, we will do this gladly. Magi, pull your magic back; we made this mess, and the Technocrats are not the enemies we've believed. It's only the ones who've been power hungry, and this time, their leader was one of us."

It feels like a lifetime passes before us, but it's really only a few moments until the first Technocrat guard lays his sword on the ground. Then another follows. Then the rest of the company. Some angrily shove their way back into the city. But soon nearly the entire army has disarmed. All the while, the magic that once made the air fizz is drawn back. There are Magi dissenters too, who run into the forest. We'll have to deal with them later. But for now, the tension on the plains finally begins to clear.

For the first time in over a century, Magi and Technocrats regard each other across the battlefield, but not with hatred and animosity. With curiosity, and mostly, regret.

THE NEXT DAY, AFTER ARO HAS OFFICIALLY

taken the reins at the Palace and we've all gotten some sleep, I find him in the lower levels,
addressing a group of researchers. He seems more
self-assured than I've ever seen him. His pale blue eyes
glow with excitement.

"My parents gave Darian free reign to assign you whatever
projects he deemed necessary. But many of those were in service
to his own selfish goals and not the greater good. That's why
we're putting a stop to them as of today. From now on, those of
you who've been working on the new energy generator Darian
demonstrated a few weeks ago will be reassigned. Most of you are
not aware of this, but Darian created it to drain magic from Magi
prisoners." He notices me at the back of the room, and a small
smile flits over his face. "We will not be pursuing that any further.
We're now allies with the Magi and will not conduct any human
experiments in these labs. Is that understood?"

Most of the researchers gape, shocked by the revelation, but
there are a couple who are not so surprised. Some must have been
in on the full extent of the project in order to help Darian build
those awful metal boxes. I make a mental note of who they are.
Our new alliance will be an adjustment for all of us, and I need to
mark who I can and cannot trust.

"I require an answer," Aro says.

"Understood," is the unanimous response.

"Good, thank you."

One woman in the center of the crowd raises her hand. "What
project will we be assigned to instead?" she asks.

"We've made many new discoveries lately, not the least of

which is that both Technocrat and Magi have the same ancestors—who could use magic on all things, living or otherwise. We'll have several new research projects, including investigating those bloodlines, determining how they diverged and how they might be merged again."

Catoria peels off the wall behind him, bending her head toward the group in greeting.

"This is Catoria. She is highly knowledgeable about alchemicals. She will be leading a new research project and can offer insight into the bloodlines as well."

Catoria wanted a new life now that her duty to the Sanctuary has been lifted. Aro was more than happy to oblige. She can make this program her own.

Aro lets Catoria take over and joins me in the doorway. "Come with me," he whispers in my ear, and I slip my hand into his. Warmth tingles through my fingers, along with a jolt of happiness. I can walk through these halls for the very first time without any hint of fear.

He takes me on a route I know well. One I've missed. When he opens to the door to the garden, I inhale deeply, absorbing the scent of lush flowers and foliage. The sun illuminates the many shades of green, shot through with reds, yellows, whites, and my favorite blues and purples. Aro's arms curl around my waist, and he rests his chin on my shoulder.

"For a while, I thought I'd never see this place again," he says quietly.

"Me too," I say. I should never have allowed myself to get attached to this place, this boy, but I did.

And I don't have a single regret about either of those things.

We sit on the bench in the center, the same place where we ate lunch together so many times. Something flutters in my stomach.

This garden is packed wall to wall with the ghosts of our memories and strange, secret courtship.

But there was a reason I went looking for Aro this morning, and it can't wait a moment longer.

"Aro, I want to do something for you."

He tilts his head quizzically at me. "And what would that be?"

I take his hands in mine. "Zandria and I are supposed to begin healing the Heartless children, but I want to use the Heartsong on you first. You deserve it the most. If you're going to be king, you should be whole."

When we finally deciphered the Heartsong, I wanted to use it on Aro right away. The only reason I didn't was in case we needed to show the people of Palinor that he was Heartless first in order to win them over. It's been chafing at me ever since.

His expression softens, his eyes sparkling earnestly. "Aissa, I'm already whole."

I frown. "What?"

He laughs softly. "I've been thinking about this too, ever since Catoria first mentioned that spell back in the Sanctuary." He shakes his head. "I'm in no danger of dying now. My heart may be made of metal, but it will keep functioning as long as we both live. It's part of me. The technology and the magic you gave me to keep it running—they make me me. If I'm going to rule over this land and both our peoples, it's fitting for pieces of each to live in me. It isn't a flaw; it's an advantage. It puts me in a unique position to understand both. I don't want to risk forgetting that."

I gape at him. "But . . . I thought you wanted a real heart."

He shrugs. "Once, yes, I dreamed of that. But the truth is, I have one. There's no reason to worry about it stopping, yes? And even if I had a flesh-and-blood heart, we'd still be bonded, and the risk of dying together would be the same."

"That's true . . ." I say slowly, absorbing the full weight of his words. "The Binding rite connects us right down to our souls. That's why it's one of the few spells that can't be undone."

Aro smiles wide. "Then if anything, I'm safer with a metal heart."

I laugh. "I suppose you are."

His face grows serious. "There's something I need to talk to you about too. I've been giving this a lot of thought, and I don't believe the Technocrats' system of governance is working."

I snort. "Can't say I disagree."

"If the Magi and Technocrats are going to maintain peace, they need an equal voice." He clears his throat and bites his lip. "I plan to write this into the laws of the land: from now on there must always be a representative from each faction ruling the country with equal say and power. Aissa, I want you to be co-regent with me."

Warmth trills over me. I've been living day to day for such a long time, just hoping to make it to the next alive. I haven't given much thought to what would happen if we won. But this is a solution I can get behind. And I believe I can persuade the rest of the Magi to as well.

I've always known we were equal to the Technos; having that officially acknowledged will go a long way to healing old wounds.

I kiss Aro, taking him by surprise and making him laugh. He pulls me into his arms, and my skin tingles pleasantly. "Yes," I say. "I'd be honored."

It has been two weeks since the standoff between the Magi and Technocrats on the plains outside the city. My sister and I have kept our promise, and the Magi and Technocrats have kept theirs. Word of what transpired—including the murder of the royals by their most trusted advisor—spread like wildfire throughout the city and beyond to anyone who didn't witness it themselves. According to our Technocrat allies, Aro's claim to the throne is widely supported, helped along by the fact that Zandria and I have spent every day since healing Heartless children. It's a taxing, complex spell, but we've managed to heal five children a piece every day. It will take us a long time to get through all of the afflicted, but we've been working with the sickest first to buy a little time for the rest.

We've just said our goodbyes to the last two children of the day and their parents, who tearfully hugged their children to them as they thanked us. I think, perhaps, they don't quite believe it's real until it happens. Hope is a fragile thing, and the disappointment if it didn't work would be too crushing to bear.

Sometimes we can't help but get swept up in their gratefulness too. The chance to use our magic not just for devious things, but out in the open and to do good, is truly intoxicating.

Exhausted, my sister and I rest on the cushions in the small room in the Heartless hospital that was set up for the purpose of our task. She groans.

"There are more Heartless children than I ever realized," she says. "I mean, I knew by the numbers you told me about that it had to be a lot. But seeing each and every one of them brings it to another level."

"When we're done, there will be none. And if any more are born with lingering aftereffects of the alchemicals Darian put into the water, we can heal them immediately. They won't have to live with those monstrous devices inside them." Not like Aro did, not like Leon's daughter or Darian's wife. No one else will be subjected to them ever again. We have the power to change that. Our magic has made it possible.

"I still can't believe Aro turned down a real heart," Zandy says.

I laugh. She has said this almost every day since I told her. "I was taken aback by it at first too. But he's right—he doesn't need it with the Binding rite in place. And I can appreciate that he wants to remember what he almost didn't have. He doesn't want to take a single thing he has now for granted. Not like he did before."

Aro told me of his childhood in the Palace. As the prince, he received just about everything he desired, except his freedom and an assurance he'd live to take the throne one day. He had the best of everything, but his parents didn't understand how to love someone like him. Thank the Anvil he had people like Leon in his life.

Zandria smiles slyly at me. "All I care about is that he doesn't take you for granted." She pauses. "And that he doesn't rule like his parents."

"Oh, he definitely won't do either of those things, I'll see to that." My sister throws a pillow at me, and I catch it at my stomach.

My sister grows more serious. "I've not always liked Aro, but I've seen him with you and working with the Alliance. I believe he will be a fair ruler."

I raise an eyebrow. "That is quite a concession, and I'm glad to hear it. Now, have you considered my proposal yet?"

Zandria props herself up on one elbow and faces me. "You mean the one where you've offered me a cushy job in the Palace?"

"It will probably be a lot less cushy than you think."

After I agreed to be Aro's co-regent, I asked Zandria to be captain of the Regency Guard—a hand-picked group of Technos and Magi who will be sworn to protect Aro and me, and all of Palinor's citizens.

"As long as I get to choose the members of the guard myself, I'm in. Someone needs to look after you, and the Anvil knows Aro can't do it."

I laugh and throw the pillow back at her. "Absolutely. You can pick anyone you like."

She grins. "Then I'll start making my list."

A few hours later, I find myself inside the Technocrat throne room for the first time. But it's very different than I imagined. Months ago, I feared one day being dragged into this red-marbled room and imprisoned in a terrible metal suit, never to see the light of day again.

Instead I'm here with Aro at my side and a crowd of courtiers I've only seen and never met until recently. They'll do anything to curry favor to the point of irritation. I'm beginning to understand why Aro always went out of his way to avoid them when we'd sneak through the halls, yet they're important nonetheless. We need their backing to ensure the support of the entire city. The deaths of the king and queen sent shockwaves through Palinor, but these courtiers wasted no time mourning. They don't care who has magic and who doesn't; they only care about money and power and where they can get it. Ours has become a delicately balanced but mutually beneficial arrangement. A dance I'm still learning while Aro begrudgingly goes through the motions he knows well.

But so far it has worked. They're delighted by my magic and Aro's bizarre situation of being kept alive partly by machine and partly by magic. They see it as a good omen for the future and their own prospects. Like them or not, they're on our side, and we need to keep them there.

The courtiers line the room alongside our friends like Vivienne and Leon and about half the remaining Magi, including Remy, Owen, Catoria, and everyone we rescued from the dungeons. In the wake of the revelation about Isaiah's death and Darian's betrayal, the Magi turned to Remy to guide them. He and the rescued Magi have persuaded them to recognize me and Aro as their ruling co-regents. We may not always have gotten along, but his heart is good, and he truly wants what's best for the Magi.

I know Remy well enough to know that he'd have no qualm telling them—and me—if he didn't believe this was the right path forward.

Owen will be joining the Regency Guard under Zandria's command. He'd walk off a cliff at her direction, if only to make her laugh. He's grown on all of us, becoming almost like the brother I never had, and much more than that to my sister.

Leon Salter stands a step above us on the dais with the thrones. In his hands are two crowns, which he crafted with help from Catoria: each one uses platinum and the black, shimmering marble from the ancient Magi. Aro's is a band made primarily of platinum with a thin strip of black throughout, leading to the center of the crown with the Technocrat sigil imprinted on it in gold. Mine is mainly crafted of the black marble, with a platinum circle in the center imprinted with a carved black-marble tree.

My hands tremble unexpectedly. I reach for Aro's, and he squeezes mine with a broad smile. All we've worked for is finally coming to fruition.

"Regents," Leon says, holding up our crowns. "As Master Mechanic, I've been chosen from the Palinor guildmasters to grant you your titles and crowns. As decreed by King Arondel, son of Damon and Cyrene, the monarchy has ended. Instead, a new system of co-rule, a regency, will take its place in perpetuity. From now on, Palinor will always be governed by a representative of the Magi and the Technocrats until such a time that we find a way to make our bloodlines one again."

Leon places a crown on each of our heads, then addresses the crowd. "I present Regent Arondel and Regent Aissa."

The response is raucous and louder than I expected. "Long may they reign! Long may they reign!"

Aro lifts our clasped hands and we beam at each other. Our love, our reign, is the perfect blending of magic and technology.

From now on, we're no longer Technocrats or Magi, but Alchemists.

Acknowledgments

THIS BOOK SERIES HAS LIVED IN MY HEAD AND HEART FOR A VERY long while, especially this second book, and I'm overjoyed that it is now out on bookshelves. The world of *Twin Daggers* and *Heartless Heirs* is one that's dear to me, and while saying goodbye to these characters is bittersweet, I'm pleased with how they ended up. I hope you are too!

I'm so grateful to the many people behind the scenes who made this journey possible. My particular thanks the following:

My intrepid editor, Jacque Alberta, and the wonderful team at Blink YA Books. Thank you so much for giving this duology an excellent home!

My ever-awesome agent, Suzie Townsend, her fabulous assistant, Dani Segelbaum, and really, the entire New Leaf team because they're just the best in the business.

My family! None of my books would get written without my awesome husband, Jason (it's hard to feed a toddler and type at the same time, you know?). Without his support, this story wouldn't be possible.

And thanks so much to you, readers, for going on this journey with me and Aissa, Zandria, and Aro. I hope you enjoy reading about them as much as I did writing about them.

Twin Daggers

MarcyKate Connolly

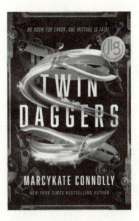

Aissa's life is a web of carefully constructed lies. By day, she and her sister
Zandra play the role of normal young
Technocrats eager to fulfill the duties
of their new apprenticeships. By night,
they work for the Magi's spy organization, which seeks to overthrow the
Technocrats who subjugated their people. Soon Aissa is given
her greatest mission: find and kidnap the heir to the Technocrat
throne, who is rumored to be one of the Heartless—a person
born without a working heart who survives via a mechanical
replacement—and has been hidden since birth.

Aissa has never been one to turn down an assignment, even
if the hunt is complicated by a kind Technocrat researcher who
is determined to find a cure for the Heartless. But when Zandria
is captured, Aissa will do anything to get her sister back. Even if
it means abandoning all other loyalties ... and risking everything
by trusting the enemy.

Available wherever books are sold!

BLINK®

Connect with MarcyKate Connolly!

Website: www.marcykate.com

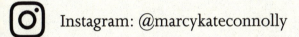 Instagram: @marcykateconnolly

Twitter: @marcykate

Facebook: @MarcyKateConnolly

Goodreads: www.goodreads.com/marcykate

MARCYKATE CONNOLLY is a *New York Times* bestselling children's book author and nonprofit marketing professional living in New England with her family and a grumble of pugs. She can be lured out from her writing cave with the promise of caffeine and new books. *Twin Daggers* is her debut young adult novel, and she's also the author of several middle grade fantasy novels including *Monstrous* and *Ravenous*, and the Shadow Weaver series. You can visit her online at www.marcykate.com.